Betrayal at the Arrow—B

JACK F. KIRKEBY

Published by Jack F. Kirkeby
Mission Viejo, California, 92692

All questions or requests concerning the publication or copyright of this book should be directed to the publisher by email to info@jackkirkeby.com.

This book is available for purchase at Amazon.com and an electronic version will be available as well.

Cover Design by Mark Worcester
Illustrations by Matthew B. Guccione

ISBN: 978-0-692-13234-0

DEDICATION

This book and the other two books of the Trilogy are dedicated to my Kirkeby and Worcester Families so that they may continue to enjoy stories of the West.

CONTENTS

ACKNOWLEDGMENTS

To my beloved wife, Priscilla Kirkeby, I owe much for her tireless support and professional editing during the writing of this novel. And to my son-in-law and good friend, Mark Worcester, I owe much for the book cover design, and the publishing of this book. Without these two, this writing would not be in print.

1 | MY DAD IS MISSING

The Marriage of George Bentley, a Wyoming rancher and Betty Harris, the daughter of Steve Harris, a retired educator and ranch owner, was the feature article in the Glencoe Herald on the first day of April, 1955. The ceremony took place in a little church located in the small town of Walnut, Wyoming.

The article read:

Not in recent years has there been the excitement over a marriage of two of our local folk as with that of our own Betty and George. Their courtship started with a chance meeting in Rosey's Café in Walnut a short two years ago. It suffered through misguided local bias that touched on the bigotry still existing over the marriage between Indians and whites, and the trauma of a violent invasion into the area from a gang of city criminals, intent on the acquisition of the Arrow—B ranch.

Most of us know George, born on the Arrow—B to Richard Bentley, an immigrant from Scotland, and White Dove, the daughter of an Arapaho Indian chief. What some of us may not know is that Betty lost her first husband through a hunting accident. Her mother died of natural causes when she, Betty, was only seven, which might explain why she had been hesitant to enter the world of dating since moving to the Walnut area with her dad a few years ago. The wedding will be followed by an Indian ceremony to take place in the nearby Arapaho Village. It

1

was learned by this writer that the newly-wedded couple will honeymoon in San Francisco, then return to the Arrow—B later this month. From all of us that call you friends, George and Betty: God speed, come back to us safely, and we wait eagerly for your return.

The Harris ranch lay a few miles south of Walnut. It was small by any measure, and supported perhaps three dozen head of cattle and a half a dozen horses. Steve Harris had mostly worked his cattle alone or with just one hand. Spike, the one ranch hand, lived in a four-person bunkhouse and generally shared meals with Betty and Steve. On the departure of Betty from the ranch, there were just the two of them, and they were to share cooking etc.

The morning after the wedding Steve went into town, and as usual entered Rosey's Café for coffee and a bit of gab with that charismatic café owner, who greeted him with a smile and a question, "Hi, how lonely is it Steve?"

"Plenty, Rosey, but I'll live. Betty's life has to go on. She is too vital a person to pine the loss of both her mother and her first husband, Paul, forever."

"So, who does the cooking?"

"Me and Spike share."

"Oh."

Steve, hearing humor in that 'oh', said, "Alright Rosey, so we'll find ways to do this thing, so . . . it won't taste very good." Rosey poured more coffee, Steve blew across the top of the steaming liquid, "What do you hear now about yesterday?"

Rosey smiled, "Some fer, some agin, you know what that's all about."

"Uh huh, won't the town bigots ever give up? It's been twenty-five years since Dick Bentley dared marry an Indian. These diehards around here still call George a breed."

"That's funny, George spent five years in an eastern college, and excelled in all areas of study. The college big wigs are still expounding on that one. I read the monthly alumni sheet from there. There isn't one of these idiots that can hold a candle to that one."

Rosey got a whimsical look about her, "George is not only smart but just look what we women see: he's over six feet, innately handsome, with a steady look about him, caring, and canny to boot . . . what are your plans now that Betty's gone?"

"I'm not sure, Rosey, I may go back to teaching. Two men, Spike and me, soon run out of things to talk about. When George and Betty return we'll have a family discussion over that one." Steve smiled a bit, then, "It's been hard, Rosey, I've given Betty away twice now. I sure hope it works. I couldn't do it a third time."

George and Betty spent the better part of two weeks in San Francisco. They returned to the Arrow—B, and once again took up the reins of running a western cattle ranch. Betty's call to her father found him not at home. She waited a time, and then tried again with the same result. It was nighttime now, there was no logical reason for him to be out on the range. She had a little nervous twinge, tried to shake it off and failed. She went to bed, awake and troubled.

George was already up and gone out on the range when Betty rose and called Dorothy, the local switchboard operator, and asked if she knew where her father was.

"I sure don't, Betty. He doesn't answer his phone. I've had several people try to reach him with no success."

"Thanks Dorothy, I think I'd better drive over and see if he's okay." She hung up, then found Mary Ellen, the ranch cook, "Mary, I'm going over to Dad's ranch. He's not answering his phone. Tell George when he comes in." She got into the ranch pick-up and headed out.

Betty drove up the short driveway to the Harris ranch house. She got out of the truck, and entered the house by the front door. She was already nervous and the silence within gave her the shivers. She called out, then went from room to room . . . nothing. In the kitchen were dishes and cookware showing an unfinished breakfast. Her heart thumped, and her breathing became rapid. She went to the phone. "Dorothy, I'm out at my dad's house, Dad isn't here. Could you see if you can find the Sheriff. I'll wait here." She next put in a call to the Arrow—B and informed Mary Ellen of the same.

Sheriff Bill Williams received the call at his office in Walnut. He listened to Betty on the phone, then said, "Give me 20 minutes, Betty, don't leave, I'll be right there." The Sheriff turned to his deputy, Leon Roberts, and said, "Leon, Steve Harris is missing from his ranch, call Dorothy at the switchboard and tell her what has happened. I'm heading for the Harris Ranch. You stay around the office."

A short time later found the Sheriff driving up the Harris Ranch driveway. Betty met him at the door. She was visibly distraught. She motioned him to come in, and said, "I don't know where Dad can be. He'd never leave dishes and food on the breakfast table and go out. There's something else, Dad always kept a sizeable amount of cash on hand. He kept it, along with the family jewelry in the bottom of the chest of drawers in his bedroom. The money and jewelry that were there are gone."

The Sheriff said, "Let me look around, Betty, maybe we can find a clue as to where he is. Try to calm down a bit. We'll do everything we can to find him. Show me where he kept his money."

Betty led the Sheriff into the bedroom, pointed to the bottom drawer, and said, "Dad showed me that when you remove the drawer you found that space underneath that made a good hiding place for money and other valuables."

"Do you know how much money or what other valuables he kept there?"

"I don't know exactly but I would guess it might be around a thousand dollars. He used to keep my grandma's rings there too. They were to be passed on to me when I got married."

The Sheriff asked, "Where do you suppose Spike is?"

"Lately Spike's been looking for a place to start a small ranch, like a spot where he could build a house and raise a few cows. He might have been away."

"Did he know about the money cache?"

"I don't think so, but he might have tried to figure out where my father got the cash to meet his wages every month. I trust Spike though, I don't think he would do anything wrong against my dad."

The Sheriff's mind scudded along over the people he knew around about the area. He went outside, checking for any unusual disturbance of the grounds around the house, nothing. Stepping over to the corral, he saw three horses munching away at their portion of hay that had been put out earlier. He saw nothing unusual here. He went back into the house. Betty stood quietly in the kitchen, her eyes misty, her countenance questioning. Sheriff Williams felt the worry, the emptiness that was there and a bit of inadequacy in himself that he could not help somehow. "Betty, I want you to come out to the tack shed with me. I need to know of anything unusual or out of place there."

She nodded her head and followed the Sheriff out to the open-sided shed that served as a shelter for the horses as well as a place to hang saddles and other paraphernalia needed for the care and use of the ranch riding stock. There were three stocky wooden pegs protruding out from the back wall, two of them supported saddles. The third was empty. Ropes and bridles hung from smaller pegs. Haphazardly strewn across the floor was a rope. The Sheriff asked Betty, "Do you see anything wrong or unusual here?"

After a moment of hesitation, Betty said, "Dad would never throw a rope on the floor. He was almost sure to have coiled it and hung it up along with the others." She continued, "The two saddles are mine and Dad's. Everything else seems to be in order."

"Were the ropes all about the same length?"

"He did seem to keep things even and equal, even the length of his ropes."

"Was there a ranch dog, Betty?"

"When I last saw my dad he told me that Andy, our dog for many years, was sick and very old. He was here when we left on our honeymoon."

The telephone rang, Betty picked up the receiver. George's voice said, "Betty?"

"George, we can't find Dad, please come, I need you."

"Is there anyone with you?"

"The Sheriff's here. I'm really frightened for Dad. Please hurry."

George came and drew Betty to him. He felt her fear and whispered, "We'll find Dad." He turned to the Sheriff, "What do we know?"

The Sheriff brought George up to date then said, "We all need to calm down. I'm sure there's a logical reason for Harris not being here."

George was silent, recalling that time, twelve years ago, when he returned from college to find his father dead of a so-called accident. That wasn't an accident then, and it looks like Steve Harris's disappearance wasn't either. He comforted Betty as best he could, held her close, feeling her shake with fear. There was dark here. He sensed evil, and he knew what the demise of Betty's father would mean to his wife. George and Betty walked outside circling around to the rear of the tack shed. Scrawled on the back wall was the image of a snake, and written below, a poem:

Snake . . . Come crawling
There's fire in your eyes
Bite me, excite me
I'll learn to realize
The poison transmitted
Brings eternal flame
Open me to heaven
To heal me again.

Looking down, one could see a five-foot patch of loose dirt. Betty gasped when she saw it. She clung to George with desperate strength. George gently extradited himself, all the time speaking softly. Returning to the house, he asked the Sheriff to come out and take a look, which he did. The Sheriff asked, "Do we have a shovel somewhere?"

Betty, seeing what the two men were doing, put her hand to her mouth as nausea flooded her body. A short time later as soil was shoveled out of the way the red brown hairs of Andy the ranch dog appeared.

As George drove Betty back to the Arrow—B, Betty sat somber and oblivious to the world around her. George reminded her of his love, promised to do everything possible to find her dad. She offered little or no response, and the ride home became one of silence.

2 | A THREATENED ROMANCE

George thought of the first time they met in Rosey's café. Betty was beautiful, albeit she was still mourning the loss of her husband, Paul, in a hunting accident. For the following two years their love grew until it finally overcame the terrible loss that Betty had endured.

Betty lost her mother at an early age, lived through the accidental death of her husband, Paul, and now feared the loss of her only remaining family member. The trauma of the possible demise of her father now seemed more than she could handle.

In a way, Betty's mind shut down. She sat alongside her husband of just two weeks with a blank look on her face, out of reality. Once, on their drive home, George thought he heard her whisper, "They killed Andy...."

George parked the car in the ranch yard, went around to the passenger side and helped Betty out. She allowed him to guide her into the house, where she stood staring at *nothing*. He seated her in a chair facing the valley through the picture window of the big room, then called Mary Ellen up from the cook shack. "Mary, will you prepare something light for our evening meal, and bring it on up."

Mary glanced at Betty, "Is Mrs. Bentley alright?"

"Steve Harris is missing. I think Betty is worried for her father."

"Oh, I'm so sorry. I hope he is found soon . . . Mrs. Bentley must be terribly upset, her father means everything to her."

Betty came to George at a time when she needed someone, someone to help put behind the tragic death of her husband, Paul. It had been two years since Paul's demise and Betty's acceptance of another's love.

Not knowing is sometimes worse than death itself. The finality of the end of a life is a closing thing. The not-knowing lingers. Betty was in shock. Her body functions continued but her mind closed down. George spoke to a deaf ear. He finally backed off, waiting for Betty to awaken. The hours went by and then the days and weeks.

A ranch survives when humans perform. The Arrow—B claimed its owner, and George turned to doing. For Betty, there was Mary Ellen, who watched over her and cared while George was out on the range. Doc Morrison came, felt himself lacking, and said to George, "Betty seems comfortable to remain away from all of us right now. I don't know how long it will last, or what to do for her."

George asked, "Are there any specialists in this field nearby that we could call on for help?"

"The one I'm thinking of has a practice in Cheyenne. You'd have to take Betty there. Let me touch base with him; we went to medical school together."

The Sheriff did what he could about finding out what happened to Steve Harris. He initiated a missing-person report and contacted sheriffs in surrounding counties and those agencies that might help, or that might have some related information. He spoke to other ranchers in the area looking for anyone that might have a problem with Steve Harris, or for itinerant workers that might be suspicious, but those inquiries went nowhere. He even spoke to the tribal council of the nearby Indian tribe, receiving little or no help there. Then he half closed the book on Steve's absence, feeling that he had done everything he could, and there were other matters of import that needed his attention.

George Bentley, faced with a depressed and almost comatose Betty, saw to it that the Sheriff wouldn't forget that Steve was missing, which in time irritated the Sheriff to no end. Their phone conversation one-day went like this: "Sheriff Williams speaking."

"George here, anything happening about Steve?"

The Sheriff was silent for a moment, then, "We discussed that yesterday George, I can't spend my life on a missing person who might have gone off on his own. If I hear anything, I'll call you." He placed the receiver firmly on its cradle.

A frustrated George looked across the room at Betty. He felt inadequate, unable to help his wife. He crossed to her, talking softly to a deaf ear.

The trip to Cheyenne was just under 400 miles. George and Betty left the ranch early, stopping only once for gas and food. Betty sat stiff in her seat, not speaking or touching. She showed a coldness that lately had begun to feel like a permanent wall, letting no one in. They checked in to a motel on the outskirts of Cheyenne for the night.

Doctor Edmond Lewis, M.D. a highly-respected purveyor of clinical psychiatry greeted Betty and George as they entered his office. He seated Betty and asked George to wait in the outer office while he examined Betty. He had received and reviewed a report from Dr. Morrison earlier. He began speaking of mundane things like the weather and the trip from Walnut, then began asking questions concerning family matters. "Tell me about your mother, Betty."

"She died when I was only seven."

"I read that, Betty, I'm asking, what was she like, what things did she do that you liked?"

A tight-lipped Betty sat quietly, starring into the room

seeing nothing. The psychiatrist continued to question. Betty remained silent.

George and Betty stayed in Cheyenne for two more days, spending an hour in the morning and an hour in the afternoon with Dr. Lewis. Finally when it came time to leave for the ranch, the psychiatrist gave George his assessment: "Betty cannot face the loss of one more person she loves. There will always be fear of another loss in her mind. She, therefore, denies love from anyone or to anyone. If her father turns up, maybe she'll begin to recover. Hard to say. But unless that happens, it is doubtful that her condition will change much for a long, long time."

George asked, "Is this a depression?"

"No, but to you and others, it may look like depression. She suffered an emotional trauma, a series of them really. The result of these traumas is actually a very deep, very profound phobia, but Betty isn't afraid of people or things, she's terrified of relationships and I'm afraid that means you."

George Bentley, with his father and mother gone, and now it would appear the de facto loss of his beloved wife, Betty, felt a hollowness, a sense of futility, which he couldn't share with Betty or any other person. In his sadness, he buried himself in the hard parts of running a western ranch, leaving the ranch house early, husbanding his herds, and often eating with the hands. Betty spent much time alone, calling for Mary Ellen only when she needed something.

One night when George came home late he found Betty gone. Pete came up from the cook shack when he saw his boss. "Boss, Betty lefta' hour ago, I think she's gone back t' er ranch."

George nodded, "Do you know if Spike is back from his vacation yet?"

"Yeah, he's there now."

"I'm glad she has someone there, I need to know she's not alone."

George didn't give up on Betty, but when he called on the Harris Ranch, only to face a cold, non-responsive Betty, he left frustrated, trying to understand what had happened to the love between them. He returned to her again and again, sometimes to see that she was eating and functioning well, or to try to ignite the magic that had slipped away. It was a hard time for George. He was not used to failing at anything he did. The weeks went by and then the months.

George Red Fox Bentley began to take it out on those around him. One day while tending to his favorite horse he abstractly pushed her head away while she was asking for attention. Pete, who was standing by said, "That hoss a yers seems to know when somethin's wrong. You just rode her pretty hard, and she's asking for a reward."

George glared at Pete, "Then you take care of her." He dropped the reins, turned and went into the ranch house.

Soon after the disappearance of Steve Harris, George had contacted the Arapaho Council, asking to speak before the next session. In time he received notice to attend the bimonthly meeting of the tribal elders, held in the Arapaho Great House. Since the death of Chief Running Deer the Tribe no longer had a Chief per se. Governing was done by a body of Council members, with no Chief. By repute they showed little emotion or often would not divulge what they were thinking, especially when facing a non-Indian. The experience of trying to get a point discussed, had frustrated many. This was not news to George, but he felt that, as an honorary member of the tribe he had some kind of an edge on this matter. When his turn came to speak, he rose and took a position in front facing the Council. He spoke in a low voice, first thanking them for this opportunity, he said, "Elders, most of you already know why I'm here. The absence of Steve Harris from his ranch, and the real possibility that he might have been killed, is a matter that needs your attention in that evidence indicates Indian involvement."

"Do not get me wrong, the sign and poetry of the Snake Medicine Card left at the Harris ranch site was put there for the Sheriff to find, with a purpose to point at and implicate our nation's involvement. Elders, this is a serious matter, and I am asking that you consider evoking the medicine of the Owl, as well as opening a dialogue with the white man's law. We will always be suspect until the real story is learned. Law enforcement outside the Reservation needs to know that Reservation police will cooperate to find and bring to justice those responsible for this crime."

There was silence from the Elders. They glanced between each other, they glowered at George, and they made no response to George's appeal.

George continued, "Steve Harris has always been a friend to the Reservation peoples. During your battles over water rights he was there for you. Help where you can to locate Steve and or his killers."

George left the meeting with little to show for his effort to enlist the aid of the Council. They would, of course, deliberate among themselves, take plenty of time, and probably remind each other that the incident happened outside the Reservation, and therefore should not be of their concern.

3 | FUTILITY

White Dove, John Running Deer's only offspring, died when her son George was twelve years old. Richard Bentley, George's father, was killed just prior to George's return to the ranch from college. Following the departure of Betty from the Arrow—B came the news of the death of John Running Deer, George's Indian grandfather. He was eighty-two, and as a tribal leader he had helped shepherd his people through those difficult years when they were forced to transcend from a nomadic life style to one of agrarian farmers. The passing of George's grandfather temporarily took his mind away from Betty and her denial of their love.

Ceremonies for the passing of John Running Deer were conducted by his own Arapaho people, and symbolic gestures by the nearby Shoshone. He was buried on the Reservation. A low fence surrounds his grave.

George would miss his grandfather who always listened to what was said, gave advice when requested, and through his stories, told of his ancestors. Together they had explored the surrounding natural world, the grandfather teaching the ways of the Arapaho, the young man soaking up everything he saw or heard. The bond between them was strong and would endure.

Once while returning from visiting Betty, George stopped in for mid-morning coffee and a chat with Rosey. It was in between breakfast and lunch, so Rosey came out from the kitchen holding her big coffee-pot, and two cups. She sat George down and seated herself facing him.

"Hi."

"Hello Rosey."

There was eye exchange, a moment of dead silence, finally, "Do you want just coffee, George, or is it so bad that you don't wish to share?"

George mused for a moment then said, "Considering the efficiency of the county wide communication network we have, I'm sure you know all about what's going on between Betty and me."

"Yeah, and I also will miss your grandfather John. Listen, George, you have been dealt a tough package, I know that. You can't do anything about it. Just remember that you have friends throughout this county. We need you in our lives."

George was silent for a time. His mind was sweeping over the last few years, and his strong love for Betty that came as he struggled with the problems of his ranch. Rosey was that special person that always seemed to be there when a friend was needed, and indeed he needed a friend, "Rosey, it's hard, very hard. You were here and saw how strong our love had become. You helped us get over the rough times. Yes, Rosey, it is simple to ask why, to a very complicated matter. This is not Betty's fault. She has lost too much and I know now of her real fears. The loss of her father was a tragedy and she is afraid to lose me. In defense, she has put me out of her life.

"I too have lost, Rosey, first my mother then my father and now my grandfather, they are all gone. And it seems I've lost Betty too. There is no one of my family left."

Rosey reached over and touched his hand. She said, "Be mindful, George, you have many friends who would miss you if you were gone from us. Give us a chance!"

"Thank you for that, Rosey."

George continued to visit Betty as often as the running of the ranch would allow. Gradually, and without really understanding what was happening to him, he began accepting a life without her. The routine of ranch life demanded strict adherence to the business at hand. Stock had to be provided for, fences mended, and living conditions for the ranch personnel looked after. His visits to the Harris Ranch became shorter and fewer.

4 | BETTY

The George and Betty affair had been lengthy and very romantic. Betty still carried the hurt and shock from the loss of her first husband, Paul, whom she had loved passionately. She moved to her new romance cautiously. The electricity that happened during the first meeting between George and Betty soon tapered off while they took time to learn about each other. Still there were moments of question. Would the accidental death of Paul linger within Betty, and affect a new relationship in her life? George recognized Betty's bruised persona, and respected her need to remain uncommitted. It took nearly two years for Betty to give herself fully to another human being. When the private moments came, and the fire of love took place, it was complete and full. The engagement time was short, and the community exhorted over the prospect of two of their favorite people joining in matrimony. This became a time of excitement, especially for the women who are always more romantic, and took this opportunity to live a bit away from the humdrum of ranch life.

Following the death of Paul, Betty had moved into the Harris Ranch with her father. There she had become an integral part of ranch life, taking her turn at caring for livestock, mending fences and such. She had stayed, more or less, away from the other ladies of the county, except for her occasional visit with Rosey when she came into town. In fact, Rosey became her only confidant.

After the disappearance of her father, Betty retreated to the Harris Ranch. Once again she made only one contact beyond the confines of the ranch. That was Rosey. Spike, the one ranch hand, pretty well handled things about the ranch which allowed Betty time to do the ranch shopping, and which always resulted in a visit with Rosey.

One of these early summer shopping trips to town found Rosey and Betty chatting as they always did, and skipping by the discussion of the weather and other mundane stuff, Rosey asked, "How are you, Betty?"

"I'm fine."

Rosey studied Betty; there seemed to be something changed, something not Betty here. She calculated time from their honeymoon. "You're pregnant, Betty."

A startled Betty asked, "How can you tell, Rosey?"

Rosey was silent for a time, then, "Have you told George yet?"

"No ... I'm due to see Doc Morrison this afternoon, and I will not be telling George. Will you keep this thing to yourself?"

"Of course, if you want it that way, Betty."

Betty walked up the short path to Walnut's only medical facility, noting the weathered sign hanging from a rafter near the front door. This was not the first time she had been to see this man, and she knew of his reputation as having birthed most of the babies in the area for the last fifty years. Still she had trepidations about being here. She followed the instructions printed on a small framed notice to enter, which caused the bell at the top of the door to announce her presence and sat down on a convenient chair.

Still thinking of the uncanny ability of Rosey to spot her pregnancy, she wondered how many others might know? Telling George was not an option, but not telling him also ran the risk of him finding out from someone else. Carrying George's child so complicated Betty's life that she sank further into a psychological fog.

Emma, the doctor's wife, came into the front room that served as a waiting room, nodded to Betty and said, "Henry 'll be right with you Betty." A few moments later, Emma invited Betty into the examining room, sat her down and left.

Doctor Henry Morrison was fully aware of Betty's psychological problems. He smiled and asked Betty, "You look well, what can I do for you?"

"I think I'm pregnant."

"Well that we won't know right off, Betty. Tell me what's happening to you?"

"I missed my period for the last two months, and I seem tired all the time." Betty gave a short laugh then said, "I just came from seeing Rosey, she just looked at me and guessed."

The doctor said, "Rosey seems to have special intuitive powers. We'll do some tests, in the meantime, Emma has a diet to give you, and we need a specimen from you. Go home and get some rest. I'll call you tomorrow."

The doctor did call as promised, and told Betty, "Yes, you are pregnant." As she hung up the phone, she fell into a deeper depression.

5 | JOAN LA CROSS

Joan La Cross and George Bentley met at the University of Vermont. Joan came from upstate Vermont where her parents owned a small dairy farm. She was a warm outgoing college student, softly beautiful, and popular around the campus. The friendship she shared with George was strong from the start, to say the least. There was no formal commitment, just trust and respect between them. They dated on occasion but stayed a bit apart when it came to discussing a future together.

At the time of George's departure from the university for his father's ranch in Wyoming, Joan had suddenly discovered more than friendship for George. Following graduation ceremonies from the university in 1952, Joan returned to her room in the dormitory, sat on the bed and deliberated. With George gone, she felt a void, a time of emptiness, she was sad. She was puzzled at first but reasoned it out: "I must be in love, geez."

George had departed for Wyoming ten days before graduation to attend to his father's passing, and to matters concerning the ranch. Joan had seen George off to the airport. There were unspoken promises, a kind of "we'll see you again" but no plans as to when or how. Wyoming was two thousand miles away. She lackadaisically packed and left for her parents' farm in upstate Vermont. She went by bus, and her mother picked her up at a nearby bus stop. "Hi Mom, it's good to be home, how's Dad?"

"Not that good. And along with the physical stuff, he's a handful. You know your Dad. I'm sure glad you're here."

"Oh Mom, Dad has always been demanding of us, but I know he loves us. I'm sorry you've had to do it alone though, maybe I can help."

"Joan dear, tell me about that young man you liked, will he be coming back after tending to his father's funeral and all?"

"I don't think so Mom, he'll be busy running a ranch. . . . I don't know I'm so confused. I think I love him. He didn't seem to return the favor. It's two thousand miles to where he is. I've just spent four years watching and sometimes dating this man. He was busy and I likewise. I can't see it ending this way. There has to be more."

Her Mother was silent for a time. "Dearest daughter, give it time, your man is facing a difficult time in his life. His father was strong in his life, it's hard to understand that he is gone, and the last of his family. If you feel you love him, try to understand him."

Charles La Cross, Joan's father, had acquired a sizable piece of land in upper Vermont early in the twentieth century. He met and married Renee in Montreal, Canada and moved to the United States, settling in northern Vermont where they established a dairy farm. Renee and Charles had two children, Joan and a younger brother. The farm was small, but became successful as a family business. Daughter Joan entered college with family knowledge of what it takes to run a farm business and a love for farm animals. She graduated with a degree in animal husbandry. When she arrived home her father gave her a big hug. He said, "Honey sweet, you made us proud, I am so sorry your Mother and I couldn't be there, but I'm not going out much these days. Have you made any plans for the future, I'm sure you don't want to chase a bunch of cows around for the rest of your life?"

"I'm working on it, Dad. I expect it will be fall before I hear from those who have jobs to offer. In the meantime, I will stay here with you, and help out. Maybe I might learn something."

"You know the routine here, Joan, but would you like to handle our accounts and the financial aspects of running this farm?"

"That sounds like a winner, Dad."

Joan was bored. The routine around the farm was just that, a routine. The mornings were early, the cows got milked, the dairyman came by and picked up the milk, the cows were released to pasture, and lunch was much the same each day. The afternoons were quiet, the cows tended and cleaned up as needed, and the evenings were milking time again. Saturday, an occasional movie or a barn dance, with Sunday to church for sure.

She needed more, and she knew what it was. Her time at home, helping her Mom with Father was done with love, yes, but she needed more. One day in early fall her mother said in a firm forceful voice, "Joan! we are not a people to willy wally around. For the past week or two you have been depressing to be around. You look like a sick cow. For heaven's sake go out to your man. We'll survive."

Joan's eyes glistened. She hugged her mother, and said, "You are so wise, Mom."

Joan had been keeping in touch with her college friends. It was a bit like a closed circuit group that passed a word around whenever anything happened to one another. So the word went out that Joan would be looking for a ride out to Wyoming. Of course there were busses and trains, airplanes and such, but these were kids without much money, unorthodox if you will. So Joan eventually hitched a ride to Walnut, Wyoming to see the man she couldn't get out of her mind.

In the interim, and before Joan arrived at the ranch, George had fallen in love with Betty; and Joan found herself second in line for George. Well, Joan's reception at the ranch in '52 had been anything but warm in that there were no extra bedrooms in the ranch house. Whereas this was okay with Joan (spending the night with George) it didn't fit in with George's situation. By then he had learned that his betrothed was a bit possessive, and might not be enthused over another female spending the night with her man in the same building even, let alone in the same room. So much to the puzzlement of Joan, George had moved down into the bunkhouse with the hands, leaving the lone ranch house bedroom to herself. And of course, Pete, the ranch foreman, had to be cute about the matter, making pseudo remarks about his boss's prowess in attracting women, etc. George who was then trying to shepherd his ranch through skimpy times wasn't that much enthused with Pete's jocularity, had winced and said "I really don't need this. We have enough problems on this ranch without adding more."

So, this was a large county, yes, but it had an outstanding communication system, and by the time the story got to Betty it had become, "Joan spent three days sleeping with George." Hmm. Being that as it may, Joan had fallen in love with this world of ranches, mountains, big skies and honest people and decided to stay. Her feelings for George didn't change, even after he and Betty got married. She still felt love and wanted him.

Given her studies at the University of Vermont in animal husbandry, it followed naturally that Joan found a niche for herself in the field of veterinary medicine, and in 1953 she enrolled at Colorado A&M in the Graduate College of Veterinary Medicine. Located in Fort Collins, Colorado, the school was only about forty-five miles south of Cheyenne, Wyoming. This took her away from the Walnut area for much of the year, returning to Wyoming during break or summer vacations. She would do her internship with the Davis Veterinary Clinic located in Glencoe.

6 | LOCOWEED

The Arrow—B Ranch was situated half way between Leaning Mesa and Portal Mesa in western Wyoming. George Bentley, along with Richard, his father and Leonard MacLaren, his great uncle, had taken the land from nothing to a successful western ranch, along with extensive properties. The ranch butted up against a portion of the Shoshone National Forest, and utilized leased areas of public lands within the Forest for grazing herds of cattle.

The Wind River Indian Reservation touched the north boundary of the Arrow—B ranch, and over the years the two entities had acted responsibly to each other, gaining a measure of support for the other's problems. Of course, the marriage of the lead Arapaho elder's daughter to Richard, the then owner of the Arrow—B Ranch, further strengthened the ties between them.

Almost from the beginning, there had been water wars between the invading Caucasians and the Indian residents in the area. The waters of the Wind River had been in contention for more than a century, and the issue of who gets what water never seemed to cease. Fortunately, the Arrow—B Ranch had a water source exempt from Indian jurisdiction and therefore was not an issue between them. Both Richard and his son George vehemently defended the Arapaho positions on this matter among other issues that concerned the welfare of the Tribes. Richard and his son George were adopted into the "Tribe," and given all the benefits of tribal membership. Richard became White Owl and George was named Red Fox.

After making his appeal to the Arapaho Council concerning the disappearance of Steve Harris, George returned to the ranch mumbling to himself over the lack of enthusiasm or response from the Tribal Elders. Totally frustrated, he seemed to be faced with unsolvable problems every way he turned. What with some unusual problems on the ranch, and the trauma that Betty was experiencing, his usual positive mind was being tested big time. The spring of 1955 had turned to summer and the longer days allowed for more ranch work and less time to dwell on his troubles.

Pete met him as he stepped out of the ranch truck, looked at his face, and said, "I guess you really don't need this, but we have a problem that we need to look at, but quick."

"So what's the problem?"

"We got some sick cattle up on the range."

"That's just peachy, have you called the vet, Davis I think, in Glencoe, yet?"

"No, I thought you might take a look first."

George said, "This is a new one for me, I'll make the call."

George's call to the veterinary office was answered by a pleasant female voice, which he recognized. He paused, then, "Is that you Joan? What are you doing there?"

"Hello George, I'm just doing a summer thing to get some intern time. Do you want to talk to Dr. Davis?"

"Uh huh, Joan, I hope you've been well."

"I have, just hold on."

The authoritative voice of the veterinarian came on the phone, "Todd Davis, here."

"This is George Bentley out on the Arrow—B. I wonder if you could come out and look at some stock of mine? There's something going on."

"Sure, how about tomorrow morning about nine?"

Todd Davis came, and not surprisingly, Joan too. The greeting between George and Joan was warm but guarded. Their eye contact told more than the meeting of old friends. George, extremely loyal and concerned over Betty; Joan, still in love with George, knowing he was untouchable. Soon to return to the university in Colorado, Joan who would again be away from the man in her life, tried not to wish ill toward Betty, but couldn't. She could not diminish what was in her heart. She could not accept a life without him.

Todd noticed, and thought, "Something going on here?" then said, "It's been some time since you've needed me, George. You must have the healthiest bunch of cows in the county."

"Yes, well some of those 'healthy' critters don't look that healthy. I hope you can do something."

The trip in the vet's pickup out to where the infected cattle were, found Joan in the middle seat, feeling the strong chemistry of her closeness to George. It was hard for her to think about their reason for being there.

The veterinarian laughed to himself, got out of the pickup, and studied the small grouping of animals. Off to the side, George, embarrassingly silent, and Joan trying to make small talk, finally, "I heard that Betty has been ill?"

"That she has, Joan. How is it, working with Todd?"

"I learn the mechanics of things at the university, but from Dr. Davis I learn what animal care and doctoring is all about."

Todd, who had been walking among the small herd of cattle, taking notice of behavior and physical conditions asked, "How long has this been going on, George?"

"I think it started when the rains came, about two weeks ago."

"That figures, you probably haven't noticed that you have locoweed growing strong and healthy down here, and with this good wet season it will make a lot of your cows sick if you don't keep them away from here." He looked over at Joan, "Come take a look."

George asked, "Will any of these recover?"

"Not really, I suggest you market this bunch right now if you can, but get them out of here." He turned to Joan, "We need to take some pictures and get blood samples."

George asked, "Why this year, in the years I have been on this ranch, I have never had this problem before? How did the seeds get here?"

Todd said, "I can only speculate on that one, did you bring winter feed up here this winter? Could be some seed mixed in. Even bird droppings could contain seed. The point is, it's here. These cattle are sick. They won't become normal ever. They're drunk, so to speak. The poison is swainsonine. It's addictive. Left alone this pasture will affect your whole herd. Take a look, those white flowers that stick up out there are about to make more seeds."

Gordon Clyde out of Glencoe was almost a second father to George Bentley. He was the owner of the Glencoe Livery Station, and housed George through his high school days. He also ran a few beefs on Arrow—B land. From the beginning, Gordon had been a close friend and confidant to the Arrow—B owners. Now, in his mid-seventies, he no longer actively participated in the livery business. He did however, retain his interest in the equine and bovine worlds, and in particular the cattle business at the Arrow—B ranch.

Not too often any more did George call the brawny Scotsman with a problem. This was one that he needed help with. He put in the call. "Hello Clyde, George here, how's retirement from the world of horses?"

"I'll survive, any change with Betty?"

"Negative, this is a tough one, and I'm not sure I'm prepared to handle. It's been over a year now, and many visits to the head doctor. How's the wife?"

"She's fine, but you didn't call me up for a discussion of

our girls. What's on your mind?"

"Yes well, we've got locoweed growing in the pasture."

"That's not great news, have you contacted the State Board of Agriculture?"

"Yeah, they told me to keep livestock away from the stuff. This I already knew, they didn't seem interested beyond that."

"That figures, the farther one gets from the action the less concern. The State is not equipped to understand a local problem, and is a toothless tiger anyway. How big an area are we talking about?"

"I don't know yet, I'm seeing their white flowers all over the place. They stick up like white flags. Our Vet tells me that this will happen in a year that has lots of rain and a mild spring like this one. It's into too much of my pasture to fence off, and my hands can only make a dent in the problem. Besides, cow hands don't like pulling weeds much."

Gordon said, "I hear there are lots of Reservation Indians unemployed. Will your finances cover hiring a bunch to dig this stuff out?"

"Not bad, Gord, that might work if the Council of Elders will do something in a reasonable amount of time, which is doubtful. You know them. The last time I asked the COE for help on finding information on the death of Steve Harris, it took three weeks to tell me no, it was none of their business. I can't wait three weeks."

Gordon said, "You know the drug and alcohol problem they are having is directly related to unemployment, and I hear that's like 25% on the Reservation. Can't we get the Bureau of Indian Affairs to stir someone up on the Rez to hurry a bit, and clear us for hiring some of those unemployed Indians? How many do you think it will take to grub out what you are seeing?"

"Oh maybe twenty, but my relationship with the BIA hasn't been that great since I pressed Washington to investigate their activities out here. I really don't think they like me enough to help me do anything. In fact I believe they would like to see the Arrow—B go under."

Gordon said, "How about going outside the Rez for this one?"

"That would be interesting, it would put me between a rock and a hard place: I go outside Rez and I alienate the whole Indian world, and if I don't I grow lots of locoweed?"

"I see your point, George, let me see what I can do from this end. I'll give you a call in the morning."

Moving one thousand-pound critters that don't want to be moved is a bit of a challenge. The ranch had always handled this problem by pushing and cajoling them to do it on their own four feet. The hands of the Arrow—B moved the main herd away from the Locoweed, and then tackled the eight affected animals with gun and pickup.

On the morning of the third day Gordon called. "Howdy, George, getting enough exercise out there? It must be lots of fun grubbing out weeds."

"I guess I'll have to listen to your ill humor and insults in order to find out what you called me about. Let's see now, it's been six months since your retirement, do you still smell like a horse?"

"Do you think you can handle twenty Indians for a week or two?"

"The question now becomes when."

"Like tomorrow."

"How'd you do that?"

Gordon laughed, "First off they will be working for me as you seem to have managed to make yourself justifiably unpopular with the BIA. Second, yours is not to know the who, but I'll tell you how. The BIA reports to the U. S. Department of The Interior. I know a guy up there that owes me a favor."

"I see you haven't lost your talent for arm twisting. I remember that once or twice before you have saved our bacon out here. The next question is how am I going to house and feed these guys?

"I think we should let them return to the Village each night, and can't you activate your chuck-wagon?"

"Uh huh, how about transportation? The ranch pickup can maybe handle ten in the open bed."

"Yours is not to worry, I'll take care of that one. See you tomorrow. Be ready to feed twenty."

7 | MORE THAN FRIENDS

The first person Joan La Cross met in Walnut, or in the entire West for that matter, was Rosey. The meeting took place in Rosey's Café, and both took an instant liking for each other. So on a weekend, when she could get away, she boarded the shuttle bus to Walnut for a visit with Rosey, and it was not long after the "how are yous" were over before the subject of George came up. Rosey asked, "Have you seen George since you came?"

Joan answered, "I went out to the Arrow—B to look at some sick cattle with Todd." She paused then said, "It's difficult for me, Rosey, you know I love him. It's not fair, what Betty's doing to him, and I can't help." There were tears showing in her eyes.

Rosey touched Joan, feeling the pain there. She withdrew her hand, looked into two moist eyes, and said, "I too have agonized, Joan, you know how much these two mean to me. I have looked to my church for understanding, and I am trying to shake off a feeling of darkness."

Joan spoke through her tears, "But Rosey, how long must he suffer? You know this man, he will be infinitely loyal to Betty. What if she doesn't recover?"

There was a time of silence between them, then Rosey said

"Joan, George is a man who is very positive. He will find a way to both, care for Betty, and make a meaning to his own life. All of us need love, George included. If he cannot find it with Betty, he will with someone else."

With help from Gordon and the Rez, George had fought off the locoweed over the dry summer months and now it was getting toward fall. The annual rodeo events brought togetherness to the community and a celebration time for the ranchers and miners in Contra County. Joan was there, soon to return to Fort Collins, and the university, where she would continue her studies toward her doctorate of veterinary medicine. She met with George one more time before departure.

George spotted Joan as he entered the Beefsteak Café in Glencoe. Both had been spectators at the annual rodeo, and were on their way home, so to speak. George surprised Joan with a hello, and a smile.

Joan turned and answered with her eyes, brushing back a wisp of auburn hair that had fallen away from its assigned position.

George asked, "Can I join you, Joan?"

Joan nodded then, "Do you like what happens to those critters forced to perform at a rodeo?"

"Well, not really, Joan, but my riders look forward to this every year, and after all it is a tradition started long ago to display those skills a hand needs to do his job. So, will you be heading back to Fort Collins now?"

"Yes, but it is getting harder and harder as I'm learning more here than in some classroom elsewhere. I spent the early evening last night tending a mare birthing her first foal. Something I won't forget for a long time."

George was silent for a while, then, "It is good, Joan, that you feel as you do. I feel the same, each creature on the ranch is nurtured by the hands. It is always sad when we have to send them off to market. The rodeos, while a part of the West, may someday be gone or at least tempered." He studied the woman sitting across the table, remembering those college days when they were close. "Have you met anyone new in your life?"

Joan avoided the question. "Rosey told me about Betty. It must be very difficult for you."

George asked, "Are you leaving for Fort Collins today?"

"Yes, in about an hour."

"May I drive you to the airport?" he smiled, "Do you remember driving me to the airport when I left college for the ranch?"

"You had received news of your father's death, it was a time of us parting, and a time of challenge for you."

There was a quiet time as they drove to the Glencoe Airport, each with their private thoughts and emotions. Nearly at the end of their twenty-five-mile trip, George asked, "When will you return, Joan?"

"Oh! If I can drum up the fare, I'll come back for a short stay at Christmas, if not, I'll stay put until the end of the spring semester." Boarding time came and with it a light kiss from Joan. George felt the warmth, at the same time experienced a tinge of discomfort. His love for Betty, still strong, but beset with futility and frustration. Was this going to be his life, or will he once again be whole, with a partner in life, giving to, and receiving as love partners do? It had been almost two years now? He watched Joan board the plane, then turn around at the top of the steps and wave.

The drive, from Glencoe to the Arrow—B, found George depressed over his personal life. As he drove along the narrow two lane highway he tried to shake off those negative thoughts, and prepare himself to face the everyday challenges of running a ranch. By the time he reached home he was ready to function again, and he buried himself in the affairs of his ranch. Pete met him as he drove in. "Hi boss, how'd things wind up, I had to leave early?"

"Great, Pete. The guys did good. Everybody won something."

Things on the ranch settled down, giving George time for a well-earned vacation. Considering Betty's condition, he hired an extra hand for the Harris Ranch, explaining to Betty that he would be away for a short time, and wanted to be sure that she had a presence to call on if need be. Without thinking about it, the person he hired turned out to be a woman. Betty, who had been living in a man's world, welcomed Sadie on to the ranch, and they soon became good friends.

From the start, George had offered a reward for information leading to the discovery of what happened to Steve Harris. He felt that the answer to Betty's mental state was solving the problem of her father's disappearance, and he constantly reminded Sheriff Williams to do something more than create a file, or mark that file, "Case closed" and file it away. This, of course annoyed the crusty old Sheriff to no end, and threatened their friendship. George continued to needle, and the Sheriff refused to even talk to him. Rosey got into the act when the Sheriff was in for coffee one day, she asked him, "Are we making any progress on the Steve Harris case?" The Sheriff exploded all over Rosey, and stomped out of the diner without paying his tab.

After returning from Glencoe and the fall roundup, George buried himself in the everyday work of preparing his ranch for the approaching winter. On a trip to Walnut to pick up supplies, he stopped in to see Rosey. It was off-hours, and the café was empty, so Rosey sat down with George to a mid-morning cup of coffee. Rosey asked, "How'd it go at the Rodeo?"

"Great, Rosey, our hands did real well and all four came away with some prize money . . . I ran into Joan leaving for Fort Collins. She will finish her studies and get her doctorate this coming June."

"Yes I know, she came out here last week, and we chatted a bit. I think she intends to become a full-fledged veterinarian out here somewhere."

"She'll make a good one, Rosey."

There was an awkward silence between the two. Finally Rosey said, "You still have feelings for Joan?"

"Rosey, you know I will never give up on Betty. Now, more than ever she needs someone."

"Yes, it would be like you to be that way about Betty." There was a long pause between them. Each with their own thoughts.

Rosey got up and busied herself with filling sugar bowls and salt shakers. She knew the torture that lived in George. She studied him closely as he sat quietly seeing nothing, and she watched him as he left the diner.

8 | RANCH UNDER SIEGE

Winter on a western ranch was as one, a resting time from the open range chores, but two, a grueling work time for ranch hands doing the mundane tasks around the ranch. It is always cold in wintertime on the range. The buildings would be called "cozy" but one can't spend much time there and do the winter chores. There is the spreading of winter-feed, water sources to keep open from freezing, and critters to husband through the winter. In stormy times the hands hunker down, and travel—to and from, ranch to ranch or town to ranch—was often restricted. Keeping the roads clear for travel in wintertime becomes a joint effort of the ranchers and miners.

George Bentley authored the weekly Walnut Newsletter among other periodicals around the State. He enjoyed doing this as it gave him a first-hand look at what was going on. He often crossed bases with Ruth, Reverend Thomas's wife and Rosey, whose café was the town's meeting place and privy to everything happening around the county. There was little going on that these two didn't know about. The newsletter told of births, deaths, weddings, etc. and usually contained an editorial from George. Writing for George was a way to release him from some of the tensions and frustrations he was experiencing. Peter White, the ranch foreman, pretty well handled ranch matters, so this allowed George time to move around the county and observe the pulse of the area. On one of these times, when he sat across from Rosey nursing a morning cup of coffee and munching on one of her famous cinnamon rolls, Rosey said, "I hear the price of beef is off big time, George. How's this hitting the Arrow—B?"

"Not good, Rosey, we'll survive of course, but there are some out there that won't. I'll know more after this afternoon's Cattlemen's Association meeting."

"That's nice, are you telling me that that bunch of drinking buddies actually accomplish something in their monthly meetings?"

George mused a bit looking deeply into Rosey's eyes. "You're right on, about that one, Rosey, if it isn't about sheep verses cattle or farmers infringing on rangeland, they don't do much. I have trouble bringing up serious issues and getting a meaningful discussion going. However this affects their pocket books, maybe they'll get engaged.

"Rosey, the real issues at times like these, are big versus small. The small ranchers can't afford this kind of trouble. They need a hand right now. It used to be that the banks would help them out through a rough period. Lately that isn't happening. I'm going to the meeting this afternoon, and I expect to be talking to deaf ears."

"You covered that one pretty well in this week's newsletter, George." Rosey paused for a time, then said, "We women read your writings with a passion. Don't give up on that one. We'll be talking about this, and who knows, maybe we can help."

George left the café and headed for the church. He found Ruth getting ready to handle a Sunday potluck. She took off her apron and sat down with George. She said, "The reverend thinks you should come to church once in a while. I think, after reading your last article he feels much as you do, 'concern over the plight of the smaller ranchers,' and your presence on Sundays would help put the message out." She smirked a little, "Tom seems a bit nettled that he doesn't see all of his following every Sunday."

This month's Cattlemen's Association meeting was held in Glencoe's city hall building. Ranchers from all over the county attended, and Rosey was quite right, it was more like an excuse to 'let it all hang out' for a day, than discussions related to ranching or mining. Many checked into the Glencoe Hotel or a nearby motel to avoid long turn-around trips back to their ranches in one day. It was cold outside and most came wearing sheepskin jackets and caps with flaps to cover ears as needed.

The meetings convened at ten a.m. and after the pledge of allegiance to the flag and the invocation, business began. Most present were anxious to get past the business and enjoy their time off from the daily humdrum of ranch life. In time, George was recognized by the chair and he rose to address the gathering.

"Fellow ranchers, I think we should discuss the issue of dismal beef prices. If what we are now offered for our products doesn't improve before next spring, there are many here that won't survive. I ask the chair to open a discussion on this matter as well as the availability of short term loans to carry some of our members over this coming winter."

"The chair will so open. George, we are all affected by the low price for beef. Just what do you propose to do about it?"

George answered, "First off the Arrow—B doesn't have a problem sitting out for a better time to sell beef, and I would guess there are others here that can do the same. However, this is not the case with many of the smaller ranchers in our county. In the past one could go to the local bank for a loan to tide one over. In that most of the local banks have been bought out by large institutions, and they aren't inclined to loan unsecured money, I don't see this happening now.

"Prices are so low that selling now would bankrupt many of the small ranches. I think this association should consider supporting its members through the winter."

After a few moments of silence a member stood, chuckled then, "There are some here that might not feel put out if that happened, however, I see your point. Do you have a plan that we might discuss?"

George, answered, "First, let's hear from others."

The ensuing discussion took the better of an hour, with no concession of opinions from those present. George came away empty, but still concerned over the issue and its effect on the small rancher. His feature article in both the Walnut Weekly and the Glencoe Herald, read:

A Look in the Mirror

Since the price we are offered for our beef has managed to sink to a level below the cost of growing it, I am asking myself why do I suffer through miserable below-zero winters and 100 degree summers? We do this because we have chosen to. We like it this way. In other times when we make a profit and can financially sustain our chosen life style, the frigid winters and hot summers are but a nuisance and we discount the inconvenience. We are a community made up of ranch owners, cowboys, miners, and families. In a sense we are one family. We have mutual problems just as we have mutual successes. No one in our community is really alone nor should they be.

Now this Wyoming community is facing one of those tougher times when the markets for our product have dried up and some of us face a financial setback. It is not a serious problem for most of the larger ranchers who can wait out the depressed beef market, however it is close to a disaster for some of the smaller ranchers.

In the past it was possible to borrow from the bank to tide one over, but that source is not lending to the little guy these days. Those who traditionally supported the ranchers, large or small, are gone now in favor of a large institution, an ocean away from the action, and which looks at things with a jaundiced eye.

We have a choice, we can let things fall as they may, or act as a community and help each other. No one questions the generosity of this community. That attribute of my fellow citizens has long been established, though we sometimes forget or are not aware of a neighbor's needs, and that neighbor is sometimes too proud to ask for help when he needs it.

Are each of us looking at others in our community that we may know when they are in need?

GB

Well, Reverend Mathews wasn't exactly the fire and brimstone type, but at times he could get a point across firmly and clearly without sounding like a grammar school teacher scolding a ten year old. His Sunday sermon following George's feature article went like this:

Getting our priorities straight as a community in the eyes of God is the reason we are called Christians. We look out for each other as we stretch out our hands to touch families in times of need. This church has always been a "mission-oriented" church, especially giving to peoples of the world who have less than we do in America, people in African and Asian nations especially who are suffering from wars, famine, and starvation. We sometimes forget that we have those at home, too, who are in need of help, maybe not as crucial as in a war-torn area, but just as important.

When people in our own community have grave needs, we have to be good neighbors. Often in small towns like ours obvious needs hide themselves even as desperation sets in but no one wants their neighbors to know. They suffer in silence and are too proud to ask for help. Let's always be sensitive to our neighbors' needs, for being good neighbors is what God has always wanted for us.

The Bible tells us "Do unto others as you would have them do unto you." And as Luke in the New Testament says, "You shall love the Lord your God with all your heart, with all your soul, with all your strength, and with all your mind, <u>AND</u> love your neighbor as yourself."

Go forth today and carry God's love and joy with you. Remember the Golden Rule ... there is no more important commandment God has left us. We are all neighbors and we all need each other at all times in our lives.

Ruth Mathews joined Rosey at her café the morning George's article came out, and it was no surprise that they would get to talking about the small ranchers' financial crises. The situation for many would certainly test their will to the breaking point, and the women of Contra County were well aware of this.

Whereas the role of women in the masculine dominated society of the time was generally submissive, when they felt a need, they would step out of those traditional ways and state their views to their menfolk, sometimes with a solid impenetrable front that their men knew better than to cross. Firmly, as is normal with this spread out community, most issues, large or small, manage to find their way into every corner of the state without help from the radio and newspapers. It might be said that there was some kind of an underground telegraph system in play. So everybody has an opinion, and everyone has to voice their own understanding of what should be done.

At the next meeting of the Cattlemen's Association the question of financial help to the small ranchers was vigorously debated, and it was obvious that some power beyond a church sermon or a news editorial was in play. In time a consensus in favor was reached and the matter of what to do, and who would do it came to the fore. Whether it was from respect or otherwise, George was selected to follow through on the matter, and told to come up with a plan. It was sort of a "You started this thing. You do it." And the boys went back to the bar.

George mused to himself about the "let-George-do-it" attitude of most, then set out to make as simple a plan as possible, as anything more would be difficult to sell to this bunch.

Back at the Arrow—B, George asked Pete up to the ranch house, sat him down over a late cup of coffee and some conversation. He asked, "What do you hear from some of our nearby neighbors over the lousy beef prices right now?"

"Some ain't gonna make it through this winter."

"So would any of them take a little help if offered?"

Pete chuckled, "Shore, if'n it war their idea."

George thought for a moment, "Imagine yourself running a few steers, expecting to sell some via the fall roundup to carry you over the winter and this cash source dried up.

What would you do?"

"I dunno, I guess I'd fold up and try to find a job workin' for someone else."

"How about if we let this roundup slip by, you get a small loan on your marketable stock to tide you over, until the price of beef gets better, and we all benefit?"

"That sounds like it might work."

"Thanks, Pete, would you spread that around a bit for me?"

That was the way of things in the world of cattle, horses, and ranches in a time of economic downturn. Those that had gave a helping hand to those in need. On the other hand, there was that sticky matter of 'big versus small' where personal mindsets were involved.

9 | NOT MY DAUGHTER

The Robinson Ranch lay halfway between the bend in the Little Wind River and the city of Glencoe, just south of the edge of the Wind River Indian Reservation. The Robinsons settled there, generations ago, and the present resident, Lester Robinson and family have carried on the culture and traditions of their ancestors. Lester, a crusty old rancher, rules his empire of several thousand acres, with an iron hand and the several employees know it as did his family. He and his wife, Amelia, had only one offspring, a girl named Amy.

Amy, the apple of Lester's eye, now 18, was a free spirit, and in a way reflected her father's ways, was just now beginning to take issue over her father's sometimes dictatorial commands. Her mother tried to explain to Lester that his daughter was an adult now and needed to be treated as one. When Amy found a young man to date and perhaps more, Lester almost had an occlusion and forbade Amy to see her new friend. Albeit the boyfriend was just out of high school, and was punching cows for George, the owner of the Arrow—B.

George Bentley had dealings with Lester over the "Be kind to the small guy" program. Lester considered himself of the old school, and felt little compassion for the small ranchers.

To him they were infringing on his ranchland even if they were not. However, the pressure from others in the ranching world and his wife and church got too much to handle, and he succumbed. When it came to his daughter however, that was a different matter! He would never allow his daughter to go out with a cowboy.

The program that George laid out was indeed simple. A man with cattle needs cash. He borrows what he needs from one who has, putting his cattle up as collateral. It was like putting his cattle in escrow. All this is done in someone's kitchen with a minimum of paper, and sometimes with just a handshake. Lester finally endorsed the plan after much bluster and gesturing.

So when George asked Lester how Amy was doing, as in "Does she have any plans for the summer?" Lester gave him the eye like 'it's none of your business.' George got the message and backed off. The two men rose from the table where they had been discussing the subject at hand and as they shook hands Lester said, "I hear that Mrs. Bentley has been ill. I hope she has recovered."

Taken by surprise George hesitated a moment then smiled and said, "Lester, I guess I'm about as sensitive about that subject as you are about Amy. Betty is not well. She has lost all of her family and cannot risk the loss of anyone else in her life. She has chosen to live alone on her small ranch. I visit her as often as I can. As to my question concerning Amy, I am looking for a young person to act as an out of the office news finder, a cub reporter, so to speak. From what I hear, Amy has sort of been leaning in that direction during her high school studies."

"Who did you hear that from? It seems that you know more about my family than I do?"

Sensing a bristling Lester Robinson, George said softly, "It is not, nor will it ever be, for me to infringe on your family's privacy. In answer to your question, I have asked the high school counselor of the graduating students for a possible candidate to fill my needs. Amy was highly recommended."

"My women folk have never worked to make money. I take care of that. I will not permit my daughter to do otherwise."

George drove back to the ranch, his mind in contest with that of the man he had just spoken to, musing to himself of the human side of it all: A father that loves his daughter deeply, and won't let her go: a man of principle, who is now facing an age-old problem, and knows not how to handle it.

During graduation week, the Glencoe High School counselor had an early appointment with Amy. She waited patiently as the youthful looking school official studied her records. He looked up with a smile and said, "You seem to have worked very hard this last year, Amy. Now it is time for you to decide what you will do from now on. Have you given any thought to going on with your education?"

"I have and I think I would like to teach."

"An education degree then, any particular subject?"

"English."

The counselor studied Amy for a moment, "Looking at your grades, you would make a good one." He shuffled some papers on his desk, selected one to study, then turned back to Amy. "The only thing we have to offer here in Wyoming is in Casper, and that is two years only. You can get by with that here in our State, but it would be better for you if you went out of state to an accredited four-year university."

Amy asked, "What choices do I have out of state?"

"Colorado A&M at Fort Collins has a fine School of Education. Would you consider going that far?"

Amy left the school office and caught the shuttle bus out to Walnut, where someone from the ranch would pick her up. While waiting for a ride home, Amy stopped into Rosey's for a cup of coffee and a bit of conversation, which found her walking into the café shortly after nine a.m. The café was empty of customers. Rosey met her with a hello and a smile.

"Sit down, I'll pour the coffee, and I have some new cinnamon rolls waiting to be eaten." She looked at the pile of pots and pans from the morning breakfast time, then at her visitor. She said, "Sometimes this business gets to me. That stack of stuff on the kitchen sink gives me the blahs."

Amy asked, "Do you do the cleanup all by yourself, Rosey?"

"Not usually but my help is gone for the summer. She won't be back until the fall, and I haven't found anyone to help during the summer."

"Rosey, I want to go off to college in Fort Collins this fall, and I need money. Could I work for you this summer?"

"Sure, hon' … can you go for eight to ten hours a day for the summer?"

"If that's what it takes, Rosey."

"Okay, Amy, start tomorrow. Come at eight, you can have breakfast here if you want to."

Amy arrived home to find her mom giving dinner instructions to Maria, the Mexican cook. Her dad was still out on the range. She waited until her mother was finished with Maria, and said, "Hi, I just came from Rosey's, she wants me to work for her during the summer."

Her mom said, "That's fine with me, Amy, but your dad is going to blow up at that idea. What will you be doing?"

"From what I could see, washing up stuff in the kitchen. I'll be taking her usual helper's place, who is away for the summer. Will you help me with dad?"

"No, Amy, one of the things that happens when we make adult decisions for ourselves is that we also have to face the consequences by ourselves. Your father is a proud man, he will object to what you wish to do, but he loves you. Listen to him, but stick to your guns."

"Gee, Mom, I've already upset him by seeing Cliff. He doesn't think he's okay for some reason."

"And he won't change that one either. It's because he loves you and that nobody is good enough for his daughter to go with. Have patience, my dear."

Lester Robinson arrived back at the ranch house late, tired and dusty from a tough day out on the range. He washed up, changed his working clothes for something more comfortable and joined the others in the dining room. The meal proceeded in its usual form, and during one of its lulls, Amy said, "I found a job today, Dad."

Lester looked up from his dish, his fork suspended, and his eyes telling of his indignation at the usurping of his authority. "Just what kind of work?"

"I'll be helping out Rosey at the café."

"Did Bentley put you up to this?"

"What? No, it was my idea, I will be going to Colorado A&M at Fort Collins this fall to take a major in education."

"Oh, and who helped you make that decision?" Lester looked over at his wife, "What do you know about all this?"

Amy interrupted, "Mom had nothing to do with my decision, Dad. Teaching is what I want to do. I need to go to a university that has and gives degrees in that field."

Lester said, "Going to a university is one thing, but I will not permit you to wash dishes or wait on tables for my friends and neighbors. That's out, do you understand?"

He studied his daughter for a moment then, "And while we are about it, you are not to see that cowboy, period!"

Tears showed in Amy's eyes, she jumped up from the table and ran out of the room. Amelia stared at her husband, then after a moment, said, "Lester, Amy is an adult now, you are treating her like a child. When are you going to let her go? Your daughter is fully capable of facing the world without our help or interference." She stood up, turned and left the room. She made her way to Amy's bedroom where Amy was sitting quietly, holding back the tears.

"Amy, your father loves you. Give him time, and he'll come around. Go ahead with your plans, I'll handle Dad."

10 | A CHILD IS BORN

George Bentley was a tough western cow man, but he had a softer side, built in by a loving and caring mother. White Dove's untimely death years before left a deep sadness in her boy and it changed his father, Richard, forever cementing the bond between father and son. White Dove's death also brought George closer to Chief Running Deer, his grandfather. From these two men, George became both strong and caring. From them he learned the meaning of family love and loyalty.

For George, his commitment to his first true love, Betty, was complete. He remained devoted to her during the years of their courtship and their legally constituted marriage despite the painful fact that Betty did not return that love. Deeply fearful that she might lose another person of her family, Betty rejected love and companionship from all. She lived on the Harris ranch with a live-in companion. George visited as often as he could, but at times Betty would simply call to him from the bedroom, "I can't see you today," or they might have a short discussion concerning finances or the needs of the Harris Ranch. Steve, the ranch hand, managed to take care of the ranch needs with occasional help from one of the Arrow---B hands.

On one of his visits to Betty at the Harris Ranch, George stopped on his way back to the Arrow---B at Rosey's for a cup of coffee and some conversation. Rosey called from the kitchen pass-through opening and said, "Come on in honey, the coffee is fresh."

"Hi, Rosey."

Rosey came bringing a basket of cinnamon rolls and a large enamel pot. She poured and asked, "What brings you to town, hon?"

George, with a blank look on his face said, "Been out to visit Betty."

Rosey noticed the blank stare, "You worried about Betty?"

"Uh huh, she seemed unusually guarded, almost afraid of me."

The conversation switched to other matters, Rosey careful not to step too far into Bentley privacy. George, mumbling about the expected drop in beef prices and such, was kind of talking around what was on his mind.

Intuitive Rosey asked, "Did you two talk about the baby today, you and Betty?"

"What baby?"

"Betty's pregnant, didn't you know?"

"Oh. ... She didn't tell me. Are you sure, Rosey?" Rosey immediately felt heartbroken for the rift between her two young friends but tried not to show it.

"Doc Morrison came by this morning. He said she is coming along just fine."

"That sure complicates things, Rosey."

"I wish I could help, George, but the best is for me to stay out of the way."

The news of Betty's pregnancy brought both concern for Betty and worry over whether Betty could care for a newborn. As the time for birth got closer, George's concerns grew. George hired a full time live-in for Betty, and their child was born at the Harris Ranch, as was customary in those days. From the time of the birth, George was denied access to see his new daughter Eva. Sometimes when he visited the

Harris Ranch he heard his baby cry and gurgle through the closed door to Betty's room. His need to see and hold his daughter in his arms was heartfelt. He worried for Betty, but now he found himself blocked from seeing both his betrothed and his newborn daughter.

George, in his sadness, turned to other aspects of his life, running a large cattle ranch, and hunting and fishing in the nearby mountains as his time allowed. There was a hollowness in him that never went away. He became terse toward those around him, giving no quarter to those who might violate his standard of performance. The weeks went by, and then the months and still he had no one to carry in his arms and no one to care for. His marriage to Betty had come with the commitment to love and care for each other always. It seems it was not to be.

11 | AMY AND CLIFF

Clifford Upton, Amy's boyfriend, handsome to a fault and innately intelligent, standing a towering six foot four in his stocking feet was the undisputed athletic hero of Glencoe High School. The two young people did things together. Amy was the more forward of the two, often challenging the more bashful Cliff into exploring the physical aspects of dating. By the time they were eighteen the relationship had grown into one of first love, and would last into their later adult lives. They were giving both sets of parents nightmares. Since there is no way one can influence eighteen-year-olds who know everything and have found love, beyond locking them up, turmoil often prevailed.

So when Mr. Upton found out that Cliff had spent the afternoon in a motel with Amy, the relationship between Cliff and his father disintegrated to the point that Cliff gathered up some of his clothes and moved out. Now it's not uncommon for local eighteen-year-old young men to knock on a ranch door looking for work, George Bentley hired Cliff to work at the Arrow—B ranch for the summer. Word got around as word does, and one morning George answered the ringing phone with a gruff, "Bentley here."

"Bentley, are you harboring my son out there?"

"It would be helpful if you told me who you are."

"Peter Upton, Bentley, I hear that you have given my son a place to stay away from his home. I want him back here as of now."

"If you are referring to one of my cow hands named Cliff, yes, he's here. As he came here looking for a summer job, and I needed a hand, I hired him."

"Well you can just un-hire him. I'll come out to your place and pick him up."

"Come ahead, Pete, he's out on the range fixing fences. As for me, I hired the young man, he's doing good work, and I'm not about to fire him. What's your problem?"

"My problem is that you are butting into my family business. Get out of the way Bentley."

"Now simmer down, Pete. Come out and talk to your son if you will. I'm out of that one."

The Upton ranch pick-up found its way on to the Arrow—B ranch yard and an angry Peter Upton emerged from behind the wheel. He climbed up the three steps that led to the front door and pounded away. George opened the door and said, "Pete, you're going to have an occlusion if you don't calm down. I'll take you out to where your son is working, and you can talk to him."

A silent Peter Upton climbed into the ranch pick-up and the two men drove out to where Cliff was fixing some broken fence wire. He got out of the car, walked over to where Cliff was working and said, "Get your ass back home where you belong, Clifford, you need a lesson in behavior, and as far as you shacking up with that slut is concerned, you're going to be sorry about that one." He turned to George, "Pay Cliff what he has coming. He's going home."

Cliff said, "That sounds like you, father, dictating what you want me to be, and how to behave. It won't work this time. And as for telling me who I can see, forget it, I'll see anyone I care to. I'm staying here as long as Mr. Bentley will have me."

Peter Upton was a big man, hard muscled from wrestling

livestock, and strong willed to the point of pain for anyone disputing his way of things. He towered above his son, reached to grasp him. Cliff sidestepped, dodging away. Peter swore, then stared at his son, "You choose to do this, then you are totally on your own. You needn't come home again ever!" He turned away.

George felt sadness for both the father and the son. He thought of his own life, and how happy he would be to have a son, to have loved ones in his life, to again do together and plan together with another person. He finally said, "Cliff, ride on back to the ranch house, I'll drive your dad back."

George turned to Peter, "Let's get things straight, Peter; I don't wish to take your son in any way from you. I've hired Cliff for the summer. My word to your son is like a written contract. Young people need to know that we adults are true to our word. As long as he does the work I ask him to do, he stays. If he fails to keep his end of things, he goes. This young man wishes to go to college, and he is trying to earn money to do that."

They started back to the ranch. There was clouded silence in the car as they drove. Peter didn't need to verbally express his dislike for George, and that he, George, was out of order allowing Cliff to stay. George could feel it. Peter's mind-set was focused on how much he had been injured and how wrong everyone else was. Back at the ranch Peter climbed into his own pick-up and drove off, not mentioning his son as he left.

Things settled down on the Arrow—B, George had little contact with Cliff. Peter White, the ranch foreman, pretty well handled the men and their assignments for each day. Amy and Cliff did, as lovers do, meet as often as they could. The four parents settled into some kind of acceptance of what their offspring were doing. With the fathers it was a need to keep peace in the house, with the mothers, a more mature understanding of being young and wanting to get away on one's own.

12 | A TROUBLED NATION

The Arrow—B Ranch, through time and toil, had evolved over the years as one of the larger land holdings in the Wind River area. George Bentley the owner and manager of the huge spread was an honorary member of the nearby Arapaho tribe, living on the Wind River Reservation. As such, George was inherently sensitive to its whims and moods, its troubles and health as a nation.

When it became a troubling time for the tribe due to alcohol and drug abuse, George took notice and vowed to do something to alleviate the problem. He postulated that the high unemployment rate on the Reservation was primarily responsible for this, and that fixing this would go a long way toward a solution.

George's voice was generally heard on this matter during the bimonthly tribal council meetings. He engendered and encouraged discussions related to drug abuse and or excessive drinking by tribal members. The council would listen, and nod their heads, but would, or could, do nothing beyond that, so, substance abuse remained a major issue with the tribe. While the Reservation police struggled to take care of the drinkers and the users, it was undermanned and undertrained to make a dent in the drug and alcohol issue. The idle let it all hang out in large numbers, and paid the price: moral and ethical breakdown.

In time some of the problems flowed out of the Reservation and into the surrounding white world. The northern edge of the Arrow—B was within shouting distance of the Reservation, and there were no fences or physical features to accurately determine just where you were. People moved back and forth easily, giving no thought as to whose property they were on.

The Arrow—B staff consisted of an olio of talents with skilled personnel to handle the livestock, and less-skilled hands to fix the fences and chop the wood. All were treated well, and most wished to stay where they were: working for the Arrow—B. Several of these were from the Reservation, and for the most part were fine employees. George made it a point to know each of his ranch hands, and each for his or her value to the ranch. He also encouraged his neighbors to do the same. The fact that George moved about the state tasting events to discuss in his bylines carried in the Glencoe Herald and elsewhere gave him the opportunity to feel the pulse of the community, and he always pressed on the matter of employing tribal members when help was needed.

On a day when nothing was happening, George took himself up to the water-tower for a look see. Tommy Little Feather was cleaning out the sluice that led to the water tank. George watched for a moment or two, considering the feelings of the person he was watching: a little bit awed, not quite sure of himself, maybe a little concerned that he might do something wrong. He said, "Tommy, did you know that John Running Deer was my grandfather?"

Tommy looked up in surprise, "No Mr. Bentley, I was not told that when Mr. White hired me."

"Well, Tommy, my tribal name is George Red Fox Bentley. I learned much about our nation from my grandfather. I still miss him now that he's gone." After a few moments of silence he said, "Tommy, when you finish here I'd like us to visit together for a few moments."

George found a flat rock to sit on, and waited while Tommy finished his assignment. Tommy kind of embarrassedly found a spot opposite and sat down across from his boss.

George asked, "Do you have parents living on the Reservation?"

"My mother is there, but my father is gone."

"Oh, that's too bad … do you visit your mom on your day off?"

"Well, yes, she needs me to be there once in a while."

"That's good, Tommy, do you meet others while you are visiting the Reservation?"

"I have friends there that I sometimes do things together with."

"Do some of them drink alcoholic drinks, or take drugs?"

"I think so, although I don't actually see them do it."

"What do you think about this, Tommy?"

"These are my friends, I don't wish to talk about them."

"This is right, Tommy, I would never ask you to talk against your friends. I wish though, that I could help in some way. It is very sad for me to see our families being destroyed by drugs and alcohol."

Tommy Little Feather sat in thought. George finally said, "Tommy, as you go about doing your jobs here on the Arrow—B, think about this and if you have any ideas that you think might help, come and see me at the ranch house. I'll listen."

It was several weeks before Tommy took the risk and knocked on the ranch house door. It was evening. George opened the door, looked down at the hesitant Indian at his doorstep, smiled, and invited Tommy to come in. They sat down across from each other, and George said, "Tommy, it is good to see you, have you something to talk about with me?"

"Yes, Mr. Bentley, can I call you Red Fox?"

"I would feel comfortable if you do."

"Since our conversation at the water tank, I have taken

notice of the troubles you spoke of. I have seen several of my friends in such trouble. I still like them as friends, but I would like to help them recover their person and their dignity. How can I do this?"

"This is not easy, Tommy, some are caught in a web of abuse to their bodies through the use of alcohol or drugs and cannot escape. For these we can only hope that the Great Spirit will show mercy and peace to their lives.

"For others we can try to guide, through our own actions, showing our concern and our friendship. It is not an easy path to follow as some may reject your counsel. It will be up to you whether to risk friendship or accept the demise of that friend."

Tommy Little Feather was silent. He went over in his mind what his employer had said. Certainly he was right, he would be ridiculed by some.

"One thing more, Tommy, remember, drug abuse is illegal, this will make it even harder for you when you find one of your friends using." George was silent for a time, then said, "We come from a strong people, Tommy, do what you think is right. You can live with that."

George wrote in his weekly by-line:

It is time, we who conquered, appeased and regulated our Indian population living in the nearby Wind River Reservation, take a look at the physical and psychological aspects of those who live there now.

We can continue the long-standing bias against those we have placed in a space that we have directed and largely ignored, failing to understand that they, like ourselves, have needs, both physical and psychological; or we can recognize them as fellow human beings with all that this implies: Humans who have problems just as you and I, humans who wish to be part of the productive world, humans who have families to love and support.

We know of the alcohol and drug problem among the tribes. Can't we ask why?

There is little doubt that a sizeable part of the human mantra includes more than the duty of living. One must include the pride of doing, the satisfaction of contribution, and the peace of knowing you are appreciated by others. That is what all of us need, to feel good about ourselves, to know we have added something, to see what we ourselves have been responsible for: a purpose.

When one is unemployed it is hard to see one's purpose. When one is unemployed for a long period, the damage is even worse, and that's what is happening in the Wind River as well as other like Indian Reservations. With unemployment on the Wind River tottering at 25 % plus, five times the national average, the sheer number of the idle tests the community. The idle quickly turn to substitutes, alcohol and drugs, for the lack of meaningful purposes.

13 | BONES

Amy as a teen living on a ranch, learned to ride early in her life, and this part of Wyoming was incredibly beautiful to ride in. It followed, then that whenever both Amy and Cliff could match their times off, they would end up on a trail someplace together. Riding off south toward Portal Mesa they would skirt the bottom of the alluvial fan that separated Portal and Leaning Mesas, then climb the gradual uphill trail that led to the highlands. Water and grass was plentiful along the way, so that took care of their mounts, and Rosey would have provided food for the day. These were special times for the two lovers, and they usually pushed a day into fifteen hours depending the time of year. Exploring the nooks and crannies of the Wyoming wilderness was a bonus, and often turned up some surprises.

On one of these trips, Amy who was sitting on a rock looking at their back trail spotted something that seemed out of place to her, something dead white where there should have been brown. She said "Cliff, I wonder what that is," pointing at the object. Cliff walked down and took a look. Half buried in the side of a dry gulch could be seen the top of a human skull. Cliff scraped away some of the sand, and found a fully clothed human skeleton. He turned and climbed back to where Amy sat and said, "Someone died down there, you're looking at the top of a man's skull."

Amy sat silent for a moment, then, "Hadn't we better tell the Sheriff about this, Cliff?"

Dead bodies usually stir law enforcement into some kind of action and that did in fact stir Bill Williams to lower his feet from their place on his desk, put down the novel he was reading and start for the Arrow—B. George was out on the range when he arrived, and the Sheriff waited impatiently for him to return.

In time, George rode up, dismounted, took care of his horse, then walked over to where the Sheriff was waiting, and said a casual, "Hello Bill, what brings you all the way out here?"

"Yes, well I hear that you have another dead body to show me. That sounds normal for you. I seem to remember that you produced several of those things a few years back. What took you so long to do your thing?"

"Well, I was just helping the law do its job, and those other dead bodies were really bad people. Honest Injun, Bill, I didn't have anything to do with this one."

"Oh funny. Let's go look at the alleged body."

George said, "Knowing your devotion to riding a horse, I have one saddled and ready to take us to where the body is."

The Sheriff grimaced and asked, "What's the matter with cars?"

George answered, "Can't do, this is an off-road thing, horses will have to do, unless you would prefer a fifteen-mile walk."

Cliff led the Sheriff and George up to where the body lay and the Sheriff, after dismounting, knelt down alongside the corpse. He postulated that the body had been buried, and that recent rains had uncovered, and exposed the remains. He spoke as he further uncovered the body, "It looks like this happened a long time ago. There's a good possibility that a crime has taken place here, however, it is doubtful that we will be able to determine who the perpetrator was."

George said, "Don't you think it might be helpful if we know who this guy was?"

"The other bodies you produced were fresh and within wagon distance from civilization. This one isn't. The immediate problem is what to do with the body. I don't want to leave it here. We need to move it to the medical examiner's office. D' you have any ideas?"

"No, that's your bailiwick; you used to be good at that kind of thing. It'll be good seeing our elected Sheriff earn his keep for a change."

"As usual, you can't stand being civil, and have to be full of wisecracks. The next thing I'll hear from you is to tell me what my job is, and how I'm failing to carry out my duties."

"Okay, Bill, simmer down, I get your point. No, I have no idea how to get this pile of bones down, where you, the law, can do its thing. Let's get off this mountain, it's getting late. We can't do anything about it today."

The next day a team consisting of the medical examiner, a photographer, a member of the nearby Indian Tribe and the Sheriff was assembled. The assemblage wound its way, all mounted, up to the burial site, and observed, photographed, and recorded, then unceremoniously placed the remains in a body-bag The remains were taken by horse-back down the trail to the Arrow—B where they were laid in the bed of the ranch wagon for transport to the medical examiner's facility in Glencoe. In that the apparent crime had taken place outside the Indian Reservation, there was no tribal interest.

It was a full three weeks before the medical examiner's report was made available to Sheriff Bill Williams. The report identified the remains to be those of Steve Harris, Betty's father. Positive identification was made using dental records. George received the call from the Sheriff, "George Bentley here."

"George, we just got the medical examiner's report. The bag of bones we brought down from up on the mesa was what's left of Betty's father."

"Confirmed?"

"Uh huh, Steve's dental records confirmed. I haven't told Betty yet. I kind of thought you would want to do that one."

George said, "Well, one of us better do the telling soon. I don't want her to hear it from the underground telegraph we have in this county. She's really not talking to me much these days, but this must be done. I'll ride over and talk to her tonight, but I think you should make it official and call her tomorrow."

"Will do, talk to you tomorrow."

George found Betty removing nettles from the front legs of her favorite mount. He watched her for a few moments then said, "We've found your father's body."

Betty looked up, tears forming in dark empty eyes. "Are you sure it's dad?"

"Yes, Betty, the medical examiner, based on your dad's dental record, positively asserts the identification. You will receive a call from the Sheriff tomorrow with details. You'll need to view the clothing and some items that were found."

Betty nodded, then turned silently away. George waited a bit then said, "Betty, I don't like the idea of you being alone tonight. I'll sleep in the bunkhouse. If you feel uncomfortable I'll be here for you."

Betty stood, flipping her tangled hair behind an ear and said, "Do as you wish, I won't need you. I can handle it." She dismissed him with a flip of her head, and entered the ranch house.

George paused for a moment, looking toward the ranch house and thinking of his daughter whom Betty had refused to let him see. He decided that this was not the time to press Betty on that issue. He said, "I'll leave in the morning then, Betty."

The Sheriff's call to the Harris Ranch was brief, stating that Steve's body had been recovered, and would she join him for the trip into Glencoe to meet with the medical examiner?

Betty answered, "Alright, Sheriff. When do we do this?"

"I can pick you up tomorrow morning around eight, Betty."

14 | PARENTS IN CONFLICT

Doctor Henry Morrison had presided over the birth of Eva Bentley. It was early in the year 1956, and at the request of the mother, he did not inform George of the birth. He did, however, issue a birth certificate as required by law. George had been expecting the event, as he had known of Betty's pregnancy since that day in Rosey's Diner in September of the year before. Betty refused to include George in any of the happenings around her pregnancy, and he got what information he could from Rosey. Now that his daughter was born and real, he felt it time to press the issue, especially after delivering the news to Betty about her father's remains being found on the Arrow—B.

This was a difficult decision for George, as his love for Betty and the knowledge of her psychological difficulties made him cautious of doing further harm to her, however his paternal impatience finally won out and he decided to act.

The legal firm of Emery Forbes Esquire located in Walnut, Wyoming had become Forbes & Forbes, Attorneys at Law, located in downtown Glencoe. In that the Arrow—B Ranch had always depended on this firm to handle its legal matters, it followed that George would go there for counsel concerning his daughter Eva.

By appointment George sat in front of a dining-room-table-sized desk facing a diminutive Peter Forbes. George recalled an earlier time when Emery Forbes's office was in the second story of an old brick school building in Walnut. That room was small and smelled of varnish and cigar smoke. Emery's son, and the environs he had surrounded himself with, did not follow his father's frugal ways. Peter asked, "Mr. Bentley, what can I do for you?"

George said, "Peter, we are almost family, call me George. I have known your father since I was ten. The Arrow—B has used your father and his skills for decades. How's your dad anyway?"

Peter, who had learned much about the law, had learned little or nothing about people. His well-disciplined mind was having trouble relating to the casual Wyoming persons he had to serve. He sat behind a huge empty office desk fully suited with bow tie and cufflinks, a bit frightened that he might do something wrong, and showed it. He answered, "Father is well. Would you rather speak to him?"

George sensed Peter's discomfort, mused to himself concerning the generation of youth facing the real world they knew nothing about, said, "Peter, no, you will do fine. I'd like to visit with your dad sometime though. Give him a hello from me. I have a family matter that I need your help with."

Peter Forbes retrieved a legal pad from within a drawer, placed it on the desk and studied George with a questioning look.

George said, "I am concerned for the safety of my baby daughter who is with her mother. Her mother is under the care of a psychiatrist. Mrs. Bentley and I are legally married, but estranged and not living together. Mrs. Bentley has denied me the right to see my daughter. I need to know what rights I have, as a father. I need to know if the law will recognize my right to see the child, and to make certain that the child is protected, and if necessary give me custody of my daughter. And of course, based on what you tell me, I expect to take such legal action as is appropriate to protect my daughter, and to gain access to her."

Peter said, "Yes, well first we need to agree on a fee. Second, we need to gather the facts and confirm the status of you as the father of this child and your wife as the mother."

George smiled, thinking to himself something like, this youngster is right out of school, following the rules and procedures he was taught. I wonder how smart he is? "This is understood and will be handled. My questions are, do I have a case, and second, will you take this case on if I do have rights regarding my daughter?"

Peter said, "The answer to your first question is complicated, and that's why you are seeking legal assistance. The answer to your second is yes, if we agree on a fee."

George said, "I see your point. Alright, tell me about fees."

Peter, now feeling a bit more confident, said, "We can do this on a retainer basis, or pay as you go. We agree on a "so-much-a-month" retainer amount which would terminate when the case is settled, or you can pay hourly fees for all of my time, whatever that may be. In either case, court costs and any expert's fees will apply as a separate item."

George thought for a moment then said, "Suppose you bill me by the hour with costs until you can answer my question, do I have rights? Then we discuss the other. Can we do that?"

"Yes, of course. I'll need to prepare some documents and plan a sequence of actions. This will take the better part of this week. I'll inform you by phone when our next meeting will be."

A little more than a week after the meeting with Peter Forbes, George received a phone call from Peter. They set up a meeting to be held at the ranch and the meeting would include Peter's father Emery. The two Forbes came out in their family station wagon, and were seated in the grand room of the recently enlarged Arrow—B ranch house. The room sported a huge picture window set to view the valley below, with two flanking chairs set to allow occupants to enjoy the splendor of the landscape.

Afternoon coffee materialized out of nowhere, served by a young Indian woman. Pleasantries were exchanged and the business at hand started. The young attorney's questions were carefully phrased to provide him with what he needed to represent George and establish a foundation for legal action.

In time, and when Peter was nearly finished, George stated, "Peter, I understand what must happen here, but I must also guard the health and welfare of my wife. Therefore, I will consult with our psychiatrist before we proceed. I will not destroy Mrs. Bentley. At the moment, please get me the answer, what are my rights?"

Emery Forbes, who had been silent to this point, said, "George, you will have to also consider the welfare of your daughter. This may come down to which is more important to you—your wife or your daughter. You can't have it both ways."

George said, "That I know, let's proceed as directed, maintain my privacy, and I will let you know what my decision is as things unfold."

George contacted Doctor Lewis, the psychiatrist, by phone. The matter of Betty's mental condition and whether she could tolerate losing her child was discussed. Doctor Lewis said, "Mr. Bentley, in order to give an informed opinion such as you are asking, I of course, would have to see the patient again. And even if we did have Mrs. Bentley start seeing me again, I could only give you my opinion. If you ask me whether she is able to raise and nurture your child safely or not, I would still have to give you an opinion. If you proceed with legal action to get your child placed under your care, the court might ask for my opinion. In either case, declaring Mrs. Bentley unfit to raise your daughter is not only hard to prove, but if you are wrong the consequences to you could be staggering."

Doctor Lewis continued, "I know I haven't been much help. Have you been in touch with an attorney? I suggest you do not inform Betty until you know exactly how you will proceed. If she spends too much time worrying about court proceedings, it won't be healthy for her."

George hung up the phone and considered what he had just learned. It was not a nice, easy, comfortable situation. He was not a person to dwell on the negative, but this was a problem that was not going away.

Emery Forbes called, "George, I think we should get together. Do you think you can meet me at Rosey's in Walnut at ten tomorrow?"

"Can do, Em, I'm buy'n."

Rosey sat the two men down, poured coffee, left a menu, and returned to her kitchen. Emery said, "George, Peter is a bit hesitant to do anything that isn't flat out according to the book, so I thought you and I might move around that stuff a bit. Now Judge Hastings, who happens to be a good friend of mine, knows that the real world is here and things need to get done. He also knows a bit about you and Betty. Well, I had a drink with him last night and your name came up. Turns out Hastings has some thoughts on your situation." Emery smiled, ignoring the obvious judicial slip.

"As I said, Peter is a bit sticky when it comes to skirting the letter of the law. Off the cuff, the judge told me that if a case such as this came to his court, he would first assume that the father has the right to have a presence in his child's life. Denial of that right would probably cause the court to issue a clear custody order that would be kind of like a restraining order, probably a shared custody program; that is, if both parents are proven sane and capable of taking care of the child. In the case of a parent having custody who is not able to adequately tend to the protection and nurturing of the child, the court might direct that the child be reared elsewhere."

"What I hear Emery, is that I must make a decision which

is bad one way or the other, further injury to my wife versus the welfare of our child."

Emery said, "Uh huh."

Rosey came by and asked if they needed more than coffee. She mentioned those cinnamon rolls that were smelling-up the room and testing the staunchest of sensory organs. George glanced up at Emery and said, "It always is wise to come here at the right time of day; of course, Rosey, bring more coffee too." He said to Emery, "Do you suppose the court would go along with placing a nanny in the house with Betty?"

Emery said, "That's a novel idea, do you think Betty would go along with that?"

George said, "Well, she might, and then I could tackle the matter of sharing my daughter, knowing that there was a responsible person in the home."

15 | TO CLAIM ONE'S OWN

George first reinforced his direction to his attorney, not to take any action until he approved. Second, he placed a call to Dr. Lewis in Cheyenne, "Dr. Lewis, this is George Bentley, I need to discuss a matter concerning Mrs. Bentley."

The Doctor asked, "Can you be more specific?"

"Well Doctor, as I spoke of before, Mrs. Bentley and I are estranged, she has birthed our daughter, and she has denied me access to that daughter. I need to know if her mental condition is such as to endanger that child."

"Mr. Bentley, I can only give you an opinion, and only after I have given her a full examination again."

George thought for a moment. The Doctor asked, "Are you still there?"

George said, "Yes, I can figure that one out, however I don't think I can get her in to your office again."

The Doctor said, "I don't think that I've ever made a house call before, however, I need a vacation, and I now have an associate. How's the fishing out there?"

"Great. How about free board and room at the ranch, as long as it takes?"

Doctor Lewis came to the Arrow—B, and stayed for a full

seven days. His fishing lasted from early each morning till noon. Each afternoon he would drive out to the Harris ranch and observe and counsel Betty. In the end he prepared a written report concerning his findings. The report was his opinion, of course, as he promised. He summarized his findings in a brief statement:

Mrs. Betty Bentley is suffering from extreme paranoia brought on by the loss of persons close to her. At this time she is unable to overcome these personal tragedies, and return to a degree of normalcy. The paranoia exhibits most notably as a phobia directed specifically to her husband, George Bentley, and more generally results in the avoidance of any long-term relationships. While the paranoia appears mild on the surface, it hides and remains deep within. In my opinion she is nonviolent, and would not knowingly bring harm to anyone including her daughter.

George read and reread the report from Dr. Lewis. He wasn't sure that it helped him make a decision concerning his daughter. He still had the problem of potential "injury to Betty, should the court decide to mandate shared custody." In the end he put in a call to his attorney. "Peter, I would like to proceed with legal action regarding my daughter. When can we meet to discuss the details?"

The meeting took place at the attorney's office. Peter Forbes asked, "Do you wish to seek custody of your child as against Mrs. Bentley?"

"Peter, yes, however for shared custody only. There is to be no mention of Mrs. Bentley's psychological condition, and it is not to include any reference to possible child endangerment. It is my opinion that a child needs both a mother and a father.

"What happens next, Peter?"

"We prepare and file papers, and wait. The judge will decide when and how he wants to hold a hearing, and whether he wants to hear testimony or take other evidence from the petitioner, that's you, and the respondent, that's Mrs. Bentley."

"And then?"

"In most cases of this nature, a hearing by the county judge will ensue, and will be held, perhaps in the judge's chambers or in open court. Both the petitioner and the respondent with their respective attorneys will be present. But I should warn you, even though this is a court case, the judge has a great deal of discretion in how he proceeds, and his primary responsibility is to look out for the best interests of the child, your daughter. Once this gets started, you can't really stop it until the judge is satisfied that the child is safe and properly cared for."

George said, "I expect no less. And you said the respondent will have to be in court? That's going to be interesting, I haven't been able to get Betty away from her ranch for months."

"Yours is not to worry, she'll be there."

Betty received a personal summons to appear in court and to respond to George's formal petition, relating to her alleged denial of the father's right of access to and possible custody of their child. She studied the official document, shivered, feeling a sense of darkness and fright. She sat for a time, puzzling which way to turn. She needed a friend. Rosey was the only one she could think of, but even she posed a problem. Rosey was also a good friend of George. Never had she felt so much alone. The summons directed her to appear in court before a judge in just ten days.

Betty's call to Rosey came late in the afternoon. It was a time when Rosey was free for a few hours, and she answered, "Hi 'Bet. How are you, and what's going on?"

"Rosey, I need to see you. Can I come by, have a late dinner there, and sit down with you for a time when you can?"

"Of course Betty, but it'll be late. Why don't you plan on staying overnight with me. I have lots of room and I would enjoy your company? Oh and bring Eva. She is such a joy."

Betty drove the fifteen miles into town and parked in front of Rosey's Cafe. She lifted Eva out of the clothes basket where she had been riding, tucked her blanket around her little body then entered Rosey's Café. Rosey and her helper were just finishing the after-dinner clean-up, she came quickly from the kitchen and took Eva in her arms. Betty sighed, "Thank you Rosey, Eva and I will sit at the counter until you're through."

"I'm through, Betty, but you need some food, I'll fix you something."

"No thanks, Rosey, I'm not hungry." She took Eva back into her arms, looking solemn and away.

Rosey sat on the adjacent stool, "Would you like to tell me a bit about what's going on in your life? Sometimes it's good to have someone to talk to."

Betty was silent, patting Eva softly and murmuring unintelligible sounds. Rosey waited a bit, then, rose, reentered the kitchen and filled two mugs with coffee. She asked Betty about cream or sugar, came back to her stool, and still silently waited. Betty remained quiet, finally Rosey said, "Betty?"

Betty fumbled through her bag, pulled out the summons and handed it to Rosey who glanced at the official document. "Oh, Betty, I'm so sorry to see this." She was silent for a time, drawing close to Betty, recalling the warmth and happiness she knew of both George and Betty. Finally she said, "Betty, it is a fine thing that George feels so strongly, and so proud of both you and Eva. He will always love and protect both of you."

Betty was silent. Her eyes seemed empty, unseeing, and not comprehending. She asked, "What should I do?"

Rosey was silent, now realizing the depth of Betty's depression. She rose, went into the kitchen and spoke to her help, then called George at the ranch. "George, Betty is here and I am worried for her and Eva. I'm going to drive her home and stay with her until you come. She needs someone to be with her right now." She turned to Betty and said, "Yes

Betty, you will have to appear in court. It is important that the judge hears your side of the story." She took Betty by the hand and led her out to her car, then drove her out to Betty's ranch. Eva rode comfortably in her mother's arms.

George drove up the gravel driveway leading to the Harris ranch house. Rosey met him as he stepped up to the ranch house doorway, she said, "I'm glad you're here. I need to get back to the café, and prepare for tomorrow's breakfast bunch. I hope you can help Betty, she seems in some kind of a trance. I'm driving Betty's car so we'll have to sort the cars out tomorrow."

When Rosey was gone, George entered Betty's bedroom. Betty cast a frightened look at George cringing and wrapping her arms around their child.

George said, "Betty, I'm not here to harm you or Eva, I'll be right outside your door tonight. If you need me just call." With that he left the room, and made a place for himself to sleep for the night. In the morning, he rose, started the coffee, and was just about to do something about breakfast when a young Indian girl came to be with Betty. She would spend the day helping Betty with Eva and tend to some of the chores.

George listened to the soft sounds coming from the bedroom as Betty took care of their child's needs. He did not enter or interject himself into Betty's world. He took heart that their child was safe, and felt he could leave freely.

Betty appeared in court as required. A court-appointed attorney was present to act in her behalf. Judge Hastings had taken care of this a few days earlier when his clerk advised him that no papers had been filed by an attorney on Betty's behalf. The four, Betty, her attorney, George, and Peter Forbes met in Judge Hastings's chambers. The opening plea from the petitioner was presented by Peter Forbes:

"Your Honor, at this time my client, Mr. George Bentley, is estranged from his legal wife, Betty. Mrs. Bentley has borne a child of their marriage. Mr. Bentley has made frequent requests to Mrs. Bentley for access to or visitation with his legal offspring. Mrs. Bentley has repeatedly denied that father any access whatsoever to their child. It should be noted that in no way does my client wish or intend to take the child, Eva, away from her mother. He feels that a child needs both a father and a mother. Mr. Bentley only wishes to share the responsibility and love for that child. My client respectfully requests that the court direct the respondent to allow a natural relationship to exist between the father and the child."

The Judge turned to the attorney acting for the respondent and said, "Have you conferred with the respondent, and if so, what is her position on this matter?"

"Your Honor, yes I have, it is the firm desire of my client, Mrs. Betty Bentley, to insulate their child, Eva, from her father on the basis that Mr. Bentley is a known killer, and she is fearful for the influence of the petitioner upon their child."

"You have facts to back this up?"

"Yes, Your Honor, the records show that Mr. George Bentley has been responsible for the deaths of several persons."

Judge Hastings studied Betty for a moment. "This is your statement, Mrs. Bentley?"

"Yes."

"Where is your child now, Mrs. Bentley?"

"She is at home on the ranch with a caring person."

"The Judge said, "Alright, I don't feel informed enough to make a ruling at this time." He looked at his desk calendar. "It is the order of this court that we meet again in ten days. Both parties are ordered to be here then and at any further hearings unless I say to the contrary. At our next meeting I want to see the child, the caregiver, all present; and I want to see or hear any evidence of alleged killings by the petitioner that respondent wants the court to consider in this case, and any and all evidence and material available that either party wants me to consider regarding this petition by Mr. Bentley.

Oh, and one more thing. The petitioner's papers say that the respondent has been treated by a psychiatrist recently. I'm not pre-judging, but I'm putting you all on notice that I intend to speak with this physician and determine whether we need any medical testimony regarding the care or safety of the child. This hearing is hereby adjourned."

Judge Ralph Hastings was well known in Contra County and beyond. He was a strong proponent of the American family unit, constantly trying to glue broken homes together, with a pretty good track record at doing just that. In this case he had personal knowledge of both the petitioner and the respondent, and his ruling would be made more difficult than if these two were strangers to him. The concern for promoting a unified household then, shifted to the issue of how best to serve the child's interest and future.

The waters became even more muddied when he considered the reported mental condition of the respondent. This equated into, the love of a child by a mother verses any danger to that child from that mother—a mother who seemed less than psychologically stable. He considered a change in venue but rejected this idea on the grounds that his knowledge of the principals in this case would enable him to make a more informed ruling than a stranger from somewhere and by someone unfamiliar with local personalities and their needs. Judge Hastings, having warned the parties, deemed it prudent to touch base with Betty's psychiatrist. His call to Dr. Lewis, the clinical psychiatrist treating Betty, resulted in a statement to the effect that, in his opinion, Betty was non-violent and would probably never place her child, Eva, in danger.

And so, with an 'opinion, and a probable', Judge Hastings would still have to make a decision on his own, unless the lawyers decided to bring him new evidence. About now he wished this was a jury trial and he could squiggle out of the tough decision here. But he couldn't.

The second gathering took place in Judge Hastings chambers, off of a hallway behind the courtroom, on a somber day, a bit chilly, lacking warmth from the declining sun. The attendees were equally somber, each traveling down different paths of emotional engagement. Present were Betty and George Bentley, the young Indian girl, Chloe, acting as a helper to Betty in the care of the baby Eva, Eva Bentley, Peter Forbes, and the court-appointed attorney for Betty. When all were seated, the Judge, settled into his swivel-chair behind an ancient gnarled desk bespeaking of the no nonsense personality that sat there. In the ten days since the last meeting of this case, he had acquainted himself with as much information pertinent to this litigation as he could find. He said, "Alright, I will have to rule on the evidence presented here today, each of you who testifies will have to be sworn in. We'll do this as informally as possible, but when anyone except the lawyers speaks, know that you are giving sworn testimony." He rose, went to the door and yelled out, "Virginia, come on in and bring our bailiff."

In time a diminutive figure appeared at the doorway and took a seat off to the side. She looked up at the six foot four icon of the county court system, Judge Hastings, and with pencil poised over a ragged, well used note pad asked, "What'll it be Ralph?"

The Judge ignored the obvious lack of formality and tiredly said, "Virginia, just do your thing will you, we need a record of what goes on here. Where's our bailiff?"

"We couldn't find 'im, he's probably out on a coffee break."

The Judge said, "Alright, then, let's get started and see how far we can get without our bailiff." Judge Hastings looked at the young Indian girl and asked, "What is your name?"

"I'm Chloe Little Bird."

"How old are you, Chloe Little Bird?"

"Chloe hesitated then said, "I think I'm fifteen, but I'm not sure."

The Judge said, "Well, fifteen-year-old, who looks like a twelve-year-old, take Eva out into the courtroom, and watch her during these proceedings." He shuffled some papers on his desk, selected one, and addressed both the counsel for the petitioner and that of the respondent, "Let's keep this simple, we all know the issues involved. Forbes, tell me something I don't already know."

"Your Honor, my client, George Bentley, reiterates his claim for the right to visit his daughter, and be a part of her growing years. He stands ready to respond to Your Honor's questioning."

The Judge smiled, "That's keeping it simple alright, but it's not helping me adjudicate this case. You're saying you have nothing new to add to your client's petition?"

"Only that Mr. Bentley continues to be concerned for both his daughter and his wife, as she has chosen to live alone with their child on the Harris Ranch. He has frequently visited the ranch to check on and see to ranch matters, and of course, ask to see his daughter. Said requests have, to this point, been denied."

The Judge turned to the counsel for the respondent, Betty Harris, "Do you have anything new to add to your client's opposition to this request?"

"No, Your Honor, but Mrs. Bentley is anxious to conclude this hearing and return to her ranch with her child as soon as possible."

The Judge said, "Alright let's all have a cup of coffee or whatever. We'll have to wait until the bailiff shows, and can do some swearing in."

The bailiff came. George was duly sworn in, and Judge Hastings began his questioning. "George, when did you know that Mrs. Bentley was with child?"

"I can't be sure, Your Honor, but I guess it must have been about four months or so before our child was born."

"So, how did you find out? Did your wife tell you?"

"No, Mrs. Bentley did not tell me." George kind of laughed, "The moccasin-telegraph, maybe."

"How often do you visit the Harris Ranch, and check on things there?"

"Once, sometimes twice, a week."

"When was the first time you saw your daughter?"

"Just an hour ago, Your Honor."

Judge Hastings hated what he had just heard. Here were two people he knew very well. It was hard not to like them both. They were the sweethearts of the area. Now they were in trouble. The magic that had brought them together was seemingly gone. He turned to the counsel representing Betty, "On the telephone you mentioned some documents that might have a bearing on this case. What do we have?"

"Your Honor, I have certified and valid copies of news articles that chronicle the killings and violence that the petitioner, George Bentley, has engaged in. And I ask you to take judicial notice of these killings to the extent you participated in your judicial capacity during those times. Clearly, Mr. Bentley is prone to violence, and that is what the respondent, Mrs. Bentley fears, should her child be exposed to Mr. Bentley."

The Judge was quiet for a bit, recalling the incidents that surrounded the killings that were referred to. He was there. He was the jurist that heard the evidence in criminal cases, and he was the one that served during a difficult time in Contra County. A time when evil people invaded, and it was the time when rancher George Bentley defeated that evil. The Judge asked, "Are these documents dated, and if so, when did those alleged killings take place?"

"They are, Your Honor, the events took place in 1952."

The Judge said, "I wish to question Mrs. Bentley. In view of her psychological history, I have spoken to her psychiatrist. He feels that she will have no problems in testifying." He nodded to the bailiff, who waited as Betty took a seat in front of the judge's desk, and then administered the oath.

The Judge said, "Betty, your attorney has stated in a brief that you fear for your child should she be exposed to Mr. Bentley. Do you confirm this?"

"Yes, your Honor."

"And yes, in what is this fear founded; that is, what makes you feel this fear, Betty?"

"My husband has killed, I don't wish for my child to be exposed to killing."

"Betty, you were certainly aware of those referred to killings before you were married, why do you feel differently now?"

Betty was silent for a time. The Judge waited patiently then, "Betty?"

"The loss of my father has changed things. My child is my whole life."

"I'm sorry I have to ask this Betty, but has your husband ever struck you or threatened you in any way?"

"No." Betty looked over at George then down at the floor.

"Has he ever threatened baby Eva?"

Betty looked back at the judge and said, "No."

"Betty, your child may not feel the need for a father in her life at this time, but all too soon she will grow, and perhaps look for her roots. What will you tell her when she asks about her father?"

Betty was silent, the judge restated his question. Betty remained silent. Finally the Judge said, "Alright Betty, that's all for now."

The Judge said, "Bailiff, do your thing. Let's get George sworn in." He waited until George was officially under oath then said, "Hello George, how's ranching these days?"

"Ranching's fine Judge, it's the price of beef that's making trouble."

The Judge said, "I've been hearing a lot about that lately, how bad is it?"

"Plenty, most of us will survive, but it won't be easy."

The Judge shuffled some papers, found what he wanted, and said, "I find it difficult to learn of the split up between you and Betty. I have known both of you for a long time. I suppose no one can change that except you two. So be it; I'm asked to make a ruling here, and I will hurt one of you in doing so. George, do you have anything to add to your formal request since the last time we met?"

"Not really, Ralph, except that I am also saddened that we are here. I cannot accept that a child of mine would be out of my life forever. Eva is the result of a mother and a father. She is entitled to both."

The Judge said, "Alright, I'll deliberate through tonight. My ruling will be phoned to each of you tomorrow, and I'll follow up with paper."

Judge Hastings deliberated for a full three days, alerting both George and Betty of his delayed decision. When he had his ruling ready and in writing he called each, and set up a meeting. When all were seated he spoke:

"In that there are personal reasons for the estrangement toward the Petitioner by the Respondent which are beyond the scope of the pleadings in this case, the following ruling deals only with the welfare and custody of the child, Eva Bentley.

"I hereby find that the child Eva will be best served by the participation of a father, that is, her biological father, George Bentley, in her life as well as her mother, Betty Bentley. I further find no evidence to support the assertion by the Respondent that the Petitioner, George Bentley, poses any danger to the welfare of the child. It is then hereby directed that the Respondent, Betty Bentley, is to have primary custody of Eva Bentley, but that the Respondent is to allow the Petitioner, George Bentley, to share custody and to have physical contact with their child. This need be handled at all times with the interest and safety of the child Eva Bentley in mind. Visits to see and be with his daughter requested by the father will be honored by Mrs. Bentley. This should happen informally and I don't expect any disputes. But if the parties can't agree on visitation issues, you lawyers come back and see me and I'll straighten things out. My order is interlocutory and is not meant to be a final order. I will retain jurisdiction over this matter in order to protect the interests of the child."

16 | PETE AND ROSEY

Peter White had joined the Arrow—B family almost from the beginning. Richard Bentley hired him when he had just turned sixteen, and he became the mainstay of the Arrow—B ranch complex early on. He acted as ramrod working with his boss, not for him. As such the Bentleys, both George and his father, Richard, provided for Pete's retirement in a separate account. This was in the form of a percentage of the ranch profits, and by the year 1957 this account had grown to a nice fund for Pete.

One day when George was 'tidying up' the ranch finances for the month he noted the 'Pete retirement account' and considered that Pete should now start to enjoy the fruits of his long years of service to the ranch, and retire. Now it wasn't that easy to tell a loyal employee that he should retire, which might sound like "we don't need you anymore." So on the way to do his monthly money matters with the bank in Glencoe, George ruminated over his dilemma for the two hours of traveling to and from Glencoe, coming up with no ideas at all. When he got to Walnut, he stopped in at Rosey's for an afternoon cup of coffee.

Well George took the end seat at the corner, near where the huge black coffee pot simmered, leaned over and poured himself a cup of the black acidy brew. He was just into his first swallow when Rosey stuck her head out through the counter pass-through and said, "Hello George, what brings you into town today?"

"Just passing through, Rosey, what's going on around these parts?" He drank more from his coffee cup.

Rosey looked hard at George, shook her head and said, "You must have something plenty serious on your mind not to complain about that coffee. It must be plenty lethal by now. I made it at six."

"That's awful, Rosey, I'd hate to try a bluff on you in a poker game. You read me like a book."

Rosey smiled, then, "I'll listen if you need me to."

"Yes, well it's this way, my dad set up a retirement fund for Pete before I was born, and I kept it up. It has grown to quite a sum, and I think Pete should enjoy some of that money. So how do I tell Pete he should retire, without him thinking we don't need him any longer?"

Rosey answered, "Well don't you need him anymore?"

"Of course we need him, Rosey, it's just that money sitting in a bank just benefits the banker. Pete deserves to benefit from his money which he has worked hard for really."

"How about a long vacation?"

"He wouldn't take one unless it had horses and cows in it. Oh, that gives me an idea. He really should have a spread of his own. There might be something I can do in that vein."

George was just sitting down to one of Mary Ellen's steak and egg breakfasts at the ranch when Pete did the same and sat across from him. George said, "Mornin' Pete, what's on for today?"

"Nothin' special except that I need to have a check out at the line shack. I'm sendin' two riders out there to have a look."

"Well the reason I asked is that I want to do something about that up-high area between Portal and Leaning. You know the place we never seem to have time to cover. Do you have any ideas?"

"You know, boss, I'm frustrated about that one too. It could only be solved if'n and when we put someone out there, permanent like."

George said, "How'd you like to do that one yourself? It looks like great pasture, and I'm sure water is nearby?"

Pete looked hard at his boss. "Who'd handle things here?"

"Well, you of course. You give the orders like always, and I'll see that things get done until you get things started out there."

"Well it might work."

"You know, Pete, that place has no value to me as it is, and I really don't need any more real estate to take care of. What if I deeded that section over to you, and as you go about fixing things up there you know you'll be building for yourself. You can work out there whenever you feel you have time away from here."

On a Monday, early in the year 1958, Peter White went into Walnut to pick up Arrow—B mail and some supplies. As always, he stopped in to see Rosey. Rosey usually took Mondays off, and when Pete knocked on her door she opened the door and said, "Hi" and waited for Pete to speak.

"Hi Rosey, are you in for a ride and a picnic?"

"Sure, Pete, what's up?"

"I just have somethin' to share."

Rosey packed a lunch, and Pete drove them out to the area that George and Pete had discussed. They found a shady spot under a tree, and Rosey spread out a blanket and food. She said, "This is nice, Pete, why today?"

"Well." He paused, then, "We could make a small ranch here, and I wanted you to see it."

"You said 'we', Pete is this a proposal?"

"Well, I've always wanted to but I didn't think you would go along. Now that I might have a place, maybe we could make it our place?"

"Of course, Pete, I've waited a long time for you to ask."

17 | LOVE AND BELONGING

Joan LaCross tidied up her living quarters and arranged with a neighbor to tend to her mail and water the geraniums that stood on her balcony wall. The letter from her mother about her father's illness came as a surprise. She had to withdraw most of the money from her account at the bank to pay for her fare to Vermont, and to her parents' home. Her thoughts, as she took her seat on the plane, dwelled on her father, of course, but they were intruded and intermingled with what was currently going on in her life. In truth she was grasping for an answer as to who she really was. Joan was deeply in love with a married man, a man with a baby daughter. She was at that time in life when she felt the need for someone close; she was in the middle of serious study related to her professional goal and she worried for her mother if her father died.

Whereas she slept much of the six-hour trip to her home, her mind strayed back to Wyoming. It was there she knew she belonged. It was there where the man she loved lived, and it was there where she was forming into Joan the person complete with a goal and the determination and urgency to get there.

Joan speculated on the after-happenings should her father

die. Certainly her Mom could not live alone. In short, she and her mother needed each other. These two and her brother who lived in Boston were all that were left of the La Cross family. Would her mother leave her beloved Vermont and join Joan in Wyoming?

Joan used almost the last of her cash to pay the taxi driver that carried her out to her family home. She eagerly walked up the short walk to the front door and tried to enter, finding the door locked. She knocked and waited. There was no response from within. She fumbled through her purse, found her house key, and let herself in. She went into the downstairs bedroom, where her Mom and Dad slept. The room was vacant yet busily alive with an unmade bed, a dresser drawer half open, and a bed pan on the floor. Her heart thumped then skipped a beat, her mind raced through the possible explanation, and her hand covered her mouth as she gasped. She entered the kitchen and there found the note. It read:

Dear Joan, Your father has taken a turn for the worse. I've gone with him to the hospital. Come as soon as you can., Mom.

The La Cross farm was located just outside of town. It was small by any standard, and had not been worked for several years. The farmhouse stood close to the county road, and broke the level landscape with its two stories, bedecked with two brick chimneys. The barn in the rear had been modified to house two vehicles.

Joan left the kitchen and opened the garage door. The family car was there. She rummaged around the driver's side and found the spare key. She backed out and drove into town, and to the hospital.

The small one story hospital serving the community of Bristol, Vermont and the surrounding farmlands was located at the edge of town. Joan drove into the parking lot, parked and entered the reception room. The receptionist who happened to be a former classmate of Joan, said, "Hi, Joan, you've come a long way. Your Mom and Dad are in room five down the hall."

Joan found her Dad's room, opened the door and moved quickly to her Mother's side. She kissed her and said "Hi, I came as fast as I could."

Joan's mother, Renee, said, "Oh, Joan, thank goodness you're here. I need you terribly."

Joan sat on the edge of the bed and took her father's hand. She noted the rise and fall of the covers and knew that her dad was still alive. She asked, "Mom, is Dad just resting or is he comatose?"

Her Mom sighed, then, "He hasn't spoken to us for over a week, it seems more than sleep. We think he can hear though. The doctor said his time is close."

"How long have you been here, Mom? You look tired, are you taking care of yourself?"

"I don't want to leave Dad. He might awaken and find I'm gone."

Joan said, "Mom, you need to keep your strength up. That means food and rest. You probably haven't eaten well either." She helped her Mom up, and the two found their way out of the hospital to a nearby café. They were seated in a booth facing each other and reminisced about earlier days. They ordered from the menu, and Joan said, "Mom, I'll help with Dad, now that I'm here." Joan and her mother returned to the hospital. They watched father and husband, Charles La Cross, for a time.

The doctor came in. Joan said, "Doctor, I'm Mr. La Cross's daughter, what's happening with my father?"

The doctor glanced at Renee. She nodded and said, "This is my daughter; please tell us about my husband."

"Miss La Cross, your father has terminal cancer. It has advanced to a point of no return. He has very little time left. There is nothing more we can do for him."

Joan and her mother were both there when Charles La Cross died. They were there for each other, and together they planned the funeral services. When all was over it became time to look to the future for Renee La Cross. Joan was the first to speak of her mother's future. She would be living alone on a farm, she could not drive, and her two remaining family members were her daughter who was attending college 2,000 miles to the west and her married son, living in Boston. The relationship between Renee and her daughter-in-law was not a friendly one, the thought of her living under the same roof was not an option.

Whereas the discussions concerning Renee living alone versus the other option, moving to Wyoming to be with Joan, were considered during the rites and ceremonies that took place after the death of Charles, nothing had been decided. Joan felt very strongly that her mother should not stay on the farm alone. On a morning after the ceremonies marking the passing of her father were over, Joan said to her mother, "It is time for me to return to my studies at the University, Mom. You must make a decision about your future here in Vermont. I don't think it would be good for you to live here alone. I'd like you to come with me."

"This is hard for me, Joan, here is where all my friends are, where you were born, where your father and I fell in love. I'm not sure I could leave all this behind."

"Mother, suppose you come with me, stay for the winter with the option to return here if that is your choice. Would you consider that?"

"What do I do about my home and farm here?"

"I hope you don't mind, mom, I did some checking with the realty people in town. They suggest we lease the farm for a year while you are in Wyoming with me. We would put your things in storage where they will be safe. It will also allow me to finish my studies at the University. It would be good, mother, for me to have you there while I finish my education. What do you think?"

"Well dear, that's a lot for me to think about. Give me a day or two, this would be a big change in my life." Renee took two days to decide. In the end she was ready to go west with her daughter for a year. For the next two weeks she and her daughter gathered her personal items, some to go with her to the West, some to be placed in storage in town, and some things that had no personal value given away. They would drive the family car.

Renee's brother living in Boston, who was in the real-estate business, would handle the leasing of the farm while Renee was away.

18 | DRIVE TO WYOMING

The family car, a Chevy Bel-Air station wagon, was new with less than a thousand miles on it. Joan looked at driving to Wyoming as an adventure. This would be the second time she traveled by auto from her home in Vermont out to Wyoming. Her mother wasn't that comfortable at first with the idea of two women driving alone for 2,000 miles, even if it was the middle of the twentieth century. But Joan's enthusiasm won out, and it was all go.

The farm animals which included two barn cats and a big red Irish setter became an issue between the two women. In the end it was decided to leave the cats on their own as they seemed to be able to feed and care for themselves most of the time anyway. Clancy, the Irish setter, was a different matter, and would travel to Wyoming with Joan and her mother.

On the day of departure friends and neighbors waved and saw them off. Renee faced west with misty eyes.

That first day on the road in the station wagon was driven much in silence between Joan and her mother. Both were in their own world, reviewing those years of family life, and the strong presence of Charles La Cross in the family who was gone now. It was the first leg of a two-thousand-mile journey which would take the two women from Vermont to the mountains in the West. They traveled about 200 miles a day, stopping a time or two along the way to savor the people and the lands they were passing through.

Before departure, Joan had called George at the Arrow—B and informed him of their plans. George said, "Why don't you plan on coming to the ranch first. You are welcome to stay here until you have made other plans."

"That's nice, George, I was kind of worried about arranging things. We'll try not to stay too long, and perhaps we can be a little help somehow while we're there."

"Drive carefully, Joan, and call me once in a while and tell me where you are."

A twinge of excitement invaded Joan at the thought of spending time on the ranch near the man she loved, and it stayed with her, growing, as she got closer to the Arrow—B. She admonished herself for the carnal instinct she felt regarding Betty, which conflicted with her sense of right and wrong. Whereas the excitement and wonder of travel through new vistas and the anticipation of the next dip-in-the-road carried through for the 2,000 miles Renee and Joan traveled. At the end of each day Joan's mind drifted on to her love for George.

With Renee, the driving was a time to remember, a time to grieve but also a time to heal and view the future. From the start though, Renee sensed the conflict she saw in her daughter. Puzzled, she bided her time but finally asked, "Are you in love, Joan?"

Joan, taken by surprise, said, "There has always been a question in my mind as to how you are able to read right through me. Sometimes you seem to know me better than I do myself. Yes Mom, I am in love, but it's not right. I will suffer to see and be close to the man I love during our stay at the "Arrow—B, as he is untouchable. Regardless of his feelings for me, he will remain loyal to his wife, Betty."

Joan's voice dropped to a hoarse shaky whisper, "Oh Mom, my man has much to handle with his wife. She is in some kind of psychological shock caused by the death of her last family member, her father. She has categorically denied George. Now there is a child conceived on their honeymoon. She won't let him even see his daughter. I live through his sorrow. I think bad thoughts. Yours and Dad's teachings didn't prepare me for this."

"My dear daughter, love is a wonderful thing, but tangled and abstract if it is one way. Is your love this way, or is it returned in kind?"

"Mother, I don't know, his loyalty to Betty wouldn't allow him to tell me of his feelings that way. All I do know is that he is terribly unhappy. He needs someone to love him, and Betty isn't doing that. He is not a person to stay negative or to live with adversity for long. I am willing to wait. If I can help him past this bump in his life, I'll do what I can."

"My dearest daughter, my heart is saddened for this. I want so much for you to find happiness. Perhaps time will help you find your way."

Renee, as a passenger for the two-thousand-mile trip west, began to heal from the loss of her life's partner. Their trip took them past the Ohio River, over the Mississippi and on to the Great Plains. It was not until she saw the distant mountains, low on the horizon, that she began to understand her daughter's apparent love for the West. By the time they reached the Arrow—B ranch she was totally in awe of what she had seen.

Joan watched her mother's gradual release from the tensions of those last few years of caregiving to her ailing husband, and in a sense understood herself better. When she drove under the Arrow—B sign off the highway Joan resolved to accept a time of patience in her life, a time when she must stand by and avoid doing anything that might put pressure on the man she loved.

Joan and Renee drove into the Arrow—B early on a Sunday. George met them, greeting them both with a welcome hug, and a light kiss to Joan. He said, "Just leave your car where it is and come on in. We've been expecting you." He led them into the ranch Grand Room. Renee stepped into a new world for her. The grandeur of the vista displayed through the wide window made her gasp in wonder. When she had regained her composure, she said, "Oh Joan, now I understand why you wish to live in this country. Only God could create such beauty."

Joan said, "Yes Mom, this is not like our home in Vermont. It's different. It's too bad Dad couldn't be here to see this."

George said, "You are both very welcome here. Leave your things, we can attend to them later. You may want to clean up a bit after your morning's drive."

Joan smiled a thank-you and said, "I'm afraid I have tested Mom a bit on this road trip, considering that she has never been west of the Ohio River before."

Renee said, "Yes it was scary to me, maybe for the first few days, but when I actually saw what I had only read about, and that was when I was a youngster, I could become disloyal to my native Vermont."

George said, "Well there's room for both on my list, as you know I spent the better part of five years attending the University of Vermont."

Joan and Renee stayed a short two weeks at the Arrow—B Ranch, then set off for Fort Collins and the University of Colorado. The two women settled into Joan's apartment, adding a few touches to make Renee comfortable, and Joan checked into the University continuing her studies of veterinary medicine.

Renee found new life: without her friends of fifty years, away from her church, and those daily happenings of yesterday. She endured, and moved forward, soon learning to love the West as her daughter had.

19 | THE WEDDING

The magic that brought Pete and Rosey together was born of years of casual opportunities, but as both were busy doing their things, a wedding was pushed aside, always with a "wait a while" attitude from each. The catalyst, of course, was when a bashful Pete felt he had something to offer Rosey. In truth, Pete was very much a romantic. Now it is sometimes a long space between talking and doing, weddings tend to wait for seasons or spring or something. Rosey, intuitive as she was, gave Pete plenty of time, and Pete always the considerate one, didn't press the matter. In the meantime, the community waited and planned. This was to be the event of the decade to the folks of Contra County and elsewhere nearby. So when the day was finally set, the doers of Walnut and surrounding areas formed a committee to handle "after ceremony stuff." There was a lot of "stuff" in the minds of the women, and they stirred their menfolk into action.

On a breezy Sunday in the spring of 1957, a nervous Peter White walked from the groom's room with his best man, George Bentley, to the altar in the front of the church. They stood with Pastor Mathews waiting for the matron of honor, Ruth Mathews, and the bride, Rosey. In time to the strains of

"Here Comes the Bride," Ruth preceded Rosey down the aisle, and the bride was accompanied by Sheriff Williams who was giving her away.

Reverend Thomas Mathews looked down at a radiant but plainly dressed Rosey, and Peter White, in his best Sunday, going to church, garb. The small country church was filled to capacity with some needing to stand in the rear. The Reverend couldn't help but comment, "It seems to require a wedding or a funeral to make some of us come to church."

There was a humorous murmur emanating from the attendees, then an expectant silence, while the Reverend studied his agenda for the day. He leaned his spectacled face forward and said, "Let's get on with the ceremony." He studied the congregation for a moment. "I don't think there is much I can say about this union which you don't already know, as these two have already endeared themselves to all of us. To say we wish them the best is an understatement. Peter White, as a young man, came to us many years ago, and I can't think of a single time when he was not helping someone, or giving of himself when a hand was called for. Rosey, who cannot think well of our Rosey? She has been there for each of us at one time or another. God bless each, and may they live in happiness together."

With the words, "I now pronounce you man and wife" and the subsequent "Peter, you can now kiss your bride" came a humorously raucous emanation from the assemblage as a bashful Pete succumbed to the not so bashful Rosey's strong embrace.

The people of the ranches work hard, endure long hours in sometimes not-too-friendly weather. Celebrations, such as the wedding of two favorite folks draw all, not only for the event itself but a chance to let it all hang out: an excuse, if you will. The wedding of Rosey and Pete was no exception, and the community responded with vigor.

The church garth took the brunt of the gathering, sprouting tables, chairs, makeshift furniture, and piles of food. A fleet of pick-ups crowded around the area, some with tailgate down providing tables for the celebrants.

20 | FOLLOW THE STONE

At the time of the disappearance of Steve Harris, and the investigation thereof by Sheriff Bill Williams, much energy and effort was expended by all to alleviate the trauma suffered by Steve's daughter, Betty. Nevertheless Betty remained emotionally comatose to those around her and dwelled outside the world, so to speak. During the initial investigation however, and before Steve Harris's body was found, Betty told the Sheriff that her father kept a sizeable amount of cash below a dresser drawer in the bedroom; and she spoke of family jewelry that was kept there as well. The Sheriff procured and documented a list of said jewelry from Betty, which list was made available to lawmen in surrounding towns and counties. Since jewelry is easily identifiable to dealers, jewel thieves most often take stolen jewelry apart, removing stones and sometimes resetting them in other settings. This is all good and well except that there are some stones that catch a jeweler's eye for what they are, champions.

One piece in the Harris's collection was one of those 'champions,' a one and a half carat diamond delicately blue, flawless, and expertly faceted, more a museum piece than a finger decoration. The stone was brilliant, cut and faceted by the best artisan in the industry. Its flawless color gave it an aura and made it a piece that many would give their eye teeth to own. It was that kind of a stone. So into the second year after the death of Steve Harris, a jeweler named Sol Silberstein in Cheyenne was asked to evaluate a family's jewelry collection for insurance purposes, and he stumbled, should we say, on a very large blue tinted diamond. The object he held in his hand was a one and a half carat diamond tiffany set finger ring, far more of a treasure than he carried in his store, and too fine a stone for the setting it was in. He examined the piece through his loupe, noting its clarity and faceting. He sighed, then called to his associate, "John, c'm 'ere a minute." He handed the ring to John, "Take a look at this."

John looked, whistled and said "Where'd this come from?" He took another look and said, "That's a beauty."

Sol said, "I found this in amongst a whole bunch of mediocre pieces which came from the Double U Ranch just east of Glencoe. We are supposed to come up with a collection value for the court. This piece doesn't belong in this collection. I don't think the owner knows what this is."

"So how do we come up with a figure, considering that this would be a known specific item with its own name and ought to be in a museum someplace?"

"I think we should call our Sheriff on this one. The Double U owner, Arthur Anderson, died last week, and the heirs live in the East somewhere. The estate is in escrow, and this package came to us as part of that estate."

The Double U Ranch was small by any standard. Its very existence depended on the charity of the Arrow—B owner, as it lay in the foothills just west of the Arrow—B spread and was cut off from water during the summer months. As needed, the Arrow—B owners had always granted access to water for the Double U.

Now that the Double U ranch was up for sale George Bentley considered the purchase of the land and buildings thereof. After the rightful heirs, living in the East, had removed personal items from the property, George and the Sheriff paid a visit to the Double U. George did his thing, evaluating what was there, so that he could make an informed offer for the property. The Sheriff was there at George's request for law enforcement observation. They finished, and started for home, the Sheriff driving, and George sitting quietly alongside, deep in thought. George glanced over at his longtime friend, remembering the earlier times when they both were younger and contentious with each other. He said with a smile, "How'd we ever get along, you with your bristling personality, and me with my insults?"

The Sheriff chuckled, "I was faced with a smart-ass kid, unable to simmer down, and I jumped on it. By the way, do you know Silberstein, a jeweler in Cheyenne?"

"Uh huh, so what's with Sol?"

"He called me last week about a diamond ring he ran across. Said it had all the reasons for being in the stolen category. Do you still have that list of jewelry missing when your father-in-law disappeared?"

"Yes, of course. That's interesting, do you know where it was found?"

"It ended up in Sol's place along with some minor pieces for estate valuation. Sol was inventorying and evaluating some items found in a small safe on the Double U."

"So, let's do some matching. You know I haven't thought much about that jewelry collection because of my problems with Betty."

The Sheriff said, "I'm going over to Cheyenne tomorrow, why don't you come along, with your list."

George and Bill entered the Silberstein Jewelry store and after old-friend hugs Sol said, "Come on back to the coffee pot and we can talk."

The Sheriff said, "Let's see that ring you called me about."

Sol used a soft black cloth to rub the ring and stone out of habit, then placed the cloth on a work bench, and gently set the ring on the cloth. He put a jeweler's loupe in the Sheriff's hand and said, "Take a look." The Sheriff did, and so did George.

Bill said, "So you know, I don't know anything about this stuff. Tell me what I'm looking at."

"This is one sweet rock, perfect in every way. Worth lots, and has no reason to be in this collection from the Double U. Further, it's in a cheap, poorly-crafted, fourteen-karat yellow gold setting, the kind we might use for some kind of smaller semi-precious stone, like maybe an aquamarine. That should raise a question in anyone's mind."

George, who had been silent till now, produced his list of items missing from Steve Harris's collection. One of the items listed was "A large diamond ring, set in white gold," and with a written statement, "This ring is to be passed on to the first natural born female grandchild in my family." It also contained a certificate of merit and size, which was consistent with the stone on hand. George looked at the Sheriff, "Do you read what I read?"

There was a moment of silence from the Sheriff, then, "Yes, I'm interested, does this mean you'll be bugging me every day, or will you cool your heels, and wait, like any other citizen?"

George said, "So just because we found that pile of bones up in the mountains doesn't mean we should consider the case closed. Now we have a new lead and we need to go forward and see how this connects to Steve's death, right?"

"Yes, well it's hard to question a dead man, what other idea is stirring around in that convoluted mind of yours?"

George said, "Well you might consider questioning the man's heirs as a starter, it seems a bit odd that the family didn't know about the diamond."

The Sheriff said, "It's too bad you didn't take up law enforcement instead of raising cows, as usual you are giving me instructions on how to do my job."

"Well you sort of asked this time."

It was two full days before Sheriff Bill Williams placed a call to George Bentley out at the Arrow—B. "George, no need to get a swelled head about this, but I'm booked to fly east and talk to the Anderson Family. I asked Silberstein not to say anything about the diamond until I have a chance to talk to the family."

"Thanks for your concern over my head. Do you need me to do anything while you're gone?"

"Uh uh, I'll keep you informed."

"Fly well."

Arthur Anderson's will was written on the back of a large envelope. It was short and specific. It simply directed that all of his real and personal properties, whether at the Double U Ranch or elsewhere, were to be divided into three parts, one part each to be given to his son and two daughters. It was signed by him and entirely written in his own handwriting, which made it legal as a holographic will under Wyoming law even if it hadn't been witnessed, which it had been, by a neighboring small rancher and the rancher's wife. The trouble started with, how do you divide miscellaneous assets into three parts without selling them on the open market first, and then dividing the money received from the sale? While the heirs all lived in the East, Mr. Anderson's son made the trip west to close up his father's affairs, to get himself appointed by the court as the executor and to choose a Wyoming resident to act as the agent who would legally handle things: selling the property, all the regalia, the furnishings, and such personal property as would be appropriate. Before he left for home, Anderson's son left the jewelry with the Silberstein Jewelry store for evaluation at the suggestion of the court. He was not aware of the diamond piece, its origin, or the value it represented.

Sheriff Williams, by appointment, met with Arthur Anderson's son. They discussed the matter of finding stolen jewelry in Arthur Anderson's possession and the legal issues involved. Returning home after a quick turnaround, he called George. "Bill Williams here, I'm back."

"So, what did you find out?"

"I don't think son Andrew knew anything. My guess is that Arthur accepted the ring for some kind of service, not knowing the ring was stolen."

"That makes sense. Arthur was a good man. But the trick is to figure out what kind of service Arthur could give, big time."

"That might be helpful. Have any ideas?"

"Why don't we start with Anderson's bank account?"

"Yes, well I'm sure the courts will give me authority to delve into a private citizen's personal life, especially their financial activities. Are you kidding?"

"So, twist a few arms, you used to be good at that kind of thing."

The Sheriff stared up at the ceiling, "Your complements frighten the hell out of me. I have such a nice job, and I expect to retire in a year or two, perhaps you would like me to retire early, on demand."

George said, "Now Bill, isn't there a way? We need to know who needed money, and where they got it from."

"I'll think on that one a bit. In the meantime I have the problem of what to do with the ring. Certainly it doesn't belong to the Anderson family, although I can see them taking issue there, unless the state can prove conclusively that stone is positively the same item as in the Harris list of stolen items. That may be hard to prove. By the same token, the question of where did rancher, Arthur Anderson, get the ring? The ring will have to stay in escrow until rightful ownership can be established. My job is to conduct some kind of an investigation for the purpose of determining what criminal acts have taken place here. The court will have to decide the fate of the stone."

"That's nice, Bill, the case of a stolen gem takes precedence over the murder of Steve Harris?"

"You have such a nice way of telling me what my job is. I

see you haven't done away with your smart-aleck ways."

"Sorry, I get carried away sometimes. Bill, my life's been all screwed up since Steve was killed. I can't let it go." He was silent for a moment. "I'd like to visit the Double U again. Maybe we can find something related to a friend of Anderson's."

"So, what for?"

"Well, Bill, small ranches generally pay cash for everything. I see no mention of cash being found. I think there is a connection there somewhere."

The Sheriff said, "How serious are you about buying up the Double U? That would make it easy, you could take the place apart if you owned it."

"Nice thought, but time is of an essence here, like tomorrow."

George and the Sheriff entered the Double U ranch house. Their search was methodical, thorough, and revealed nothing. They had been there for the better part of the morning and were getting ready to leave when a large rat came out from under the bed, scurried across the floor, and out the open door. George said, "Where'd he come from?" They took another look under the bed. Behind and hidden from view was a passageway into the wall area. A loose piece of wood was pushed aside showing a Maxwell House coffee can. The rat apparently had been using the loose board as a doorway into and out of its nest.

The can contained two hundred sixty U. S. dollars plus an IOU in the amount of 1,000 dollars signed by a Miles McKinney and payable to Arthur Anderson. George said, "I'm sure that our diamond ring was used as collateral. It doesn't seem logical that a man with two hundred sixty dollars to his name would lend a thousand to anyone without some kind of assurance that he would get it back."

The Sheriff said, "Seems as how."

"We have a name."

The Sheriff said, "I'll work on it, George."

21 | A NIGHT TO REMEMBER

Sheriff Williams had some business to do in Glencoe, and so did George. After the discovery of money and the note in the Double U ranch house wall, the two rode together into town, the Sheriff checking with local law enforcement, and George checking with the Cattlemen's Association. George finished his business there, and then stopped in to the Davis Veterinary building. His subconscious mind led him there, while he consciously made up a somewhat minor reason for doing so, like he needed more vitamins for his pregnant mare that was having difficulty. Todd was out front when he came in the door, he produced the requested pills, saw a kind of hollow look about George, and smiling to himself, said, "Would you like to take Joan out to lunch? She's been here since the wee hours this morning doing some tests for me, and I want to get her away from it all for a time."

George's subconscious mind tweaked at the thought of seeing her, which he consciously denied, reminding himself of his vows to Betty ... so they went out to lunch together.

At an earlier time these two were very close. Yes, they once had a physical experience with each other, but it was a time when each had other interests and needs, and neither had thought of a life together or marriage. The sudden death up on Portal Mesa of George's father, and the need for the new man on the block to suddenly become a western rancher, further postponed anything more serious than friendship. Betty came into George's life soon after his return from college to the Arrow—B Ranch in Wyoming. Their romance was instantaneous at their first meeting, and the community at large soon looked to these two as their favorite lovers. The marriage ceremony of George and Betty had been an inspiring event, full and rich. Joan suffered the loss of her father and then suffered more because she had truly fallen in love with George.

George Red Fox Bentley was a man needing to love and to be loved in return. This did not happen, and the man suffered. The magic that had brought Betty and George together cooled, and died of itself. The woman collapsed within herself, and the man, loyal to his vows to that woman, was beset with a pause in his life that he didn't expect or need.

George and Joan finished their lunch, which had been one of guarded conversation by both, and walked on back to the veterinary building. Todd met them with a message from Pete out at the Arrow—B. "Pete wants you to call before you leave Glencoe."

Pete answered George's call, "Boss, that prize steer we have coming is due in tomorrow morning. Why don't cha pick 'im up afore yu come on back?"

"Sounds reasonable, Pete, I'll see you about eleven tomorrow, then." George hung up the phone with a kind of wistful idea, thinking dinner with Joan? He waited until Todd was out of the office, then asked Joan, "I have to stay over tonight, will you join me for dinner?"

"That's nice, George . . . Where are you staying tonight?"

George didn't answer the question. "I'll pick you up at six then. Do you like steak at the Cattlemen's Steakhouse? That's about all they serve there."

Two friends sat across from each other in the local purveyor of the famous Wyoming staple, beef. "Tell me what's going on in your personal life, Joan, anyone new?"

Joan demurred a quiet "no," studied George and said, "I am remembering the times we spent together in college." She paused. "I guess I haven't the right to wish them back."

There followed an awkward silence, finally George said, "I too remember those times with much pleasure. My father's death, no his murder really, the 2,000 miles we were apart, and the problems of running the Ranch, all occupied my mind to the degree that what we had together suffered."

Joan was silent for a time. "And then along came Betty. You broke my heart you know."

"Were you in love with me? I didn't know."

"I thought I was, George, I guess it must have been one way, and that doesn't work."

"Perhaps in time we will have a future together, Joan."

Joan asked quietly, "Will you stay with me tonight? I need you."

The morning found George and Joan breakfasting together early, after which George headed for the livery stable, and Joan to her job at the veterinary clinic. Their night together had been fulfilling, each parting with the warm feeling of love. George had discovered feelings for Joan that went beyond what he had felt during their college days. Whereas he retained his concern and feelings for Betty, he found himself less troubled by his loyalty and concern for his estranged wife than his conscious mind would allow. The light kiss between he and Joan, as they parted, promised.

George walked into the livery office, sat down opposite his friend Gordon Clyde. "Hi, I need transportation for me and a big animal out to the ranch."

"So, how was your night with Joan?"

George groaned. "This county has a communication and

spy network that is so good and so fast that the U. S. Government should take note for defensive purposes. It's got to be better than anything they use. I wonder if it's gotten to Betty yet?"

Gordon smiled, studied George's face which was still in a trance over his night with Joan, said "You must make a lousy poker player; sure, I been wanting to visit those cows of mine out there anyway. Where's the big animal?"

"Coming in on the morning's freight. Bring your biggest, he's 2,000 pounds."

22 | JOAN THE VET

Joan La Cross finished her studies at Colorado A&M but received her newly minted diploma from Colorado State University since the Colorado legislature had voted to change the name in her final year. She returned to Glencoe as a Doctor of Veterinary Medicine in the spring of 1957 skipping her graduation ceremony, but too late for the Pete and Rosey wedding. Her graduation ceremony was less important to her in that Todd Davis needed help at the veterinary hospital, and Joan availed herself to bring relief to an overworked Todd. In the following weeks, Todd made the move to open a satellite office in Walnut, and put Joan in charge. The veterinary clinic was located in an unused freight building, built before surface vehicles were moving beefs from ranch to market. Whereas there was still a need for rail services, that business end could be handled elsewhere. The building was copious, like a barn, and Joan started her business in one end, expecting to utilize more space as needed. In the first week it sported a desk and telephone, and of course, the first person she talked to in town was Rosey, but she didn't need a phone for that.

Joan entered the café, sat herself on a seat at the counter, and waited. Rosey came out from the kitchen, and said, "Hi,

Joan, what brings you out here so early?"

Joan answered, "You might as well get used to it, Rosey. I'm going to be the new kid on the block. I'm in the old freight building down the street."

"This is news, tell me about it."

"Well, Todd is opening up a satellite office out here, and I'm the 'man' in charge."

"That's nice, I'm happy for you. The rest of the folks out here have needed someone closer than Glencoe for a long time. Where are you staying?"

"That's why I'm out here today, I owe mom a visit out at the Arrow—B, where she is staying in the ranch guest house. I thought I'd get someone to take me out there for the night." She did a half laugh then said, "I might have to learn to ride horses again."

"That's a funny. I can picture you on a horse with your little black bag rushing to resuscitate a newborn calf. Since you sold your car, just how does Todd expect you to get out to a problem?"

"Todd is nice, Rosey, He put me on a budget to start things out here, and I'm going to ask George to put an article in the Walnut weekly. I suppose though, it will be a while before the folks out here trust me to care for their animals."

"From what I hear, Joan, you've already gotten a start on that one." Rosey studied Joan's face a bit. "How will it be with you, seeing George again?"

"I can handle it, Rosey. It's so unfair, though, I have to admonish myself all the time not to think bad when it comes to Betty. Right now I'm filled with things to do, things I must learn about animal care, animal owners and their feelings about me being responsible for their herds and flocks." That'll take my mind off George for a time. You know, Rosey, I can't stop loving him. Perhaps things will work out some time."

"Why don't you stay with me tonight, and I can do without my car for a few days so you take it in the morning and drive out to the ranch."

"That's an offer I can't refuse, can I help some way today?"

Joan drove out to the ranch early the next morning. The ranch buildings now included a small guest cottage located just below the main structure, and accessible to both the main building and the parking and corral areas. One could walk from the parking area into either the main building or the cottage directly. Her mom met her at the cottage door. She said, "Joan dearest, what a pleasant surprise."

"Hi Mom, you look well. I have wanted to find time to come out sooner but couldn't until now. I have some news for you. I'll be starting a satellite office in Walnut for Todd."

"That's nice, then you'll be living in Walnut?"

"Uh huh, right now I have an army cot in the old freight building in Walnut. I expect to change that ASAP. This is very nice here, Mom." She lingered a bit over kissing her mother's cheek. "How often do you see Eva?"

"George picks her up on a Friday, and returns her to Betty Monday morning."

"Gee, how does it feel to be a mom again?"

Renee La Cross smiled, "When George will let me, it's fine. George is very devoted to his daughter, and spends all of his spare time with her. I don't remember your dad ever changing a diaper even."

"Yes, George would be that way, is he home?"

"He's usually gone by now. This sure is a big place. George took me around in the pickup last week. The ranch seems endless. Did you see George when he was in Glencoe last week?"

. . . "Uh huh."

An astute mother noticed the pause and quiet words. "And?"

"Mom, you're not being fair. You really don't want to know."

"No, I guess I don't. Sorry. I want so much for your happiness, daughter."

George arrived home at noon, hungry and tired. He took care of his horse, washed up at the pump, and entered the cook shack. Joan was there, bigger than life, her mother too. He joined them, "Hi. What brings you way out here, Joan?"

"Hello to you, George. Oh, I wanted to see Mom, it's been a long time since my last visit."

Renee said, "Joan has some good news."

Mary Ellen came, poured coffee for all, and waited.

George stirred in some cream and sugar, his mind darting back to that pleasant time with Joan in Glencoe, and looked quizzingly at her.

Joan said, "You know that old empty freight building in Walnut, well it's now The Walnut Veterinary Clinic."

George asked, "Will you be working out here then?"

"Todd has asked me to set things up, and, yes, I'll be doing my thing here, now that I'm a Doctor of Veterinary Medicine."

George said, "That's nice, where will you live?"

Joan kind of laughed, "Right now I have an army cot in the freight building. It's a bit basic, I know, but convenient."

Mary Ellen said, "That's good news, we need you out here."

George said, "The last time I was in that building it looked more like a barn than an office building."

Joan said, "I can handle it, just bring your sick cows in."

23 | WATER FOR PETE AND ROSEY

Pete began to build his ranch house, torn between his time ramrodding the Arrow—B and the time he needed to spend building. He didn't know there would be this conflict, however he handled things pretty well, keeping in mind his loyalty, and concern for his longtime authority over the main ranch.

Rosey started looking for someone to take over the Café, with the thought of living with Pete when the ranch house was habitable, the definition of which meant more than four walls. Pete, a longtime bachelor, living in a bunkhouse, wasn't too sure of himself and in his new role as a husband, stumbled. One day on a picnic at the building site, Rosey asked Pete, "How soon can we move in, it's coming in to the cold time, and we need to cozy up for the winter?"

Pete hesitated then, "I'm not sure, Rosey. We have propane for cooking, the telephone company has brought a line up here, and the electric company promises this fall but we still need to haul our water."

"Oh, and I suppose we'll have to do an out-house thing until we get water?"

Pete nodded, then said, "No Rosey, I won't have you do that."

George came for a visit at a time when Pete was working on his ranch house. He smiled as he watched his ranch ramrod and good friend work, "Pete, it sure looks good. Has Rosey been out here to see this lately?"

"She was here yesterday."

"So, what did she think?"

"She seems to like it so far."

George scratched his head, waited for further comment, got none, then said, "What's the problem, Pete?"

"Well, I mentioned doing an outhouse until next spring, then finish off the bath and toilet. That seemed to go over like a bawling cow at two a.m."

George laughed. "Welcome to married life. Yours is not to worry, Pete, Rosey is a special person and so are you. You two are going to do fine together. You can fix this water problem. There's water down there, you just have to dig for it. I know the guy with the water wand in Glencoe, I'll call him."

George's call to the "Junk & Stuff" business in Glencoe found Mike O'Neal, the owner. George said, "Hi Mike, George Bentley here. Do you still do wells and find water?"

"Shor do, what d-yu need, George?"

"You know Pete, my ramrod, well he's got a small spread up just below Portal Mesa. He needs water. Go help him out, charge it to the Arrow—B."

"How far do I go, all the way to his building?"

"Talk to him about that one, you know he got married to Rosey and, well, they need water for cattle and indoor plumbing for the house."

"Gotcha."

Mike O'Neal had been doing "water" for the ranchers and miners of Contra County for as long as anyone could remember. He was a colorful character, so to speak, from Scotland, unmarried, and on perpetual retirement. Likeable and considered a vital part of the County business activities, he got away with being a prima donna in a he-man's world. So when George told Pete that Mike would come out to do his thing, Pete laughed and said, "You s'pose he'll bring that divinin' rod a his, I always wondered if that worked or is he just plain lucky?"

"Yes well, one way or another, he usually finds water, in spite of his weird ways. Anyway, we don't have a choice, he's the only one in town."

Mike came out to the Arrow—B, brandishing his divining rod like a catholic priest swinging his censer. Pete met him in the ranch yard, and they drove together out to Pete's spread. Pete watched, skeptically as Mike did his thing. In time Mike said, "We can do this one of two ways, dig the well close in, keeping the need for long piping at a minimum or digging our well up a ways with long pipes to bring the water down, thus providing water pressure to the system. How much money do you want to spend?"

"Tell me what my options are."

"If we do it here you will need a large tank and a pump. There's water here, I need only go down 40 or 50 feet. Pumps need electricity, how will you handle that one?"

Pete thought for a bit. "Show me where we should put the well, and tank close up. How big the tank should be for stock and us, and how much it'll cost?"

Peter White finished his house in the fall of 1959. Rosey made a home out of 'the house that Pete built.' Rosey retired from cooking for the folks of Contra County, and sold her café, but she didn't retire from her place as confidant and active participant in county goings on. George's article in the Walnut weekly read:

For all of us who call Walnut and the surrounding ranches and mines home, the retirement of Rosey is sad, but it shouldn't be. This vibrant and warm person has touched all of our lives. She has been there for each of us when we strayed, when we suffered, and also when we prospered. Rosey had a way of listening, saying little, but always making us feel better and stronger. She has kind of a magic about her. Rosey's Café will still be there, yes, but Rosey won't. We should feel happy for this charismatic icon of our social world, wish her well and thank her for her many years of giving to each of us. God bless you, Rosey, stay well and happy in your new role as wife and homemaker.

24 | A FOREMAN TO BE

Running the ranch without Pete ramrodding was going to be a bit of a problem for George. He had always known that this day was coming, and he had given much thought on the matter. He had two choices, train someone or do it himself. Over objections from Pete, George finally said, "Pete, you have a wife now, you have a home away from here, and you need to let go here at the Arrow—B. We will survive."

Pete completed his ranch house and one day told Rosey that things were right for them to move in. He held Rosey's hand as they entered, and an appreciative Rosey smiled her pleasure. Pete, with help from George and two ranch hands from the Arrow—B, had transported furniture and such from Rosey's home in Walnut out to the ranch, and Rosey began to make a home out of a house.

This was not an easy time for Rosey. She needed to divest herself of both her café and her home in Walnut. She had made that commitment to retire from the rigid schedules and work that she had kept for many years. She was comfortable with Pete, and the love between them grew as they worked together. The building included two bedrooms, a large main room featuring a fieldstone-faced fireplace, and a picture window viewing the valley below. A copious kitchen was there to accommodate Rosey's cooking skills and also to handle visitors or ranch celebrations or special events. The bathroom, located between the two bedrooms did indeed offer "inside plumbing," the water system having been completed as Pete directed. It had taken the better part of a year to build his ranch house, Pete doing much of the construction, while he hired folk around him as needed to handle that which he himself could not do.

The Arrow—B hands had been selected and honed over the years into a fine force, one that could almost function without daily instructions from a ranch foreman or the owner. George knew this, and depended on his hands to do their thing well. However he also knew that the time would come when he would again need a strong skilled manager, and one qualified to cross the boundary between himself and those that did the hard stuff: working with the animals, fixing the fences and chopping the wood. With this in mind, he asked Pete what he thought about Cliff, who had been working on the ranch for over a year. "Pete, how's Cliff been working out?"

Pete said, "Just fine. Why, is his father giving you trouble again?"

"No, he's going to have to stay mad until he gets himself figured out. He really has a great son, who just wants to succeed. No, Pete, I'm thinking that Cliff is about your age when you came to the ranch. Do you think that in time he might be able to handle our hands?"

Pete thought for a moment, "Wal, he's been workin' hard, he learns fast, and all of that, but do you think he could handle the older guys in the bunk house?"

George said, "I kind of think he could, he stood up to his father, who didn't like him working as a cowhand. I don't think he likes being stepped on, and can handle the men well."

Pete said, "He seems to have a level head on him, do you want me to help tell him what the real world is about?"

"Hell no, Pete, it's better that he gets in trouble and learns it that way."

One morning, George joined the hands in the cook shack and asked Cliff who was sitting across from him to stay put, and when the rest left he said, "Tell me what you intend to do in the future, I'm sure you don't want to stay a cowhand forever?"

"Mr. Bentley, my dad wants me to go to college, I don't feel good about spending more time in school. I like ranching from what I have seen so far."

George studied Cliff for a few moments. Cliff sat quietly, then, said, "I know I'm a long way from owning a ranch, raising cattle, and building that kind of a life for myself, but that's what I think I would like to do."

"Cliff, would you consider a position as ranch foreman sometime in the future, as a step toward having your own ranch?"

"Yes sir, I certainly would."

"Fine, Cliff, but I suggest you continue your education also. Try reading anything concerning ranching, and management. When I think you are ready, I'll give you the chance to foreman this ranch."

Amy had been helping out at the Café for the summer. During that summer she stayed with Rosey, and Amy had become like a daughter to Rosey. When fall classes started at Glencoe Junior College, Amy left. Now that she was gone, Rosey found less reason still for continuing in the café business. She placed an announcement in the Walnut Weekly of her intended retirement after a sale of Rosey's Café, and another in the Glencoe Herald for the sale of said business. The beloved Rosey the café owner had become Rosey the homemaker. The transition was complete when Rosey finally agreed to sell Rosey's Café, however, Rosey's position in the County, as counselor and confident to most, remained. She was visible in church, in all community affairs, and often encouraged and hosted visits to their ranch.

25 | THE RESERVATION CONNECTION

George called Sheriff Williams, "Hello Sheriff what's new on the Steve Harris case?"

The Sheriff answered, "I suppose you had to make this call, if ever you called friendly like, I'd fall off my chair. What's your problem, you know as much as me that the link person is a Miles McKinney who is nowhere."

"So what are you doing to find 'im?"

"I don't find people, the Missing Persons Bureau does that stuff."

"So, do we just wait, or apply some kind of reminder to the MP bunch?"

"George, they're supposed to do their thing without prompting. When they have something, you'll be the first to know. Now, how will we know what's going on when Rosey is gone?"

"I don't know why I should expect to get a straight answer from our duly elected Sheriff, but let's play that one again. Are we not actively trying to find out who caused the killing of Steve Harris, a respected resident of our county? ... And I expect we haven't heard the last of Rosey? Speaking of that venerated icon of our community, do you suppose you can lower your feet from your desk long enough to meet me at

Rosey's for lunch today, she isn't closed yet? I'm buyin'.'"

"Sounds good. See you there at twelve."

George arrived at Rosey's first and drew himself a cup of coffee from the pot sitting on the counter. The café was filled, and in the words of some past bard, Rosey was "As busy as a one-armed paper hanger with the seven-year itch." She saw George at the counter, nodded and went back to her culinary efforts. The telephone sounded, and she wiped her hands on her apron, lifted the hand set off its hook and said, "Rosey here."

The Sheriff came on the phone and said, "Hi Rosey, is George there?"

"Uh huh. You wana talk to 'im?"

"No, just tell him I'll be a little late, say like a half hour."

Rosey informed George of said, and returned to the kitchen. Her helper for the day handed George a handwritten menu, and left to serve others. George drank more coffee, glanced at the menu and when the Sheriff showed up, said, "Hi, I assume you had some kind of Sheriff business this morning. What's goin' on?"

"I received a rare call from the Reservation police. They want to have a pow-wow. Something about booze, and how it gets to the Rez."

George said, "That's interesting, when I bring up the subject of alcohol at the tribal council meetings, I get ignored. I guess the problem of alcohol and drug abuse is getting too much for the Reservation police to handle. You know how much they want our law enforcement to stay out of Reservation matters, they must be plenty desperate."

The Sheriff said, "I really can't help them anyway; what they want me to do is against the law here."

George mused, "When grandfather Running Deer was alive, we could help solve some of these things. Now, it's like all Indians and no Chief. And nothing happens by committee. This is not a new problem. The cause is two-fold: first is medical, the second is unemployment. People with nothing to do sometimes turn to drugs or alcohol to crutch them through life. I suspect that is what made someone go after Steve Harris. He was known to have a stash of cash."

"At least we agree on that one, George, I'm sure there is a connection here. In as much as you can dig into things going on in the Reservation better than me, I've been expecting something from your end. The moccasin telegraph doesn't know I exist, and we both know it's the best source of info around."

"Well the MT seems to avoid the subject of substance abuse on the Rez, Bill. I can't even get the blink of an eye out of the Indian Council members when I bring up the subject. I do agree, however, that there has to be someone on the Rez that is in the know, and also has a drug problem. When we find out who that is, we'll maybe find the killer of Steve Harris.

"The note we found in Arthur Anderson's bedroom wall was signed by a Miles McKinney. That doesn't sound Indian. I think a breed or non-Indian did the killing. That person may not be on the Rez. He may have had help from an addict living on the Reservation though."

Rosey came out from the kitchen wiping her forehead with a tired looking dish towel. She looked at the two, George and Bill, smiled and said, "You two must have made up, I can't remember ever seeing the two of you sitting together this long without one or the other of you storming out in frustration or something."

George smiled, looked up at Rosey and asked, "How's married life, Rosey?"

"I'd like it a lot more if I could finish off the sale of the Café."

The Sheriff and George didn't meet again for the next two months. Although the subject of the Harris killing bugged Sheriff Williams big time, he could do nothing more than hope another clue would surface. He had responded to the

Reservation police regarding the sale of alcoholic beverages into the Reservation, explaining that he could not interfere with commerce in any way, but that if they could identify those on the Reservation that might be desperate for illegal substance of a kind as to commit a crime, he could, perhaps, help. This brought on a silence and glum looks from Reservation police.

The summer drew to a close and with it the fall roundup on the range after which the Rodeos took place, when ranchers and cowboys gathered for a few days to compete and relax from the hard labors of ranch life. It was here that cowboys from all over the state assembled, displayed their skills and perhaps came away with some prize money. And so it was at the Arrow—B.

The hands of the Arrow—B traveled to Glencoe for the games, leaving a skeleton crew to keep things in order, and handle any problems that might occur there. George would be there at the Rodeo on the final day to record and write about the highlights of the events. Left at the ranch, on that day were the two women, Mary Ellen, and Joan's mother Renee, along with the child Eva plus one of the hands. Renee would look after the toddler, Eva, just two years old.

26 | INTERLOPERS

Mary Ellen was just finishing clean-up of the evening meal when a soft voice came out from nowhere. It said, "Keep looking straight ahead, Mary. It would be dangerous to you if you know who I am. Walk into the store room, and don't look back." The voice followed, closed the door and slipped the padlock over its cradle.

Renee La Cross, with Eva in her arms, answered a knock at the front door of the ranch house to face a large man wearing a handkerchief mask and pointing a pistol at them. Renee gasped, quickly brought her left hand to her mouth, and stumbled aside as he pushed them inside. The man guided them into the bathroom, closed them in and placed a chair against the door knob.

Both women had been admonished to keep silent, and both did for almost an hour. Finally Mary Ellen felt the intruder was gone and took the risk. She screamed as loud as she could, and a ranch hand heard her. He came into the cook shack and let Mary Ellen out of the store room. They went directly up to the ranch house. What they found was a tearfully frustrated Renee and Eva in a trashed house. Renee went to the telephone only to find it inoperative. The ranch station wagon was in Glencoe with the rodeo bunch, so Mary

Ellen climbed onto a horse and rode over to a neighbor and called George in Glencoe. She found him at the Cattlemen's Café. He listened, swore, and called the sheriff in Walnut. "Bill, we have trouble on the ranch, I'm two hours away, will you go on out and see what's going on?"

Sheriff Bill Williams pulled up in the ranch yard, and stepped out to meet two highly upset women, who finally calmed down enough to tell the story of their ordeal. He entered the house, took a look, and asked Renee "Do you know if George had any cash stashed in the house anywhere?"

Renee thought for a moment, "Only that I suspect he did, as he made payroll in cash from his office which is in the rear of the main room."

The Sheriff turned to Mary Ellen, "Tell me what the man looked like, Mary."

"He was big, wore clothes that didn't fit, and had his face covered." She thought for a moment, "He spoke as if he were acquainted with everything here and who we were. He called me Mary, and sounded like he knew his way around."

"Have you ever heard that voice before?"

Mary answered, "He was speaking through a cloth. It sounded muffled, that's all I can recall."

The Sheriff retrieved his camera from his car and started to take pictures of the trashed rooms in the ranch. Ranch hand Eddy traced the telephone line and found where it had been cut. He came into the ranch house and told the Sheriff.

George found the Sheriff sitting in the cook-shack having coffee with the two women. He joined in and asked, "So tell me what happened."

The Sheriff rose, and led George into the ranch house. George took a look at the mess, noticed that the ranch safe had not been opened, whistled, and asked, "Where was Eddy when this happened?"

The Sheriff said, "You'd better ask him, George, it seems

he was invisible until he heard Mary Ellen's scream."

George said, "Well that's just peachy, let's get him up here, I didn't leave him here to be invisible. By the way Bill, did you notice the hoof prints on the side of the house? We never ride horses up there. Probably two riders from what I saw."

Eddy joined the group at the mess table, and George asked "Where were you when this all happened?"

"I were down in the far corner of the pasture and didn't hear nuthin."

George said, "Two riders came out from nowhere in broad daylight, enter the ranch house, stay for a half an hour and you didn't see them. Or did you?"

Eddy shifted himself on the bench he was sitting on and remained silent, averting George's eyes. George said, "Okay, go on doing what you were doing, I'll want to see you after the Sheriff leaves . . . Bill, let's take another look outside and around."

The Sheriff said, "Yeah, I did see those hoof prints like you said. I just wasn't sure if they were yours or theirs. Here's where you come in. Aren't there one or two of the old ones still alive in the Tribe able to follow a trail? How about Black Raven, is he still alive?"

"He's got to be over a hundred by now, and since I haven't heard otherwise, I guess he's still around. I'll check . . . Let's take a look."

The two men moved outside and the Sheriff pointed to some horseshoe prints. George studied them for a bit, and said, "I'm not too good at this stuff, you're right Bill, I'll look for one of the tribe that might still be able to follow a trail. If you're through here, I'll clean up and see what's missing."

George began putting things back in order. The more he worked through the mess in his office, the madder he got. A thought began to cross his mind, the intruder seemed more interested in the contents of his files than money, although the petty cash in his desk was gone too. Fortunately much of the ranch cash was in the safe.

George had a special relationship with the Sheriff. Their

respect for each other had grown over the years, albeit the testy Sheriff was a bit biased where 'Whites versus Indians' were concerned. So in any case of crime, George knew where Sheriff Bill Williams stood. While he worked, he mused to himself over what he knew the Sheriff was thinking, like *the number one suspect has to be one of those living on the nearby Reservation.* George considered this, of course, but couldn't see one of his own people in this light, although he knew for sure there was enough of a drug and alcohol problem on the Reservation to generate theft in the interests of needing cash to support a habit.

Since the death of Grandfather John Running Deer, it had been difficult to reach anyone by phone on the Reservation. The ship of state, so to speak, was in the hands of the council, which met about every two weeks. And nothing much ever gets done by committee anyway. George was a special entity within the confines of the Wind River Reservation. He is honored as George Red Fox Bentley. He is privy to events taking place on the Reservation, and encouraged to attend Council meetings. But his counsel is more often heard and quickly forgotten than to effectively trigger action. So George knew that unless there was a typhoon or an earthquake, the sitting council members would end up doing nothing.

In frustration, George found Tommy Little Feather who was doing some fence work and asked him to sit for a bit and chat. Tommy complied, sitting on a nearby bale of hay facing his employer questioningly.

George asked, "Tommy, do you know if Black Raven is still alive?"

"I'm not sure, Mr. Bentley, he moved up into the hills some time ago, and as far as I know, he's living with a grandson."

"Tommy, would you find out for me. I have a need to hire one with the old skills, and if Black Raven is gone, perhaps there is someone else that can do what I need. Take the rest of the day off, pick a pony of your choice, and see what you can find out."

Tommy nodded, and got up.   George added, "Take another day or two if you have to."

Whereas Tommy Little Feather had become a loyal and hard working part of the Arrow—B, he was careful not to play the part of "spy" on his own people. George was aware of that, and never expected nor asked Tommy to violate this premise. So in his attempt to help his boss locate someone from his tribe to do "spy" work, Tommy had to come to terms with his conscience first.   He went through the machinations of thought, balancing "for or against" then chose to comply with Red Fox's request.   There was trust here.

Tommy first went to John Running Deer's sister, who he knew still lived in the village. His knock on the door was answered, and a pleasant person said in the tongue of the Arapaho, "Come in Little Feather, I have been expecting you."

Taken by surprise he asked, "How did you know?"

"Little Feather, the women of our tribe will always talk to each other. Information is passed from teepee to teepee as it happens. Red Fox is a favorite of ours, and we already know of the trashing of his house. Do you have a message from Red Fox?"

Tommy said, "Yes, he wants to hire a person with the old skills. He asked me to find Black Raven if he was still alive, or someone else with the old skills if he was gone to the Great Spirit."

"Tommy, yes, Black Raven is still alive, however he no longer can leave his home, and would not be of value to Red Fox. Perhaps, though, he might know of one still active from a time gone by. We can ask him."

Tommy rode up the dirt path that led to a small building, the place where he had been told to find Black Raven. His knock was acknowledged and he was invited in. Black Raven welcomed him and pointed to a chair. He looked at Tommy expectantly.

Tommy said, "I'm Tommy Little Feather. Red Fox asked me to find you. He asked if there was still someone here that could follow a trail."

Black Raven hesitated, then said, "And if it's yes?"

"I was instructed to have that person report to Red Fox at the Arrow—B Ranch."

Black Raven was silent for a time, studying the young Indian standing before him. He finally said, "It is best that Red Fox meet with me. Please inform him of this."

A frustrated George Bentley, ranch owner, and by decree and ancestry, a full- fledged member of the local Arapaho Tribe, first went to the home of Chief Running Deer's sister, Sarah Golden Poppy. His knock on the door was promptly answered, and after traditional greetings he asked, "I wish to speak with Black Raven, however I am not learned in the language of the Arapaho. In that you are fluent in both English and Arapaho, would you accompany me to act as interpreter?"

George and Sarah made the trip to Black Raven's home. The brother and sister greeted each other with a flurry of Arapaho, then Sarah looked inquiringly at George and asked "My brother is well and asks of yourself?"

George answered, "I am well, but I once again have need for your expertise. My home has been invaded. I sought a person that might help in finding out who did this. It is too late, now, as the trail is cold."

Sarah interpreting said, "Red Fox, your request was considered, but there are no tribal members outside of us elders that know the skills you are asking for and we don't go out at all anymore." She paused, looking her visitor in the eye, "But it's a fact that when anything negative happens in or near the Rez, it is always considered our nation who is to blame. The crime you speak of took place outside the

Reservation. If we are involved, it is our nation that must respond." She hesitated for a moment, "Certainly we will seek answers here, but only if we're involved. We don't like what happened in your home either ... look to those who bring drugs and alcohol to our young people. They pretend to be our friends, and at the same time make money from our suffering and demise."

"Black Raven, yes, but we cannot find the pusher, the alcohol supplier or the thief, when our people hide and protect these evil doers. There has to be some help to the neighboring white law-enforcement from our tribe. This is not a matter of loyalty to our cause, it is vital that we do something beyond this. The distrust here is wrong. They cannot do anything about the criminal who plies his trade within the Reservation borders unless they have access to the errant tribal members who can identify those who need to be found and made to pay the consequences."

George waited as Sarah spoke to Black Raven. As she spoke George read Black Raven as he nodded and showed expressions of agreement or dissent. When Sarah again turned to George, he sensed the frustrations of the one before him, and knew that nothing would change. She said, "My brother is tired now. He wishes us to leave. He has no answer for you."

George Red Fox Bentley was not used to frustration about anything. Now he had both his problems with his wife, Betty, and a hopeless concern over the Arapaho people in his life. His call to Bill Williams, the Sheriff, was equally frustrating. "Hello Bill, George here."

"Hello yourself, what's going on that makes you make this call? I'm sure it's not about my health."

"Yes, well this citizen is wondering if the law is doing anything about the invasion of my home?"

"You were supposed to get some help from some Indian friends of yours. What happened there?"

"We discussed the tie-in with drugs or alcohol."

"So it doesn't take a brain to figure that one out. We can't do anything about that as long as the tribe won't tell us who or where. If they want us to do something about the vermin who ply the Reservation, the Indians in charge will have to open up."

George said, "Well that's not going to happen; how about some outside stuff, like a discovery party as the bad guys cross into the Rez with a load?"

The Sheriff said, "Great idea, George, I have somewhere around 4,000 square miles to cover, that would take a task force of a dozen or more cars and twenty working three shifts. I'm sure that the county Supers would approve, especially if it's for the good of the tribe." He chuckled, "I can't even get them to approve a two dollar raise for my deputy."

"Suppose I tell you when and where, can you handle a bust? I might have a way to narrow things down a bit."

"Uh huh, you've got the ball."

The Wyoming Cattlemen's Association meeting for the month of January tackled the problem of sheep stripping the range grass down to the roots as usual. The problem got smaller as there weren't that many ranchers that had seen any sheep lately, and most wanted any problems to go away so they could do their dinner and bar thing. George waited until the chair asked "Any other business?"

George said, "The drug and alcohol problem on the Reservation is getting worse. In that some of us might be a target for users who always need cash, and also in an effort to show our Indian neighbors a sign of good faith, I ask the chair to open up a discussion on the matter."

The Chair said a tired, "The chair so opens, George, what's this all about?"

George said, "In that the Reservation is surrounded by our ranches, drugs and alcohol have to come through these private lands of ours. They come via unscrupulous two-footed lice sneaking through our ranchlands, usually at night.

"Certainly the person or persons that invaded my ranch house represented one or more users looking for money to support a habit. There's little we can or should do within the Reservation, but we might try stopping those coming through with contraband."

The Chair interrupted, "George, what is this leading up to? It's the Sheriff's job, not ours."

"I agree with that, however we have a minimum of law enforcement in this county. We voted it that way, and for the most part that's fine. I'm suggesting that our Sheriff can't do anything about the bad people slipping through our ranches unless he knows where and when. We haven't given him enough personnel to cover even half of our county. Here's where we might be able to help. As a community of ranchers and miners we pretty well are everywhere, and for the most part are aware when someone crosses into our space. I'm suggesting that a call to our Sheriff would be in order when some interloper is noticed. The Sheriff has promised to respond, and maybe we can catch some of these people."

George added this, "Yes, I have a personal interest here, and a 'not-so-funny' dogged attitude, but I don't like someone messing up my home and stealing from me. We are reminded: 'Drug addicts are always needing money,' and will steal to get it. There are many druggies on the Reservation. Let's keep our eyes open and when we see something, call the Sheriff."

The Chair asked, "Since we are talking about night time mostly, will the Sheriff answer a phone call at say 2 a. m.?

"Yes, well we all know Bill, he'll grumble a lot but in the end come around. Just call him at any hour."

The Sheriff was eating breakfast when the phone rang. His rough "Sheriff Williams," was answered by "George here, Bill, I just had a call from our line shack. Our man is watching a man edging off of Leaning Mesa. I'm going out there and take a look. I told my man to do nothing, just stay out of sight until we get there."

"O-Kay, George, just look, don't take any action until I get there."

George drove the six miles to the line shack, entered, and joined the hand watching the mountainside. He could see a lone figure on horseback winding down the switchback trail. He said to his ranch-hand, "Saddle up one from our stock. I want to meet that rider before he enters Reservation space."

George mounted, and made his way along the bottom of the alluvial fan to the spine of the descending highlands. He waited behind a huge boulder cast down from the massive volcano activity of an earlier geologic time. The rider rounded the corner of the rock to face George blocking the trail. The rider totally surprised, pulled up, reached for his rifle, which motion stopped as he faced George's pistol. George asked, "Going somewhere?"

The man, sitting on a tired looking bay, was dressed in jeans and a checkered shirt which showed under a thick outer garment, and he wore an off-white baseball cap which sat upon a mop of black hair. He asked, "What's this all about? What d' yu want from me?"

George answered, "Just what do you have in those saddle-bags?"

The man answered, "That's my business, who are you, the law? If so show me some ID."

"This pistol's my ID."

"The law might consider this as an unlawful act, and I'm sure they'll find out."

"Yes, well I'll take that chance. Now get down off that horse, slowly. I've got nothing to lose if this gun goes off, as you say I'm already breaking the law."

"You're bluffing." He started to back his mount.

George fired his pistol. The bullet whizzed by the man's cheek and he yelped in fright, then did as he was told. George sidled up alongside the man's mount, lifted the flap on one of the two saddle bags, and took a quick glance inside. He saw items within that needed a closer look, then decided to wait until they reached the line shack, and let the flap fall. He ordered the man to dismount, then, with the man walking in front, and his horse tethered to George's saddle, they wound their way down the trail to the line shack. Ed, an Arrow—B hand, was there. He tied the hands of the walker, and handled the two horses. A short time later the Sheriff drove up. He looked at the figure sitting on the ground. "So, tell me what's going on here?"

George said, "Found him coming out of the Rez. and thought we might have a little chat. Take a look in those saddlebags."

The Sheriff walked over and opened the flap, first on one then the other. He looked up at George, "Don't see anything here, George, what's your point?"

"Point is, Bill, they're empty, and he has lots of money in that belt of his. I think we caught him on the way out."

"So what's that mean? I can't arrest someone because they have cash, even if there is a question as to where they got it."

"Uh huh, even I can figure that out. You might ask him what he's doing here; it's early morning, he's riding out from the Reservation. He's obviously been doing business of some kind, and I don't think it's trinkets for the Indians."

"George, some people never change, you've been telling me what to do ever since we met twelve years ago. I don't get mad like I used to, but this time you're pushing a bit too far. However you did it, holding this man is against the law, and I have to uphold."

"So uphold, do you want to tie my hands and lead me to jail, or are you going to just warn?"

"Oh for craps sake, untie the guy, put him on his horse, and send him on his way. We don't have anything here." He paused, then reached into his car and retrieved his camera, took a picture of the man on the ground and asked, "What's your name mister?"

There was silence from the oily looking lump of humanity sitting on the ground. George said, "Yes, well he didn't say much to me either. I suspect, unless you use a little pressure, he will remain nameless."

"Uh huh, well I'm not going to do that." The Sheriff looked hard at the suspect; then went to the man's saddlebags, rummaged through, finally found an envelope addressed to an Eddie Black. He said, "Now Eddie, I recommend you don't show up on or near the Reservation again soon. Now get on your horse and go," which the suspect did.

George watched as the man rode away, then, "Bill, we both know that that man's a dealer. If ever I see him again, I don't promise to call you."

"Yeah, and if I see something outside the law, I'll arrest."

It was a full week before the Sheriff got word of a trespasser moving toward the Reservation at twilight. It came from a small rancher located close to the Bar County line. The Sheriff picked up Deputy Roberts and drove out to the reported sighting. This time the Sheriff caught up with a vehicle traveling along Foothill Road. He turned on his siren and the vehicle drew to a stop. Leaving Roberts in the car, he approached the driver side of the vehicle from behind. The vehicle suddenly sped off, causing him to scramble back into his car and follow. The offending vehicle raced ahead with almost a mile head start, heading for Glencoe.

The Sheriff swore, then while Roberts drove, he called the Glencoe police. Reaching the desk he said, "This is Sheriff Bill Williams, We have a vehicle traveling on Foothill Road heading your way. I need to question the driver, can we have a road block where the road comes into town? I'm following, and should be there right behind him."

The desk Sergeant said, "Can do, Bill, I'll get on it right away."

Bill Williams was not exactly gentle when he pulled the suspect out of his car. The man complained bitterly, declaring abusive police tactics, and his rights. On arrival at police headquarters in Glencoe, the suspect was booked, charging him with one count of resisting arrest. The suspect's car was impounded. It was almost dark now, and the Sheriff opted to stay in town for the night, and question the suspect in the morning. He would also be going through the suspect's vehicle with proper witnesses and a warrant.

Morning found Bill Williams talking with Chief Richardson over a cup of coffee. The Chief asked, "So what made you go after this guy anyway?"

The Sheriff answered with a bit of humor, "You know big George out on the Arrow— B, he got hit one day while he was away. They messed up his house real bad like. Well, he speculated that drug and alcohol users on the Reservation were the culprits looking for cash to buy drugs. Then he stirred up everyone in the county to look out for strangers at strange hours. This guy is a stranger, driving in a strange place at a strange hour.

"So, me being the Sheriff, everyone expects me to patrol 4,000 square miles, capture the pusher or pushers, bring them into court with solid evidence for convictions, and I suppose, the incarceration of these lice. This guy acts like he's scared and I think he knows where the body is buried. I haven't looked in his car yet but we might find some evidence that will be of value."

The Chief said, "Yes, I know George, he's like a dog with a bone. You can bet he won't let this thing die until someone pays the consequences. I wouldn't want him for an enemy." He guffawed, then said, "You mind if I joined you looking inside that car?"

"Not at all, bring that finger print man of yours, we might find more than just a lowly drug pusher here? These guys are usually expendable, and don't have very healthy lives if discovered."

The car proved to be empty of any illegal material but had been "borrowed" without the owner's knowledge. The suspect would be moved to a Glencoe jail; and would be facing grand theft charges there.

A disappointed Sheriff was sitting at his desk in Walnut when George walked in. He asked the Sheriff, "So you caught-up with one, how's that working?"

"About as well as I expected from one of your ideas. The suspect turned out to be a car thief, and there were no drugs found in his car."

"So tell me about the arrest."

"He was arrested in Glencoe, I caught up with him there."

"You were chasing him?"

"Uh huh, I was on foot approaching his car, and he sped away. Richardson's crew stopped him and held him for me."

"Sounds like he was awful scared, Bill; do you think maybe that he did have drugs in the car, and got rid of them out the car window while you were climbing back into your vehicle?"

"You come up with more maybe's than anyone; it's too bad we can't arrest them all on the basis that 'maybe they are guilty.'"

George went over to the perpetual coffee pot simmering on a small table in the corner of the office, poured himself a cup, tasted it, and said, "Ach, how can you drink this stuff, and keep a stomach? . . . Why d' yu think he was so anxious to get away?" George sat down facing the Sheriff with a quizzed look. "Could he have thrown something out the car window without you seeing it?"

"Yah, I've been considering that possibility."

"Do you suppose it's still there?"

The Sheriff thought for a few minutes, considered telling George to go fly a kite, as he didn't take to being maneuvered into doing what he should be doing anyway, especially from George. "Well if we did find it we couldn't pin it on this guy anyway."

George said, "That's certainly true, Bill, but a stash of heroin is worth a lot of moolah. Besides, the crumb-bums that manage to get runners to deliver, don't like it much when one fails. I'm sure if our man was free he would lead us to where the drugs are."

"So he's not free."

"I seem to remember a dozen years ago when a couple of dummies were in Richardson's jail. The mob bailed 'em out, and a couple of weeks later they were found dead of 'no air.' I expect whoever's running drugs here will do the same."

The Sheriff considered this for a moment, then, "I could talk to Richardson. He doesn't cater to drug dealers much, and might cooperate."

"Yes, and I expect someone will come and bail this guy out like before. I expect they will head for the stuff, and I also expect the man who ran has a short life ahead."

The call to Chief Richardson of the Glencoe police was timely, as a short time later, bail for the suspect was posted. Chief Richardson informed Sheriff Bill Williams by phone of the posting, then took his time releasing the suspect. As expected, the suspect and the man who posted bail drove down Main Street and turned onto Foothill Road proceeding out toward the point where the Sheriff had first stopped the suspect. In that Foothill Road is a dead end road, it was easy to control by law enforcement, and the Sheriff along with two members of the Glencoe police force were waiting when the vehicle returned. The suspects surrendered in the face of several long guns aimed their way. On examination, a sizable package of heroin was found in the car. Both faced charges of possession and would pay much....

27 | A LOVE GONE AWRY

In a sense, George Red Fox Bentley was a leftover from a time when adversity produced strong persons, accepting what they were dished out, and going forward with their lives. His struggle to overcome the sadness brought on by the mental breakdown of his bride of only two weeks, the untimely death of his father, the death and mystery of his father-in-law and good friend, Steve Harris, all tested him. It had been a few years since Betty had succumbed to a mental breakdown. In spite of engaging a well-qualified psychiatrist to treat his bride, nothing had changed with Betty after three years and indeed he had been advised that her condition might possibly never improve.

Whereas counsel had indicated that Betty was non-violent, and would certainly not harm their child, Eva, George worried. On his weekly visits to the Harris ranch where Betty opted to live alone, he did what he could to help her, and, of course, pick up Eva for her time with him. It was on one of these visits that he noticed a dismal dark condition of the home. He stayed a while, drawing the curtains, picking-up misplaced items, half eaten pieces of fruit, and washing dirty dishes. This made him even more worried. Early on he had provided daytime help for Betty. Chloe, a young Indian girl, had been there during her summers, but when school started she didn't come.

On one Sunday night George returned his three-year-old daughter to her mother. When he walked in, he found Betty in bed. Dirty dishes, and an unkempt bedroom further piqued his mind, and he hesitated to leave Eva, albeit the law had said he must. Spike, the ranch handyman and wrangler, was outside when George came out of the ranch house. George said, "Spike, I'm worried for Mrs. Bentley, would you kind of look in on her from time to time, and call me if you think she needs help."

Spike said, "Mr. Bentley, she doesn't make herself available much except on payday. She used to work our stock, just like a hand, and now seldom even gets on a horse."

"Spike, call me if you feel something is wrong here. I would appreciate that."

George could neither leave his daughter in an environment and care condition that questioned the welfare of that daughter, nor could he physically remove their child, Eva, from her mother for fear of further psychological injury to that mother, Betty. Joan's mother, Renee, came to mind, she had been caring for Eva when she was with George on the Arrow—B and was very fond of her. He returned to the ranch, found Renee, and said, "I am concerned for Eva. Her mother is not well, and I think needs someone with her right now. Would you consider doing this until I can find a better answer . . . I'm not sure what that will be yet, but things can't go on like they are?"

Renee said, without hesitation, "Of course, George, I love your daughter, and feel responsible for her anyway. I'll stay with Betty as long as it is necessary."

"That's very kind of you, Renee . . . Let's try to make Betty feel comfortable with your 'visit.' I don't want to upset her if at all possible."

Renee called Betty, "Hi Betty, I'm on my way to spend a day with my daughter in Walnut. Would you like me to stop on the way back?"

Betty answered, "That sounds nice, Renee, and I know Eva will be pleased too."

Renee drove the ranch station wagon into Walnut and to the old freight building where Joan had her office and veterinary clinic. She found her daughter treating the Arrow—B ranch dog, Clancy, for a rattlesnake bite. The dog was strong, and it looked like he would survive. And, of course, mother had to ask her daughter if she had seen George lately.

Joan, who was hurting more and more over her love for George, who seemed out of reach, didn't need that question, and snapped, "Mom, I'm not going to go there." She went on with preparing the snakebite antidote for Clancy. Renee stood quietly, then was about to turn and leave, when Joan said, "I'm sorry, Mom, I'm kind of sensitive where George is concerned. It's nice to see you, I'm just right for lunch, and Rosey's in town. We'll meet her at the café, the new owners have opened it up for lunch." Joan finished with Clancy, put him in a large fenced area within the building, and joined her mother for a walk to the café. They entered under the large, 'NOW OPEN' sign and, spotting Rosey at the counter, joined her. After the hellos and hugs were over, they moved to a booth and started that phenomena, women's talk, which went on and on. It was Renee, of course, that brought up the subject of George, and Joan once again bristled. Rosey who was always good at listening, sat quietly remembering the times she was friends with both Betty and Joan, and knew of the tangle and real life drama that was happening. She understood Renee's conservative views, borne on the shoulders of righteous family traditions, and the struggle for her to understand. Rosey had watched and helped Betty recover from the death of her first love and husband, Paul. She had empathy plus for Betty, but stepped beyond that to recognize the need of a normal life for George, a life with love, warmth and the progeny that he deserved. She said, "I think it is time we give thought to what is happening to

George. Through no fault of his own, he is being denied happiness and fulfillment. It is wrong for any of us to moralize when we aren't wearing the shoes. Where true love and commitment exist, isn't it better that we try to understand, rather than condemn?"

There was a time of silence. Finally Joan reached over and took her mother's hand, looking into her eyes for a sign of acceptance. There was none. Renee asked, "Have you been going to church, Joan?"

Joan was silent, her Mother stood and said, "I need to be at the Harris Ranch now," and left. A tear formed and fell on Joan's cheek. Rosey took a tissue from her purse, reached over to Joan and touched that tear. Rosey said, "Joan, try to understand; your mother is faced with strong family traditions and moral values that will not accept the real life happening in your life. She loves you as she always has. It will take time for her, but she will change."

Renee drove into the Harris Ranch yard, parked and entered the main building. It was dark and gloomy inside, and she heard Eva sort of half crying. She stepped into the bedroom and found the child sitting on the floor. Betty looked up from a rocking chair where she swayed back and forth, smiled and said, "What do you want?"

Renee didn't answer, she picked up Eva, comforting her, and asked Betty if it was time for her nap, and had she eaten lunch. It was then, when she didn't get a response from Betty, that she began to understand the extent of Betty's illness. Certainly, Betty was not able to care for Eva, let alone herself. Renee did what was needed, caring for both Eva and her mother. She slept in the second bedroom with Eva.

It was a full week before George came again to the Harris Ranch. Renee waited at the door when he stepped out of his car. She said, "Hi."

George stopped, "You look worried."

"We need to talk." She indicated away from where Betty could hear. They moved off. "Betty is sick, George. She can't live alone, let alone care for her child. My being here is temporary, and is not solving the problem. She needs professional help."

"Yes, Renee, I think I know, and I certainly won't expect you to suffer, caring for her. I'm embarrassed now to have left you to face this thing. I have already made arrangements for a fulltime care nurse here." She should arrive this week."

Renee studied George's face then asked, "How long has she been this way?"

"This started the day we returned from our honeymoon and found her dad missing."

"Oh." Renee silently calculated the years George had been alone.

They entered the house, and found Betty playing with Eva, she looked up at George, smiled and said, "You don't need to take Eva this time. Renee will help me if I need her."

George first contacted Dr. Lewis. "Hello Doctor, this is George Bentley. Would you consider making another visit to see Betty? There seems to be a change in her behavior since you saw her last. . . . The fishing's been great lately."

"Hello to you, George, what kind of change?"

"The best I can tell you is that she seems lost from reality."

"Can you be more specific?"

"I have a court order allowing me to share in the care of our child, Eva. I don't think Betty can handle Eva's care let alone care for herself any more. She seems to have a lack of concern either for her own daily life functions or those of our three-year-old child. I am concerned for the safety of Eva, and, of course for Betty. I cannot defy a court order, and place my child in a safer environment without the approval of the court, and they will require some testimony from a professional."

"You're not giving me much to go on, however, if you can hold on for a bit, I'll check my schedule, and my associate to see if I have a time for a visit. Yes, I would like to do a fishing trip out there again, we'll see, I'll call you back."

Dr. Lewis's call came the next day. "George, I cannot stay a whole week with your wife as before, but perhaps over a long weekend. If this is okay, I'll drive over next Thursday and stay until Monday morning."

"Sounds fine, come ahead; the red carpet's laid out."

As before, Dr. Lewis did his fishing in the mornings and met with Betty in the afternoons. He didn't say much, just listened. Sunday night he wrote his report using the ranch typewriter. The next morning he handed George his written report.

To whom it may concern: At the request of Mr. George Bentley I have examined Mrs. Betty Bentley, the wife of George Bentley, following his reports of her possible nervous breakdown, and I report on her diagnosis and prognosis here. My findings, after three extended sessions with the patient, indicate severe paranoia and a detachment from reality. My examination together with my review of the patient's medical records show a deterioration of like symptoms that the patient experienced over two years ago. These symptoms and her current condition are emblematic of a long-term or permanent pathological dissociative fugue disorder in the patient. To say it another way, the patient has a personal identity or sense of herself, but she does not see much of the world around her and she has no capacity to understand another's view or situation. The patient also displays a lack of emotion. Mrs. Bentley definitely shows symptoms consistent with the above diagnosis and prognosis, and she should not be living alone.

Edmond Lewis, M. D., Clinical Psychiatrist

28 | A DIFFICULT PARTING

George read the report that Dr. Lewis gave him, and he reread and reread it. First off, he knew he couldn't expect Renee to care for Betty for long. Second, he saw less and less of a future life with Betty. There had to be a way to relieve himself of that burden. After three years, nothing had changed, and by nature he could not face a negative life which it looked like he was slated for.

First things first, the matter of live-in help for Betty had to be his first priority. An even more pressing and related problem would be Betty's acceptance of such a person if he did find someone. He placed an ad in the Glencoe Herald, promising board and room as well as a wage. The ad read:

Wanted, A person or couple to live in and perform domestic duties and care for a disabled individual. In the case of a couple, the man needs to be handy around animals. Applicants can apply by mail or phone to The Arrow—B Ranch, No. 1, Arrow—B Ranch Road, Wyoming.

George next called Peter Forbes, his attorney, and made an appointment to discuss his legal rights concerning his marriage to Betty. His third phone call was to Renee at the Harris Ranch. Renee answered the call, he said, "Renee, I'm advertising for help in caring for Betty, I hope to find someone soon. Can you hold on out there for a bit longer?"

"Of course, George, I'm okay out here for now."

Emery Forbes, Peter's father, was in the office when George's call came in. Peter took the call, listened, checked his calendar, and answered with a date and time. He returned the receiver to its cradle, paused thoughtfully then said, "That was George Bentley, Dad. It's funny, that you should talk about him last week. We haven't heard from him for three years."

Emery smiled, then said, "Peter, as you know, George and I go back a long way. I was speculating with myself as to how long George could stand being without love, family, and progeny, so to speak. I calculated that it was about time for him to run out of excuses, and bite the bullet. He has no future with Betty, and must need something to happen. Nothing has in nearly four years."

Peter said, "Maybe you should handle Mr. Bentley."

"Not on your life, Peter. He's all yours."

Peter said, "Why do I feel I'm being tested?"

The father said, "You're doing just fine, son, you might not have much heart yet, but you're gettin' there."

George came to Forbes & Forbes; it was early and Peter, who really wasn't an early person, was nursing a cup of coffee, trying to look awake and alert albeit he didn't feel that way, offered George coffee. In time the two began to discuss marriage, divorce, and such. George asked, "Peter, I need to separate, legally, from my wife, tell me what this involves."

"We file a complaint with the court that must allege legal 'cause' which is your justification for a separation, and we state any anticipated spousal response. Sometimes couples agree to separate, even though a complaint has to be filed by one party first."

"So what happens next?"

"You discuss the issues with me so that I can prepare the complaint and a brief that explains our legal justification and any evidence that we have to back it up."

"Peter, what do you need to know?"

"First off, will this be done in concert with Mrs. Bentley?"

"I suppose not, I haven't discussed this with her."

"Will you be speaking to Mrs. Bentley about this in advance?"

"Peter, you know about Betty's psychological problems, and that any question posed regarding her marriage would be lost, in that she probably doesn't even recall being married now."

"We need to discuss matters such as on what grounds are you basing your complaint for an order of separation. Remember, the legal cause for separation or divorce is essentially the same."

George let out a long sigh, then said, "Peter, I'm asking you for help here. You know that Betty has been under the care of a psychiatrist off and on for over three years. You also know that we have not had a de facto marriage, and it's been void of any marital relationship, physical or otherwise except for our honeymoon. Whereas I will always take care of Betty, I need to be legally separated from her so that I can go on with my life."

"Well, I still have to ask these questions. We need to establish grounds, that is, legal cause that justifies either an order of legal separation or the dissolution of your marriage to your spouse. The court may look askance at your unilateral request to break those bonds that took place when you were married unless we can provide recognized legal cause why this separation should come to pass. I may know, and for that matter, agree with what you want here, but in the final analysis, it will be up to the courts to decide. If the paperwork I submit is too weak, or the underlying facts supporting the cause can't be proven, you will lose. Now, tell me, why do you want to separate from Betty? Or would you prefer to divorce her?"

"How do you want it, off the record or what the court needs to know?"

"Mr. Bentley, you should trust your attorney. I work for

you, and I need to know everything in order to properly represent you. Anything less will work against you. So, first, do you want a divorce or just an order of separation which would leave you still legally married but not responsible for each other?"

After a pause, "A divorce."

"And why do you want a divorce?"

George answered, "The love that brought Betty and me together, and caused us to marry, is gone. It became unilateral immediately upon the disappearance of Betty's father. That was just two weeks after our wedding.

"I need to go on with my life: a wife who is a partner, a friend and will bear children and establish a home."

"When did you know the futility of your marriage to Betty?"

"Upon receiving a report from Dr. Lewis, her psychiatrist."

"And when was that?"

"The last report came just a week ago. It stated quite clearly that Betty was in a mental state such that she fails to recognize reality, and there is a question as to her ever recovering from this syndrome."

"All right, George, I'll need a copy of that report, and any other info you might think of.

"George, you have a child with your wife. What harm do you think you would bring to that child, not having a mother and a father?"

"That problem has happened already. Betty is unable to care for our child. I've been concerned to the point that I've provided in-house care for Eva, however, Betty may not always accept someone living in the ranch house with her. At this point, a good friend is with her, but that will end soon. My effort to find a person or couple to live at the Harris Ranch and look after Eva is in progress."

"So you have two reasons for wanting a divorce then. I'll prepare a brief and present it to the court, stating these reasons. The court will require proof, evidence that is, of what you have told me."

"Peter, I need to have something definitive happen here soon. My child, Eva, must be provided for and protected, and my own life channeled toward family, love, and security for that family. I cannot do this the way things are now."

Peter stumbled a bit, "If you are asking me to hurry up, sure, however the courts and the legal processes don't recognize a need for speed, and they aren't known for their alacrity. One has to cool one's heels where the legal stuff is concerned."

"Well, will Judge Ralph Hastings get into the act? He knows this family fairly well and might hurry things up a bit. Can we kind of let him know what's going on somehow."

Peter smiled and said, "That's close to a legal no-no, but has some merit."

"So what comes next?"

"I prepare, and then call you for an okay and some signatures. This goes to the court for the under-types perusal after which your case will be reviewed by a judge. Hopefully Ralph."

* * *

Judge Hastings, senior jurist, had been turning over more of the workload that appeared on his case docket as he grew older. Contra County allowed him to hire one "pro tempore" or temporary judge to hear cases and lately Judge Hastings had been referring most of the new case filings to his colleague, Dean Brooks, Judge Pro Tem. On a Monday morning in March he scanned those items shown on his to-do list, and ran across the complaint and paperwork from attorney, Peter Forbes, on behalf of Plaintiff George Bentley seeking a divorce from his wife, Betty. He spoke a silent oath, opened the brief that Peter had filed with the more form-like complaint, and started to read. A short time later he called in younger colleague, Dean Brooks. He said, "Dean, I got a problem, George Bentley, a good friend, is asking the court to grant a divorce from Betty, his estranged wife. I must decide whether I am too close to these two to handle their case. In that I ruled on the custody of their child a few years ago, I am more familiar with this case than you or anyone else for that matter, and can better serve those involved. Do you have any thoughts on this matter?"

"I have a full schedule for the next few weeks, Ralph, does that help you make a decision?"

"That kind of gives me a way out as there's a request for shortened notice on this one, justification for which is a child's welfare. Still, I wonder if there were an appeal of my ruling, how the appeals court would view my personal knowledge and friendships with both parties here? My closeness, that is."

"Ralph, you have to go with what you believe, regardless. Unless you have some financial connection or obvious bias, it's going to be up to you to decide whether to recuse yourself. If that steps on someone's toes, that's tough. Besides, if you decide to recuse yourself, it will pass the matter on to me, in which case, I'll consult with you anyway. So, bite the bullet, and suffer. . . . Do you really think that Betty would pursue an appeal?"

"Maybe not, but if she gets an attorney, he might talk her into it since Betty is not institutionalized. And from what I've heard, George doesn't want her to be either.

"I'm still troubled as I was there when these two were born, followed them through their growing years, and on to when they got married. Now I must decide what happens to their marriage and child. The complications of this case are many and the positions are strong for each party. Neither of these two has broken any laws to this point.

"I'm concerned, of course, for the child, Eva, and that may be the deciding factor. She's three now, and has endured a split family. Now I think she needs both parents, or we might say, both a father and mother, in her life."

Dean asked, "How serious is Mrs. Bentley's mental illness?"

"I ruled a couple of years ago that she is not a hazard to the child's life; now it seems that I may have been wrong or that the situation has changed. I will be checking with her psychiatrist, of course."

* * *

There were two applicants for a live-in person or couple to satisfy the need of someone to care for Betty, one of which turned out to be Amy Robinson. The other, a couple, were not married, and seemed to be vague about their understanding of what their capabilities were. George also worried over Betty's feeling about two unmarried kids living in her home. He interviewed Amy who was now nineteen. "Hello Amy, I understand your job with Rosey is about over I talked with Rosey yesterday. She sure thinks a lot of you. What had you planned to do before you read my ad?"

"Mr. Bentley, about the only jobs available right now are waitressing, or clerking. I'm really not enthusiastic about either, but I need money for school this fall."

George smiled, thinking "This kid is on the way." He said, "Amy, this is a tough one, you'll be running a household, plus acting as a caregiver for Betty and giving help with our baby, Eva."

"My time with Rosey was sometimes from five a.m. to nine p.m. Some people really don't know what it takes to run a small café. All that folks see is the finished product. I think I can handle this one."

"So how do you intend to continue your education if you take this job?"

"I really don't have a choice. Attending any accredited learning institution is expensive. I have to have money to do that. I'll take the job first, and perhaps correspond where it is practical until I have money to physically attend."

"Okay Amy, let's go see Betty. You need to be accepted by her."

George and Amy drove into the Harris Ranch parking lot, and moved to the ranch house entrance. Renee answered their knock. After hellos and 'how are things' were over, George asked to be alone with Betty. George entered the bedroom where Betty was reading a magazine. He leaned down and said, "Betty, Renee will have to be leaving you soon. She has family matters to attend to . . . I don't want to leave you alone when she leaves, and finding someone to take her place needs to be a person to your liking, someone who cares for you, and someone whom you care for."

Betty was silent, George said, "Betty?" Betty remained silent, George said, "Alright Betty, there's someone I want you to meet." He went to the door and asked Amy to join them. He introduced Amy, and left the two alone.

About an hour later, Amy came out from the bedroom where she and Betty had been talking. She said, "We need some coffee with a snack, Betty and I have more to talk over."

Renee said, "Betty seems to prefer women, George."

"Uh huh, I hope this works. I've taken steps to separate from Betty, Renee. She seems to reject me. I'll always take care of her, but I also need a life."

Renee asked, "Have you told Betty yet?"

The crisp "No" told much. George left it there, and Renee was careful not to press. She felt of the torment that must be with George. She also knew of what was happening between her daughter and this married man. It was hard for Renee, conservative, raised in the church, and family oriented, to accept her daughter's love of a married man. She said, "It looks like Betty and Amy have found something to like about each other. And Amy wasn't shy or worried handling Eva. That's good news."

George said, "Indeed it is, Renee, I've found Amy a thoughtful and caring person, and I think, just right for what we need."

On George's next visit to the Harris Ranch he faced Betty

and told her of his plans to end their marital relationship. He had conferred with Dr. Lewis on the possible injury to Betty over a divorce, and was assured that little harm would come to Betty when she learned of George's intentions. He said, "Betty, you know that I will always be there for you." He paused, reaching for Betty's hand. She let him touch her and nodded. George went on. "I've decided that we should separate. I feel it would be better for both of us, as we can't have a normal life together, that is, physically join, and have mutual goals."

Betty pulled her hand away, "Yes?"

"Nothing much will change, Betty, I'll still visit here, Eva will still be here with you for now, and Amy will care for you and Eva here."

Papers arrived at the Harris Ranch, directing Betty to appear at the county court house. As once before, Betty felt a tinge of fear, a nagging sense of aloneness, a hollowness, a helplessness. She sought out her friend, Rosey.

Rosey came to find Amy sitting quietly alongside Betty, who was lying curled up on the living room sofa. She kneeled down in front of Betty and asked, "What is it Bet?"

A silent Betty handed the summons and court documents which she had been clutching, to Rosey.

Rosey spread out the crumpled summons from the district court, quickly read the contents, and groaned. She took Betty's hand and said, "It's alright Betty, we can do this together." Betty was silent. Rosey stood, and she and Amy moved into the adjoining room where Eva was napping. Rosey asked Amy, "How long has Betty been this way?"

"Mr. Bentley was here yesterday. After he left I felt a change in Betty, and when the court order came this morning, she seemed to withdraw into a different world."

"Has she taken food, or done any of her normal activities?"

"No."

29 | A DAY IN COURT

Rosey drove into the Harris Ranch yard, stepped up to the front door to face Amy and the ranch dog, Charlie. Charlie did his usual woofing, then smelled Rosey up and down. Amy waited for Charlie to stop his investigation, then said, "I'm glad you're here, Rosey, you need to talk to Betty, she seems a bit confused about today."

"Hi." Rosey studied the earnest young person in front of her for a moment, then said, "Let's step outside where we can talk . . . Tell me about Betty."

"Rosey, "I'm not sure I can do this thing." She showed signs of concern and doubt.

Rosey asked, "Why do you think that, Amy?"

"I feel inadequate and almost helpless at times with Betty. She is such a lovely lady. Sometimes though, she steps out of this life into another world. I know I should be doing or saying something at these times, but I stand there mum."

"Amy, it's not easy to do adult things with heart. You have much to offer. You are compassionate and understanding or you wouldn't be concerned as you are. Take hold of this one, you'll be surprised at yourself. Betty is an unfortunate event in all our lives here, but the real loser has been George. If we can make things just a little easier for this man, we will be doing that adult thing which defines us."

"Rosey, you have always been able to make me feel better about myself. I hope I can live up to your expectations. Thank you, Rosey."

Rosey took Betty's arm and seated her in the car. They drove to the Courthouse, and parked. The two sat in the car for a few minutes while Betty busied herself adjusting her hair, applying lipstick and then through pursed lips, signaled she was ready.

Rosey said, "You look nice, Betty."

They entered the courthouse and were directed to Judge Hasting's chambers. George was already there along with Peter Forbes, his attorney. They were all seated and in a short time the Judge, without ceremony entered the room waving all to remain seated. He took his seat behind his huge ancient desk, adjusted his spectacles, and proceeded to recognize each person in the room. He explained that the informal meeting was both a pre-trial conference and an emergency hearing on the Plaintiff's request for temporary orders pending a trial. He then confirmed Peter as the attorney for the Plaintiff, and next asked Betty if she had an attorney. Betty was silent, and the judge repeated the question. Receiving no answer, he turned to George, "Betty should have a lawyer here to protect her interests and represent her. If she won't hire one, the court intends to appoint one. What do say you, how do you want it, George?"

"Ralph, I'll always take care of Betty, with or without her having an attorney. Is one absolutely necessary?"

The Judge ignored the informality, and said, "I know you are sincere, George, but in the eyes of the law, and based on what's in your filing, yes, she needs an attorney. And I'm inclined to have that attorney send you the legal bill for now, at least until we get to the property division issues in this case."

George persisted, "It seems kind of a waste of the family assets. Would it not be better just to divide things up, assign responsibility here and now and we can all get on with our lives."

The Judge sighed, he said, "It doesn't work that way, George. If you two don't agree on a divorce, we'll have to have a trial to determine if there is cause to grant a divorce. And that's before we get to the property issues." The judge frowned at Peter, annoyed that he had to explain this to Peter's client. "Now what's it going to be, you find an impartial lawyer for her or I do it? Make up your mind."

"I suppose we can't use Peter to represent both Betty and me?"

"You know better than that, George."

"Well, I just thought I'd throw it out there . . . So you better go ahead and do what needs to be done. I don't know any other lawyers beyond Peter here."

"The court will, and since the Defendant is not represented by an attorney here, this hearing is adjourned. The court will notify date and time of future proceedings, at which time counsel for both Plaintiff and Defendant must be present."

Judge Hastings tried to find an attorney to represent Betty Bentley. After a frustrating week calling lawyers he could trust with a divorce case, he turned to his young colleague, "Dean, do you have time in your schedule to represent Betty in the Bentley divorce case?"

Dean smiled and answered, "Uh huh, I figured you'd come to me sooner or later. This county has plenty of land lawyers and water law specialists, but darn few who know their way around a divorce case with property division and child custody issues. Okay, yes, how much time do I have?"

"How about a week?"

"Boy, you're real anxious. Why the big rush?"

The Judge answered, "There's a three-year-old kid that needs some thought right now. As you know I ruled Mrs. Bentley capable and willing to care for the child, safely that is. Now according to a written report from her psychiatrist, I was either wrong or Betty has gotten a lot worse."

"Okay, I know almost everything I need to know already, I'll spend some time with Mrs. Bentley, of course, and then I think we'll be ready."

Judge Hastings ordered a second hearing. It took place a full week after the first, and included the two litigants, their legal representatives, Rosey, and the court recorder, Virginia. When all were seated the judge said, "First, I'm not going to recuse myself in this case even though I know both the parties very well, and yes, I know them both and like them equally well! There is nothing about my experience with either party that would lead me to favor one over the other. And if I recused myself every time I knew someone in a case this court wouldn't get much business done here. Hell, I live in this county, and I know most folks. Some I put in jail, some I award damages to or against. People get in trouble or have disputes and my job here in this county is to make sense of it in a fair way and bring justice to folks. Now anyone here who has a problem with any of that, well you can file a motion and put into the record anything you like. Just let Virginia know and you'll get a hearing. Now let's get started.

"The court assumes that the attorney for Mrs. Bentley has had sufficient time to confer with his client and to proceed with this litigation, is this correct?"

"Yes, Your Honor, I have spent time with my client."

The Judge took off his glasses, grimaced at the young man where he sat, then, "That's a kind of mealy-mouthed answer, are you satisfied enough with your defense to properly represent Mrs. Bentley?"

"I think so, Your Honor."

"Mr. Brooks, are you ready or are you not?"

"Yes, I'm ready."

"Mr. Forbes, do you have any comment at this time, has your client tried to settle the fault issues and the financial issues in this case directly with Mrs. Bentley?"

Peter Forbes nodded. "Mr. Bentley has suffered during

their marriage, yes, but he has stated many times that he will always provide and care for his wife and their child."

"Okay, then let's consider a summary ruling by the court, without any kind of a public trial per se. What say you to this idea, Mr. Bentley?"

"I would like that, Your Honor."

"And you, Mr. Brooks, can you speak for your client on this issue?"

"My client has so indicated."

"Alright. Suppose we take a break now, this will give you time to discuss this approach with Mrs. Bentley. Let's meet back here at two p.m."

Court reconvened at two with all parties and seated in the Judge's chambers. The Judge asked Dean, Mrs. Bentley's attorney, "Is your client willing to accept a summary ruling from this court on the fault issues, and to forego and waiver her right to a public trial on fault?"

"Yes, Your Honor, she is ready and willing."

The Judge said, "So be it . . . Mr. Forbes, state your case."

Peter Forbes shuffled some papers in his lap, then rose to answer.

Judge Hastings said, "Oh for crap sake, Peter, sit down and state your case on the legal issues of fault and cause for the divorce."

"Your Honor, my client, Mr. Bentley, has waited patiently for normalcy in his marriage to Mrs. Betty Bentley. The Plaintiff acknowledges, of course, that the marriage was consummated. But Mrs. Bentley has consistently denied any close relationship, either physical or emotional, with Mr. Bentley since their return from their honeymoon nearly four years ago. These facts are demonstrated in the sworn affidavit of George Bentley which is on file with the court. As a result, Mr. Bentley has endured a life void of the human condition that love and marriage usually bring. He has waited patiently for Mrs. Bentley to recover from her depression or mental disorder, but to no avail. This is clear evidence of abandonment of the marriage by Mrs. Bentley.

"Additionally, the Court is in possession of documents provided by Mrs. Bentley's psychiatrist, the latest of which diagnoses a very serious mental disorder and it further projects the very strong probability that 'Mrs. Bentley may never recover from her mental illness.' Your Honor, Mr. Bentley needs to again feel whole, have someone in his life and start a family. He feels totally responsible for his wife's welfare, but he has been denied all the rights of marriage in Wyoming, and there is ample cause for granting a divorce based both on abandonment and on mental illness under the revised Wyoming statutes. Stated simply, Mr. Bentley has the legal right and need to go on with his own life."

The room was silent for a time . . . the Judge asked Peter if he was finished, then turned to Dean and instructed him to address the issue at hand. "Tell us, Mr. Brooks, why this divorce should not be granted for cause on the grounds of abandonment or mental illness?"

"Your Honor, whereas Mrs. Bentley feels the detachment from her husband, and admittedly seems to have little or no emotional attachment to Mr. Bentley, she is concerned about losing the umbrella of protection that Mr. Bentley has provided. This protection is a form of relationship and she places great value in this. She is also concerned over the status and operation of the Harris Ranch. She sees a rider from the Arrow—B working her ranch, and this worries her. She needs assurance that Mr. Bentley will have no legal ownership of or interest in the Harris Ranch because of her marriage to Mr. Bentley.

"Also she is concerned for their child, Eva, and wishes to retain half custody of their child.

"To make this all clear, Your Honor, Mrs. Bentley wants these property division and child custody issues to be resolved before a divorce is considered."

Judge Hastings ignored the instruction he had just been given, thinking, *I'll let that one go by for now.* He turned to George Bentley and asked, "Do you have any comment pertaining to what Betty's attorney just said?"

"Only that I intend to remain responsible for Betty's welfare, whether the court grants a divorce or not. Ownership of the Harris ranch is held in the name of Betty Bentley, and I expect it to remain that way. I've been providing a ranch hand from the Arrow—B to assist Betty in the care of her ranch."

The Judge said, "Mr. Forbes and Mr. Brooks, I know you two gentlemen are smart enough to see a consensus forming here. So before I make my ruling on the divorce, I want you to work through a settlement of the property division issues. Use a mediator if you have to, but come to an agreement, put it in writing and have it notarized, then bring it to me. I'll take it under advisement along with the other issues in this case and I'll rule as quickly as possible."

A week went by and the two attorneys complied with the court order. Judge Hastings, now in possession of the proposed property settlement between George and Betty, as well as the psychiatrist's report on Betty, chambered himself and reviewed the various issues of the Bentley case. The stickiest of these was the welfare and care of the child, Eva.

At this time, some care for the child was handled by a paid companion for Betty in the home, and the parties were in agreement that George would continue to pay for this care. The Judge knew of Amy, the caregiver, and he knew she would be gone in the fall. The issue of Betty's psychological status came into play here, where it concerned the care and safety of that three-year-old child. The papers he held in his hand didn't really solve that problem. Betty still expected to hold on to her child. One solution to this problem was to institutionalize Betty. Betty was an enigma: she, as one, was loved by everyone she came in contact with, and two, it seemed, a danger to herself as well as her daughter, if left to live alone.

The Judge put in a call to Dr. Lewis in Cheyenne. When the operator put through the call, he said, "Dr. Lewis, this is

Judge Hastings, I'm the presiding district judge in Contra County, Wyoming, and I'm overseeing the divorce and child custody issues in the case of Bentley versus Bentley. I'm in receipt of your latest report concerning Betty Bentley. I've a question to ask concerning this person."

Dr. Lewis answered, "Yes Judge, I met you once when I visited the Arrow—B, what is your question?"

"It seems that according to your report, Mrs. Bentley would not be able to safely care for her child on her own. Is she also a danger to herself without companionship or some care?"

"If you are asking if she should be institutionalized, probably not, if she has live-in companionship. But without someone there she could be a danger to herself."

The Judge asked, "Is there any treatment available for Betty's condition, and if so, have you tried such?"

"Mrs. Bentley lives nearly 400 miles from my office. Whereas I have traveled to her home twice, it didn't allow me to treat her condition. However in accordance with what I know from other similar cases, the answer has to be, perhaps. We wait in hopes that the mind will heal. Based on the time that has elapsed here, it is doubtful."

"Thank you, Doctor."

Judge Hastings decided in favor of the Plaintiff and granted a divorce, but he conditioned his Judgment on the provision that the Plaintiff, George Bentley, provide in-home companionship and care for the Defendant Betty Bentley as long as she needs it. George was given primary custody of the child, Eva, but Betty was to have the child in her home, subject to companion care, on a regular basis as the parties had agreed in their written settlement agreement.

30 | A TIME OF HEALING

George was in his office when Judge Hastings called. The Judge said, "George, I'm granting you a divorce from Betty with the proviso that you provide a qualified in-house companion for Betty for as long as it is necessary. You get primary custody of your child, but Betty is allowed to see her as you have agreed. If anything changes with regard to the child's care, or with Betty's care, I expect to hear about it." He was silent for a moment, "I had a choice, George, either it was this way or we would have to institutionalize Betty . . . and I don't think any of us want that."

"Thank you, Ralph. This must have been very difficult for you. And you know I would take care of Betty without any court order anyway."

George Red Fox Bentley had loved. That love had been deep, powerful and committed. It was gone now, yes, but its loss haunted George. It left a hollow where joy could have been. He had really never lost hope that his betrothed would recover, and that love would be real again. Whereas the legal release from the vows of matrimony brought some kind of closure to that love, he needed to pause and reflect, and be away.

At the evening meal George said, "I'll be leaving in the morning for a time in the mountains. I'll do a little fishing, and perhaps bag an elk."

Mary Ellen, the ranch cook, asked, "How long do you expect to be gone?"

George smiled, "Well if you haven't seen me in ten days or so, you can begin to worry."

It was early on a midsummer morning that George headed out on Nellie for a time alone in the nearby mountains. Tethered behind them trotted a pack horse named Cloe, shaggy and not too happy with what was on her back or the time of day. Mary Ellen had helped her boss fill saddlebags with food and gear, and she watched as he placed a bedroll behind his saddle. She said, "I don't suppose you know where you will be staying tonight?"

"Not really, Mary Ellen, I'll be somewhere up in those friendly mountains."

"That sounds like punishment to me, sleeping on the ground and all that out-in-the-open stuff. Do you really want to do this thing?"

George smiled, nodding his answer.

Mary Ellen said, "Take care."

George rode for a few miles, dismounted and spared the two animals for a bit, repeating this pattern until they were just beginning to climb the steeper trail. It was noontime and they stopped for lunch, Nellie and Cloe munched on what sparse vegetation there was to offer and George ate a Mary Ellen sandwich from his saddlebags. They resumed their trip upwards, and when nightfall came, they found themselves in a niche of the mountain where George set up dry camp for the night. He shared the water in his canteen with Nellie and Cloe, ate from his saddlebag, wrapped his bedroll around himself, and slept a tired body through the night. Morning found them on the way early again. At noon they found a small stream disappearing into a crevice in the granite shelf.

The water was clear and cold, bespeaking of purity and bounty offered away from man's world.

George was beginning to feel close to nature, and the wonders of the natural world began to blot out those human discords of his life. And so it was as they continued upward until Nellie neighed, stopped, and lowered her head to nibble on some vibrant green grass. George let her have her own way for a bit, then urged her on up the trail, looking for a permanent campsite. The warmth of the day faded away as evening found man and beasts together in a small grove of hemlocks where they spent the night.

On the third day they found a fine campsite. It had water, shelter, and seclusion. Close by was a mountain meadow rich in summer grass, food for the horses. Weary from the long day of riding, George picketed the two horses, ate cold from what Mary Ellen had packed, rolled himself up into his blankets, and fell into a deep sleep.

The morning was cold, George shivered as he left the warmth of his blankets, recalling with some humor what Mary Ellen had said. He rose, made a fire, a pot of coffee and cooked oatmeal for breakfast. He spent most of the day working to make the camp supportive of his needs. When the chores were done he took time to read one of the novels he brought along.

Camp life requires that one spend a good deal of the day doing the survival things, food preparation, etc. George felt himself melding into the natural world around him. He did short trips each day to explore and enjoy the way of things where there were no humans. Night time was a time for looking at the stars, and listening to the night sounds. He often thought of Joan now, as his commitment to Betty as a partner in life was gone. The vision of Joan and their college years together kept flashing in his mind. The days passed and he was beginning to consider his trip back into the human world. George had not been alone these days in the wilderness. He watched as the creatures of the woods gradually became used to his presence and returned to their lives of survival and procreation. He trapped the rabbit, and the marmot, and fished the upper lakes and streams.

On the morning of the 8th day, he decided to leave for home the next morning. He had just finished breakfast and morning chores when Nellie, out in the meadow, gave out a gruff neigh. George walked down to the edge of the meadow where the horses were, peered through the foliage, and saw two riders moving into the open meadow. They had entered close to where Cleo and Nellie were, picketed and eating. They rode up, shook out their lariats and tossed loops over Nellie and Cloe, drawing them in close.

George stepped out into the open and confronted the two. "Where do you think you're going with those, they're not free stock."

The two men looked at each other. One pulled a pistol from its home on his hip, pointed it at George and said "They look free to me, good bye." They turned and rode away, taking the two horses with them.

George was unarmed, his revolver and rifle were a hundred feet away. He swore. It was a good sixty miles away from civilization. This was not nice. He cursed, blamed himself for letting this happen. He returned to camp, stood looking at his temporary home, and decided he had no other choice but to hoof it out; and the sooner he got started the better. He calculated he could walk perhaps 20 miles a day in that it would be almost all downhill. This is if he didn't take much time for food or other necessary human functions. Squeezing out a minimum of 20 miles per day meant three days. Still he looked where the two men and horses disappeared. If he faced a sixty mile walk anyway, then he might as well chase the two bums that knowingly left him on foot.

So a furious man jury-rigged a back pack from his bed roll, filled it with food, tied in his second blanket, stowed everything else in the crevice of a big chunk of granite, and started out following the very visible tracks made by four horses and two men. His pistol rode snugly in its holster, and his rifle was strapped across his back. It was then shortly after nine a.m. It was early summer sporting long daylight hours. George, raised in part by his Arapaho grandfather, toughened along the way as he grew, and seasoned on a western ranch, was an entity of strength, both physical and mental.

This was an easy trail to follow. George easily kept pace with the riders, often taking shortcuts, and always keeping his quarry in sight. Early evening found the riders coming up to an old miner's shack, they dismounted, and tied the horses to a hitching railing and starting cooking their evening meal. George watched from cover and waited. He rested and ate from his backpack.

It was dawn when George caught up with the two riders. He had walked all night under a full moon. He stepped on the bulging belly of one of the sleeping riders, pointing his rifle at the other, and said, "On your stomachs, the party's over." Two startled men raised up, then looking into the muzzle of George's rifle, did as they were told. George cut short pieces of rope with which he tied his prisoner's hands behind their backs. He said, "We used to hang horse thieves, but they tell me that's against the law now, however, since we are three days from the law, no one would ever know. Well let's see, you two idiots would leave a man sixty miles from nowhere on foot. That's nice. Let's do the same for you."

George contemplated how to get everybody down the mountain. Three days of watching these two was going to be risky. He would need sleep, and if he lost control, he would be dead meat, that was clear. He decided to leave them on foot as they had done to him.

George saddled Nellie, went through the gear and food of the two riders, taking what he needed for his trip down the mountain. He tethered each animal, one to another, making a train of four horses led by Nellie, untied one of the rider's hands, and said, "I won't forget either of you two. If you insist on doing dumb things, I'll find out, and you'd better watch out." He then started his train down the mountain leaving the two afoot.

31 | THE DEMISE OF TWO HORSE THIEVES

At the end of the second day, away from the high country where George left the two riders to figure out how to reach civilization without mounts, George and his train of horses plodded into the Arrow—B Ranch yard. Pete was the first to stick his head out from the mess hall, where Mary Ellen was serving the evening meal to the ranch hands. He gave George a questioning look, waited for an explanation, and helped handle the stock. George said, "I got bushwhacked by two dummies. These two horses were theirs once. They're walking down the mountain."

Pete said "Oh." He paused a moment, "I gotta hear about this one . . . I guess you're hungry, I'll finish here, go on in. Food's on the table."

George entered the cook-shack and joined the others at the long table, where food, in large bowls, circulated among the hungry. Cow hands aren't particularly communicative, especially when they are filling their bellies. The four at the table looked up, went right back to the food, and more or less waited for their boss to share about his time away. Pete entered and joined the others, looking enquiringly at George for some kind of story about how he ended up with four saddle horses when he started off with two. Mary Ellen came in from the kitchen brandishing a huge pot of coffee, and noticing George, said, "Welcome home boss, tell us about your vacation. Did you see any elk?"

George put down his fork, which was stuck in a chunk of pot roast, half way to his mouth. He said, "Uh uh, no, but I ran into a pair of rats." He went on eating.

Mary Ellen poured coffee around and returned to the kitchen mumbling something about the modesty of some men, who seem to want to keep the rest of us in the dark, when she knew there was something going on. "A pair of rats" from George, she thought, has to be two bad guys for sure. A few minutes later she reentered the room with another platter full of beef stew, "So tell us about the two rats." Which he finally did.

George's call to Sheriff Bill Williams went this way:

"Hi George, how was your tryst with nature, did you bag an elk? Some fresh meat would be nice."

"No, but I have some work for you to do. I expect that fat ass of yours needs some relief from its place in your swivel chair, so where'll it be, here or there?"

"You always have had such a talent for insults. I don't know why I expect you to change, what tu ya wanna see me about?"

"I got bushwhacked sixty miles up in the mountains. It disturbed my vacation plans."

"So file a report with the State Police."

"Well that's just peachy, while the State Police makes up its mind to do something, gets a posse together and finally makes a move, the summer will be over. These bad guys will be long gone by then. . . .Why don't you come on out tomorrow, plan on staying for dinner and cribbage. I got some stuff to show you."

"The last time we did that cribbage thing, I lost my shirt. I'll bring my own cards, I think yours are biased. Okay, I'll see you about four."

George came out to the ranch yard and met the Sheriff as he stepped out of his station wagon. The two men moved to the ranch patio, George found some cold beer and began to tell his story. Sheriff Bill asked, "How'd you ever catch up with these guys, mounted yet?"

"They weren't in a hurry, and I was."

"In boots?"

"You forget, I went through the Arapaho school for survival when I was small. I always carry a pair of moccasins, just in case. I had a full moon to help."

The two men went out to the pasture, looked at the two horses in question, found no brands or other identification, and returned to the patio. George dumped the contents of a saddlebag onto the patio table. He said, "I collected this from the bad guys. From this stuff we know who they are, we know about where they are, and we know they'll have to come out from the wilderness soon, or they'll starve. I left them with nothing, no guns, not even a pocket knife."

The Sheriff half laughed, "Seems I remember you doing something like that once before when a pair of idiots hit you over that hard head of yours and left you to die in the desert. Okay, so it shouldn't take a ten-man posse to handle this one, how about you and me. I'll deputize of course."

"Well I kinda thought I'd get with the Tribe first, they don't like strangers messing around in their sacred area much, and usually know when someone does, and where. They didn't bother me, I being one of them, so to speak. Two men on foot, sixty miles from nowhere can't go anywhere fast, so let me see what I can do that way first. How about some food, and cribbage?"

Chief Running Deer, George's grandfather, had died in 1955, over four years earlier. His position as tribal leader had never been filled, rather things were decided by the tribal council, essentially a committee which was never very fast, and often inconclusive. Nevertheless, George contacted Sarah Golden Poppy, John Running Deer's sister. He said,

"Sarah, there are two renegades messing around in our sacred grounds. Would you pass the word around. The Sheriff needs to pick them up."

Sarah said, "Red Fox, we have been watching them as they came down through our sacred burial grounds. I'm sure they would want to be captured by one of your white brothers rather than by one of us. Our medicine man has a somewhat disturbing reputation with intruders."

George said, with a bit of humor in his voice, "In that case, since these two were going to leave me sixty miles from nowhere on foot, I think we should leave them in your capable hands."

"I don't think even my brother would buy that one, as he would carefully stay away from the white man's law."

"Sarah, can't you frighten them a bit, like hold a war dance or something? By the time we take a legal stab here, it'll be turned around and I'll be accused of stealing two horses."

George never did find out what happened to the two horse thieves up in the Arapaho sacred burial grounds. When he and the Sheriff picked up the two men the next day, they seemed anxious to cooperate, looking back toward the trail they had just left with frightened eyes, and shudders.

32 | RANCH TIME

Ownership of the Arrow—B was the product, reward if you must call it, of hard work, sweat, and determination of three strong people: George Bentley, his father Richard, and his uncle, Leonard Mac Laren. Each had contributed much toward the enterprise, and each took a great deal of pride in what they did. George, who had returned from college in the East after the death of his father, learned the cattle raising business quickly, and continued to grow the dynasty that was the Arrow—B. As the years passed the ranch holdings grew. In the year 1959, this rancher, George Bentley, faced difficult personal problems as well as the constant demand on his managerial skills, and as the rule goes, *'If you want to get a job done, go to a busy person'*, and George was usually busy. Be that as it may, George was not one to avoid problems or any of the complexities of life, rather he faced each logically and did the hard stuff himself. When it came to his personal troubles, however, his changed relationship with Betty, whom he loved passionately at the start of their marriage, was difficult to embrace, and he had a hard time turning to another. He stewed over his reasons for his divorce from Betty.

There was that subconscious tingling somewhere in his chest for Joan, which his conscious mind denied. To further make him oblivious to the true love that had grown between them, George continued to deal with Betty's needs. Somewhere in the back of his mind he wondered whether he still faced potential claims from his ex-wife to an interest in the Arrow—B enterprise. So George didn't pursue any sign of romantic feelings toward Joan, and Joan wondered why not.

The summer faded and the fall chill was early. The business of cattle raising became hard, and the people responded. The peripheral activities consumed everyone as the storekeepers, the schools and the town's leaders dug in for the winter. And so it was with Joan, now a fully licensed veterinarian, who tended to the health needs of the animals of the area.

Pete and Rosey were building up their ranch together. From time to time Pete would need help with the heavier tasks like constructing out-buildings for which he would hire an extra hand or two. Rosey was there to support her man in any way she could. Her visits into Walnut were usually dictated by their needs for supplies. When in town, Rosey always visited with Joan. On one of these visits, Rosey said, "What do you hear from George these days, Joan?"

Joan was silent. She went on refilling their coffee cups and in a time sat down opposite Rosey.

Rosey looked into two moist eyes. She saw the hurt that was there.

Joan finally said, "Rosey, it's been so long. I had to live with his marriage to Betty. I watched as her illness came on and how he suffered, and now I'm waiting. You know Rosey I have loved this man for a long time. It is so hard."

"Joan, your man is honest and loyal to his betrothed, a quality rare in a man. It is hard for him to break his once strong commitment to Betty. He will, and he must. This man demands positive, and this he has not had."

A time went by and then Joan asked, "How are things going out there at your new home?"

"Just fine, Joan, can you break away to visit us soon? We're finally ready to have visitors."

The Arrow—B owners had always done things that were necessary to further the Ranch's interests. Throughout the years they had accumulated real estate as it became available, and now the Arrow—B was a sizeable spread. Most of the documentation, concerning those land acquisitions, were recorded, of course, but there were a few loose ends where word of mouth or a hand shake took hold and were never officially documented, the result of earlier ownership missing a cabbage patch or two.

Ranch records from Leonard Mac Laren's early days through today had been placed in the cavernous old Diebold iron floor safe kept in the ranch house office, which nobody had looked at for years. So when a registered piece of mail arrived claiming a large portion of ranch lands, George called attorney Peter Forbes, made a date for Peter to come out to the ranch and review those musty records that were in the ranch safe.

Peter came along with his father, and after some ranch hospitality they opened the safe, and started searching through its contents. Peter had learned to keep his records clean, carefully filed, and precise. What he was seeing was anything but that. He pinched his nose and said, "It is doubtful that we can use any of this, the law won't recognize hand written promissory notes written on the back of a farm tool flyer a hundred years ago."

His father, who was seated at a nearby table laughed to himself, and thought, "Peter is about to find out what the real world on a western ranch was, early on, and today's western mindset concerning a man's word; today's people out on the range haven't changed much. Oh my."

George said, "Peter, I'm paying you to protect this ranch. Do you want the job, or don't you?"

A red-faced Peter stumbled for words, glanced at his father, and said, "Yes sir, my apologies, there was no offense meant."

George had never gone beyond the cash box, which was squeezed onto the top shelf of the safe. Loose papers and old ledgers were stuffed in anywhere they fit. At the end of the day the three men had separated the inconsequential items from the legal or meaningful papers, some of which were yellow with age. A map of the existing ranch holdings was drawn, and acquisition documents assigned each to its specific area. The claimant's area demands were then placed over the map. In that most of these records were copies of official ones located in the state depository, Peter had himself a messy problem. First he must verify the authenticity of what was there in front of him. Second, he needed to search elsewhere for corroborating evidence of George's ownership of the land in question.

Peter and his father stayed overnight at the Arrow—B. A light snow had fallen during the night, and there was frost on everything outside. Peter shivered as he walked down to the cook shack for breakfast. He joined his dad at the table, looking a bit off the main line. He said, "Sure glad I'm not in the cow business. This looks tough."

"Uh huh, and the folks out this way kind of fit that description. They're tough, but they're good people. You 'll never go wrong making friends with any of them."

Peter said, "Mr. Bentley has a serious legal problem, I sure hope I can help him."

"Peter, you'll do just fine. I think from what we saw yesterday, you will need to ask the court for a time extension. You better plan on a month of discovery, and whatever other time you will need to prepare. This guy looks serious. He must have something to back up his claim. We need to find out what that is."

Peter smiled and said, "Yes Dad, even I can figure that one out. I plan on visiting the County Hall of Records as soon as I have a viable list of ranch documents. Yesterday was only the start. We're talking about fifty or sixty years of people doing stuff informally and sometimes by the seat of their pants."

"You're going to need help, can you have your part-time secretary be full-time?"

"I plan on it."

* * *

Ruth Mathews, the minister's wife, was, as one, totally in love with her aging husband, and two, a sometimes critic of his "hellfire and damnation" mind set. So when George went for a divorce, and finally got one, a sanctimonious Tom Mathews leaned a bit heavy on George reminding Ruth, "A marriage vow is forever." Ruth, who was a people person, liked by everyone, and sometimes open with her criticism of Tom, took issue with her rigid husband, and openly approved of George's divorce.

Whenever Rosey, with her wonderful intuitiveness and love for her community, came to town for supplies or a visit, she stopped in to see Ruth. They were good friends, and would engage in more than "Women Talk." One of those meetings went something like this:

Ruth said, "Hi, what brings you to town, Rosey?"

"Hi yourself, I just needed to pick up some supplies, what's new?"

Ruth answered, "I guess you've heard, George finally got a divorce from Betty."

"Uh huh, it's been a real tough time for George. More than three years of plain misery. Why does this kind a thing always happen to the good guys?"

Rosey put down the coffee mug she had been nursing. She studied Ruth for a moment. "I wonder what it does to a young man to be in love, get married and right away be denied any sex or any other physical touch with his betrothed for three years? That would be real mean for any man. And George was not going to break his vows either. I'd bet on that."

197

Ruth said, "I sure am glad he can now begin to live, and have some happiness." She gave a little laugh, "Tom doesn't think that way. He sometimes overlooks human needs, and I get lectured on infidelity. He doesn't believe in divorce."

Rosey said, "Yeah, I can just see Tom playing the right or wrong part. But we all love Tom and most of us understand him. . . . You know, Joan's in love with George. Do you see her once in a while?"

"Not too often, she's building a business, and spends double time doing just that."

Rosey said, "The last time I saw her she was almost in tears. George hasn't called or seen her since the divorce. I'm sure underneath he loves her. You know these two went to college together, and had a thing going there. I think this man is having trouble separating himself from Betty, psychologically that is. He's not in love with her anymore, but he still cares."

Ruth asked, "Can't we do something to get these two together? They would both be happier."

Rosey thought for a moment. "Pete and I have been thinking of asking George to come out and see the ranch house. I maybe could invite Joan at the same time. I've got a big rooster waiting to be roasted, a little relief from beef that we eat every day."

"So how do you plan to get these two alone when you get them out there?"

"Pete an' I'll work that out."

Ruth said, "Sounds like a plan, I'll loan Joan the parish car for the trip she doesn't have a car yet. Just tell me when."

On one early spring Sunday, George drove the ranch pickup out to Pete's spread. When he entered the ranch house, he found Joan in the kitchen helping Rosey with the dinner. He glanced at the two women, quickly understanding that Rosey set this up to get Joan and him together. Overcoming his natural instinct of not liking to be maneuvered, he smiled, and said, "Nice, Rosey, you haven't lost your touch." He moved to Joan, "You look beautiful as usual. How's our new Vet doing?"

Joan pushed back a strand of hair from her forehead, looked in surprise at seeing George, turned and glanced at Rosey. She smiled and said "Nice." She turned back to George, "As a new man on the block in Walnut, I'm doing okay. Most of my work gets me out to ranches with sick animals. Yours seem to be eternally healthy."

Rosey found something to do in the bedroom. George studied Joan's face. He saw misty eyes, a whimsical look, and came to her. He touched her nose, and placed a light kiss on her lips. She waited a bit, then, reached up and pulled him to her. They parted, George whispered, "I didn't know, Joan. You know my life has been so mixed up for so long, I've not wanted to share. Maybe now I can go forward."

Joan said, "I knew you before Betty came into your life. When you left me in college to see to your father's death, I knew. I knew it was one way then, but I always carried the hope that someday we could find love together."

George said, "Yes Joan, I too have wanted this. It has been hard, both legally and morally for me. Now that the one, legal matter, is satisfied, the other will come to pass."

Joan showed tears of joy, she dabbed her eyes with a corner of the apron she was wearing. She touched his lips with her finger. He responded by taking her into his arms.

* * *

A young attorney, Peter Forbes, not quite sure of himself yet, tackled the job of land acquisition by three different Arrow—B owners over some sixty years. Since his father told him in so many words that he was on his own, and if he failed, it was his own fault, and if he succeeded, it was to his credit, not his father's, he, Peter, felt he had no choice but to protect his client with vigor. It took him the better part of a week to confirm the legality of what they had found in the old Arrow—B iron safe. He also verified that there was no apparent documentation of the lands in question. Knowing the Arrow—B, and its reputation per se, he was sure that his client was in the right, and that the claims from another for certain parcels of land within the boundaries of the Arrow—B were false. In frustration, he consulted with his father. He asked the question, "Are there historical records of land transactions that you know of other than what's in the Hall of Records depository in Glencoe?"

"Peter, the existing HOR was built in about 1938, previous to that, records were kept in an old building somewhere in Glencoe. I assume, when the new building was ready, the records in the old building were retrieved and included in the new building's files. You might check that one out."

So, Peter went back to the Hall of Records, the history of which he found to be in the Glencoe City Hall's files. Approaching the desk clerk facing the entrance to the City Hall he asked, "Do we have city history records here?"

A smallish pert-looking personage nodded and asked, "Sure, what do you want to know about?"

Peter answered, "Glencoe City history."

"Oh, that's in our fire proof safe room, however the history section of the Glencoe Public Library has duplicates for public needs, have you checked there?"

"Miss, this is a legal matter, I will need to see original copies."

He waited . . . finally the young person in front of him saw that he wasn't going away. She pressed the switch on her intercom. A voice answered, and she said, "There's a man here insisting that he must get into our secure document room. He won't go away."

Shortly a bald-headed, bespectacled man emerged from the rear, obviously annoyed, he said, "What's your problem, young man?"

Peter handed the man his business card, and asked, "Who am I speaking to?"

The man smiled, and said, "Call me Stanley, so you want to get into our records, for what purpose?"

Peter answered, "A legal matter which may or may not concern Glencoe history."

"So go check with our library. Our city history is all there for the public."

Peter said, "If I find what I need, I'll still have to come back here for verification. You need to remember that your public has undisputable rights when it comes to viewing public documents."

Stanley bristled, he said, "I'll pass this through the mayor. For now, the answer is no. We'll be in touch."

Peter studied the man in front of him, nodded his head, turned and silently speculated, "This man is protecting himself or someone else from something. I'm sure that when I get into those city files I'm going to find something fishy."

A frustrated Peter left City Hall, and walked over to the nearby public library. He came up to the vacant checkout desk, slapped the desk bell, and waited. A young person emerged from a rear room, approached Peter, and asked, "How may I help you?"

"I'd like to know a bit about Glencoe history, please point me in the right direction."

Peter, at twenty five, was handsome, seemed in control, and the young person noticed no wedding ring on his finger, ogled, and said, "Follow me." She unlatched the swinging half door into the checkout area, and then into a closet size space labeled "County History." She remained, closing the door. A puzzled Peter asked, "Is it against the rules for me to be in this room alone?"

The young person answered, "No, but I thought you might need help finding what you're looking for."

Peter calculated that she was about eighteen. "Well since there is room for only one of us in this room, why don't I try to find what I need, and count on you if I need to?"

"Oh, all right, I'll be right outside if you need me." She moved outside, closing the door behind her. He mused, "Gloria would sure get a kick out of this one." He and

Gloria, his girlfriend, had been going together for the better part of two years now. He sighed, planning his escape as he read into Glencoe's dusty past.

About all Peter got for his time in the library was where the old library was and when it was born and died. So he exited the library's tiny storage room sidled past the young library aide with a thank you and a quick smile, then walked over to the old building site, where stood a barn-like structure at the back of the town's farrier shop. Since its demise the building had been serving as a storage area and contained multiple items that nobody wanted. There were also bales of hay to support the farrier's business.

Peter found no one there, a sign on the front door read, "Call for service." A phone sat on an adjacent ledge. Peter called, a gravelly sounding voice answered, "Geoffrey here."

Peter answered, "This is Peter Forbes, Attorney at Law. I'm searching for information regarding land ownership history in Contra County. I'll need access to the building behind your business, in that it was once the records depository for this county."

"So there's a key hanging on a nail just to the left of the window. Help yourself."

Peter hesitated for a moment, then, "That's nice, Geoffrey, is there a chance that you might join me for lunch. I would like to meet you personally?"

"So, I eat lunch at the old Rosey's, it's still called that, and it's on Main Street."

The hand shake was firm to say the least. Peter looked across the table at big muscles, and a beard and mustache-covered face, the setting for a pair of friendly cobalt eyes. They ordered lunch, and Geoffrey asked, "So you're a lawyer, what brings you to this creepy village?"

Peter said, "There is an ongoing dispute over the ownership of a sizable portion of the Arrow—B Ranch. I represent the Arrow—B."

Geoffrey snorted, "Bentley needs a challenge once in a

while . . . so who's dumb enough to try to get some of George's land?"

"The plaintiff is local, but I'm sure it's someone from Denver as the attorney for the plaintiff is from there . . . I have to ask, how would anyone out of state know that there was a 1,000-acre chunk of Wyoming with no official ownership on record?" Peter studied the man across from him for a moment. "How old are you Geoffrey?"

"I da no, Peter, what's that to do with what you're working on?"

"I kind of thought you might remember something of the old times, when these lands were up for grabs, and people shook hands over land deals."

Geoffrey smiled, he asked, "Emery's your dad?"

"He is. Everyone I talk to seems to know him. . . . Every time I ask him about the old times though, he tells me that I am on my own, you figure it out."

"That sounds like Emery. Give him a hello from me the next time you see him. What you want to know is not to be found here. The State Department was involved, making treaties which involved land swaps. The BIA was acting to enforce the treaties, you may have to go there." He chuckled, "We are probably talking about government lands. Knowing the three Arrow—B families, I guarantee what happened was on the up and up an up."

Peter mused to himself as he worked on the beef stew he was eating, "The man in front of him represented a generation gone by." He asked, "How long have you been shoeing horses, Geoffrey?"

"Wal, I don't rightly know exactly, but Teddy was president when my father ducked out, and left me the business. Dad made a lot of the iron fencing and other ornamental stuff around the government mansion in Cheyenne. I learned the business from him."

"So when you were a kid, was there still land swapping going on?"

"Heard about it from my dad, but it was all over when I

was a young'un."

"Did you know Leonard Mac Laren?"

"Shor, every 'un knew Len. Dad used to make trips out to the Arrow—B to do his thing out there. Have you checked with the Indian people, they might know what happened back then. . . . I know that Bentley is half Arapaho, he would have access to one of the ancient ones still living on the Reservation who were there."

Peter picked up the tab for the lunch, shook hands again with Geoffrey, and said, "Thanks, Geoffrey, I think I'll do that."

Peter found the key where Geoffrey said to look. He entered the building, studied what he saw, and an hour later exited, musing to himself, "History eludes, when things get rusty, I need people who were there." Two hours later he sat in the Arrow—B great room studying the panoramic view. As he waited for his host to join him he sat in wonder at what he saw. His thoughts were interrupted when his client entered and said, "Hello Peter, what's happening?"

Peter rose and answered, "Mr. Bentley, in the matter of Contra County officially recorded documents and records for the lands we are concerned with, I am sorry to say, I am no closer to establishing legal ownership than I was when you hired me. We are talking about a time when the Arapaho and the Shoshone were negotiating with the BLM over the size and shape of the Wind River Reservation. Things were done with a handshake, and paper didn't always follow. It appears that the properties you hold involved one of those handshakes."

"Peter, tell me about the claimant that is pursuing this suit. Who is he, and what grounds do you think he has or feels he has to the ownership of a piece of my land?"

"Mr. Bentley, as near as I can find out, he was a records clerk working for the County Hall of Records. He resigned a few months ago. It's likely that he discovered the lack of formal documentation for title to the property in question through his access to historical records while working for the Contra County Hall of Records."

"We have a name and address?"

"We do."

"So one of us has to be a detective, Peter, this needs follow up. Most wrongdoers in these parts are either revengeful over something or have a habit. We need to find out which."

"Well that brings me to the reason for this visit besides bringing you up to date. The man in question lives on the Reservation. Since you have a closer knowledge of that part of the world than I do, I thought you might do the sleuthing there." Peter continued, "It is interesting how a local nobody suddenly has enough money to hire a high end eastern law firm. Perhaps there is a tie-in here."

"Peter, that sounds reasonable, so give me what you have so far. I'll see what I can do on the Rez. You're doing good Peter, do what you have to, and keep this thing open. We'll need time to learn the whole story."

33 | THE SEARCH FOR THE SUPPLIER

George knew the mindset of the Arapaho and Shoshone living on the Wind River Reservation well through his attending Arapaho Council meetings as an honorary member. He knew that, as a whole, they wished to be invisible to the Caucasian world around them. Further, finding someone in charge was almost impossible. The person he was looking for had a Caucasian name, as well as an Indian one, and his suspect was probably using his Indian name.

Ranch hand, Tommy Little Feather was wrangling a raw colt in the at-home corral where George found him. He watched, and thought about the value of a loyal employee such as Tommy. They had talked before, and, whereas Tommy was true to his people living on the Reservation, he also understood the substance abuse problems of his people. He did his best to persuade and help those he knew were in trouble, to live a better life. As a result, he was sometimes the recipient of abusive dialogue and lack of understanding from fellow tribal members. This he expected and took the risk, so to speak.

Tommy's dislike and concern for those who promoted drug use on the Reservation became a common bond between Tommy and his employer. They could communicate, a process rare between the ranching people and the Indians living on the Reservation. Tommy controlled his animal, closed the gate to the corral, and joined George. George said, "That was a nasty one, Tom, you did it well. Come on up to the house when you're finished here."

Tommy came, removing his chaps as he climbed the steps up to the ranch house front door. He was admitted by the housekeeper and was seated in the front room before the big window overlooking the valley. George joined him there, and the housekeeper served coffee to the two men.

George said, "It's been too long, Tommy, since we talked about the drug and alcohol problem on the Reservation. Are things any better than they were?"

"I think so, Mr. Bentley, but my people now know where I stand, and I'm sure they sometimes protect their friends, so I no longer am in on things."

"Tommy, if you have helped only one person it has been worth the effort. I think you have done more good than you know. . . . Along that line, I'm looking for one who may or may not be from the Reservation. He goes by the name in the white world of Jake Hunter." George handed Tommy a photograph which contained five individuals standing in front of the Hall of Records building in Glencoe. George said, "One of these might be the person we are looking for. Does anyone there look familiar?"

Tommy studied the photo, and said, "I'm not sure, Mr. Bentley, maybe if you let me have this picture, I can find out."

"What I need to know, Tommy, is that person taking drugs or using alcohol beyond his ability to function. If it turns out that he is a tribal member, I will talk to the Council myself. I think that this person intends to do harm to this ranch, and that he is being forced to do this by some very bad people who have supplied him with drugs. And maybe he owes them money too."

Tommy was silent for a few minutes. George knew this man very well. He knew of the struggle that was always present where tribal loyalty conflicted with what he was asked to do.

George waited. In time, Tommy asked, "Mr. Bentley, what will happen to the man, if you find him?"

"We are looking to find the bad people, the pushers, those who supplied, and addicted this man to using drugs. Punishment to the errant tribal member will be up to our Council." It is the suppliers who we need to find and then to stop their illicit activities both for our Nation and the white world.

Tommy Little Feather, on his day off, usually went to his mother's home on the Reservation. He rode bareback on a pinto from the ranch saddle-stock, with the permission of his employer, of course. He carried with him the photograph of the five people. It was Saturday evening when he arrived home, and in the morning, Sunday, the family attended early Mass at the small near-by chapel. At the end of the service, while his sister and mother helped with some 'after Mass' social activities, Tommy stayed, edged up to Father Daniels, and said, "I need to speak with you, Father."

Father Daniels nodded, and when all others had departed, he led Tommy into the church office, and asked, "What is your problem, son?"

"Father, I am asked to find a person who may be a member of our Nation, and has perhaps done a wrongful thing to the Arrow—B."

"And why is it so hard for you to say no Tommy, isn't it a matter of loyalty and love for your family and Nation?"

"Yes, Father, except that there is good reason to believe that outside interests are supplying drugs to this person. As you know, Mr. Bentley has been helping to fight drug abuse here on the Reservation and I have loyalty to him as well as our Nation."

"Tommy, this will have to be a decision from your conscience of course. How will you search for this person?"

Tommy produced the photo of the five he had, and

handed it to Father Daniels, and said, "He is one of these. We're not sure which."

Father Daniels studied the photograph. "Yes, Tommy, I know three of these men. Knowing who it is will not solve your problem. You need to know and see before you can act. That is before you inform your employer, you need to be sure." Tommy and his family returned to their home on the Reservation Sunday night.

Tommy left for work early Monday morning. During the noontime meal he sat silently across from his employer, trying to say something but didn't know how to start the conversation. The two men had been doing physical, big time, and Mary Ellen's stew was disappearing in record time. Finally, George, reading Tommy well, asked, "How's your family, Tommy? Are they well?"

"They're fine, Mr. Bentley."

George was silent for a few moments. "Have you thought about what we discussed last week, Tommy?"

"Yes sir, but not knowing for sure who it is makes it hard."

George called Peter, "How's progress, Peter?"

"Nothing new, Mr. Bentley, is there any news from our friend, Tommy?"

"Tommy can't do much without knowing what the man looks like, and suggested we try to find a person in the photo that we do know at the Hall of Records who might recognize him."

Peter Forbes had an ego. He knew that something logical like this friendship thing should have been his idea and he said, "Tommy's right on, I'll check that one out right away, I'll need the photo again."

Things are never as simple as they sound, but in time Tommy received an identifiable image of Jake Hunter.

Peter Forbes had multiple reasons for proceeding vigorously in the defense of his client, George Bentley. It was his first major land case, and that alone drove him to full speed ahead. He swallowed his pride and arranged a meeting with Tommy Little Feather to discuss the issues surrounding the lawsuit against George and the Arrow—B. He found Tommy on a Tuesday morning shepherding a nervous colt around the corral. He waited patiently, noting the skill with which Tommy handled his charge. The colt bounded up on his hind legs several times and Tommy gave him rein to do just that. The two slowed their moves, and while Tommy soothed his charge, he glanced over at Peter. Peter smiled and held his ground until Tommy moved outside the corral.

Peter said, "I'm Peter Forbes, Mr. Bentley's attorney, can we talk somewhere?"

Tommy nodded, led him to a nearby table under a shade tree and said, "Mr. Bentley told me that you would be coming. I'm sad for Mr. Bentley about his ownership dispute. I hope you can succeed for him."

Peter handed the photo of the five to Tommy. He said, "Tommy, at your suggestion, we found a person in this photo who identified Jake Hunter. He's the middle person in the photo." Peter paused, noting a questioning look from Tommy. He said, "This man hired an expensive attorney from Chicago to sue the Arrow—B. At present he remains invisible, leaving the lawsuit in the hands of his attorneys. We need to make him visible, Tommy."

Tommy said, "Yes sir, Mr. Bentley told me that. We know, Hunter most likely is using his Indian name, and the Reservation where he is, is over two million acres, with dozens of small villages. Do you have any suggestions?"

Peter smiled, then said, "Tommy, I needed to tell you that we are both on the same side, and that if there is some way I can help, tell me. Also, if you find any information as to where we can find this man, call me. Oh and Mr. Bentley is convinced that drugs are involved. Perhaps this might be a help in finding him."

The ranching world knew nothing about the moccasin telegraph, only that it was humorously fast and effective. So the person who put the story on the MT used the Arapaho name for male hunter, hiinoo einen, and as it traveled throughout the county, those who were fluent in the Arapaho language, knew who to look for. In time, information from the MT found its way to Father Daniels who put in a call to the Arrow—B. A voice picked up the ringing telephone, "Arrow —B, Mary Ellen here."

"Good morning, Mary Ellen, this is Father Daniels calling from the Reservation church. Is Tommy Little Feather available, I need to speak to him?"

"Hello Father, hold on while I call him, he's out in the corral."

Tommy Little Feather came, put the handset to his ear and said, "This is Tommy, Father."

"Tommy, the man you are looking for is here on the Reservation. The Reservation police know where he is. The word is that he peddles drugs as well as uses them himself. I suggest you contact the police here. As you know Tommy, the Reservation Police don't know what to do about the drug use as well as the alcoholism here. The State Police won't touch anything that happens on the Reservation, so nothing gets done."

Tommy was silent for a moment, he glanced at Mary Ellen, who was cleaning up from the ranch breakfast. He finally said, "Thank you Father, yes I do know about my people's problem. Mr. Bentley and I have talked about this, and he has tried to help. Now he needs to talk to this Jake Hunter. I'll tell Mr. Bentley what you have told me."

George came in from tending to some wayward cattle that had wandered up a narrow gorge after some rare fresh grass, and seemingly couldn't find their way out. The three heifers had been bawling for two days, and might never have figured it out. Food and Tommy were waiting for him. He washed up at the yard pump, then plopped down at the table across from Tommy.

Tommy waited until his boss got some food inside, then said, "I had a call from Father Daniels." Tommy related his conversation.

George gave a mild explicative. 'That's fine, Tommy, I'll take it from here."

George Red Fox Bentley as an honorary member of the Arapaho Council often attended the bimonthly meetings. The Council members discussed issues such as substance abuse, but wouldn't or couldn't do anything about it. It was all blamed on the white communities around them for allowing drugs and alcohol to cross into Reservation space. So at the first meeting after the discovery of Jake Hunter's location, George again brought up the matter of substance abuse among the tribal members. There was the usual nodding of heads, and the agreement that "something has to be done," then the lead council member asked if anyone else had anything new to discuss. George said "I have more to say" and remained standing. The lead council member nodded and waited.

"We have in our midst a Jake Hunter who is evil and is providing drugs to our people. I need to face and question him, with the Council's permission of course."

The Arapaho Council was not known for its speedy decisions. The lead Council member demurred, looking to the right then to the left for any sign of approval, finally said, "We'll let you know later."

It did, in fact, take time for the council to decide, but in the end, George was given tacit approval to meet with Hunter. Said meeting took place in the Council chambers. George waited as the Reservation police escorted Hunter into the room. The man was unaware of why he was there, and he sat with a questioning look on his face.

George said, "I'm George Bentley, owner of the Arrow— B. You have initiated legal action against me. Would you explain why, and why now? This ranch has been in existence for over sixty years."

A belligerent nervous and frightened man blustered out a, "I don't have to answer to you."

George said, "Well I guarantee you'll have to answer that question if we go to court. You're on drugs, aren't you? Where do you get those drugs, Jake?"

Hunter managed out a "You can't prove that."

"Who are you kidding? It's common knowledge, even told on the MT. You're an addict, Hunter. Who's paying for those drugs? Is this so-called suit against the Arrow—B a way to pay?"

"I don't have to answer any of your questions."

"Not here, but you will have to when we meet in court. I suspect there were papers proving my ownership of that land you are suing for and you destroyed them. Is that what happened, Hunter, while you were working for the Hall of Records?"

Hunter was silent. He looked defiant, at the same time showing guilt.

George said, "Hunter, you're a nothing, some smart people got you to do this, that's for certain. You face serious questions while you're under oath in court. Expect to have a choice, tell all or lie and face perjury charges, and that spells lots of jail time. Oh, and you don't get drugs in jail. Who put you up to this, Hunter? I know a lot about the rampant drug culture here. You're playing a dangerous game. The dealers and pushers kill. They want their money. Tell us who they are, Hunter, it might save your life."

There was no response from Jake Hunter. George stood up and left the room.

Word travels around the Reservation like water down a fast running creek, and the private conversation between George and Hunter sort of turned out to be not so private. Wrongdoers and the drug cartels can't exist when they are exposed doing their thing, so pawns like Jake Hunter don't expect to live very long. And that was the case with Jake Hunter. He was found dead of a gunshot a week later.

After the interview with Hunter, George called Peter Forbes and filled him in. Peter agreed with the scenario George had developed concerning Jake Hunter's suit against the Arrow—B, but reminded him that there was really no evidence that the Court would accept here.

George considered the death of Jake Hunter as very bad news, considering that once again the link to the drug dealers was broken. The loss of a human life, of course was sad in his mind, and ridding the world of a really useless human being wasn't so morally justified. When George discussed Hunter's death with his attorney, that conversation went like this:

"Hello Peter, have you heard about the death of Hunter?"

"I just have, George, this may change things a bit."

"So, what happens now?"

"Generally the legal action ceases, unless the plaintiff has heirs and an estate representative that steps in, or if there are multiple plaintiffs, they will proceed."

"How do we stand on this issue?"

"There was only one plaintiff, Hunter, and I can't see anything in the lawsuit that mentions family or heirs of any kind. If no one steps up, the case will be dismissed."

George said, "All right, Peter, keep on top of things, and continue to be inquisitive. I'd sure like to know who did the killing, and that has to be one of the pushers or higher-ups in the drug culture. . . . I'm not forgetting the probable connection between Steve Harris's death and this one, both have drug connections."

George sat for a while, cursed the people who prospered from the weak who depended on drugs to comfort or excuse, and reinforced his determination to fight the drug culture wherever and whenever he could. Whereas Hunter's death was not that great a loss to the human race, and it may have solved the problem of ranch land ownership, it removed an important link to the drug world. He rode the range that day, his mind dwelling on and planning a campaign to fight for a drug free society on the Reservation. This strong dogma of the Arrow—B Ranch owner would dominate his thoughts and actions well into the future.

34 | TO LOVE, HONOR, AND OBEY

As the year 1959 drew to a close, Joan was happy to be done with it and to look to the future. Now, a bit peeved, she called the Arrow—B at noon, knowing she could expect her lover to be with the hands in from the range having their midday meal. Mary Ellen answered.

Joan said, "Hi Mary Ellen, can I speak to George?"

"Sure, hon, just a sec." She turned the phone over to George.

George said, "Hello sweetheart, this is nice."

"I haven't had a call from you for some time, what's going on?"

"Oh, I'm sorry. . . . You heard about the Jake Hunter killing?"

"Uh huh, what's that have to do with you picking up the phone once in a while?"

"I could answer lots, but that would become an alibi of sorts. Sweetheart, first off, probably Jake Hunter would still be alive if I hadn't questioned him. Second, he needed to be brought up to task. He was a drug addict, and most likely, a pusher. So I have on my conscience the death of a human being, which didn't accomplish anything. We needed him alive, and perhaps we could find out who's bringing drugs into the Reservation. That is frustrating to me."

Joan smiled within herself, but wasn't going to give in to George. "The last I heard there are twenty-four hours in each day, and the phone works all those twenty-four."

George said, "Can we meet and work this out? How about dinner tomorrow night? I'll pick you up at around five."

"Sure, my love, but what will we talk about, and where will we be dining in this restaurant wasteland?"

"My call."

George Bentley was not Joan's only suitor, in fact her popularity among the single males in the County of Contra had been growing ever since she took up residence in Walnut. She was not immune to advances of the eligible, even though she seemed to vigorously reject closeness from those who would wish to enter her life. She had a choice! When she learned from George that he was worried for her to the point that he stumbled over his words when confronted over the issue of telephone calls, she knew that he was in love with her, and they needed to join and live together.

So when George fretted over her tease, she became a little naughty, extracting every bit of personal glee she could, and in essence though, she wanted a commitment from him.

George came to pick up Joan as promised. She was waiting, dressed in wintry clothes: a soft deerskin parka trimmed in white fur framed a softly tanned, mature face.

His heart thumped. George was already in love with Joan. He had been stumbling along, only half accepting that love due to his once love and commitment to another. All that disappeared. A strong ranch owner and a dedicated veterinarian came together. The love would endure! Their kiss was warm and told all. George said little as Joan tucked herself into the passenger seat of the ranch station wagon.

To Joan's surprise, George drove to the Arrow—B. They entered the ranch house to find a small table set for dinner.

It was there, over a glass of wine that George proposed. It was there that their life together began and would endure.

Immediately after the announcement of the forthcoming wedding of two of the area's favorite people, the community of Walnut and surrounding area showed their approval and started to prepare. Reverend Mathews excluded. He was having trouble with his conscience, in that he recognized and believed that marriage was forever. Ruth, knew her husband well, said, "Tommy, God expects you to understand what has happened here. George will always see to the care of Betty, but Betty is ill, and will remain that way. George needs a life beyond that. He has waited patiently for Betty to recover to no avail. To make matters worse, she has rejected him, and it is time for his release from their vows. The court has removed any legal ties between them, and you should dissolve their heavenly ones too."

Reverend Mathews was silent, looking away from Ruth, his own partner for life.

Ruth studied her husband of many years. She knew what a struggle he was having. She moved closer, touching his cheeks, then caressed his forehead. She said, "Tommy, it's all right. George is a good man. He helps people wherever he can, try to understand."

Births, weddings, and funerals in the Walnut area had always depended on Reverend Mathews to handle them. It was Joan who approached the venerable Walnut church leader, asking him to officiate at their wedding. She met with a vague, non-responsive Tom Mathews, and got his suggestion that she look elsewhere, as "we may not perform the service you wish in this institution."

Word got to Rosey over the stubborn church leader who seemed set and firm in his decision, as it always does around the County. She called Ruth. They met in the old Rosey's café, which was open for breakfast and lunch only. Amy, now operating the café for the new owners, poured the coffee, and served donuts to the two, then joined them.

Rosey asked, "Ruth, what's with Tom? Everybody here wants to attend the wedding. He can't do this, can he?"

Ruth answered in a voice tinged with mirthful awe, "My husband, whom I love dearly, has very strong beliefs. I know that this one may be misguided of course, but there seems little I can do to change his mind. That will take a higher power."

Amy asked, "What does the Bible say about divorce?"

Rosey and Ruth looked at each other, both thinking something like, "This kid is telling us grown-ups—."

Ruth said, "I guess I don't know as much as I should. I know divorce is wrong, but people get divorced for lots of reasons, and I'm sure God still wants to see them in church. It's time for me to dig a little deeper into scripture. Maybe that's the higher power Tom will listen to."

Ruth, first asked the Reverend, "What will your sermon be about next Sunday?"

He answered, "I haven't written it yet, why do you ask?"

"A young woman asked me about forgiveness in the eyes of the church."

"So why didn't she come to me for consultation?"

"Tom, this young woman is, and has been, a member of this church from when she was a toddler. Her parents are the Robinsons. I think she is taking the side of George Bentley. That is, can't you forgive, and allow the wedding to take place in our church."

The Reverend hesitated, feeling a bit out of control. He said, "Ruth, the Bible will uphold the sanctity of everlasting commitment of ones that choose to wed before God. I see no room for deviation from this tenet."

"Alright, Tom, but this young woman has a right to expect an answer from you. Just what does the Bible say about forgiveness?"

Reverend Mathews stubbornly prepared his Sunday sermon, yes on forgiveness, as he needed to answer a question from one of his flock, and he felt more comfortable doing it before his congregation than facing this young person directly. He based his sermon on Luke 6:37—Judge not, and ye shall not be judged: condemn not, and ye shall not be condemned: forgive, and ye shall be forgiven—but he managed to sneak in a reference also to advice from the Apostle Paul in 1 Corinthians 7:15-16—But if the unbelieving depart, let him depart. A brother or a sister is not under bondage in such cases: but God hath called us to peace. For what knowest thou, O wife, whether thou shalt save thy husband? or how knowest thou, O man, whether thou shalt save thy wife?

Whereas he didn't specifically refer to his own dogma against divorce, which he took from Jesus's words in Matthew 19:3-9—What therefore God hath joined together, let not man put asunder—he left the question of conducting the Bentley wedding himself and in his church, open. In a sense he was justifying a deviation from his well-known stand against divorce for any reason. In the end, and after much prayer, he understood more deeply the Apostle Paul's admonition that God 'called us to peace' and saw 'forgiveness' as the link between his firm beliefs and what God expects him to do for others.

Not long before the wedding Rosey said, "Pete, Joan and George most likely will be gone from their ranch on some kind of a honeymoon for a week or two. Has George asked you to manage the Arrow—B until they get back?"

"Not yet Rosey, I'll check that out with George, He's a needen' sum un fer sure."

Over a cup of morning coffee, Pete and George sat rancher to rancher discussing the daily mini events that always pop up when two or more of the locals get together. They managed to avoid the subject of the upcoming wedding and in time, Pete got around to asking, "Any way I can help yer while you're gone after the weddin'?"

George looked thoughtfully at Pete, sipped a bit more

steaming black coffee, put his pint-sized cup on the counter, and said, "Pete, you have practically raised me, taught me everything I know or am, and been there when I stumbled. Yes, of course it would be nice for me if you ramrodded the Arrow—B while I'm gone, but you have a ranch now and lots of things to do. You're trying it alone right now but you know that can't go on for long. Let it be me that comes over to help you once in a while, as you've done yours long ago. How about this, Pete, let's throw this one at Cliff, see how many mistakes he makes. You know that's the only way. You can find some excuse to see him every so often, just in case he gets nervous or something. I'm looking forward to what six toughened riders can do to a kid put in charge. This should be fun. If he screws up, we'll know something."

"When you put it that a way, I see where you're comin' from. You gonna talk to the boys?"

"Well I probably needn't, they're mostly more interested in money and a home such as it is anyway. These are great guys, and I'll always see to their needs and desires. They're proud to be what they are. But I'll chat with them about it."

"How long do you expect to be gone?"

"I've made arrangements for a month. Cliff has to handle the payroll, or he would be toothless. We won't do any marketing for that period, and Todd will handle any animal health issues that might come up. Joan and I have been discussing a trip back to our roots in Europe." George hesitated for a moment, "I could tell him to touch base with you if he likes."

Pete smiled and said, "Let's do it like you laid it out. This sure begins to look like fun."

When the "I do's" had been spoken, the kissing of the bride, the walk down the church center aisle, a short walk to a reception in the Church Garth and the rice flung, the bridal couple scrambled into their car and escaped from the world of good wishes and issues of the day. The longstanding feelings each had for the other finally won over.

35 | TO BE IN CHARGE

George had been preparing Cliff to ram-rod the Arrow—B for some time. He knew he was young but savvy and learned fast. His high school education put him a step above the other riders. So sometime before the wedding George asked Cliff up to the ranch house for a powwow about things in general. They sat in the great room over a cup of coffee. After the work talk was over and George had measured the young man, his responses and his look, the ranch owner said, "Cliff, I will be gone for the better part of a month. By now you probably have figured out that a ranch doesn't run itself. The gahoot who sits up here has to make decisions daily or nothing gets done. Further, you can't run any enterprise by committee. So how'd you like to run this ranch for the month while Mrs. Bentley and I are away? I would expect you to make a mistake or two, of course, and you know the boys pretty well. You'll have to make payroll, buy supplies and assign someone to handle any special jobs that are necessary."

Cliff, a bit startled, asked "Do you think I'm ready, Mr. Bentley?"

"Do you think I'd ask you if I didn't?"

Cliff stood, reached to shake George's hand, and said,

"Yes sir, I would like to, I hope I can do well. Ah, will the boys accept me?"

"Alright then, you will get manager's pay for that month. We leave in two weeks. Cliff, the men you call boys are professionals at what they do. Treat them for that and they will return the favor."

36 | THE TESTING

Generally speaking most ranch hands know what needs to be done, and do their thing without the need for instruction, per se. On the day after the departure of ranch owner George Bentley for his honeymoon, Cliff Upton walked down to the cook shack and joined the six Arrow—B riders for that six o'clock breakfast. The six munchers kind of blinked a silent acknowledgment of his presence and went on with their eating, giving Cliff less than a warm feeling. He sat down and filled his plate with eggs and such that was passed to him from six silent souls, getting more uneasy by the second. The meal went on, and in time ended with some rising to leave for the day of ranch chores.

Clifton Upton was the product of a firm father expecting his son to listen, learn and obey the instructions issued. With the transition to adulthood for the son came a measure of stubbornness. Call it rebellion if you will, a not too unusual attitude for a 'new adult,' which perhaps helped shape this young man, and on the morning of the first day of his management assignment, he bridled at what he saw as envy and distrust. By the end of the meal he had decided to face it now rather than cower in fear until his assignment was over.

He said to the group, "Sit down, Mr. Bentley gave me orders to manage this ranch until he returns, and I intend to do just that as best I can. We can either manage to run this ranch together or do less for Mr. Bentley. I don't expect to instruct any of you. You don't need that, but I will manage. If I screw up, I'll pay, that's for sure."

Six seasoned ranch employees, skilled in the care and handling of cattle and associated ranch work that goes along, sat mum, attentive to a neophyte youngster announcing his intent to manage their lives for a time. There was humor mixed with a bit of defiance here.

Cliff continued ignoring the lack of enthusiasm. "Now we all know that the upper herd is running out of grass, and needs to be moved. Curley, you stay close in and take care of ranch stuff. Three of you prep the ranch wagon, trail what riding stock you'll need and head for the line shack, then the rest of us tend to local pastures as usual."

The six riders headed for the bunkhouse to do the personal stuff and get ready for the day. The conversation went something like this: "S-funny, the boss didn't tell us about this one. He's either bein' funny, or tryin' ta see what this smart-ass kid can do." Another hand said, "Yeh, maybe the boss wants to get off a horse for a while, after all, he's been punching cows for a lot of years."

"You mean, act like a cattle baron, send a boy out with our orders and sit on his behind in a big chair in a big house?"

Another guffawed and blurted, "I'd take odds against that, knowing George."

A third hand asked, Well should we help this dummy out and tell him that three riders aren't enough to do this one or let him find out all by his lonesome? Those critters are scattered all over the state of Wyoming, and just gettin' 'em in a bunch to move will be somethin' else."

Another hand said, "If we don't tell him somethin' we'll be out there for a week, and I don't like bein' away from Mary Ellen's cookin' fer that long."

A fourth rider, who had been silent up to now, said,

"Since Cliff didn't leave any room for talk, I'm fer lettin im find out all by 'imself. I think that's what the boss would want us to do, or he would have said somethin' 'afore he left." And that's the way it went.

The Arrow—B holdings had grown throughout the years to a considerable chunk of Wyoming. Owner George Bentley was a working owner, not exempt from the tough jobs, and expected no less from those who worked for him. To get to this point in the success of this enterprise, he had faced failures as well as the opposite. He fully believed that the best teacher is when you screw up. And that's why he gave Cliff a chance to do just that.

George and Joan were on their way to Europe. They expected to pretty well do the continent. That meant a month or more.

After four days, and his riders hadn't returned, Cliff decided to go on up there and see what was going on. He drove the ranch jeep, and as he approached the line shack, he could see smoke coming from the stack. The ranch wagon sat alongside the shack, and riding stock chomped away at a bale of hay lying on the ground. He entered to find all three men eating lunch. He said, "Hello" and joined the ones at the table. There was an awkward silence for a few moments, and finally Cliff asked "How are we coming?"

One of the riders said, "Not that good, Cliff, these cattle are used to having their own way, and they won't stay put."

Cliff thought for a minute, then asked, "This is not a new problem, what's different this time?"

Another rider said, "There were six of us the last time."

Cliff speculated that these three knew from the start that three weren't enough riders and they let this happen. This then was his first test, and these three were enjoying every bit of his discomfort.

The herd got moved, the ranch settled down to its routine,

and a young man grew a bit. Payday, the first and third Saturday of the month, saw Cliff reading a schedule of pay for each hand in the ranch office. He placed the indicated cash into pre-identified envelopes, sealed each and entered the amounts into the ranch records. Lunch time saw him handing out pay envelopes to a less than talkative assembly, each measuring the kid in charge for some kind of weakening or acknowledgement that he had screwed it up and found none. He joined the eaters, commenting on Mary Ellen's cooking, which brought on a bunch of nods.

By tradition, ranch activities allowed a short work day Saturday afternoon on paydays, the hands enjoying an early start for their day off, Sunday. Cliff, of course, took a turn at being with Amy, and they didn't waste the time visiting their parents. Monday came along as it usually does and the working part of life began again. On this Monday at about 6:15 a.m., one of the hands came up to the ranch house, and knocked on the door. Cliff, who was just getting ready to start his day, opened the door to face a worried looking Frank, who said, "We can't get Jerry up. He just moans and hides his face." Cliff followed the rider out to the bunkhouse and entered. He leaned over a comatose Jerry and shook him. Jerry reacted with a wave of his hand and a guttural "Go away." Cliff asked Frank, "Do you know if he was out drinking a lot last night?"

Frank answered, "He wasn't with any of us, Mr. Upton, he's always been a loner."

Cliff leaned over and sniffed Jerry's breath. Jerry didn't smell of stale beer or booze. He thought for a moment, then said, "How can a man that handles wild horses as well as he does get 'out of it' this way? Do you suppose he's on drugs?"

Frank answered, "Jerry's from the Reservation, there's a lot of that going on over there, Mr. Upton."

Cliff tried to shake Jerry into consciousness with no success. He turned to Frank and said, "Go get Mary Ellen and tell her to come on down here with a pot full of black coffee." He continued to work on Jerry. Mary Ellen came, and between Cliff and herself, with the help of lots of coffee, brought Jerry into some kind of consciousness. Mary Ellen said, "This has happened before."

Cliff asked, "What did Mr. Bentley do the last time?"

"Well, somehow we kept it from the boss. I'm thinking that was wrong. This guy is killing himself and in some ways putting the rest of us at risk."

"So if I turn him in, so to speak, I'm a heel, and if I don't, I'm not doing my job. That's my choice. I want to be a good guy to the hands, of course, but that won't solve an ongoing problem for Jerry, or the ranch."

Mary Ellen put on a wry smile, "Uh huh, you got that one right, Cliff."

The next day found Jerry on the back of a cantankerous mare, showing once again his skill and expertise when it came to the equine animal. Cliff watched, and admired. He knew that talk had never changed an addict's mind. It had to be something else—perhaps ego, or money? What would a fine horseman not want to do? Walk of course. Supposing we take him off the horse, and give him a cushy ground job, like tending the chickens or weeding the vegetable garden?

Cliff speculated at looking too officious to the rest of the hands, and decided it would be worth the risk. At lunch time he made the move, "Jerry, you're grounded for now. You'll have to do the stuff around the ranch."

"Like what?"

"Like shovel manure and stack hay, as long as you ask."

"You can't do that to me, Mr. Bentley won't like it!"

"That's my problem, Jerry, I may be fired for this, so be it. Complain to him when he returns."

About two weeks later, Pete came out to the Arrow—B as promised to see how much trouble Cliff had gotten himself into. He found all the hands, including Cliff, out on the range except Jerry and Mary Ellen. He said howdy to Jerry, and entered the cook shack. Mary Ellen and Pete had been good friends for a lot of years, and after a big hug, they sat over a cup of coffee and a stack of Mary Ellen's tall cinnamon raison muffins.

In time Pete asked, "How's 'Cliff doin'?"

"I can't believe this one, the bunkhouse bunch invited that kid to join them in their poker game last night. I think they all expected him to fall on his face, but that didn't happen."

"So what happened to make them change their attitude, the last I remember, those stubborn prideful characters wouldn't bend an inch from their own thinking?"

Mary Ellen answered, "You know, I don't quite know, but I think it was when he faced up to a drug problem with Jerry. He grounded Jerry, put him in charge of the manure and hay duty. This seemed to get Cliff a lot of respect from the bunch."

Pete guffawed and said, "Yes that would certainly upset Jerry. This is not the only time that he has goofed it. Heretofore the boys have covered for 'im. They must a gotten tired of that. It'll be interesting to find out how Cliff responds when George returns and asks why Jerry is shoveling manure."

"Uh huh."

Cliff didn't sleep much during his reign as manager of the Arrow—B. He was learning fast, but there seemed to be little things here and there that tested, one of which was the ranch bronc buster (Jerry) not being available when needed. This had made a shortage in the ranch remuda, and none of the other hands were skilled enough or did they want to sit on unbroken ponies. He constantly went out to the corral checking, worrying and kind of hoping for his boss to return soon. This was a busy time for the hands, and they needed fresh horses often. There were other things too, that made him a bit humble, but he didn't panic, and that's what George Bentley wanted to find out.

In time, George and his new bride did return, and of course he noticed Jerry doing other than working in the corral. After getting an activity and action report from his young foreman, George asked Cliff, "What's this with Jerry, he's supposed to be in the corral handling the animals?"

Cliff hesitated. He had just owned up to the things he had messed up, and this one was hard to answer. He gingerly said, "Mr. Bentley, I ordered him out of the corral when he didn't show up for work one morning. We found him stoned in his sack. I didn't think he was safe on a horse."

"We, meaning who? Who else?"

"Just Mary Ellen, Frank and me."

"And you decided to have him shovel manure?" George gave a surprised stare at Cliff. "Did he do any, 'shoveling,' manure, that is?"

"Well, he really didn't seem to have his heart in it much."

George laughed, "No, I suppose he didn't. What gave you this idea, manager?"

"My father, and an event in high school planted a dislike of drug users in my head. Dad could be very convincing at times."

"So I've noticed, Cliff, and a dislike for druggies is one thing that your dad and I totally agree on. Cliff, you made a management decision, and I must say, a gutsy one.

You have five days to solve the Jerry problem before your job as manager is over. What you did with Jerry was fine as far as it goes.

"Returning Jerry to bronc busting before your job is over is one solution. Another is to give me the job. You made a management decision, and now you have to make another. You have to find the best way to get Jerry back on the job in such a way that you retain your authoritative posture with the troops."

Whereas Cliff was getting more comfortable as time went on doing the manager thing, he was ready to give a sigh of relief when his ordeal would end, and he could go back to being 'one of the boys' again. Mr. Bentley had said, "Not so fast, Cliff."

It was two days before he decided, once again, that he needed to do an adult thing and get Jerry back where he belonged, hopefully in a manner that didn't look like Mr. Bentley ordered him to. He was nineteen, somewhat new to the world of experienced and skillful horsemen. Such men have strong convictions of their own authority over the animals they trained, which carried over into their human relationships.

Cliff thought about it long and hard. Finally, he walked down to the stable area, where Jerry was supposed to be moving hay and such around, and asked him to join him in the mess hall for a chat. Jerry complied. They were alone except for Mary Ellen, who brought out, coffee and some of her tall cinnamon rolls. Mary Ellen glanced at Cliff, guessed these two wanted to be alone and went back into the kitchen. Jerry, who loved his job on the Arrow—B, had had some shaky thoughts concerning Mr. Bentley's view of his drug habit, and really was attentive to what Cliff had to say.

Cliff said, "Jerry, I need you to get your ass back in the corral. Now we both know Mr. Bentley's attitude about drugs. I expect him to explode about that matter the next time he sees you. Cliff sounded an amused utterance then said, "My Dad and I didn't always see eye-to-eye, he was sort of one way when I was growing up, but his attitude about drugs and users got shoved into my head plenty solid. That's why I did to you what I did. Now Mr. Bentley didn't order me to put you back in the corral, but I need to. I don't want him to have to. Whether you screw up and stay with this drug thing or not is your business, not mine. Thinking ahead, it'll kill you in the end if you don't take control. In a few days, my job as manager will be over, and I'll go back to punching cows again like the rest of the bunch. I've just been doing what I was ordered to do.

"I hear that this has happened before, and that others have managed to keep it from the boss. This didn't happen this time. He knows. So get yourself back where it belongs, and face the music when the boss puts me back punching cows again."

In time, a nervous Arapaho from the Wind River Reservation, named Jerry Sitting Horse, sat across from his employer, George Bentley, in the cook shack sipping a cup of morning coffee. The two had spoken in the Arapaho tongue in the formal way of greeting by people of the Arapaho nation, then in English, George said, "Sitting Horse, you seem to have gotten yourself into a lot of trouble while I was gone. What say you to that?"

"I was only sick for one day, and unable to work, why was I treated so badly by Mr. Upton for that?"

"It's a little more than that, Jerry, I hear that this has happened before, and from what we suspect, you are into drugs. Unless you didn't know before now, druggies are not welcome here. Further, I totally approve of what Mr. Upton did when he took you out of the corral." After a period of silence from Jerry, Mr. Bentley said, using Jerry's Indian name, "Also, you have done harm to our Nation. Your friends on the Reservation must know about your drug use. I'm sure that doesn't make you very popular there either. What's it going to be, Jerry, give up the drugs or give up your job here and shovel manure somewhere else?"

"I like my job here, Mr. Bentley."

"Alright." George sat in silence for a bit, he studied the ranch wrangler. "Jerry, close to home, we think the first Mrs. Bentley's father was killed by a druggie. The killer has yet to be found. Killing is evil and wrong. Drug addiction causes people to do bad things to satisfy their drug need. That is why Mr. Upton did what he did.

"Weaker members of our Nation on the Reservation who become addicted are caught and can't get out. Keep in mind that I need you here, but you can be replaced. Now one thing more, dealers who lose customers are nasty, and have no concern over killing. They don't trust anyone lest they risk being found out. Your dealer doesn't want you to name him. Watch your back, Jerry."

37 | TROUBLE!

Joan La Cross, now Mrs. Joan Bentley, ran a functioning animal hospital business located in Walnut. Known as a charismatic, animal-loving, community-active icon, and loved by everyone in that part of Wyoming, Joan's business had grown. She had hired an assistant to handle the telephone, dispense medicine and other products, and that allowed her to attend to animals where they are, sometimes far away from the office.

George's life changed as he was now relieved from the frustrating burden of the unfixable problems with his ex-wife, Betty, and he relished his ability to love another with passion and total commitment. The training and testing of Clifford Upton for a more serious position with the Arrow—B allowed George to become more active in community affairs, and to write, which was his second love after ranching. Both, Joan and George, were strong in their own ways, but very supportive of each other.

Joan had spent a great deal of time with George's daughter Eva and grew to love her like her own. Eva now lived with her father and Joan, although Betty retained her visiting rights, albeit with supervision. Joan's mother, Renee, was quite content living in the ranch guest house at the Arrow—

B, and she delighted in caring for Eva while Joan was away tending sick animals around the county.

On an early summer day, George was in his office doing book work, and hating every bit of it. He had just come from the Reservation where he attended a bi-monthly council meeting. He reviewed in his mind the meeting agenda and the lack of firm decisions emanating from that body. The alcohol and drug problem among tribal members was, as usual, agreed on as a problem and about which nothing was done. In addition, the Reservation peoples were being visited by the NIYC—National Indian Youth Council—causing involvement in that movement by some. Whereas the NIYC was visibly concerned with Indian fishing rights, it tended toward civil rights as a basic issue. Not that the NIYC wasn't right in its endeavors, but it tended to cause unrest, and this was stirring things up also. All in all, George was totally frustrated. He picked up the ringing phone on his desk, "Bentley."

"Bill Williams here George, what's going on out there in cow heaven?"

"Yes well, we grow 'em, you eat 'em, I'm sure you're not calling to learn about the health of my cows, so to what do I owe the honor of this call from our famous sitting sheriff?"

"We got trouble up on Hamilton's spread and I thought you might be interested. Like what happened down your way a couple a years ago. Two guys powered in to Ham's ranch house, locked the women in the bathroom, ransacked the house, found some cash and left."

"Anybody hurt?"

"No, but Ham's plenty mad. If he catches these guys, he'll shoot them both dead."

"How old *is* Ham anyway, Bill?"

Bill chuckled, "That crusty old lion's gotta be at least ninety. Roberts and I went out there and caught him oiling up that old blunderbuss o' his'n."

"So, you got any clues or ideas?"

"Nothing firm yet, but Ham's granddaughter who was there said, they were masked, and talked to each other in Arapaho."

"Crap, that's the Reservation again. I was there yesterday at their bimonthly Council meeting. They all agree that drugs are a problem, nod their heads, and do nothing—which brings up the subject of Steve Harris's killer. Bill, we need to get on that again. I think when we find the answer to this one, we may be closer to finding out who killed Steve."

"Well, you're closer to that than me, there's nothing more I can do from here."

"Yah, I know, however the bad stuff hasta come from outside the Reservation. They don't grow it there. So, let's face it, greedy breeds or non-Indians from outside the Reservation are probably involved."

George, after ending his call with the Sheriff, sat in thought, going over the events tied to criminal behavior seemingly emanating from the Reservation. One could make the alibi that "bad," non-Indians, were responsible, drug pushers and dealers and the like, and the pursuit of such vermin was paramount. It wouldn't solve the matter of addiction to drugs, but it might be a start. He concluded that the only path to finding out the who, where, and how drugs reach the users in the Reservation had to be through the users themselves.

Wrangler Jerry, at the request of his boss, finished walking a new young bronc around the corral, took off his chaps, slapped his dusty sweaty hands, and walked up to the ranch house. He was admitted and seated at a small table across from George. Coffee came, and as Jerry wondered why he was there, George filled their cups, studying Jerry as he dumped two large spoonsful of sugar in his own cup. He finally asked, "How's the new bunch of broncs working out, Jer?"

"They're plenty fresh, which'll make 'em strong critters for riding, if'n I kin tame 'em down a bit, that is."

"I don't think you need worry over that one, you're good, I've never seen better, Jerry."

"Thank you Mr. Bentley, but it's no sweat for me, these animals are fine to work with."

"I need to talk to you about drugs, once more, Jerry. Something happened yesterday that looks like it is tied into persons from the Reservation. It also is certainly due to drug addicts doing bad things to support their cravings for drugs. It all points to those who introduce and supply drugs to our people. Since you have had this 'drug' experience, I need to know how you feel about it, and if you would be willing to join others of us in the pursuit and punishment of those greedy vermin?"

Jerry sat in silence for a time, he knew what his answer needed to be, but he also knew about his friends on the Reservation, some of whom used drugs. He sat in silence, looking uncomfortable.

"Jerry, you're tough, I've seen you tackle a wild animal that you could have given up on, but didn't. It's a tough thing you have to decide here. Do you do what's best for your friends or what is easier and let them get in trouble? The finality of one who bends to the falsity of the demon, drugs, is to become an outcast in society, depending on others to support and supply their needs. How much do you really care for your friends?

"Your position here will always depend on your performance, and not at all be influenced by your mindset elsewhere. This is not a matter of losing your job here."

Jerry asked, "How would I help my friends without getting them in trouble?"

"They're already in trouble. We need to find those who got them there."

Jerry nodded his head, then said, "That means, where did I get drugs when I was a user, correct?"

"Uh huh."

Jerry sat in silence. George studied the young man a bit,

then said, "Jerry, take a day or two to think this one out. It's okay. There's no pressure here."

The people of the Wind River Reservation have always been fiercely independent and very much guardians of that. Whereas there were friendships with the surrounding miners and ranchers, Reservation law enforcement would not cross the line into the U.S. Similarly, U.S. law enforcement persons had no jurisdiction within the Reservation. Rarely did the Reservation police and the U.S. law enforcement folks interact with each other. By design the off-limits sign was always up at the border! We are reminded that the Wind River Reservation represented a sovereign space, outside of the United States, without the need to obey the laws of the U.S. or the state of Wyoming.

This arrangement was sometimes convenient for wrong doers as they could move across the border with impunity, and often thwart efforts to be corralled. Both County Sheriff Bill Williams and Glencoe Chief of Police Richardson conveniently overlooked minor infractions that seemed to be connected in any way with the Arapaho or Shoshone living on the Reservation. This attitude by law enforcement was frustrating to Wyoming people, as occasionally, a rancher would miss a cow, or a miner might find a missing item in his cabin while he was below mining. There were sometimes verbal outbursts from citizens concerning the lack of action from their law enforcement.

With the death of Chief Running Deer, leadership of the peoples of the Wind River Reservation passed to the Council members, and as a result endured the problem of trying to rule by committee. George, as an honorary member of the Council, was often frustrated when matters of crime, either minor or otherwise were discussed, and for which no action would take place. This was certainly true with the substance abuse problems, which were considerable on the Reservation.

It took the action of a neophyte, Cliff Upton, to tell it as it is, and bring Jerry's recreational use of drugs up to reality: Drug users don't hear words, they need rewards. He found something stronger than words of punishment to influence the judgment of Jerry, his love of his job and the animals he handled.

George Red Fox Bentley, considered as an authority and spokesman on matters concerning the welfare of Contra County, Wyoming, knew from the start that the underlying causes of crime in the County were drugs and alcohol. The death of Betty's father, the ransacking of the Arrow—B ranch house, and now the attack on Ham's place all pointed to drugs. George wrote for the Glencoe Herald:

We are a community of strong, hard-working and industrious folks living in a not too friendly environment. The crime occurring within this community comes from without, and most of that crime is due to substance abuse. It is quite evident that the murder of Steve Harris was committed in the interest of obtaining money and most likely for the purpose of supporting a drug addiction. This crime has yet to be solved. The ransacking of homes, such as that of the Hamilton ranch recently was certainly carried out by a user. And there have been others.

Whereas the use of illegal drugs can be policed better with more law enforcement, it seems that this has become a matter of how much money we are willing to spend. Changing the mind of an addict is a difficult task at best. The real criminal, the provider, is very illusive. He is not the best of human beings, as he preys upon the weak. It is here we need apply a concerted, concentrated effort, both with money and manpower. These are evil people, who have invaded our community!

George Bentley

The County Board of Commissioners met for their regular 9 a. m.-Monday morning meeting. On the docket was the article in the Glencoe Herald concerning substance abuse and the related crime in the county. Chairman George Bentley formally opened the meeting, and went directly to the Glencoe Herald article on substance abuse on the Reservation. Discussion went like this:

The council member said, "You're right on, George, I'm

getting calls from our people. They're mad. They expect us to fix the problem.

"So what are they wanting us to do, hire more law? Every time we suggest spending money for anything, we get screams of indignation and get turned down period."

Another present said, with a bit of humor in his voice, "If we have another ranch house broken into, you bet your life we'll hear about it. I would expect us to be replaced."

"Amen."

After a short period, the Chairman said, "Okay, Williams is getting pretty old, and I would think wants to retire soon. Deputy Roberts isn't the one to take on the job, and the way I see it, even if we did a change here, the next pair would have the same problem. Richardson, seems to have his hands full here in Glencoe, and would tell us to go to hell if we needled 'im. Anyone have any suggestions?"

"Let's get Bill in here, he's the most savvy of any of us."

The Chair said, "Alright I'll call 'im, let's be here tomorrow at nine. He'll be here."

Crusty old Sheriff Bill Williams sat at the council table sipping a huge mug of steaming hot coffee when the Council convened. His countenance conveyed a bit of amusement, as the Council members took their seats. Without any fanfare the Chair said, "We got a problem, Bill. I know your department can only respond after a crime has been committed, and that's where your responsibility ends. Right now, however we need some effort in crime prevention. The drug dealers are acting with impunity in our county, and the users are breaking into ranch houses to get money to support their habits. We can't do much about, or to, the users, so we have to do something about the pushers."

Bill nodded his head, and said, "Wal, jus which part o' this 4,000 square mile county d ya want me to concentrate on?"

"Oh fer crap sake, we need ideas. I'm gettin' afraid to leave my wife alone on Friday night when I go to the club."

The Sheriff said, "Maybe we need to go back a few years.

We been gettin' softer every day. You all know it warn't this way—come trouble to any one a us. We got out our guns, took care o' problems and if there was law, we called them to pick up the bodies. For the most part we old-timers are still around, and if *not in charge,* still have a bit a influence. I don't much like the idee o' breakin' out the six guns again, but you ain't goin' ta hire more law, so we have ta do it ourselves."

The chair sighed, then said, "Alright Bill, move that forward to now. You know what's going on here. So step out of your Sheriff shoes for a time and suggest something logical, even if it's a bit on the shady side."

"So there's not that many roads into the Rez, cover those with volunteers. The lice we're lookin' fer come in cars. It's a long walk and they don't know how to ride horses. If one a us shoots somebody a little outside the rules, so what."

The Chair grimaced, stood up, pounded his gavel and said, "This council meeting is officially closed." Pounded his gavel again and said, "Nobody leave." He went over to the coffee pot, filled his cup, walked back to the head of the table and said, "Off the record, Bill is right. As long as we have drugs and alcohol abuse by twenty-five percent of the Reservation people, we have to expect drug traffic and the associated law breaking element moving through our ranches, and of course, users looking for funds to support their craving for drugs, doing bad things." After a long pause during which there were no comments or questions from the seated Council members, Chairman Bentley said in a tired and frustrated tone, "We, as the only government I can see in this county, are expected to lead and protect the interests of the folks that live here. Unless we in this room take some kind of action, we aren't doing our job.

"Sitting here and staring at each other won't do it. Time is of an essence, go home, cogitate, come back here tomorrow, and bring some considerations for a plan with you." He stood up, and headed out toward his car.

The commissioners met again the following morning. A

system of neighborhood watch was agreed upon, the Sheriff's office to coordinate. Police chief Richardson of Glencoe was asked to join forces with the Sheriff's office in that some of the drugs were shown to come in by train and he agreed to have a man meet the daily train that stopped at the Glencoe train station. In that there were usually fewer than ten passengers descending from the string of coaches each time the daily train stopped, it was not too hard to spot an unusual personage. He or she would be carrying their-own luggage and not utilizing the baggage car.

In general, the county as a whole was placed on alert. Merchants dealing with alcoholic beverages were admonished to follow the laws against providing alcoholic products to Native Americans, and it was agreed that the drug pushers doing bad things needed to be rounded up and made to suffer serious consequences. Easy to say!

George left the council chambers deep in thought, sad for those very American Indians the Council had been talking about. Yes, they were causing a problem in the white community but down in the center of it all these were fine people who once had strong living tenets and beliefs. On arrival back at the Arrow—B he sat down to write his next article for the Glencoe Herald. He wrote:

Often I wonder at our attempts to "Bring our Indian friends into the white world" with our standards of living, education, etc., without recognizing the values these people have themselves. Yes, some of those on the Reservation are in trouble, but most folks of that community of Indian people are spiritually ahead of many of us, and live by a code expressed in the TEN INDIAN COMANDMENTS:

1. *The earth is our mother, care for her.*
2. *Honor all your relatives.*
3. *Open your heart and soul to the Great Spirit.*
4. *All life is sacred, treat all beings with respect.*
5. *Take from the earth what you need, and nothing more.*
6. *Do what needs to be done for the good of all.*
7. *Give constant thanks to the Great Spirit for each day.*

8. Speak the truth, but only for the good of others.
9. Follow the rhythms of nature.
10. Enjoy life's journey, but leave no tracks.
There seems to be some magic in these ten laws. From a non-Native American view, I see words of love and concern for others, respect for one's fellow man, honor toward one's faith. People who would usurp and destroy those who live by and believe in such laws are truly evil.

If we are to get a handle on the crime occurring among us we need to go to the source. We need to conduct a war against the suppliers of drugs and alcohol to the Reservation. We are reminded that these greedy people have deliberately addicted others for their own profit.
George Bentley.

Certainly there was bigotry in the 1960s in the Wyoming region, and the marriage of Richard Bentley to White Dove early on provided grist for the mill by many who believed that Indians were a subspecies, and should be treated accordingly. The strength of the Bentleys, and their contributions to the community, worked hard to overcome this.

When George was born, a few were to call him a breed, but most didn't.

Nevertheless, George as a respected rancher still suffered the indignities and insults piled on him by a few in the area. To some, George was a breed, and they were prone to express their feelings openly.

So not everyone in the County was that enthused about some kind of major use of their money or law enforcement personnel's efforts to deal with greedy people making money off of those on the Reservation. As a result the call for 'Do it ourselves' met with a tepid reception, until it happened again to another rancher. The call to Sheriff Bill Williams to do something was anything but nice! Bill was in his office after having just returned from a scuffle with a local nineteen-year-old who had been drinking too much, answered the phone, "Sheriff Williams."

A loud, almost screaming, voice said, "Those damn Indians killed two of my herd last night. Do something! I demand protection from this."

"And who is this?"

"Elmer Emerson,"

"Simmer down, Elmer, how do you know it came from the Reservation to begin with, and second, we discussed this issue in council, and decided we needed to establish some kind of a neighborhood watch system. This office doesn't have the resources to do much here, and if you want to stay alive, join with others in the County. Watch your herd, call law if you see something out of place. The law will respond in kind."

"Well I lost two steers last night, is that out of the ordinary? Maybe the tribes expect me to feed and clothe 'em?"

The Sheriff sighed, "Elmer, just come in and sign a complaint. I'll investigate."

Via the incredible moccasin telegraph, word got around the county almost before it happened, and angry voices said some unprintable things which stirred up the unrest between those on the Reservation and the surrounding ranching and mining folk. George called Sheriff Bill Williams, "You going out to see Elmer?"

"I don't know, George, he's so mad right now, he might shoot at any one that comes into his sights, not that I blame him much, it takes a lot of effort to raise beef, and any one of us doesn't feel happy when someone steals one."

"I suppose you and I aughta go out and talk to Elmer together, but he still calls me a breed, and I don't think that old horse is going to change. When you do go out there, Bill, see if maybe some of this activity comes from outside the Rez. You better take Leon along to kind a be a witness or something."

"Uh huh."

The Arrow—B ranch had roots going back sixty years and had grown to be one of the larger ranches in Wyoming. The current owner, George Bentley, had earned the respect of most in the County of Contra, and had become a spokesman for same. In that he was born of an Arapaho princess, he also held sway with the Reservation folk. With the death of Chief Running Deer, his Indian grandfather, he really became the titular head of the tribe, which honor he really didn't want, as he was more of the white world than the other. It was not his calling to lead here. He had discussed this many times with his grandfather and again with Sarah Golden Poppy, Chief Running Deer's living sister.

A troubled George knocked on the door of the small house that Sarah Golden Poppy lived in. Answering his knock was a young Indian lad, who asked, "What do you want?"

"I am Red Fox, I wish to speak to Golden Poppy, and who might you be?"

"I am Golden Poppy's great grandson."

"Do you speak the tongue of your great Grandmother?"

"Yes, Red Fox. Wait while I tell Golden Poppy of your presence." He half closed the door, turned to Golden Poppy, and said, "Meiwoo beexouu noo'useet (Granny, Red fox has come)."

Golden Poppy, now in her mid-eighties, came to the door, "Wooukohei, Beexouu (Welcome, Red Fox)." She motioned George to come in. Over a cup of thick black coffee, and speaking through her grandson acting as interpreter, she asked, "It is good to see you, Red Fox, what is it that brings you to my home?"

"I am grateful to see you, Golden Poppy, I hope you have been well. It is a sadness that brings me to your home today. Our peoples are in much trouble, and I need tell you of this."

"And, yes, I am aware of what you are concerned with, Red Fox. People who are addicted to drugs and alcohol do bad things. Some of our people do bad things. Without those drugs and whisky that the greedy from outside provide, most of our people would not get into trouble."

"I have long been aware of that, Golden Poppy, however without the help of just a few of our people, those criminal ones could not function. It is that which I wish to talk with you about. One or more from the Reservation is acting between the drug and alcohol suppliers and those who use drugs here. I hope Tommy Little Feather will tell us who. He has used drugs procured from one of our people here. I worry for his safety."

"Red Fox, you are really from the white world. I appreciate your concern, and would do anything to assist in finding and punishing the evildoers, but you know the rules and codes that we live by here. It is not our mission to become involved outside our nation's boundaries."

"Yes, and I expect to be reminded of that when I approach the Council. Golden Poppy, we are likewise stubborn, which gets us nowhere. A dopey or drunken tribal member is unemployable, useless and sometimes dangerous. Our people are too good for that."

"What you say, Red Fox, is certainly true, but we are also loyal to each other, and there is a strong mind here to stay that way against ones that would divide. You will have to look elsewhere for answers."

After a respectful departure from the home of Golden Poppy, a frustrated George traveled back to the Arrow—B. Mary Ellen, who was in the ranch kitchen, saw George mount the steps into the ranch main room, noticed his silent glum face, poured a mugful of coffee, and put it down in front of him when he sat down. She waited, but George remained silent.

Mary Ellen was more than a cook and housekeeper, she was a family confident. She asked, "What's going on, George, you look like a lost calf or something?"

"Oh for crap sake, Mary Ellen, can't I get depressed without you noticing." He smiled and said, "Mary Ellen, you read me like a book. We have major trouble on the Reservation: tribal member or members are into drugs and are stepping out of the Rez, breaking into homes to support their habit. Leadership on the Reservation chooses to ignore the problem, and just hopes it'll go away. We can't catch the dope dealers unless we can have a look in the Reservation, and that is an unwritten no-no.

"We're not much help either, as there are a few unadulterated bigots here, who care less for what happens to the people on the Reservation. In fact, they consider what's going on out there great, just so it stays on the Reservation. Our Sheriff sits back, does nothing, and tells us that every bad thing that happens is by the tribe." He took a sip of coffee, studied Mary Ellen for a moment. "For some obscure reason I find myself in the middle of all this, and it got to me this time."

"It's funny, I remember your Dad facing down the bigots of his time. They need another lesson, and I don't see anyone else doing it but you, George."

Aside from the moccasin telegraph, the best source of information around Wyoming was women talk, or put another way, gossip. In that George was a favorite of most of the women in the county, it follows that it was soon known of his dilemma and frustrations over substance abuse on the Reservation. So Mary Ellen called Rosey, and the two decided to get together. After picking up supplies in Walnut, Rosey met Mary Ellen at Rosey's Café. Ruth from the Church joined them and the three ordered coffee and such. After the hugs and pleasantries were over, the talk turned to George, substance abuse and crime on the Reservation. Mary Ellen said, "I've never seen George so frustrated. He always seems in control no matter what."

Rosey said, "I think I know what that's all about, he finds himself between a rock and a hard place over the recent break-ins and no one from either side will do anything to try to stop it. On top of that, the few remaining bigots are chirping away again about 'it's all Indians, not our fault.' Where's the Sheriff?"

Ruth said, "I agree with that one, Rosey, after church Sunday I heard some chatter which included calling George a breed again. You'd think that by now these clouts would realize that people are people; that some people are smarter than they are themselves, in spite of what they look like."

Mary Ellen said, "George needs support, got any ideas, Girls?"

Ruth said, "I'll talk to Thomas, and see what he can do about the bigots, but at the same time we need to see what Father Daniels on the Reservation has to say. Whereas he is not a Native American, he still holds a plenty powerful sway over there."

Rosey said, "That sounds reasonable. Ruth, can you get Tom to trip on out to Father's place for a Pow Wow? If he'll do that, George could go along."

Ruth said, "I'll see what I can do; it's about time the two of them got together anyway. These two spiritual leaders want and need to comfort and nourish their followings in the same way, and between them they hold a powerful effect on their subjects. To get that man of mine to see another side to the Christian faith, is tough, but I'll work it out."

After leaving Rosey's, Ruth did some shopping at Peterson's, then walked back to the church. She found her husband in his study writing his Sunday sermon. She nodded then went out the rear exit and into the manse where she prepared tea and crackers, returning with a tray-full to the Church. She set the tray on a small table and said, "Tea time, Thomas."

Reverend Mathews glanced around, saw the refreshments, and said, "Oh, alright, Ruth." He moved away from his desk, taking his writing tablet with him. He sat opposite Ruth, seemingly oblivious to the world.

Ruth asked, "Thomas, are you having trouble writing this Sunday's message?"

Tom sort of showed annoyance and said, "It is hard to deliver a message of guidance without at the same time slapping a hand."

"I'm sure, Thomas, that those who need to hear a message of guidance will understand, and those who don't will not be offended. We all need your wisdom and spiritual guidance, especially considering the drug and alcohol troubles we find with our neighbors on the Reservation."

"Well Ruth, those on the Reservation don't hear my sermons."

"That's true, but some transgress against your subjects off the Reservation to support their habits." Ruth was silent for a time. "Thomas, how long has it been since you have spoken to Father Daniels?"

"Oh, why is that important, Ruth?"

"He would be the best one to counsel his family. You need to tell him of the problem, and offer our support."

"Ruth, you know the rules."

"And Thomas, sometimes it is wise to break the rules when it is the right thing to do. You two have been friends for a thousand years."

On this Thanksgiving week end, the Church was filled, and after the choir sang "We Gather Together to Ask the Lord's Blessing" to the strains of "We Praise Thee O God, Our Redeemer," Father Mathews stood up to the pulpit, and started his sermon, the first part of which was thanking the Lord God for this year's abundance, and the blessings of life we enjoy today. He then paused, took off his spectacles, laid them on the pulpit, and said, 'It is not sufficient that we accept the blessings of our Lord without giving to others who are less fortunate than ourselves. We are also reminded that the Lord Thy God sees all of us of all colors as one, and expects no less from us. We need ask ourselves, 'do I follow those tenets?'

"Certainly those who transgress against us need pay for their actions but we need to ask why. It is not natural for Christian souls to do bad things to others. With the recent string of break-ins and robberies in our county comes the question, why. On the surface it may look like the color of one's skin. Below it is substance abuse, and or a lack of meaningful employment. How much blame can we pile on the man who robs to feed his family, or he who has been trapped into the drug culture?

"Where employment is concerned, are we using a blind eye to color and hiring based on skill and ability? Where the other stands, the man that deliberately addicts others for his own gain, is despicable. We must find these evil ones, and put them out of business. They are worse than murderers."

After the closing prayer the Reverend invited all to the Church Garth area for a potluck, supplied by the membership. Groups soon formed, and conversations ensued. All understood what their church leader was saying, but not all agreed with his message. George Bentley and his bride Joan were there, and stood in line for coffee and such. George said to Joan, somewhat humorously, "It would be interesting to hear what those hard heads in this county are thinking after hearing this one."

Joan said, "Uh huh . . . Ruth, Rosey, and I got together a couple of days ago, and decided Father Daniels and Tom need to get together about the substance abuse issue. The two of them have more influence than any of us."

George said, "There are some real mad people out there who had their property stolen while they were out working the land or down below mining. I would think, rhetoric won't solve that one. The real thing that needs fixing is the sale of drugs and alcohol to the Reservation folks. We need to get those guys."

Ruth knew her husband well, and said nothing more about a meeting between the two church leaders. In a sense she had planted the seed and knew the Reverend would have to figure it out by himself. Which, of course, he did.

After the Sunday service, Reverend Mathews put in a call to Father Daniels. "Hello Father, Tom Mathews here. I'd like to chat with you a bit. Would you mind if I paid you a visit in the next day or so?"

"No, that's fine Tom. Come tomorrow if you can."

Father Daniels was in his study when Tom Mathews arrived. The two church leaders greeted each other, evoking reference to God for their time together, then Tom Mathews said, "Father, we have a problem. As you know Reservation folks have been crossing out of Wind River and invading ranches and miners' homes. The people on my side of the fence are getting plenty sore, and if it doesn't stop we're in for some real trouble. They 'll use guns for real! Now I'm sure most of this is due to the use of addictive drugs and alcohol here in Wind River." He paused for a moment, then, "Our Law Enforcement has its hands tied: as you know the system doesn't allow law enforcements crossing the line."

Father Daniels said, "I have to agree with that one Tom, we do have a problem. We both know what the issue is: the lack of jobs here. Idle people sometimes become frustrated and are easy targets for greedy unscrupulous bums, who purposely addict and mortify. This quickly leads to drugs and or alcohol, and that stuff is expensive and comes from your side."

"Well we need help in finding the bad guys," Tom offered, "and it's your side that won't help here. Those on the Reservation are very protective of each other. I might put it another way: they are loyal and will not turn in someone who might be involved.

"Father, I empathize with your views on the lack of jobs on the Reservation, however, as long as drugs and alcohol keep coming into the Reservation, the break-ins will continue. Can't you spread the word out to your parish that it is sometimes necessary to tell of a friend's addiction in order to destroy the source of that friend's demise? If we get a little help maybe we can chip away at the drugs and alcohol problem. In the meantime, how about some conversations with the BIA about some work for those idle ones on the Reservation?"

Father Daniels said, with a bit of humor in his voice, "I don't think you 've ever tried to get any action out of the BIA."

Tom Mathews said, "I guess it's no different trying to get any government action on anything, one has to try though, and in this case they might listen in spite of themselves, as it is approaching anarchy. One more break-in and this county will explode."

"I get the message, Tom. I'll try to meet with the present leader of the Arapaho. I don't promise anything, it's harder now than ever to communicate with them since Chief Running Deer died."

"Father, we need to find the drug and alcohol sellers. We can't do this until someone from the Rez helps us identify the bad ones."

Father Daniels's Sunday message included the following: "Each of us must follow our heart and be there for a friend. It is the best we can do, but sometimes it is not clear as to what is best for that friend. Yes, the friend who has been weak, and given in to the evil ones who has deliberately addicted that friend for his own gain, needs our support, but we cannot help him by a protective silence. Only when we know who the evil one is can we kill the evil, and help that friend.

"To do the best for a friend is to do the worst for the evil one. It is not disloyal or faithless to disclose the weakness of a friend so that one can help destroy those who would continue to prey on that friend."

She came, unsure, and a bit afraid, one Monday morning to the Church office. She knocked gently and was admitted by Father Daniels. She stood silently for a moment. Father Daniels asked, "What is it my child?"

"Father, I have a friend who is in the kind of trouble you spoke of this morning, I like him very much, and I don't wish to hurt him. He is the only friend I have, Father, it is hard."

"And it will be hard, Yellow Bird, we need to see where he meets the bad one."

"What will happen to my friend, Father?"

"Yellow Bird, your friend is already in trouble. We can't help him if we can't find out where and when he meets the evil people to provide him drugs. The White world around you has no authority here. We need to find where they cross the border, and tell the white law when and where."

The young Arapaho sitting in front of Father Daniels nodded showing that she understood, then said, "Thank you Father." She stood up, did a slight bow, and left.

38 | SUBSTANCE ABUSE

Officer Henry, assigned to meet the two o'clock local, sat on the station bench and watched as the three-car train puffed and steamed to a halt. A conductor opened the door to the center car, stepped down and placed the portable steps on the ground for use by descending passengers. A second railroad man slid open the door on the baggage car and set several pieces of baggage down on the station platform.

Nine people descended from the train, and five mounted the steps into the train to travel away. The officer carefully scrutinized the passengers, finding one he wished to question. The man made a quick move to his left, picked up a suit case from the pile outside the baggage car, and ducked into an auto that came out from behind the station, and sped away. All this seemed preplanned, the officer not informed or quick enough to react. He watched the vehicle speed off, cursed, and ran to the police station. He burst into Chief Richardson's office, and told his boss what happened.

Chief Richardson swore, reached for his phone, and called Bill Williams. "Bill, Richardson here, I think our man is here driving around. He's heading south from the train station, probably headed your way. I'm sending out a pair of units, but he's got a plenty big head start, and I don't expect to catch him. The car is a black sedan most likely rented or lifted. I'll check on that one."

"Sounds like you're right, Rich, how about if I see the car maybe I can slow them down enough for your guys to catch up. I sure can't do it alone. If these are dealers they're armed to the teeth, and won't hesitate to shoot anyone that gets in the way."

"Uh huh, Bill, we'll hurry at this end, you be careful, this is a bit out of your scope. You don't have enough assets here. I'll try to help as much as I can."

Bill Williams hung up the phone at the end of his conversation with Chief Richardson. Now he had two armed dope dealers traveling into his county. He despised those vermin who deliberately addicted others for their own gain. He had held the position of 'The Lawman' of Contra County for a long time. This one he was not prepared to handle. He really was all alone, as deputy Leon Roberts wasn't really that 'big brave torpedo' either. Leon was 'not much help when anything dangerous' came along, and would be more of a detriment than an asset in a face-off with the gangster types, and dealers in narcotics certainly fit that bill.

He picked up the phone and called George, "Hi, Bill here, what's goin' on down there in cow country?"

"My cows are healthy and wild, which keeps me plenty busy. To what do I owe this sudden interest in my neck of the woods?"

"You've got two bad guys coming down your way in a black sedan, armed, and probably with a car full of narcotics."

"Well that's just peachy, how'd they get past Richardson?"

"That don't matter, I need to stop them before they have a chance to unload their cargo."

"And I suppose they have automatic weapons, like tommy guns, which makes that shot gun you carry like a toy."

"Uh huh . . . They slipped past Richardson like he wasn't there and went speeding off our way. There's three Glencoe units chasing, but a couple a miles behind. I'm supposed to slow them up a bit, but I don't like the odds much."

"When do you expect them to get here?"

"I figure about thirty minutes or so, you don't suppose you can get that long gun of yours off the wall and meet me at house rock? I'll deputize."

"Will you have Roberts with you?"

"That's a funny, he was out target shooting the other day, and all his targets survived."

George laughed and said, "Best you have him home answering the telephone, just tell him how important that is. He's really a nice guy, we don't want to get 'im killed. I'll bring Jerry, he's great with that pistol a his, and would like a break from punching cows anyway. We'll see you shortly."

Both George and the Sheriff wanted live people. The solving of Steve Harris's murder would never happen without information, and you can't get that sort of stuff from dead people. The road block was set up to give maximum protection to both the law and the criminals. That was the way it was supposed to work anyway, however things don't always happen as planned, and when the black sedan came around House Rock, they slammed on the brakes, skidded sideways and slammed into the Sheriff's station wagon. The Sheriff cursed as did George. They ran out to the pile of broken sheet metal to find two bodies being consumed by burning gasoline. Shortly afterward, Richardson's two units arrived, and all watched from behind house rock as the gas tanks of the two vehicles exploded one at a time. The Sheriff said, "Jeeze, I'm getten too old for this kind a stuff." He said humorously, "George, you're the cattle baron here. Every bird in this county is out to get cha. Get your guns out. I'm supposed to keep the peace, and this happens. You know the syndicate will send somebody else to try to deliver. Me, I gotta get outta the way."

George said, "Now Bill, you know this county would fold up without its favorite sheriff."

"Yes well both of us know that the syndicate won't go

away peacefully after losing here. They want money, and they just lost a bundle. They've had a nice steady income from our users, and I'm expected to see this doesn't happen any more.

George mused to himself over the "Cattle Baron" bit from the Sheriff. The growth of the Arrow—B started back in the late nineteenth century, and indeed there were so-called "Cattle Barons" then, but the term had been dropped as being too abrasive to the have nots. He nevertheless knew what Bill Williams was saying: The three generations of Arrow—B owners had set claim to half of Contra County. The staff included a dozen riders, plus food people and ranch hands to care for the work at home and on the ranch grounds.

George would help the Sheriff in the form of one or more of his staff if it became necessary.

39 | RANCH OWNERSHIP

The law firm of Coleman & Smith was located on the third floor of a loft building on the outskirts of Denver, Colorado. It was small by any measure, newly formed and looking for business. Jay Coleman and Ralph Smith met in law school, and scraped up enough cash between them on graduation to rent space, and hang out a shingle. Up to now the firm had only handled mundane cases, small and yielding miniscule fees. They had to break the mold or vacate their office, and hunt employment working for someone else: a fate which they would shun. They were looking for business, any kind of business, it didn't really matter if it was a little sleazy even.

The great thing about cattle raising in the West is that the food for livestock is free. All you have to do is own a piece of real estate near a water source, and if you have enough land, you can make a living. The more land you control, the more cows, and the more cows, the more bucks. So said, there were good sized pieces of real estate acquired by some of the early ranchers, and some less fortunate, shall we say, smaller ones. Whereas there was a somewhat respectful attitude here, there was also a bit of jealously in the little ones toward the biggies. Thus the larger ranchers sometimes took on the titles of barons, and all it implied.

Jay Coleman's parents live in Glencoe, Wyoming, and when Jay graduated from law school, he obtained a license to practice law in both Wyoming and Colorado. Being of the West, Jay kept up on legal activities in both states. So every time *Baron* George Bentley added to his *Cattle Empire* in Contra County he took note. And, of course, the bigger the Arrow—B enterprise became the more of a prime target it became to the smaller ranchers and miners in the county. Jay Coleman, looking for business for his new practice, studied what was going on within and around the Bentley's Arrow—B Ranch looking for something that might be cause for legal action of some kind that would put the new partnership on the map. In time he found that the enterprise known as the Arrow—B was plenty clean and not a viable target for business. Neither were the interest of the miners.

On one weekend, Jay was home having dinner with his folks who lived in Glencoe. The conversation went like this. "How is the new Law-Man doing, Jay?"

A glum Jay answered, "Business is a bit slow, Dad."

"How slow?"

"Like we only have three clients, and they don't need our services right now."

The father said, "That sounds normal for a new business. The general rule is that you will lose money the first year, break even the second, and begin to earn something on the third. How well-heeled are you?"

"Well not that well. We really need at least one big client."

"So who have you tried?"

"We advertise in several legal publications, We're not supposed to solicit business in Wyoming or Colorado."

Jay's mother got up from the table, wiped her hands on her aprons, and said, "Have you checked on any local happenings?"

"Not really, Mom, what did you have in mind?"

Mom said, "The girls and I have been watching the Bentley divorce case. We think that Betty might have come up short."

Jay's father's mind clicked, and he smiled to himself, thinking how dumb we males can be sometimes. In their lives together, he has often listened to his life mate when it came to people. He waited for his son to respond.

Jay said, "That's interesting, but we are not supposed to solicit business, and," he grinned, "I don't think I want to test the rules at this point in my career."

On a Monday morning after his visit to his folks in Glencoe, Jay and partner Ralph sat in their office doing stuff that clerks or secretaries would do if they could afford one or two. Jay turned to his partner, "Ralph, I've read that George Bentley is getting married, and it's just a few months since his divorce from his first wife. That's got to make for a very upset former Betty Bentley. I also understand that the property settlement was considerably lopsided."

Ralph asked, "Who was the judge, do you know?"

"A Ralph Hastings, why, is that important?"

Ralph Smith guffawed, and said, "I'm not sure you want to mess with a Hastings ruling. That tough old codger rules sometimes by the seat of his pants, and usually is fair if not exactly following the letter of the law."

"From what you have just said, there may be room for movement here. The defendant is rich, and unpopular to some degree. Maybe we can stir things up and work our way into a rich settlement. What are the costs if we fail, and what do we have to gain if we win?"

Ralph hesitated, "The cost, if we fail, will put us out of business; the benefit, if we win, is great. How would you play it, Jay?"

"I'd take it any way we can get it. We're going outa business here anyway."

"So, what do we have, Jay?"

"On the surface, there was a very much unequal property settlement in a divorce case. According to my mother, Hastings may have pushed Betty Bentley into settling. And

Hastings is very friendly with George Bentley. Something smells there. If we can reopen the case, and maybe force a hearing, we might even get Hastings to recuse himself. Getting a new judge to take a look at the evidence would give us a good chance to cause some trouble for Mr. Bentley. But we'll have to go after the judge to do that, and he won't be happy."

Ralph huffed then said, "We don't care about George Bentley, or Hastings. Win or lose, they'll know we're here, better than sitting around twiddling."

Jay said, "Well it's just speculation at this point, in that we need to be invited, and as you know direct soliciting is a no-no in our business."

Jay's mother, Martha, about as solidly western as you can get, was the one who made the pies to take to a neighborhood event, called on a sick friend, or was the one to gather close-by ladies for social activities. She, of course, was a member of the Glencoe Women's Association. Martha was one of five Association members that met once a week, gossiped and played canasta. They were a little like the moccasin telegraph, seeming to be aware of everything local.

At one of these gatherings, before George and Joan tied the knot, the following conversation took place: Martha said, "For sure all of us know about the Bentley divorce. I wonder how it will be with Betty."

A second person said, "I hear that George is already to get married to Joan La Cross, the vet out in Walnut."

And another said, "If I were Betty, I'd be plenty upset. I wonder how long Betty knew of George's uh infidelity?"

Martha said, "Yes, well if he has already scheduled a wedding to this Joan, he must have been doing a lot of moonlight stuff while married to Betty, and I'm sure Betty must have guessed what he was doing some time ago." Martha paused, then, said, "Girls, I think perhaps Betty needs our support about now. Let's go pay her a visit."

Another voice said, "Some men seem to get away with

murder without paying their dues." She continued, "I hear that the property settlement gives the huge Arrow—B ranch to George, and the tiny Harris ranch to Betty. That doesn't seem fair to me."

It was a full week before the five staunch believers in women's rights found the time and vehicle to make the trip to the Harris ranch. The ranch live-in saw them coming and met them at the front door. She said, "Yes?"

Martha asked, "Is Mrs. Bentley at home?"

"Yes, but I hesitate to allow five people to see her all at once. This could upset her. Who are you people, and why are you here?"

Martha spoke up, "Miss, whoever you are, we are friends of Betty, please tell her that we are here. We're members of the Glencoe Women's Association. I think you will find that Betty will wish to see us."

"Alright, my name is Mary, and I take care of Betty. I must see that she is not disturbed or upset."

Betty met the "girls" as they entered the house. She greeted each, sat them down, and they began to chat about old times. Finally Martha asked, "Has it been hard for you, Betty, to do the divorce?"

Betty replied with a comment that was entirely irrelevant to the subject, small talk you might say.

Martha, a bit embarrassed and puzzled said, "Betty, we are concerned that you were not treated fairly by the divorce settlement. Could we talk about if for a bit?"

Betty studied her five guests for a few moments, naming each in her mind, and how and why she knew each. She turned to Martha and said, "I feel alone."

Martha said, "Betty, we are concerned with getting your share of the property involved. In that George receives the Arrow—B free and clear, and you the Harris Ranch. Did you go for that?"

"I wasn't sure what my rights were, Martha, and I went by what the court ordered. Wasn't that right?"

Martha said, "Well Betty, the five of us don't think you were treated fairly." Martha waited for a moment, then, "Did you have an attorney?"

"The Court appointed one for me, yes. I didn't know any lawyers."

"What is the name of your, court appointed attorney?"

Betty answered, "Dean Brooks."

One of the ladies said, "Oh I know him, he works for the court, and is sort of an assistant to Judge Hastings. His wife and I are old friends."

Martha asked, "Betty, how did Judge Hastings pick Dean Brooks to be your lawyer?"

"I really don't know."

Martha said, "And, of course, Dean Brooks would favor any word from Judge Hastings. Betty, I think you need an attorney that is totally independent of the court. Would you consider that?"

Betty hesitated, she thought of her daughter, who has been taken from her. She was angry now, as she knew George was about to marry again, so soon after their divorce. She looked plaintively at the five women, "Yes, Martha, do you know of a lawyer who would do the best for me?"

"The choice will have to be yours, Betty, They advertise in the Cattlemen's Journal and the Lawyer's Friend. Oh, and my son is an attorney."

Ralph Smith of Coleman & Smith received the call from Betty's live-in companion. He answered, "Coleman & Smith, Attorneys at Law."

The voice said, "Would your firm be interested in representing a Mrs. Betty Harris in an action against her ex-husband, George Bentley?"

Ralph answered, "Yes, I would have to meet with Mrs. Bentley, and discuss her case first however, before I could answer that question. I will forward a letter of introduction to my firm so that she will know a bit about us before we meet." Ralph's letter went out the same day:

Coleman & Smith, Attorneys at Law
Central Bank Building
1500 Arapahoe, Fifth Floor
Denver, Colorado

Mrs. Betty Bentley, née Harris
#1 Harris Ranch Road
Contra County, Wyoming.

Dear Mrs. Bentley:
In response to your call concerning the recent litigation: Bentley verses Bentley case. I am so glad that you did.
It is my understanding that you have met Mrs. Martha Coleman, mother of Jay Coleman, lawyer in the law firm of Coleman & Smith. She has told us some things about your recent divorce and specifically the property settlement thereof. I must say that I was shocked to hear that you did not receive half of Mr. Bentley's assets as well as very substantial, monthly alimony payments.
Our firm is staffed and experienced in the practice of representing women in cases such as yours. I know the prospects of addressing a powerful man like George Bentley in a court of law may seem daunting, but that's why you need professional help.
I would like to meet with you, perhaps at the Harris Ranch, to discuss your situation. This meeting will, of course, be at no cost to you. I will be in your area from August 10th through August 20th and if this time span is convenient to you, fine. Just call my office and inform my secretary.
I look forward to meeting you in person very soon.
Kindest regards,
Ralph Smith.

Betty had periods of "close to saneness." Whereas Dr. Lewis, Betty's psychiatrist, had testified to the extent that Betty was unable to reconcile with the present time or reality, he also said that she might slip into short periods of reality if stimulated. Betty had accepted her divorce from George, but now, hearing of George's marriage to another plus losing

Eva, she became paranoid and visibly angry, and eager to agree to be represented by almost anyone that looked or sounded legal.

The first meeting between Betty Harris, the owner of the Harris Ranch, and Ray Coleman, Attorney at Law, resulted in a contract between the two. The terms of the contract defined the goal of the legal action involved, and the fee agreement reached. The fee for the legal services provided included a small retainer and a contingent percentage amount of any settlement or judgement that awarded money or property to Betty. Ray left the ranch house with his new client's permission and authority to delve into ranch records, the prior marriage, and to file any legal actions necessary to challenge the divorce settlement and get a new trial.

Betty's new lawyers spent some time drafting a lengthy petition to set aside the divorce decree and the settlement agreement between George and Betty. They looked at property records for both the Harris Ranch and the Arrow---B. They talked to Ray's mother Martha to get gossip about the Arrow—B Ranch operations and potential value. The written settlement agreement between their client and George Bentley seemed to go against Betty, except that George appeared to be on the hook for some of Betty's expenses and care without any time limitation in the future. That part was good, because it meant that the divorce court might still have jurisdiction to protect Betty if she needed a lot more money. And as far as these two lawyers were concerned, Betty would need a lot more money! The locals also confirmed that George Bentley and Judge Hastings had been friends for a long time before the divorce case was filed. People loved to gossip, and there was plenty of that concerning George Bentley all over Contra County. They decided not to speak with Dean Brooks before they filed their court papers because they didn't want him to interfere with their aggressive new approach by trying to talk to Betty before they got to court. Brooks was no longer Betty's divorce attorney, but he didn't have to know that yet.

Their legal strategy was to go in fast and hard, make accusations against George Bentley, Judge Hastings, and Dean Brooks, ask for a hearing and present their client as a hapless, wronged woman who had been intimidated and taken advantage of by an old boys network of buddy-buddy men without understanding her rights. If they shook things up enough, they felt confident that they could force their case away from Judge Hastings and get a hearing before an unbiased judge. But due to the nature of divorce cases, they had to start first by filing papers in the court that approved the settlement agreement signed by Betty. They reviewed what was a very scant court record of the divorce proceedings, and they prepared a sworn affidavit for their new client to sign as factual support for the petition. Betty didn't spend much time looking at the paperwork, but she signed the affidavit under penalty of perjury and the once idle lawyers began to feel excited about challenging George Bentley and his buddy, Judge Hastings, in a courtroom.

Judge Hastings sat in his office reviewing the material his staff had prepared for his action for this day. The list was short, and more or less routine until he got to a stack of papers from Coleman & Smith. He saw the substitution of attorney on top of Betty's petition for a new trial and her request to recuse him from hearing the case. Then he flipped quickly to the affidavit that Betty signed and he read it. He didn't even look at the rest of the paperwork. He hit the buzzer on his desk and when his secretary answered the intercom he said, "What is this? And who the heck are Coleman & Smith?"

"I don't know. Two young guys that think they're hotshots from Denver I guess."

"Well, get Dean in here as soon as you can!"

Judge Hastings got up and walked around his office, sputtering and angry. He was too old for this. What was Betty thinking? Or was she thinking? She had accused him of bias and improper conduct as a judge! Her affidavit said that he had taken advantage of her, that she didn't want to settle, and that she was forced into it. She claimed that he conspired with George Bentley and Dean Brooks to deprive her of her rightful assets. Conspired? She demanded a new trial with her new lawyers in court to protect her from a bunch of hostile ranchers and lawyers and judges! Well, not judges, just one judge. Him.

When Dean Brooks showed up, Ralph exploded at him, and explained Betty's petition, or at least the parts he had read, before he finally settled down. He said, "Dean, find out what you can about these guys. I think they are two phonies."

"I already have, Judge. I think Betty is only their third client."

"And they need business?"

"They're having trouble paying the rent."

That seemed to make Ralph feel better. He was beginning to understand. Dean said, "Look, we both know Betty's situation, and I don't think they do. Not really."

"Well, Dean, since you don't represent Betty anymore, let's discuss this a bit." And the two men went through the legal and factual issues in the petition methodically. When they were done, Ralph said, "There's really nothing new here. No new evidence. No new legal arguments. The only thing that's new at this point is Betty saying that she was coerced into settling. Was she?"

"No, Ralph. She wanted to settle and be done with it. The courthouse scared her I think."

Judge Hastings thought about all of it. At some point, he might have to recuse himself, especially if he came to believe that Betty honestly felt bullied and intimidated and didn't really want to settle. He would have to hear that from her, even though her affidavit said as much. He said, "Forget the merits of the underlying divorce case for now. First, I need to decide whether there are grounds to even have a hearing on the settlement agreement. That way, I'll know whether I'm the right judge to hear this case or whether I should pack it all up and send it to a different county for a full hearing. I'd hate to do that to George, you know, change the venue. He's been through enough already, and he'd end up paying for all of this."

"What about these new guys in town, Coleman & Smith?"

"It really doesn't matter what these new guys want, Dean, it's Betty that matters. I'm not even sure Betty is capable of understanding any of this." Ralph Hastings decided to do his best for these two people he had tried to protect, Betty Harris and George Bentley, and that did not include recusing himself … yet. But he also didn't have to tolerate lawyers who make wild accusations, so he planned to deal with them as well.

Judge Hastings dismissed Dean Brooks, picked up the phone and dialed the number for Coleman & Smith.

"Coleman & Smith, Attorneys at Law," answered Ralph Smith.

"This is Judge Hastings. Who am I speaking to?"

"Ralph Smith."

"Two o'clock, my courtroom, tomorrow, bring your client and we'll talk about her petition."

"Judge Hastings?" said Smith. But it was too late. The judge had hung up. Jay Coleman stared at his law partner, then said, "That was Judge Hastings? What did he say?"

"We have a hearing tomorrow at two o'clock and we have to bring Betty."

"That was fast. Was he mad?"

"Couldn't tell, but I don't imagine he's singing our praises right now. Of course, if we can get him angry in court, even if he explodes on us, we're making progress. No one said this would be easy."

Peter Forbes received a similar phone call from Judge Hastings, although not quite as short, and when he called George to tell him about Betty's petition and the hearing,

George was shocked … and mad.

At two o'clock the next day, George found himself sitting outside Judge Hastings courtroom, with Dean Brooks. Everyone else including Peter Forbes was inside, and George was fuming. Peter had explained that Judge Hastings wanted the other "conspirators" outside the courtroom so he could hear first from Betty and her lawyers. But when George had seen Betty walk past him into the courtroom with her new lawyers, he also felt sadness. Betty had a vacant look in her eyes, and she turned briefly toward George but said nothing. She didn't look angry, more like she was lost.

Inside, they had covered the introductions for the record, and Judge Hastings was exceedingly pleasant and kind. This concerned Ralph and Jay who had decided to attend the hearing together as a show of force. They had expected Judge Hastings to be angry, in fact they had hoped for it. The first thing Judge Hastings did was accept the substitution of attorney request, so that Coleman & Smith was now the law firm of record representing Betty Harris.

Judge Hastings looked at Jay Coleman who was standing next to Betty, and she was seated at the table with Ralph Smith. "This hearing is going to be informal. I'm not going to consider the petition just yet. My purpose here is to listen to Betty Harris share her feelings about the settlement agreement that she signed and which is a part of the court record."

Jay Coleman objected. "But Judge, our client is scared and intimidated by this whole process. She doesn't want to talk to you. With all due respect, you are the problem your Honor. We need to have a new judge hear this case."

Judge Hastings stared at Jay Coleman for a few seconds, then, instead of getting angry, he smiled. "I'm sure that's what you want, Mr. Coleman. But I've known Betty for most of her life and she knows me. She's been an important part of this community for a long time. I knew her father, and we are all still hurting from his murder, even after all these years." He looked at Betty as he spoke, and while she mostly looked down at the table in front of her, Betty's eyes came up to meet the Judge's eyes when he spoke of Steve Harris.

"Steve Harris was a good man, and he loved his daughter. And someday, I'm sure the law in these parts will finally get around to finding the man who murdered Steve."

Betty seemed to clear her head just a bit as the Judge continued speaking.

"Before Steve was murdered, Betty met a young man and fell in love. Her marriage to George Bentley was no small matter. Everyone knows Betty here, and everyone knows George Bentley, and that includes me. We all live in this community, Mr. Coleman, and we all know Betty's pain. We feel it too. We feel a strong obligation to protect our own here, Mr. Coleman, and we will continue trying to do what is in your client's best interests, whether that relates to the divorce, her continued care and well-being, the care for her child, Eva, the protection of the Harris Ranch, or the hunt for the murderer of Steve Harris. And when we find that murderer, Mr. Coleman, we will deal with him properly and according to the law, just as we deal with all legal matters here in this county.

"Now, I don't know how you fellas do things down in Denver, but here in Contra County we like to know the truth. So, why don't you sit down for a few minutes, Mr. Coleman, and Betty, why don't you just tell me how you are feeling. Take your time. I want to know if you would like me to open this thing up and let you have a new day in court? Is that what you want, Betty?"

Betty sat very still, looking down at the table and it was awhile before she moved. When she did, the Judge thought he saw a tear at the corner of her eye, but she didn't speak. She just stood up, leaned down toward Jay Coleman and whispered in his ear. Then they all watched as she walked slowly out of the courtroom, past George, and then out the front door of the building.

Inside the courtroom, Judge Hastings looked at Jay Coleman and waited patiently. Finally, the young lawyer stood up and faced the judge.

"Your Honor, Betty Harris has terminated our representation of her in this matter. I can no longer speak on her behalf."

Judge Hastings looked at Peter who remained mum. But after a minute, Peter took the hint, stood up and said, "Judge, under the circumstances, I request that you dismiss the petition without prejudice and that this proceeding be terminated."

"That will be my order, boys. Thank you all for your time today." Then, with a hint of a smile, "Mr. Coleman and Mr. Smith, enjoy your drive back to Denver."

Later, as the two shell-shocked lawyers tried to recover from being fired by their client in open court, they considered their options. Jay Coleman faced his partner with, "What do we do now, this was your idea?"

"We don't have a client, so we don't have a case. We're done, unless we decide to sue Betty Harris."

"She did sign that affidavit, and our fee agreement, so we have her on the record. She should pay us for our time at least."

"True, but if we sue her, it will have to be here, in her town."

"Yeah, and I'm not getting the warm fuzzies from Judge Hastings."

"Well we started this thing knowing it might be trouble. Remember, we agreed that losing was probable, but that we would try to bully our way into a settlement."

Jay said, "Yes, but my mother and the girls she hangs out with didn't tell us how sick Betty Harris really is. Did you see the look in her eyes when she fired us? I'm not up for suing a crazy person."

40 | DRUG TRAFFIC

Chief of Police Allen Richardson, of Glencoe, looked through the bars of one of the city's jail cells at a shaking figure dressed in shabby dirty clothes. The man, in his early twenties, was there for the second time in a month for a misdemeanor charge of pilfering food from a local market. The Chief asked, "Tony, how long has it been since you had a meal?"

The figure in the cell mumbled incoherently, then looked pleadingly at the Chief.

The Chief walked back into his office, he called in his secretary and said, "See to getting some food into the prisoner in cell three, and then bring him into my office."

Tony from the Wind River Reservation sat uneasily across from Chief Richardson trying to still a shaking hand. The Chief asked, "Do you have a home, Tony?"

"No sir."

"Well Tony, you can't go on this way, stealing food, or anything else for that matter is against the law. Do you have relatives on the Reservation?"

Tony didn't answer. He fidgeted, the Chief thumbed the desk with a pencil, waiting. He finally said, "Tony, are you using drugs?"

The no answer from Tony said yes. The Chief escorted Tony back into the jail cell. He considered several options for Tony. This man was obviously deep into the drug culture flourishing on the Wind River Reservation. Taking drugs meant paying heavily. Where did this miserable specimen of humanity get the cash? This may explain the rash of robberies of late. He could only hold Tony for so long on a misdemeanor charge.

The Chief called his friend County sheriff Bill Williams. "Hello Bill, Allen here. How's sheriffing these days?"

"Good, how's the wife and family?"

"June's good, and the kids are an expected pain." He paused a bit, then, said, "You shoulda had a family, Bill."

"Wal, I sorta do. All the kids around here look up to the big powerful Sheriff. So what did you make this call for, it certainly wasn't about family?"

"I thought you might be interested in a man I have in jail."

"Go on."

"His name is Tony, and he's on some kind of drugs. He does little stuff, and ends up here in my jail. He looks pure Arapaho, and is scared to death."

Bill said, "Let me think on that one for a time, Al, how long can you keep him?"

"About a week."

"So, give me a couple a days, I want to check on something here before I come up there."

Bill Williams called George Bentley on the Arrow—B. He had to leave a message as George was out on the range. In time George called the Sheriff's office, and asked, "To what worthy cause do you want me to contribute this time, Bill?"

"If I ever got a reasonable response from you, I'd faint. Got a question for you, didn't you have a young Indian boy named Tony, working for you a while back?"

"Uh huh, so?"

"He's sitting in one of Richardson's jail cells. He's on drugs, and I'm interested in where and from who, he gets the stuff."

"You goin' up there to take a look?"

"Thought I would, there's got to be a pusher that comes on the Reservation to ply his trade."

George and the Sheriff joined Chief Richardson in the Glencoe police station. The Chief said, "George, I thought maybe you would like to talk with the prisoner alone. He's said nothing since he got here."

George nodded and followed the Sheriff into the cell area. The Sheriff let George into Tony's cell and left.

"What happened, Tony?" There was no response from Tony. "You were plenty good with horses. You were useful and proud. What happened?"

Back in Richardson's office, George said, "Nothing from him. And from past behavior, the residents of Wind River won't help either. They protect their own regardless. This specimen looks locked into trouble. He has no home, he doesn't take care of himself. He is entirely dependent on some vile creature making money off of his demise. We need to find out who that is, and when we do we'll probably find the killer of Steve Harris and other crimes."

The Sheriff said, "That's where we started from. There's nothing new here."

The Chief said, "I can only hold this man for seven days. We need to do something before I let him out."

George said, "Well maybe not, suppose you let him escape, and we follow. He's so knocked out right now, and is needing, he will go directly to his supplier."

"Well that sounds good in theory, just who did you have in mind?" asked the Chief.

George said, "You're not to worry, just tell me where and when you let him out. I'm sure you won't turn him loose on the streets of Glencoe. He belongs on the Reservation someplace. I can take it from there, remember, I'm half Arapaho."

"Chief Richardson twirled the pencil on his desk, and

considered this for a moment. He had to reconcile his long standing practice to stay away and out of Reservation real estate. He asked, "You want me to dump him off somewhere in the Reservation, within walking space of a village?"

"Well, something like that, You fatten him up for a week, drive him to some spot along the Reservation road, and let 'im off, I'll be nearby, awachin."

"You forget, this character has been buying drugs, the pusher doesn't expect to give them away, therefore Tony here must have to pay somehow. That means that he probably steals bigtime, and we haven't caught him at it yet. I've got him in jail here for stealing a loaf of bread. That's nothing. My guess is that he has a stash somewhere to tide him over, and the stash gets replenished every so often. I don't want to lose track of this guy either."

Bill said, "I can go with that one, Al, the space you're talking about is big and wild. Losing this guy out there would be real easy."

George said, "You guys are sure right on that one, but you forget that I have the moccasin telegraph, and it seems to know all. He'll head for his stash first, pick up some money, then make contact, and finally meet for the purchase." We need to find what that contact is, and go from there. Tony was a wrangler, and a good one, working for me. The Reservation has a big time drug problem. Fixing this one won't solve all their problems, but it will be a start to put this one out of business. I have a strong dislike for the one that got to Tony, and I might have to spend some hours on my horse or sleep on the ground to get him, but I will."

Chief Richardson said, "I'll keep him as long as the Court will let me, and then call you. I can let him off somewhere on Foothill Road. Good luck."

On the way back to Walnut, George said, "Bill, maybe we can tie this one to the killer of Steve Harris. These drug types are greedy, and the one or ones we've been looking for is back."

Bill said, "That kind of speculation is wild, that case is many years old. On the other matter, I'm a sitting Sheriff, as you have told me many times, with half a state to cover. If you want to stay out in those mountains of ours, waiting for a ghost drug dealer, be my guest."

"I'm sure glad you recognize your talent for sitting.

The Sheriff and George pulled into Walnut, George retrieved his pick-up and drove over to Joan's Veterinary Clinic. He found Joan in her office, treating a large Irish Terrier. He kissed her, getting a mild response. He said, "I see you are tied up for the moment. I could leave and see you at home."

"Oh for Pete's sake, George, stay put until I get done with Rover." She finished with her patient, put him in a large cage, giving him a last pat on his head and closed the cage door. She then turned to her husband, reached up and kissed him with meaning.

They broke apart and Joan asked, "What brings you into town, my love?"

"Do you remember a young Arapaho lad by the name of Tony that used to work stock in our corral?"

"Oh sure, and he had a parent or family member he used to visit on the Reservation. Why do you ask?"

"He's in one of Richardson's jail cells in Glencoe."

"So what's he doing there"?

"The kid's on drugs and doing bad things."

Joan, who had been married a few months now, has learned to read George quite well. She said, "This being a law enforcement matter I guess Chief Richardson will have the problem or will it be Sheriff Bill?"

"Well, it sort of got me involved."

"How, sort of?"

"I may have to spend a night or two out up in the mountains."

"And of course you'll have guns, as the bad guys will too, and they'll use them, as they don't want to be caught. I don't suppose you'd consider letting the law do this thing, we 're in the twentieth century, not the nineteenth, when the shootouts were going on?"

George laughed, and said, "Sweetheart, the man who got Tony hooked on drugs is super bad. He needs to be found, and put in prison. I'm just doing this to see if I can find where Tony gets his drugs."

"You're going to do this thing, then?"

"Well, I'm kind of committed, like I've promised."

"Oh sure, that's a typical man for you, the next thing I expect is for you to head up a posse, and ride off in the sunset on your favorite horse calling for all ill-doers to surrender."

Chief Richardson saw to the feeding and housing of the jailed Tony for almost two weeks before the law stepped in and forced him to release his prisoner. Tony spent much of that time going through withdrawals and putting on a bit of health. In that Glencoe is surrounded by Wind River Reservation land, the chief had only to release Tony at the edge of town to put him back on the Reservation. So, a larger than life Tony found himself walking down the beginning of Foothill road, toward a small Arapaho village, some five miles distant. He had water, and some food, but no money with him. He would have to walk those miles to reach his kin, and meld back into the Indian society of the Reservation.

The Arrow—B ranch had several Native Americans from the Reservation on its payroll who had relatives or close ties on the Wind River Reservation. It followed that Tony's movements were far from secret, and usually found their way onto the moccasin telegraph within hours.

So everyone knew where and when Tony went. He wasn't that welcome in the village either as they had enough people without jobs and on drugs already. So on alert from Chief Richardson, George became aware of Tony's activities and placed himself half way up Portal Mesa in a niche with good visibility of the valley below. A good set of field glasses and a bright day allowed for keeping track of Tony as he walked toward the village. Tony made for a nearby pile of rocks, disappeared in the back and soon emerged, then headed down the road. George climbed on his horse and followed, managing to stay out of Tony's view. In time, Tony stopped again by a rocky outcropping and left, or picked up something, then reappeared and headed toward the village. George decided the place to watch was along the road. And that's what he did. In time a figure atop a horse emerged from the bushes, proceeded to where Tony had stopped, dismounted and went behind the rocks, George moved down to where the rider was, and faced him as he came out from behind the rocks. He leaned on his saddle horn, pointing his pistol at the man. He said, "Just sort of ease yourself onto the ground and turn over, I'm not so sure about this trigger finger of mine."

The man did what he was told, and said, "What is this, a hold-up?"

"Not exactly, but it may seem that way, let's see what you have in your pockets." George leaned over the figure on the ground, There was some money, pocket knife, a small note book, and a stubby pencil. George asked, I suppose you're having an afternoon ride for the pleasure of it, or maybe there's something else?"

The figure on the ground answered with a curse, and promised to go to the law. "You have nothing here."

"Well, let's see, you are deep in the Wind River Indian Reservation, you are obviously not Native American, and you have been hiding in the bushes. The residents here are not known for their hospitality toward strangers, and you sure fit that bill. You just collected moola left by a known drug addict which you are supposed to deliver to a pusher, and can't, which will make you slightly unpopular in that quarter. And he likes to get his dough. Now, not too long ago, two delivery boys like yourself died of gunshot poison, and I think you might consider telling me what I need to know. If I let you go, you're in trouble anyway because I'm sure to let the circuit know that you ratted."

The figure on the ground said, "You can't prove any of this,"

George said, "I don't need to, you're in a dangerous business. Tell me the who when and where. The law will do their thing, and you will maybe not die."

After a long silence from the figure below, the man said, "I don't know much. I pick up the money here and drop it off at a spot in Picket."

"So where is that drop-off spot?"

"There is a built in compartment under the sink in the men's restroom of the Gold Strike Bar and Grill."

George was home for the evening after his time with the drug money messenger. Joan had finished at the Clinic, and there came a relaxing time for both over a glass of wine. There was the usual ranch talk, and a bit about what went on at Joan's clinic. Finally Joan asked about George's day. He told her. She put down her wine glass, faced George and said, "You mentioned a pocket knife, what else did this compliant messenger boy have on him?"

"Well, he did have a pistol stuck in his belt."

"You're going to do this stuff then, the next thing I can expect is to hear you call out 'Hi ho Silver' and gallop off to get the evil one. I bet you haven't even called the Sheriff yet."

"Joan, you know I can't leave this one. I have a young man whom I liked, ruined for life perhaps because some greedy man gets him hooked on drugs. I have one that killed Betty's father, and is invading, perhaps, my kinfolk's home, Wind River. I'll do my best to take care, but I can't let it go."

Joan was silent. She knew she must support this man. It wasn't fair, she had waited so long for him to be free for her. She went to him, sat close, and put her arms around him. "Be careful, I love you."

George called the Sheriff at his home. "Evenin' Bill,

how's things on Elm Street?"

"Just good, but I'm sure you're not interested in my domestic life, what's goin' on?"

"You know our boy, Tony, well Allen finally let him out, I followed so to speak and came up with the spot where they switch the money with the drugs?"

"Do they know you know, you're dealing with tough. Where?"

"Men's restroom in the Gold Strike in Picket. Aren't you sort of friendly with a poke that works there?"

"Uh huh, you think maybe he can watch things a bit and tell us something?"

George said, "Why don't you set it up, and see what happens."

Stanley didn't like to think of himself as a janitor but that was the way things were at the Gold Strike. He served at the bar on occasion and the tips were plenty good, so he skipped over the toilet cleaning thing, and kind of found a home there. Well he also was kind of a son to Bill Williams, the Sheriff, as Bill helped bring him up. Bill thought for some time before he decided to involve Stanley in the drug thing going on in the Gold Strike, but he finally decided to do it.

On a Sunday afternoon on the Church Garth area, the townspeople gathered for a potluck. Stanley was there and so was the Sheriff. The Sheriff walked over to where Stanley was seated and said, "Hello Stan, getting enough to eat?"

Stanley responded with a nod, and said, "Hello Bill. How's my Mom?"

"She's fine. I talked with her yesterday. She wishes you would come by more often. Things going okay?"

"Okay with me but there's a nutty one or two every night shows up at the Gold."

"How'd you like to help me with a law-enforcement job, Stanley?"

"Oh, I'd like that, Sheriff."

"This has to be very much a secret between us, Stanley, do

you think you can keep that kind of a promise?"

"I sure do, Mr. Sheriff."

"Alright, I need to know who visits the men's restroom a lot where you work. Just watch for a few days, and when you have something, stop by the office and tell me."

Stanley came up with a first name, and a plenty good description for the Sheriff, who called George and said, "We have a first name, and what he looks like. He comes into the Gold Strike almost every night."

George said with a bit of humor in his voice, "I don't suppose you'd let me suggest something? You might think I'm giving instructions to the Sheriff."

"Yes, well you do have an obnoxious way about you sometimes, but go ahead, I'll listen."

"How about we have a few drinks at the Gold Strike? Oh I think they serve a Blue-Plate-Special on Friday nights. Maybe we can get a look ourselves?"

"I'll go for that. How do you want to do it?"

"We go in my vehicle, and get dirtied up a bit. No badge of course."

"You're asking a lawman to take off his badge?"

"Uh huh, you know that's a rough place. I don't think we will be very welcome as the up-and-up types."

The hamlet of Picket consisted of a rooming house, feed store, blacksmith, saloon and a livery. The livery, since transportation had gradually gone from wagons and horses to motor bikes and half tons, was now more a garage than a livery. It nevertheless had kept its name and color. The rooming house accommodated relatives of the area folk, and overnight revelers perhaps from surrounding ranches. The Gold Strike did most of its business on Friday nights which was payday for many of the surrounding ranches.

The Sheriff and George came around seven when things were in full swing. Stanley was doing an assisted bar tender thing and managed to avoid recognizing either of them. In time a hefty looking woman acting as barmaid took their order for a pair of beers and left. The room juke-box got turned on, and country music blared out drowning any vestige of reasonable conversation.

The traffic going in and out of the men's restroom was constant and seemed normal given the circumstances. In time, George entered, securing the slide lock from the inside. He used the urinal then went to the wash basin, being careful not to show any interest under the sink.

Back to the table he said to the Sheriff, "These guys have left nothing to chance. There are peep holes all over the room, and I think anyone who goes under the sink will be spotted. Have you seen our man?"

"He's sitting over in the corner facing the men's room that you just came out of. He seemed to be awfully interested in you."

"That's nice, now what do we do?"

"We finish our beer, and leave. This rabbit is not a valid suspect at this time. We don't have a case, and we will lose what we have if we do anything."

"Uh huh, knowing who is a start, Bill." George gave a little chuckle. "Joan's giving me a hard time. She feels all this should be handled by law enforcement, and I should stop getting involved."

"So, what's her problem?"

"She doesn't like guns."

"So, we go back a long way you and I, and much as I would agree with Joan, it seems, if I remember correctly, we both treat guns respectfully. Women will be women."

"Well we need to find out more about this Joe from Picket. The only way I can see to do that is to watch where he goes when he goes somewhere. That means some kind of surveillance."

The Sheriff said, "Don't look at me, I gave up the outdoor stuff sometime ago."

"So what did we make this stupid trip for?"

The Sheriff got up from his chair, indicated it was time to

leave, and said, "I got Richardson to let me into their files. I located that promissory note. You know the one we found in that tin can in the wall at the Double U. That's the only evidence we have about that Steve Harris killing."

"Go on."

George paid their bar bill, left a tip, and the two men walked out to the parking lot. The Sheriff said, "I figure the murderer of our friend, Steve Harris, is still around. Selling drugs is a profitable business."

"This is a nasty business Bill, people get killed, and this cherub would not be particular about who. We certainly can't use Stanley or any other of our friends or neighbors without a whole lot of caution.

"We both know what's at stake here. I've been ruminating over this thing since Steve Harris was killed. He was a good friend of mine, besides being my father-in-law. It looks like you might be moving again, and I intend to get involved. You said you had a look at the promissory note left in Anderson's bedroom, anything new there?"

"There was also a study by a hand writing man, stating that the suspect was left handed, and possibly from Europe."

"That's interesting, anything more?"

"The report indicated European education based on letter shapes and the number seven. The sevens all showed a short line drawn through the stem in the written promissory note. Also, the letters sloped left, which tells us the writer was left handed."

On a Friday at noon Joan sat with Rosey in Rosey's Café, now operated by Amy for the new owners, open for breakfast and lunch only. Rosey was on her weekly visit to Walnut to pick up mail, supplies and gossip. Area womenfolk kept track of happenings and such this way, as a once-a-week newsletter didn't cover the moods, trials, and tribulations of the community like "girl talk." That is to say, it's easy to record and announce stats in the ranching and mining communities, but women want to know more, like eight-month pregnancies, or prom-night escapades by sixteen-year-olds.

Given Rosey's penchant for practical wisdom, it usually seemed like problems arising within the community had to be discussed with Rosey. Whereas her marriage to Pete took her away from availability in the community, folks still sought her out when they felt a need for counsel. Joan included. Rosey asked, "Anything interesting happening in your life, Joan?"

Joan demurred, sipped from her coffee mug, and turned the conversation another way. In a bit she said, "We all miss you when we come in here, Rosey. How's the rancher's wife holding out?"

"I miss seeing all of you like I used to, Joan, but I found a fine man. He is very good to me, he makes me feel loved and needed, and this is my new life." Rosey waited, feeling Joan wanted to tell her something, but didn't know how.

Amy came out from the kitchen with a batch of cinnamon rolls just fresh out of the oven. She said, "Rosey, I had to learn how to do this." She gave a little laugh, "Your customers of old demanded it."

Rosey asked, "How's it going with you and Cliff, Amy?"

"Fine, Rosey, he's headed for ranch management and Mr. Bentley likes him. I had hoped he would go to college with me, but that's not in the cards for him. I think we're in love, Rosey, and my dad thinks I'm still a child, which is a tough one for me."

Rosey reached over and took Amy's hand, "Hang in there kid, I'm sure your dad loves you, and is trying to protect you from his idea of a hostile world."

Amy left, and Rosey said, "These two young people have it all, the need to do well for each other. I don't think they need any advice from me or anyone else for that matter. I will sit back and watch, with interest." She looked over the top of her coffee mug into Joan's eyes, saw a flicker of uncertainty, and said, "Sometimes it is hard to stand alone on things. We, each of us, no matter how strong we feel, need to share sometimes."

Joan said, "Rosey, You knew I was struggling with

something as soon as we sat down together . . . I can only tell you how much I am in love with my chosen one, and how much I dread the thought of ever losing him. I waited for over three years to find him free and able to be my lover. Now I find a serious risk to that love, and I don't know how to handle that. I have been able to overcome the apparent conflict between fixing sick and ailing animals and raising animals to be slaughtered. That was hard for me at first, but it seems to be the natural way of things. Oh Rosey, I don't like guns!

"Well, you know of the drug abuse problem on the Reservation. George has decided to assist law enforcement in trying to capture or put out of business the drug dealers. This means putting on a side arm and packing a long barrel wherever and whenever he goes someplace. Drug dealers use guns with impunity, and mixing up in this business is always risky."

Rosey said, "And you don't like guns."

"He won't leave law enforcing to the law. And you heard about the two pushers that ended up with bullet holes in their heads after leaving a Glencoe jail? What's more, he thinks that the killer of Steve Harris has returned. That makes him fair game and a good target."

Rosey said, "I guess you are being tested, Joan, and it's within you to face this one straight on. Most of us never get a chance to love to the limit, to be tested of ourselves, or to find out really what we're made of. Somehow you will accept the needs of your spouse and tolerate. Somehow, Joan, it will happen if you truly love as you say."

41 | BIGOTRY, AGAIN

Leonard MacLaren migrated from his native Scotland to the United States in the late nineteenth century. He joined hundreds of others on the eastern seaboard, and hearing of the available land parcels under the Homestead Act, traveled west and took up ranching in Contra County, Wyoming. Utilizing adjacent government land he successfully raised cattle, started the Arrow—B ranch and added to his original homesteaded property.

Richard Bentley, a nephew of Leonard MacLaren, inherited the Arrow—B and expanded those ranch holdings. At the untimely death of Richard Bentley, George, his son became the owner, and further expanded the ranch holdings, including ranch buildings, wells, roads, and remote line shacks. This was how the Arrow—B came into being, and grew into one of the largest ranches in the West. This was not accomplished without controversy. The nearby Wind River Indian Reservation, and the bigotry that existed within the close by ranching community toward Native Americans, was ever present.

From the start, the owners of the Arrow—B respected the Native Americans, and hired them as hands whenever possible. Notwithstanding the fact that George Bentley was born of an Indian Princess, and would fit the category of "Breed," his popularity among the ranching world was for the most part good. He also led in matters of community projects. George was a working land owner. He rode hard and played the game the same way.

In his mind, bigots were fair game. So at a church potluck, one of the small ranchers in the neighborhood had too much hard cider, and sounded off about the 'subhuman Indians,' George put his fist to the man's mouth, causing the man to lose a tooth. The Reverend Tom's face turned red causing his wife, Ruth, to say, "Now Thomas, you best to stay out of this. You can do your thing from the pulpit." Rosey who was also there, understood what was going on and stayed mum watching, and thinking, *If anyone deserved getting punched, it was this man.*

Joan, who was attending to a tough birthing, heard about it of course, and when she joined her husband, murmured her approval.

Whatever the judgments by community spokesmen or gossipers came up with, by the time the moccasin telegraph had done its thing, the incident became a major item, and rekindled the age-old bigotry that still haunted a few of the folks. Now we have to know that George, half Arapaho, would be attending a gathering of Native Americans held in Chicago discussing Indian rights, and featuring the now famous advocate, Viola Hatch. The thoughtful were appreciating the plight of those from whom we had taken lands, and the bigots were calling George all kinds of names.

Rosey, reputedly the best voice in the county when it comes to bigotry, had been taking all this in, and had to say something. The Glencoe Herald, and the Walnut Weekly would print almost anything that came from Rosey, and did, after which the county began to quiet down a bit. Joan listened, and read, and commented, "This all reminds me of what I read to Eva this morning, *Hey diddle diddle, the cat and the fiddle, the cow jumped over the moon, the little boy laughed to see such sport, and the dish ran away with the spoon."*

George laughed, and said, "Your humor is right on. It's interesting that one punch in the face can almost start a range war . . . What have you heard from some of your Vet clients?"

"Most of them know how I stand, and are gun-shy when talking bigotry to me. I feel there are still a few diehards out there, and will never understand that people are people, and that this land was all theirs to begin with."

Things settled down a bit, Joan went about fixing sick animals, George ran his ranch, taking part in the grubby stuff that most ranch owners would leave to employees, and they, the hands, knew it and were very loyal to George.

42 | A STRONG WOMAN

Whereas the strong character of the early women on the plains and mountains of our West had softened a bit by the mid-twentieth century, for the most part they did their bit with vigor, raised the families and loved their men. Joan moved from the eastern seaboard to Wyoming to be near her love, and soon became a western woman. She joined with other women of the area, taking part in local activities wherever she could, and embraced the strength of those around her. Joan's veterinary training and her love for animals took her to the Todd Davis Veterinary Clinic, in Glencoe, and she went from there to open her own office in Walnut.

Sick or ailing animals can't always be brought into the clinic, so Joan would often have to travel to where they were. Joan was a very attractive woman, for sure she was whistled about, and some other expletives men might think, and discuss. Most with a bit of humor, and never intended to do what they were saying.

But there are some that would not be nice if given the chance, and that threat was always there when Joan traveled alone to a remote spot in the county. She didn't worry about it very much as she knew almost everyone in the county, and they likewise, little by little knew and respected Joan.

James and Ann Jones ran a small horse ranch located in the foothills of the Wind River Mountains. They had immigrated to the U. S. from their native Scotland, and purchased land and buildings from a widow, having to leave to live with her daughter and son-in-law in the East.

Running a small ranch in the western United States is an iffy enterprise at best, especially in the beginning, and tended to be a do-it-yourself plus an occasional temporary as needed person, enterprise, and the Joneses were just beginning to pull themselves up, when their daughter who was attending Michigan State University, called.

"Hi Mom, how are things with you and Dad?"

"Just fine, dearest, what's going on in your life?"

"I'm getting married, Mom."

Ann Jones's mind raced through twenty years of life from birth through all those precious times with her daughter. Her heart thumped, and her breath came in short bits.

"Oh my daughter, are you sure?"

"Yes Mom, he is going into the Navy, and we feel we should make that commitment now."

"How soon, Blanche?"

Blanche sort of laughed, remembering and embracing the firm teachings of her life at home. "Mom, Doug and I want to get married soon, like next week. That will give us a full month for a honeymoon before he has to report into the Navy."

"Oh, Blanche, must it be that soon?"

"Mom, I think Father would want it that way, you know how old fashioned he is. He would expect us to get married first, and sleep together next. We don't want to wait for a month. We love each other so much. Will you help me with Father?"

The call from Blanche also included an invitation, more like a demand, for Mom and Pop to be there. This started all kinds of husband and wife stuff, the one conscious of their responsibilities there on their small equine ranch verses the family need to be with their daughter on this, her most important day. Jim asked, "Why didn't she come out here and get married?"

Ann answered, "Shush, you know I have to be there, Jim, and I know your daughter would miss you terribly if you weren't there. Can't we have that part time worker from last week stay over and take care of the stock? Honestly you think more of those horses than you do of our daughter."

Jim Jones grumbled. "I don't know him well enough."

"Oh for gawd-sake, Jim, we're going, and you figure out about the horses."

Jim placed a call to the Joan Bentley Veterinary Clinic. Joan answered, "J B here,

"Joan, this is Jim out at Jones Equine Care. Ann and I are going to Dearborn to attend our daughter's wedding. We'll be gone the better part of a week, and will have to leave our handyman to attend to the stock. Do you think you could stop in sometime while we're gone and take a look to see how things are going?"

"Sure, Jim, what dates are we talking about?"

"Say, next week."

The Joneses left for Michigan on a Sunday night, and Joan made it out to Jones Equine Care Center, around noon on Wednesday. She drove up into the yard area, parked and walked up the three steps to the front door. Not receiving an answer to her knock, she walked around to the back of the house. The scene that greeted her included a large fenced in area covering a dozen acres, and a smaller corral nestled against a low hill. There was a barn to the left which sported a hay loft. Fifteen maybe twenty horses came up expectantly, and neighed in an obvious appeal for attention. Joan sighed, noticing the nearly empty water trough. She filled that from a pipe system emanating from a small water tank nestled up in the hills above. Then she took two bales of hay she found in the barn which she spread out for the stock in the open fenced in area. Now she was looking into the big brown eyes of a chestnut colored mare, while she stroked her nose. All the time speaking softly, and wondering where the handyman was that was supposed to be tending the animal? She needed help to take care of the animals here, and soon. She had other calls to make. She noticed the ajar back door, and entered to use the phone which was visible just on the wall as you entered. She got the operator on the line, and a hand came from behind and clicked the phone lever down. A voice said, "Let's not do that just yet. We need to get acquainted babe." He placed his arm around her neck, drawing her body up against his body.

Joan struggled against powerful muscles to no avail. She screamed. Her assailant took his time to further inflict control and began to make sensual touches. Joan screamed again, and bit down on the arm that covered her mouth. Hard! Her assailant yelled, jerked his arm away, spun Joan around and slapped the side of her face with force. She fell to the ground, and he was quickly on top of her. Joan struggled.

Tommy Little Feather had two passions. One was the horse and his ability to master, without breaking the spirit of those semi-wild creatures that roamed the West; the other, his seven-year-old nephew, John Wild Horse, who was named after his grandfather, Chief John Running Deer.

And so it was often that the two could be found together learning of each other and the wild things of the area. So almost always when the Arrow—B could spare Tommy, he would pick up the plucky John, and they could be found out in nature doing something natural to a person of Arapaho blood.

So this was a day when John was learning to stalk the rabbit as part of survival skills that found Tommy and John moving through the chaparral in the foothills when they heard a woman's screaming voice emanating from a nearby ranch house. When the screaming continued, Tommy told John to continue watching for the occupants of a hutch while he went to see what was causing the woman to scream.

Tommy was strong from handling thousand-pound creatures, and when he saw what was happening, lifted the man off of Joan and tossed him aside. He immediately knelt beside Joan, gently caressing, and speaking softly.

The man, about forty, bloated, and ugly, shook his head, showed fright, scrambled to his feet and took off. Tommy, gently lowered Joan's head, and thinking of his nephew, called after him. "Wild Horse, it's safe to leave what you are doing, we are needed here."

Joan stirred, rubbed her chin and sat up. She shook her head and said, "Tommy, am I glad you came. I think that man would have killed me. Can you get me to the phone?"

By the time the moccasin telegraph did its thing, no bad guy was safe in the county, and of course, Sheriff Bill Williams, was the last to hear of the attempted rape of the County's favorite veterinarian. When he called George, he found a man dedicated to his "Do-it-myself" attitude. I don't need your help. He offered the usual cautionary statement that a law man would make. And George hung up on him. That was how mad George was. Nevertheless he proceeded to investigate, interviewing those involved, which included the Joneses on their return from their daughter's wedding.

George knew what he had to do: spend some time out. This man was not going to show his face to the populous world. He would keep to the wild, and exist at night only. He would need food, and for that he would have to pilfer. George, a tough cow-man, would find him, and to George there are no rules as to what he would do to him when he did.

Joan was out for about a week. She had a large black-and-blue cheek, and didn't feel like facing anyone. She knew her husband, and nothing she could say would deter him from going after the rapist, even if it took a month of living out of doors to find him.

George first contacted the Arapaho council. The message he left there went like this, "Be watchful, there is evil in our land. Tell me when it is found, that I can overcome." Next he prepared for a time in the wilds and alone. Provisions, for a week or more, and communication with the home ranch arranged.

Nellie waited patiently as George placed two saddlebags and a sizable bedroll on her. It was early afternoon when he left the Arrow—B. He traveled to the mid highlands, to a spot that gave him visibility of much of the lower reaches of the land around. The spot he sought was well known to himself—a niche in the foothills hidden from the valley below. There was water there and grass for Nellie. He ground-hitched Nellie, and built his camp. Under half a mile away, a spur of the mountain range offered visibility of the descending alluvial fan.

His fugitive had little choice but to stay in the valley. He was on foot, not provisioned for roughing it, and frightened. By the end of the second day, George had located his rabbit. He carefully approached his man dismounting from Nellie and appearing out of the bushes with pistol in hand said, "I wish you would try something. I need to have a reason to torture then kill." He walked up close and said, "Now down on the ground." He tied the man's hands, stood him up and walked him back to where Nellie was waiting, then to his campsite.

It was late now, so George prepared. The anger within him would not be appeased easily or quickly. The creature he stood over cringed, and George studied him, thinking *how can I inflict fright and pain here?* In this he failed. He could not torture. He could not appease his anger on another. He found a level spot, spread-eagled his rapist's legs and staked them down. And that's how the prisoner spent the night, flat on his back, staked to the ground.

George woke at dawn. He did camp things, all the while talking to himself, discussing what the Arapaho side of him might do, versus what the white would. In the end, he went with the white of himself. He broke camp, freed the prisoner's feet and legs and tethered him to the saddle on Nellie's back. It was twenty miles or so into Walnut, and it was a long walk indeed for the prisoner.

Sheriff Williams made little comment as he viewed the exhausted man at the end of a rope with George at the other end. He understood, and appreciated what it must have taken his friend to bring this man in. He said with humor, "what took you so long, George?" He placed the suspect in his jail cell, then turned around and said, "How about some grub, it's supper time, we can fill out the papers later."

George smiled, "I'll go for that."

They moved on to the Sheriff's home. The cook and do everything person that took care of the Sheriff greeted them as they entered. The Sheriff, speaking in Spanish, said to the help, "Do your thing for two, George is staying." He waved George to sit down. "So how'd you find this guy, that's a big space out there?"

George munched away on a plateful of chili con carne, glanced over at the aproned man from below the border, said, "I think he is trying to kill me, this stuff is alive."

The Sheriff said, "The body gets used to it after a while. Try more water."

George said, "The point is not how I found him but how ungentle you and the court system can handle him." He gave a little chuckle, "He's lucky he got here at all."

The Sheriff said, "Well that's all up to Hastings, you know Ralph, he's not too friendly to such as this scum. I think you can relax here. How's Joan handling this? That was a close one for her."

"Good, that's some kind of woman. We been having some words about her going out to some lonely spot to tend some animal. I usually lose."

Witnessed attempted rape brings a mandatory time in the big house in the state of Wyoming, and when this one came to Judge Ralph Hastings, he was not lenient. Joan and George continued to have heated discussions over her safety. George in frustration bought her a small hand-gun that she could put in her 'black-bag.'

43 | THE WALNUT FAMILY

John Bentley was born on January 1, 1961. Eva, now a strong minded five-year-old, viewed her tiny brother resting in her step-mother's arms. She was in awe. She had been prepared for this moment by the grown-ups, and was now asking how soon she could play with her promised playmate?

The Arapaho people in the nearby Wind River Reservation celebrated with a native potlatch, held indoors in the tribal long house, and the employees of the Arrow—B ranch paid homage to their favorite Bentley, Joan, and the new heir to the Bentley dynasty.

George, the rough cowman, seemed in a trance when close to his newborn son, and when Johnny was first placed in his arms, he handled him like a basket of eggs. Joan giggled her delight at his clumsiness, knowing it was an expression of his love. She had found in his lovemaking a certain gentleness, and a total commitment to making her happy.

In the last month of her pregnancy, the Todd Davis Veterinary of Glencoe handled Joan's veterinary business when needed. Todd would continue this until Joan felt it prudent to leave her child. Todd was almost a family member, as he was Joan's first employer.

Eva started first grade in Walnut, which boasted a two

room grammar school.   Renee, Joan's mother, was there when needed, and wanted to be needed more as many grandmothers do.   She drove Eva to and from the Walnut grammar school, during the first weeks after Johnny was born.

44 | A MISSING PERSON

Sheriff Bill Williams sat at his desk ruminating over his past life and what special things he had had the privilege to participate in. It was getting time for him to consider retirement, and it was hard for him to think of leaving the life of a lawman. The allure of traveling to places he had only read about was strong, but he lacked someone to share those travels with. He was now in his mid-sixties and knew the office would be better served by someone younger. He was also thinking, *would someone else watch after his flock,* so to speak?

Deputy Roberts came to the door with the mail. He spoke, and getting no response from his boss, left the mail and departed. Bill came out of his funk and started in on the mail, most of which was routine and ended up in the round file alongside his desk.

The "routine folder" from the Wyoming Missing Persons Bureau that was distributed throughout the law enforcement world struck his eye, and he studied recent additions as well as the found persons list since the last issue, one of which caught his eye, the name Miles McKinney. He sat up, reread the name again, reached for the telephone and dialed the Missing Persons Bureau. In time he reached a body with access to current files, and pertinent information regarding found persons. "This is Sheriff Bill Williams of Contra County. I see you have a Miles McKinney in custody. I've been looking for him. Where and when can I come and pick him up?"

The telephone voice said, "Please hold on while I check." It was a full five minutes before the voice came back on the phone, "Ah he was released into the custody of a family member ten days ago."

Bill Williams was not noted for his placid nature, or for his tolerance. He exploded all over the telephone voice, and in the end calmed down and asked for the person's name. This got him nowhere, and his next phone call was to the Arrow—B.

"Bill Williams here, guess what, I just talked to the Missing Persons Bureau. They picked up a Miles McKinney, and let him go ten days ago."

George said, "Well that's just peachy. The MPB is government, that means screw-up. That sounds like normal. So how did you get to hear about this anyway, I thought you're gonna retire?"

"Well, I had my feet up on my desk as you have always said I do, reading the mail, and there it was: the monthly missing-persons report. We both know that the name Miles McKinney isn't his real name. I'm sure the alleged relative that picked him up was in some way part of the drug culture . . .I wonder how they found him? When I calm down a bit I'm going up to the MPB office in Cheyenne. Trying to do anything by remote control, never works."

George laughed, "So you're going to un-retire. Does this mean the issue of Betty's father's murder is still on your mind? It's been years?"

"Cut it anyway you want, George, do you want to go up to Cheyenne with me?"

"So when d-ya want us to go, and how?"

"How about, small plane out of Glencoe, tomorrow at nine. Get here about eight, I'll drive us up to Glencoe Air Field."

The Wyoming Missing Persons Bureau office records department sat on the second floor of the State Police building. Sheriff Bill Williams and George Bentley found their way up to face a sleepy-eyed clerk who asked, "What do you need?"

The Sheriff answered, "I wish to speak with someone here regarding a found person."

The clerk said, "Oh that would be in room four, down the hall."

Room four was guarded by a frowsy middle-aged woman who said, "If you are looking for a found person, fill out the paper on the desk against the wall, which the Sheriff did. He said, "I need to see someone about this person, Miss." She got up and disappeared through a door, returning with an official looking document. She handed it to the Sheriff saying, "This is all we have on the person you seek. This is all there is."

George said, "Miss, we need to speak to someone over this. Inform your boss that we are here."

In time George and the Sheriff were seated opposite a tired looking keeper of records wearing glasses and reading from a folder on Miles McKinney. He finally looked up and asked, "What is your interest in this person?"

The Sheriff said, with some amount of force, "You have all that information on the missing-persons-report that I filed several years ago."

The official said, "Whoa, I'm only the records-control man. I didn't do anything here."

George sat amused at the reddening face of his good friend, he of course empathized. He said, "Yes Bill, why don't you calm down?"

The Sheriff said, "Alright, Mr. Records Clerk, do we have a picture of this man and is he left handed by any chance?"

"That would be in the historical file. What is your interest here, he was placed in the custody of his brother's family.

From the information we have on file, that's legal and wise."

The Sheriff said, "In that I have a warrant for the arrest of a Miles McKinney and that was indicated on the original submission to the Missing Person's Bureau, my interest is logical, don't you think?"

The official answered, "The report we acted on was initiated just two weeks ago. It was submitted by a relative of the subject. When did you file out your MPR?"

"Here's a copy."

The Sheriff handed over his copy of the original MPR to the official, who studied it for a moment and said, "This is over three years old. After three years MPRs in this office are placed in the dead file and/or are past the statute of limitation."

The Sheriff said, "In that there was a warrant for his arrest, may I ask for full cooperation from this office in locating this man. He is wanted for murder in the County of Contra."

"Will you put that in writing, Sheriff?"

"Sure, lend me a typewriter. I'm a long way from home."

Armed with a picture, and some information concerning the alleged family that identified and took responsibility for Miles McKinney, George and the Sheriff found their way by small plane back to Walnut. They didn't talk much on the way as conversation over engine and wind noise on a small plane is limited. On arrival back to the Sheriff's office the two men, tired from the day of travel, sat in the office with a cold beer each.

George said, "How do we know it's the man we're looking for? There must be dozens of Miles McKinneys."

"Considering that you and I both believe this to be an alias, and not a name usually found in this county, don't you think we need to find another name for the man in the picture we got from the MPB?"

"So what do you suggest, Bill?"

"Isn't it likely that the man in the picture is known by

persons into drugs living in the Rez?"

George smiled and said, "If I came up with this kind of stuff you would tell me I was doing your job. Nice thinking, Bill. So where do you suggest we start? What are your orders, General?"

"If only you could be serious once . . . how about you showing the pic out and around the Rez. You can go there, I can't."

George first showed the Miles McKinney picture to ranch employees. Nothing there. Then he called on Father Daniels on the Reservation. George and Reverend Daniels had been friends for many years and they greeted each other warmly. George said, "Father, I have something on the drug problem we spoke about last time. Here's a picture of who we think is dealing drugs to Arapaho tribal members."

Father Daniels studied the photo for a time, then said, "I can't say that I've seen this person before."

"Notwithstanding the suspicion that he deals drugs to members of the Arapaho as well as the Shoshone, he is also tied in to the Steve Harris murder. Recently he showed up at the Missing Persons Bureau in Cheyenne. He was released before the law could question him. Now we need to find him again. Any help or suggestions you may have would be very welcome."

"May I have this for a few days?"

"Sure, I have other copies."

Arapaho leadership during the mid-1960s was by committee, and by tradition stayed out of non-Reservation law enforcement concerns. Likewise, the reverse was true with the surrounding non-Reservation communities.

George Bentley, now a successful rancher, respected by both communities was in a unique position being half Arapaho, and half white to cross over from one of these communities to the other. It was also frustrating. The Arapaho strongly supported their people, regardless of what they did in the white man's world. George knew he wouldn't get any help from there, so he didn't ask. He speculated that dealing in drugs had to require food and housing somewhere near where the dealer did business. This meant walking or riding a horse by the retailer.

George was fairly certain that the person identified as Miles McKinney had returned. The drug business is lucrative to say the least, and alluring for certain to ones that have learned the trade. Its legal status didn't matter, as long as you didn't get caught. George also was certain that the suspect used the name Miles McKinney easily as he had a complete set of IDs to use, which would hide his real identify.

George Bentley was not exactly the 'Dog with a bone' type, but he had his limits. Sometimes, however, injustices piqued his mind to the point he needed to do something to fix things. The fact that Steve Harris's killer had never been found, was one of those things. He mused over his friend, Sheriff Bill's sudden interest in opening up a years old murder case. Bill had told him to go fly a kite over the Steve Harris killing back then, that it was a law enforcement matter, and stay out of that business. And then there was Joan, who felt the same way or more so than the Sheriff, to be considered.

George ran a tight ship, giving to and expecting those he employed to perform well for the Arrow—B. He was a firm boss where the ranch was considered, but his treatment and understanding of the woman in his life was another matter.

They came together, as was the usual routine each day, over the evening meal. Mary Ellen, the ranch cook and do everything person, with the help of other ranch employees, would prepare and serve the evening meal. Present were Joan, her mother, Renee, George, and Eva. Young John, still in his first year of life, would be fed elsewhere. Each would talk of their events of the day, and each would express their love of family in some way or another. It was a strong love, and there was a deep commitment by each for the other.

As they began the evening meal on the day George

returned from his trip to Cheyenne with the Sheriff, Joan asked, "I heard that you did some flying this morning, what was that all about?"

"Well, you know that our friend, Bill Williams is on the list for retirement. He asked me to join him on a trip to the State Capitol."

Joan waited for something more, decided it wasn't coming and said, "I'm sure Bill didn't need you along for guidance or protection, I assume you went along for the ride maybe?"

"Well, it was sort of about the Steve Harris murder."

"So what's new there?"

"We have a picture that we think might be the man that did the killing"

"Just what do you mean by 'we' George? I thought Bill was going to retire?"

George guffawed and said, "That old soldier couldn't retire if he were ninety. He's just making talk. The board of supervisors doesn't know what to do with him. They all think he's getting too old for a sheriff's job."

"So you didn't answer my question, what about that we stuff."

"Oh, ah, he sort of asked me to check on the Reservation."

"The Law is asking you to help the Law, in what way, Dearest?"

George reached over and took her hand, smiled and said, "I love it when you do this. You have a way of showing how much you care, and at the same time keep it light. Okay, at last we know what this guy looks like. He needs to be brought to justice for what he has done, and for what he is doing to others in supplying them with drugs. Right now, there's not enough law to do it. If I can I'll fill in there."

Joan felt tears form in her eyes. She said nothing but squeezed his hand. From the start Joan had shown her dislike for guns and agonized that her love might become involved, and somehow she would lose him. Renee listened quietly, feeling she was in on a private conversation, and shouldn't be.

The routine around a working ranch of the size of the Arrow—B is often hectic depending on what gives with fifteen-hundred-pound animals in the hundreds mulling through their sometimes not tranquil activities. There are bulls doing noisy and violent things in competition, there are cows giving birth who sometimes have difficult times, and there are animals that get into trouble in odd places that need help. There are times when everyone on the ranch has to do double duty, and one of those times started the day after George returned from Cheyenne. All hell broke loose! Even Mary Ellen got into the act. So it was a full two weeks later before George found time to think about Miles McKinney again. That explosive time just past had left George with a sense of emptiness to be filled with something else. His mind raced back to his once friend, Steve Harris, and his untimely death. He could not let it go. Yes it is a law problem, but the law needed help, besides the law wasn't too thrilled about spending resources on a four year old crime.

Sheriff Bill Williams had held down the position of sheriff in a county of several thousand square miles for several decades. This was real serious crime, however, and he didn't have the resources to cope. We are still halfway into yesterday when horses and sheriffs and posses were in play, and it takes more than a lawman in a station wagon to cover the ground in a manner needed to be successful. Both the Sheriff and George knew this, and it was not unusual for the law to deputize as needed. And this time, George asked to be deputized. Of course this upset Joan, and she told him so.

First he asked Tommy Little Feather up to the house. They sat on the outside at a table with an umbrella overhead nursing a cup of coffee. After the little talk was over, George asked, "Have you seen the dealer that you used to do business with when you go home to the Reservation?"

Tommy answered, "Mr. Bentley, since I stopped doing that kind of thing, I haven't been in on the drug business going on there. I'm trusted, but not."

"Yes, I would expect it would be that way." He handed the picture of the suspect to Tommy. "We think this is the man that killed Steve Harris years ago. Do you recognize him?"

Tommy studied the picture for a long moment. "The man I knew always kind of hid his face, but I do think he had a mustache and some hair on his face. A little like what I see here."

"Tommy, this person is really bad. If you have any knowledge about him, please let me know. Will you do that?"

"Yes Mr. Bentley, but I can't promise to if it involves my village."

45 | THE LINE SHACK

Returning from the north area of the ranch, one of the Arrow—B riders came up to the ranch house. He spoke to George, "Mr. Bentley, there seems to be someone using our line shack."

George, in a surprised voice said, "Tell me about it."

The rider fidgeted hat in hand, said, "Whoever has been there not only has been using supplies but they leave a mess. Our riders would never do that."

George thanked the rider and told him to ask Pete to come on up. "You come on back, I want you to tell Pete what you found."

The three sat on the ranch patio. George said, "Okay Herman, tell us what you found."

Mr. Bentley, the inside chopped wood was almost used up, the kerosene supply for the stove empty, and the shack looked unattended. We always make it nice for the next hand to come."

Peter White asked, "Was there ashes in the fireplace? Was they warm?"

"There were ashes, but I didn't check them."

George said, "Pete, I'm going up there and take a look; this sort of falls into something I've been looking at lately.

Set me up with Nellie for a trip up there, I'll leave in the morning. I expect to be there for several days, so have Mary Ellen do her thing in my saddlebags."

Joan was into the birth of a calf mothered by a first-time parent, doing everything possible to not help. The accompanying groans, moos, and moans seamed endless, and the stress on any closeby human, intense. It was almost seven in the evening when she slipped into the driver's seat of her pick-up and headed for the Arrow—B. Mary Ellen had been warned that Joan would be late and had held up serving the evening meal accordingly. So it was well after eight when dinner was served. The discussion of an unruly animal birth event wasn't exactly the best topic to begin the evening meal with, so Joan asked, "What's new in the ranch world?"

There wasn't any real hurry by anyone at the table to respond, and Joan looked from her mother to George, then at Eva. She laid down her fork, looked hard at George, "I know the purpose of sitting at this table is to fill our bellies, but that I can do almost anywhere."

George smiled, "Well if you skip the fence fixing, cow gathering, and culling, I did have a visit from a hand that said he thought someone was using our line shack."

"So, is that a baddie or don't neighbors share that kind of thing?"

George said, "Well yes, but neighbors don't use up everything and leave dirty dishes, so to speak."

Joan ate her dinner in silence for a bit, then, "That sounds like stealing, have you told Bill, it sounds like a matter for the law?"

"Well no, I feel I should take a look out there first, then I'll call 'im."

"So are you going tomorrow?"

"I plan on it, yes."

Joan said, "It seems that if Bill had you go all the way to Cheyenne with him, you would have him join you going out to the line shack to help you 'take a look.'"

Mary Ellen came into the dining room with a tray full of

desserts. She offered them around, and when she came to George she said, "Pete tells me that you will need food for a time up at the line shack. How many days do you expect to be gone?"

Joan said, "Yes George, how many days do you expect to be gone?"

George said, "I wouldn't have a shot at getting away with being devious with the woman in my life even if I wanted to, which I don't . . . I wanted to leave that one open, as I hope to find out who's living off the supplies we leave at the line shack. Mary Ellen, put enough out there for five days."

Joan considered going a little deeper into the matter then thought it would be better to wait until they were alone. She was getting ready to discuss her own day when Renee said, "Joan dear, why were you so late tonight, did you have a problem at the clinic? You look terribly tired."

"Sure, Mom, but it is not an appropriate subject for discussion at the dinner table."

Finally alone with George, Joan said, "Why are we doing this thing without Bill? You know how I hate the gun thing and all?"

"Joan, I'm certainly going to involve Bill. He needs help though, and I intend to give him what he needs. So, what happened to you today, you looked like you'd been dragged through a rat hole or something?"

"That was a neat way to change the subject, and yes it wasn't the best of days for me. Have you ever been around when a cow is trying not to birth her calf, with blood and amniotic fluid all over everything? Well this took the better part of three hours."

"Oh."

"Getting back to talking to Bill, how do you expect to discuss what you find with anybody for that matter, when you're incommunicado, so to speak? So I guess you'll try smoke signals maybe and if that doesn't work you figure on fixing it yourself?"

George knew he wasn't going to win this one, "I'll call Bill."

Their marriage was now into its second year, and each had learned the needs and moods of the other very well. Joan now understood her husband's need to overcome adversity and injustices with or without the law when it wasn't available. She smiled and leaned over to give him a kiss.

George placed his call to the Sheriff. "Hi Bill, George here."

"So what's with cow punching these days?"

"We punch 'em, you eat 'em. Something's been going on out at our line shack that I thought you might be interested in. You know the Miles McKinney case we were into, and as to where he spent time in the county, well you know that line shack we have up north, it's been used a lot lately and not by my guys."

"So one of your neighbors needed a stayover for a night or two."

"Our kind of neighbor would have cleaned up before he left, and resupplied what he used."

"So you think that our Miles boy has been using your line shack for a base to hit the Reservation addicts?"

George said, "Could be, I'm going out there tomorrow and take a look, do you want to join me? After all, you do get a bit upset when I do something you feel is a matter for the law."

"Sounds like a winner as long as I don't have to sit on a horse for half a day. Do you want I should pick you up in the morning?"

"Uh huh, come early if you want, and have chow here."

George and the Sheriff drove out to the line shack. Panting with excitement, Charley II, the ranch German-Shepherd, rode along with his head out the window, enjoying the wind, and looking forward to whatever his nose was telling him lay up ahead.

On arrival at their destination, the Sheriff parked a distance away from the building, and the two men looked outside and around the line shack before entering. Once inside they read the signs of occupancy, and formed a picture in their minds of the last occupant. He had to be from a world other than the surrounding rural community. He would be unaccustomed to the local code of trust and consideration for your neighbor, and he took what he wanted with no intention of paying for it, or the needs of the next occupant. Charlie entered the shack and started a nosing action, sniffing everything from the wall bunk to the chair seat. George watched said, "That dog sure smells something he thinks we want to know about. Maybe that's a way to follow Miles. I think this is our man, Bill. He's here to do business, not for his health."

"Yah, even I can figure that one out. You got any ideas?"

"Well as long as you ask, yes, I was going to hide up in that special place of mine and see if I could spot the guy entering the shack. Joan convinced me to call you first saying it was a matter for the law. So now I'm out of ideas, and I'm sure this character has seen us and made off."

The Sheriff chuckled and said, "That's interesting, do I hear a bit of disagreement between you two? Something about don't do it yourself maybe?"

"Your humor is noted. You'd give another he-haw if you heard her mention smoke signals, and bows and arrows. That's some kind of woman, I'm married to, Bill, and you know it. I kind of think she expects us to do this thing, but come out alive."

"Well I kinda wish it that way too, but why didn't you arrange this a few years ago? I'm getting too old for this stuff."

George said, "We need to find a way to catch, or whatever, this character, and I expect if we aren't careful we will get shot at. Drug dealers carry guns and won't hesitate to use them if confronted."

"So what's with this big dog of yours, I'd hate to meet him

solo if he didn't like me. D' yu think he might follow a man's trail?"

"Uh huh." George led Charley over to the bunk once more. He made sure that he got a good nose full of the bedding. "Let's see where he takes us."

Charlie sniffed around the perimeter of the line shack clearing, finally heading off, sniffing all the way. The two men followed, and in time came close to the Reservation boundary. George reached out to Charlie, snapped a leash on, and said, "Not so fast, dog."

The Sheriff waited, looking at George, "That dog sure wants to go on?"

"Yes, well he's not gonna, that's no-no land, and we'll have to figure some other way."

The Sheriff said, "You and your hoodoo stuff, in the meantime we have a shot at picking this chum up."

"Not much chance of that, Bill, he can see us and the reverse isn't so. We know two things we didn't know yesterday, he's back here dealing again, and he lives in the bushes and my line shack. I don't cotton to sharing my line shack, or watching good people get popped. Now it's time to figure out how this low life gets the stuff, and make him pay."

The Sheriff grumbled something unintelligent like and thought *I shoulda quit two weeks ago, then knew he couldn't.* He said, "We stopped them once before when they brought drugs in on the five o'clock special. I don't think they'll try that again, the railroad people don't like them much and gave us a hand. Do you remember?"

George said, "If we rule out walking or riding horses, that leaves auto or small plane. I'm thinking car might be too risky, as we might throw up a road block like we did once before, and they don't want to be caught with heroin on board. Do you suppose they make drops from a small plane?"

"Could be, but they have to get the money out, how would they do that?"

"I think maybe I should talk to some of my relatives on

the Rez about that one. If there were small planes involved, they would know about it.

Charlie was straining to scramble forward, bouncing up and down and sort of yelping at his restraint. George said, I don't want to lose this dog. If he goes after wat's out there, he'll get shot."

With a shudder the Sheriff said, "You worry more about that dog than about my hide. You don't s'pose our delivery boy is somewhere in the Rez, doing his thing, and we caught him at it?"

"I expect that might be so, but I don't cotton to go after him here and now. He has all the bullets, and we have none. He can see us and we can't see him."

The Sheriff said, "I agree with that one, let's head back."

46 | DRUGS, AGAIN

By custom, George always called on his great aunt, Sarah Golden Poppy when he visited the Reservation. The day after George and the Sheriff went out to the line shack found George receiving a warm greeting from Sarah at her home. A youth of the tribe was there who spoke both English and Arapaho, and acted as interpreter as needed. After the respectful formalities were completed, Sarah asked, "And to what purpose have you come, Red Fox?"

"Golden Poppy, we have an evil one preying on some of our people again, and I've come to ask you a favor." Golden Poppy waited silently, George continued, "We suspect drugs are being brought to our people by small plane. We need to know if this is so, and where they have enough flat land to land and take off."

Sarah said, "We have always had some here that have strayed, and become dependent on drugs. Why this time, are you interested?"

"This time, Golden Poppy, we believe the killer of the rancher Steve Harris is the evil one here in our Reservation. This is a white man's problem, yes, but this man has killed, and is profiting at the demise of some of our people. We need to keep it there. I am only asking for information that may help us in finding him."

"Have you spoken to the Reservation Police, Red Fox?"

"No, as I know what their answer will be: It is a white man's problem, not ours."

Sarah Golden Poppy, the sister of the deceased Chief Running Deer, was in her early nineties. She had lived through times when the Arapaho were a prideful people, often mistreated by United States government officials charged with their welfare. Suspicion and mistrust often prevailed between the Arapaho and the White World. On the Reservation governing was carried out by a Council with little authority. Council meetings usually said lots but did little. She said, "Red Fox, what you ask is possible but will not be shown. Listen to the words of the moccasin telegraph."

Cowhands usually carry a pistol stuck conveniently in a holster on a hip. The weapon was not a weapon per se, but was there as part of their work equipment. Beyond steering an ornery bunch of thousand pound animals around, it was good at getting to snakes, or an occasional mountain lion. So when Cliff was spending his allotted time away from Mary Ellen's cooking up at the line shack, and someone took a potshot at him, he was ready to shoot back.

He was lucky. The shooter was about to be discovered, and probably only wanted Cliff to duck and not see him. Cliff checked his pistol, but decided to head back to the main ranch post haste. Whatever, it was a shaky experience, and one that George wouldn't want to happen to one of his employees.

George had a problem, this pesky interloper needed to be gathered up and placed behind bars. This was, as Joan kept reminding him, the twentieth century, not the eighteenth or nineteenth.

Heeding his knowledge and understanding of Joan, after two years of married life, George came right out and told her what was going on.

She listened quietly, then said, "And?"

"I can't endanger my employees with this kind of thing, Joan. I have one of two choices, handle it or go out of business."

"This means a time away from here, in the wilderness exposed to an unscrupulous person, ready to kill you if he could. Is that true, George?" Her eyes were dry, she must support the man she loved. It was hard.

George didn't leave for a few days. He finally heard through the moccasin telegraph of a small plane landing on a level spot in the north. This provided the assurance that drug traffic was happening once more, but with no physical proof. During this time the line shack was unattended by Arrow—B riders, so it was fair to assume that the quarry slept there. It was very early when George picked his way up the side of Portal Mesa, found his acre of grass for Nellie and a small stream for water. Once again he watched the valley below. And then it happened.

47 | CAPTURE

Nellie snorted, George looked up to see a man coming out of nowhere brandishing a pistol. He grasped the leather thong attached to his binoculars, swung the binoculars as hard as he could at the assailant. The binoculars hit the arm of the man so hard that he let go of the pistol. George propelled his 220 pounds of pure muscle at the man, pounding him with well-aimed and hard fists. The man responded in kind. The fist fight was long and bloody, with no holds barred. In the end, the man lay face down spread eagle, with his hands tightly tied, and a tired and breathless George standing over him. George said, "It was nice of you to find me, finding you would have meant me sleeping on the ground some more." He then took care of Nellie, who had been nervously snorting and stomping during the fist fight. He patted her, brushed her, found some oats in a saddle bag, all the time talking softly in her ears. When finally she calmed down, George loaded his prisoner on her back and walking, started down the trail toward the Arrow—B. Past the switchbacks and into more level ground George switched with his prisoner and rode aboard Nellie, with the man tethered and walking.

Joan was home when her battered husband came into the ranch parking area. She ran out to him and asked, "What happened to you?"

George quipped, "Well you didn't want us to use guns, so this is what using fists will do."

Joan said, "Oh for God sake, let me start cleaning you up. You sure took it in that right eye, and your whole face for that matter."

George smiled his "Yes dear."

George placed the call to the Sheriff, filled him in and asked him to come get the prisoner. The Sheriff came, it was chow time, and Bill, the Sheriff, sat with the family at the long table in the ranch house. The prisoner enjoyed the company of two devoted Arrow—B types that didn't like him much, and would for sure not let him get away. The conversation between mouthfuls went this way: Bill said, "You messed up his face so much I can't be sure he's the man in that picture we got from the Missing Persons Bureau."

"Well I don't like being a target for a pistol shot. Maybe I should have been nice, and careful with his face?"

"So what am I supposed to put him in jail for, he hasn't broken any laws that I can see?"

"How about, assault-and-battery? He come after me with all, and meant to kill."

"So do you have any witnesses?" He continued, "The real job will be keeping him some place that he can't wiggle out of, including the law, before we have a chance to hear his story. Somehow our friends in Glencoe seem to let bad guys go before we can even talk to them."

George said, "Yes, and if I file an attempted murder complaint, it won't stand without at least one witness. That'll get him free again."

Joan said, "Do we know what he's been doing for the last three years?"

The Sheriff said, "That's an interesting question, Joan, why do you ask?"

"Bad people try to be invisible, and that's hard to do in this small western world of ours. He had to sleep and eat somewhere."

George said, "You're right, Joan, which means he was either in the drug business, employed some way or in someone's jail. From the looks of him, and from the battle he put up, it was more than peddling drugs." He turned to the Sheriff. "How about posting his photo in law enforcement offices, and see what we get?"

"Well, I did that three years ago, and nothing happened. Joan has a point, however, we need to find out what he's been doing for the last three to four years. That may tie him into the murder of Steve. When and why did he disappear?"

"That doesn't solve our immediate problem, what do we do with him now. If the law screws up again and turns him loose, George will be constantly in danger. He tried to kill George and failed. He'll surely try again if given the chance."

Joan asked, "Why George?"

Morning found the Sheriff talking to Chief Richardson. "Good morning Chief, Williams here."

"Good morning to yourself. I assume you have some kind of a problem or you wouldn't call this early. Your nickel."

"Between you and Bentley you make me really an important part of things . . . I have a prisoner that I need to park some place for a time."

"So bring 'im on up. I do have an empty space."

"Well this is a little different, I want to bring him up there at night, under an assumed name for a fictitious crime, and we also need to keep him incommunicado."

"I thought you were going to retire, Bill, you sound serious like."

"Yes, well I just want to tidy things up a bit, before I walk. Is eleven tonight okay?"

"Do you care to tell me why all this secrecy stuff?"

"Uh huh, well we think this is the guy who killed Steve Harris. We need some time to prove it."

"For you, I'll do it myself, this sounds interesting. See you tonight."

The Sheriff then called George, and filled him in. "The

fewer people that know what we are doing the better. Don't even tell Joan or any Arrow—B person. I'm going to keep Roberts out of the loop too. Will you join me tonight in getting Miles up into one of Richardson's jail-cells?"

George drove up to the Glencoe police station with the Sheriff holding rein over a bound and gagged prisoner. Chief Richardson met them, and installed the prisoner into a jail cell. The now-ungagged prisoner, started mouthing off, and the Chief reminded him that noisy people don't get to eat much. Miles quieted down and the Chief joined George and the Sheriff in his office, took out a bottle of scotch and poured. He asked the Sheriff, "So what gives with this foul mouth?"

"You remember Steve Harris, and his murder years ago? That crime has never been solved. This guy looks like the killer. All indicators point that drugs on the Reservation were involved. Well that drug business which had abated after Steve's death, recently got going big time again, and this guy may be a known drug dealer. Further, he is left handed, and writes European style, which connects him with the Harris murder in another way.

"As you know, we've been watching things going on around the Reservation as well as we can, so when George found that someone was using his line shack to sleep and eat in, he got on his horse and went out there to see what was going on. In addition, someone took a potshot at one of his employees, and that made him upset beyond rational and he loaded his guns, shall we say. And then someone took a shot at George himself. This guy you have in your pokey is that man. If we or the court turn this scum loose, George's life won't be worth a plug nickel. Now you let me rummage through your records awhile ago, and I came up with the only clue to Harris's killer: a promissory note to a deceased small rancher for a thousand dollars, signed by a Miles McKinney. Could be an alias, I know, but it shows a left-handed signer, and this guy is left handed. Also the hand writing on that promissory note, per a certified hand writing person, shows a left handed signer and a 'European style and influence.'"

The Chief poured another round from his bottle and said, "So you have a thug that is probably guilty as all hell of murder, it's hard to prove, and you don't want to turn him loose." He laughed and said, "And now you've gotten me into it. Thanks a lot."

George said, "Bill's working on it, Chief. If you have a problem with holding this no name, I'll file attempted murder charges."

The Chief responded, "You are telling me that you haven't even filed a complaint against him, and you put him in custody? What did he do?"

So George told him, pointing to his black eye.

The Chief said, "And I suppose you have no witnesses?"

George said, "Uh huh."

The Chief said, "I guess this all happened fast. Why not tell all, so I can handle Hastings a bit? I'm sure he's going to give me one for violation of something."

The Sheriff said, "Chief, we need to know this man's whereabouts and activities since he left this area. We are sure he's been trafficking in drugs since his return. We have a good picture of him that can be used on a wanted poster. How about you getting it out to the law enforcement world. Maybe we can learn what his real name is?"

"I have to think a bit on that one. You guys want to stay the night at my house, or drive back to Walnut?"

"We better get on home to keep our trip secret, or something."

The wanted, dead-or-alive poster was a uniquely nameless sepia, as one might expect a hundred years ago, and spoke of the need to be aware of his desperate character. Nothing much happened for two weeks, and Chief Richardson got to champing at the bit over what to do about the man in his jail. He called Sheriff Williams, "Mornin' Bill, Richardson here."

"Yes, well I kinda expected your call, any word up there?"

"Not really, but I expect to hear from the Court over holding a citizen without bail for this long."

"Can't we do a protective custody or something?"

The Chief said, "Hastings would see through that before it got off the ground even. No, if you intend to keep me quiet much longer you better come up with something legal."

"Okay Chief, I'll work out something and call you in a day or two."

Sheriff Bill Williams was, in one sense looking forward to retiring, and yet not willing to relinquish his long-standing position of authority in Contra County. He was also bugged by the unsolved death of Steve Harris on his watch. On the morning after the call from Chief Richardson he sat at his desk with his feet up, thinking humorlessly of George, and his comments regarding feet on desks, and how much he had learned to like and admire George. In that moment he gave up his present plans to retire, and picked up the phone, called the County Commissions office and informed them of his plans to continue as Sheriff for the time being. This suited the County Commission just great as there was no one in sight willing to perform sheriff duties as well and as cheaply as Bill. He called George. "Just had a call from Richardson. Got any ideas?"

"So, any sign from our poster?"

"Nothing yet, and we better do something but soon."

George was quiet for a moment. "I think I'll file assault and battery charges, and see if we can stretch his time in jail a bit. We still need more than we have to go after him for an old murder. One piece of paper won't do it."

No sooner had he hung up the phone call with George, Richardson called. The Chief asked, "Have you tried forensic?"

The Sheriff answered, "You mean, finger prints, blood types and all that stuff, not really, but it's something to work on. Speaking of what we know about the killing, Chief, that would all be in your files up there in Glencoe."

"So, come on up and take a look. There's maybe what you're looking for."

48 | JUDGE HASTINGS

Attorney Peter Forbes had been handling the legal business for the Arrow—B since his dad's retirement some time ago. The call from George Bentley to represent him in a case of assault-and-battery was unusual in that he was not really practiced at defending individuals from physical harms, rather he protected the Ranch and its holdings from monetary losses and other damages per se. George, when he made the call assured Peter that he would do fine.

Peter drove out to the Arrow—B and with his legal pad and pen ready sat across from George over a cup of late morning coffee. He said, "You really don't need an attorney for this one, Mr. Bentley, you can do it yourself."

"Peter, call me 'George,' everyone else does. Yes, I know that. Now let's talk about what I need: time. I need to keep the subject in question in jail as long as possible. Now, I can't control that. That's your kind of thing."

"I'll need to know why, Mr. er George."

"We have very convincing evidence that this is the person who killed Steve Harris. We feel going to court at this time with what we have might fail due to the need for more evidence. We don't want to take that risk."

Peter said, "I'll do my best, however, you know Hastings.

He sees through purposeful delays like you can't believe."

"That's your problem, Peter. You know what I want, do the best you can and keep me informed."

As often happened, Peter and his father, Emery, discussed cases that Peter was engaged in. And the matter of assault and battery charges against the man in jail went like this: Emery said, "I heard that you went out to the Arrow—B today. What's going on out there?"

"Mr. Bentley asked me to file an assault and battery complaint on his behalf against a man that's in jail for another reason right now."

"So, that's interesting, he could have done that without your help. He's not one to waste money. What else did he say?"

Peter said, "You seem to know this county and its people awfully well. I would hate to be an opposing attorney in a case where you were involved. He wants time. I have to find a way to keep this guy in jail regardless until another case is solved."

"And?"

"The case he and Sheriff Williams are trying to solve is the murder of Steve Harris."

"And Bentley is like a dog with a bone, he won't give up. I believe he is right here. What do you have?"

"He's in Richardson's jail, has been invisible for several years. His alias is Miles McKinney. He deals in drugs, and he has customers on the Rez."

"That's it?"

Peter answered, "Well, we do have a piece of paper in his handwriting that pretty much ties him in to the murder."

"So, are you going ahead with this, now that he's in jail?"

"Mr. Bentley feels that this is not enough, and he might get off and scram. I agree. We need more."

"So, who's looking for more, that's not exactly an attorney's job?" Emery sat in silence for a bit. "Peter, this is one for us. I'm here ready and able to help if you need me. I liked Steve Harris. If there is a shot at finding out who killed him, let's give it all we've got."

Peter looked at his father in surprise. He kind of half laughed and said, "Up until now if I had a question or needed support you've told me to figure it out for yourself. Now, without me asking, I'm offered help." He waited for more from his Dad.

Emery sat for a moment, then asked, "How'd this guy end up in Richardson's jail anyway?"

"Oh, the suspect surprised George and put a gun in his face. George disarmed him, beat him up in a fist fight, and hauled him off to jail."

Emery smiled and said, "That sounds like George, it also sounds like attempted murder. But if George really wants to buy time, maybe we can slow this down even more."

"What do you mean?"

"Once you file a complaint for A and B or attempted murder, the prisoner is going to get a bail hearing of some kind, Hastings will see to that, and this whole thing gets public real fast. If the evidence for attempted murder is weak, and if this is really just an A and B case, maybe with trespass thrown in, Hastings might have to grant bail."

"Yes, I see. This Miles McKinney might get out, especially if he has friends in the drug business that will post his bail."

"So what about asking Dean Brooks to issue a material witness warrant, to hold this guy as a witness in the investigation of drug traffic into the Rez?"

"That's brilliant! But wouldn't that be a federal investigation because of the Rez? Richardson would have some explaining to do?"

"Son, that's why you need to be there to talk to the judge. Criminal jurisdiction around here overlaps a ton. It will be perfect for causing delay and holding this guy. For example, if the alleged crime is by a non-Indian against a non-Indian, even if it happens on the Reservation, the state has jurisdiction, not the Reservation or the Feds. After that, it all gets murky. Maybe the U.S. Attorney in Cheyenne will need to investigate too. But as far as we know, this drug trafficking is being done by outsiders, and they use our client's ranch, so the state and local guys can investigate, including Chief Richardson and Sheriff Williams."

"I'm starting to catch up with you. We argue that without the material witness warrant, this guy will disappear and won't be available to testify against the drug traffickers. And if that doesn't work, I file the complaint for George for A and B or attempted murder and string things out."

The father smiled and managed a nod of approval. "But remember that this stuff will only buy time. George is going to have to come up with something on this Miles McKinney in the Steve Harris murder, or Judge Hastings is going to step in and clean this up real fast."

Peter met with Chief Richardson and got him on board. Then they went to find Dean Brooks who was sitting as Judge Pro Tem and explained the Chief's need for a material witness warrant to hold Miles McKinney. Peter explained that he had been asked to assist by his client, George Bentley, because the Arrow—B was being used to move drugs into the Reservation. Dean Brooks asked the Chief if he intended to file criminal charges on the witness, particularly because he'd heard of the fist fight between George and a guy on his ranch, probably this guy, and the Chief answered as Peter had suggested in private, "Not at this time Judge, he's just a witness that could easily disappear as he has done in the past." Dean Brooks granted the material witness warrant and authorized Chief Richardson to hold McKinney in his jail for thirty days.

Judge Hastings didn't miss much that went on in his court even if it was a minor assault and battery case. Over a morning coffee time he said to Dean, "So I heard Bentley got into a fist fight. I'd hate to have been the other guy. I also heard that the other guy is sitting in jail." He poured himself another cup of coffee, dumped in more sugar and said, "Is the guy going to be charged? There must be more to the story. What's the rest of it, Dean?"

"I issued a material witness warrant for thirty days so Richardson could hold the guy while they investigate drug trafficking that may be happening through the Arrow—B land and into the Reservation."

"That sounds slippery, Dean. What happened between George and this 'witness'?"

"Well, apparently, George went looking for whoever was using and fouling up his line shack, and found this guy. Something happened between them. The guy had a gun. George brought him in, but maybe George is more concerned about the drugs than a scuffle or a gun or whatever. I really don't know."

"Great. It's your job to know, Dean. Why not charge the guy with something? Assault and battery or a fire arms violation?"

"Yes, well between Richardson and Williams, they've been screwing around with the man in jail. Now because they know we would force them to show cause, they do this thing. Peter Forbes even said they would report the state investigation to U.S. Attorney in Cheyenne because of the Reservation."

"So why do they get a whole thirty days?"

"Honestly? George and Sheriff Williams both feel this is the man who killed Steve Harris, and they need more evidence to prove that."

"Okay, Dean, I see where you're coming from, and I don't want to interfere here, but would you mind if I made a suggestion?"

"I'd welcome that. What do you have in mind?"

"Bring these cahoots in here, and let's find out what's really going on. We can either help them or not."

Dean said, "That's not bad idea, why not include Bentley?"

"I go for that, and Peter and Emery Forbes too. You set it up."

Judge Pro Tem Dean Brooks found a time when all could meet in an antechamber just off of Judge Hastings courtroom in the Contra County Courthouse. Present were Judge Hastings, Chief Richardson, Sheriff Williams, George Bentley, Emery Forbes, Peter Forbes and Dean Brooks. Judge Hastings got everyone comfortable with coffee and doughnuts, and said, "Alright, Emery, this whole 'material witness warrant' thing has your handwriting all over it. But that's not why the Chief is holding this guy in his jail, is it? Explain why I shouldn't get upset over these guys playing cutesy with the court?"

Emery said, "From what I hear, Judge, there's evidence of murder on the books against this hombre that's in jail. Also, this guy was carrying a gun and tried to use it on our client. It's time to take this guy seriously."

"So, why all this secrecy stuff that is secret to me only, as everyone else seems to know about it? What's the crime we are looking at here and where's the evidence?"

Emery answered, "Sitting in Richardson's jail is a man that seems to be tied into the Steve Harris killing, and that's all I know."

The Judge turned to Chief Richardson, "So why is this to be kept from the Court, Chief?"

An embarrassed Chief Richardson answered, "Williams and George asked me to hold the prisoner a week or two until another crime committed by this man could be solved and charges brought. Their request did sound a bit sneaky but I kind of went along with their thinking as they showed me their case, so far."

"So, Sheriff, what is your excuse for starting all of this, which I wasn't supposed to hear about?"

Sheriff Bill Williams grimaced. "Well Judge, Bentley and me came across some stuff that ties this criminal into the Harris murder; it's pretty conclusive to us, but probably insufficient for a conviction in Court. We just wanted more investigation time, that's all. We didn't want him to go free until we could look some more."

"Well that's just peachy, you all kept me out of the circle on purpose, and I am supposed to overlook your devious souls. Show me a reason why I shouldn't order him released right now."

George said, with a bit of humor in his voice, "Judge, we just didn't want you to suffer an embarrassment at having to er twist the law, so to speak."

The Judge said, "That's a big one, what other illegal stuff are you three doing behind my back?"

Chief Richardson said, "None that I know of Judge. We were thinking of using a little pressure maybe?"

The Judge grumped and asked, "Would it be too much to ask one of you to show me that evidence that made criminals out of all of you?"

Which George did, starting with the fistfight.

Now it's not too often that the Glencoe Herald has much to put in large print on their evening edition, but the meeting of these special people at the request of the venerable Judge Hastings did just that. The writer got his info from one of the Judge's staff, and made a field day of that, expanding it a bit, calling into question whether the man in jail was a witness or a criminal, or both. Whereas Judge Hastings agreed to continue the material witness warrant and the witness's stay as a guest of Chief Richardson, he groaned over the publicity of such. He, of course, had some conversations with his staff over this, but didn't call anyone down over it, and he let Chief Richardson and Peter Forbes know that he would have to cancel the material witness warrant soon.

So, Peter Forbes did file a complaint on behalf of his client with facts that would easily support an assault and battery charge, but asking for a charge of attempted murder involving the use of a pistol, against the man in jail. Evidence listed in the complaint consisted of colorfully described faces and bruised knuckles plus the aforesaid firearm. And all that found its way on to the front page of the Herald, the reason being the now almost universal local opinion that the man in jail was the man who killed Steve Harris. Well that's the way of things in Contra County where an unsolved murder is always a prime target for discussion and action if it comes back into the limelight.

Betty Harris Bentley lived on the Harris Ranch along with a live-in. The ranch was operated and manned by members of the Arrow—B, with profits going to Betty, all as a result of Betty's court settlement with George. Betty remained mentally unstable, and cognizant of little that went on around her. Her live-in companion, however, helped Betty bridge the gap between fantasy and reality.

When the issue of the man in Richardson's jail started to circulate throughout the County, Betty's live-in did her thing and informed Betty of said, and of the implication that this was the man who killed her father. The reaction from Betty was startling to say the least, leading to disturbing and violent thoughts within an already unstable mind. Her call to George on the matter showed irrationality and really a demand that the prisoner be executed.

George tried to calm her, "Betty, this is being handled by the law. We have good reason, yes, to suspect that this is the man who killed your father, and are taking serious steps to prove him guilty of that."

Betty's response indicated disbelief and not understanding. George was sad, going over in his mind their time together, short as it was, and resolving once more to take care and protect Betty.

Small town newspapers don't often have electrifying events to portray in their chronicles so the story of a man in jail suspected of murder got their attention. One editorial shortly after the meeting in Hastings's antechambers and the subsequent assault and battery charges, went like this:

GUILTY BUT UNPROVABLE!
LAW ENFORCEMENT UNABLE TO COME UP

WITH MORE THAN A STRONG SUSPICION

Handwriting is not enough. The story starts with the death of Steve Harris over five years ago. The killer vanishes. A viable suspect appears on the horizon and blunders into the hands of the law. He is tied to the crime through his handwriting, so shown by a certified handwriting expert. Law enforcement has appealed to the County District Attorney to indict. The D.A. asks for more evidence. Where do we go from here, folks? We all want this crime to be solved! Law enforcement is frustrated. They truly believe the man they hold in jail is guilty. The court says, "You can't hold him forever." Time is running out.

Betty had been following the case of the man in jail, a suspect in the killing of her father, all along. One day she went to that secret place on the ranch, found her father's pistol. She fondled it a bit, put it back quickly, and shuddered. She knew it was there, she knew how to use it, and she was still suffering mentally from the loss of her mother, then her first husband, and then her father. When the Glencoe Herald with the big headline concerning her father's death came out, she was thoroughly convinced that this was the man who killed her father. After calling George again she found him sticking to the letter of the law, *a person is innocent until proven guilty*. He didn't tell her that he personally felt that this was the man or that they were all searching for proof of his guilt. He felt it dangerous for Betty to stir up feelings about the death of her father all those years ago.

That didn't go, as Betty called again. It came at a busy time. He answered curtly: "Betty, we are holding this man, and we must let the law run its course." He hung up the phone and thought, *Maybe I had better pay a visit to Betty. She sounds pretty much upset.* He finished the chores for the day, which were lots of physical stuff, and he wasn't particularly looking forward to a trip to the Harris ranch. Mary Ellen watched out of the kitchen window as George unsaddled his horse, fixed a quickie cold meal for him while he washed up, and sat him down at the kitchen table. They both knew he was to go to the Harris Ranch, and Mary Ellen knew not to converse unless he started it, which he didn't.

Seven o'clock found George sitting across from Betty at her kitchen table, a rarity, as Betty wasn't that friendly about having George there. She said, "What do you want?"

"Betty dear, you sounded upset on the telephone, I thought I should come."

Betty got up and produced the Herald headline concerning the man in jail. She said, "I want my father's killer to pay."

George said, "This will be done providing he is found guilty of something."

"And what if he is found to be not guilty?"

"He would be set free, Betty, that's the law."

"Is there a chance that that could happen?"

"Yes, Betty, there is."

Betty stood up, turned away. George asked, "Would you like me to stay tonight?"

"If you wish."

George stayed the night. Amy was there to stay with Betty in the morning when he drove back to the Arrow—B. He was thoughtful and concerned; while Betty had a live-in, he was not sure she could remain, without more serious mental care.

Earlier, law enforcement had circulated throughout the area a wanted dead-or-alive poster of the man in Richardson's jail. As a result, it appeared that this man had indeed been invisible since his return to Contra County until he showed up dealing drugs in the Reservation again. Peter kept on top of this one through the Missing Persons Bureau. Unfortunately, the recent publicity made Judge Hastings uncomfortable, so the judge decided to have a meeting with the witness and relevant law enforcement parties to determine whether the man actually knew anything relevant to the pending "investigation" of drug trafficking. Peter saw this as an opportunity to do some digging, or if the witness refused to cooperate, then he would have to be formally arrested and charged with something. Either way, it was a chance to ask the man some questions and to cover Judge Hastings rear with the local paper and the citizens of Contra County.

The meeting took place in the same antechamber where Judge Hastings had met with the law men, George, and the lawyers. Present at the meeting were Judge Hastings, the witness, alias Miles McKinney, a court-appointed lawyer for McKinney, Chief Richardson, Peter Forbes, his father, Emery, and George Bentley. The witness sat handcuffed at a large table facing Chief Richardson and Peter Forbes, the Judge sat at the head of the table, and the others found chairs around the room.

Judge Hastings spoke first and looked at the witness. "I'm Judge Hastings and I'm the judge who authorized the material witness warrant. This is not a hearing and you are not charged with a crime. The purpose of this meeting is for the police to ask you some questions and figure out what you know about the movement of drugs in our county, and for me to listen. Your attorney there can tell you that this is a good thing because I'm the one that decides whether you should continue to sit in jail for now. You are not under oath. Chief, take those handcuffs off the man so he can relax. He's not going anywhere."

The Chief did as he was told, then said to the witness, "I've asked Peter Forbes here to handle the questions, so you listen to him."

Peter began, "What is your real name?"

"Miles McKinney."

"For the purposes of calling you something then, that is what we will use. But we know that is an alias, and we are entitled to know your true name."

"That's my true name."

"When you were detained, you had been on Arrow—B land. What were you doing there?"

"Minding my own business, until George Bentley attacked me for no reason."

George started to get up to say something, but Emery grabbed his arm and he sat back down.

"So, you were trespassing on Mr. Bentley's land?" Peter continued.

"Maybe I got lost."

"What were you doing when you got lost?"

"Just out for a stroll I guess."

"You had a gun on your person when you were detained. Do you always take a gun on your strolls?"

"The gun is for snakes and such." McKinney looked at George and smiled.

"Are you aware that drugs are being smuggled into the Wind River Reservation in the area where you were out for a walk? Are there people in the drug business that you're afraid of?"

"I don't know nothing about no drugs!"

"Was there some other reason that you attacked George Bentley with your gun up near the line shack on the Arrow—B ranch?"

"That man hit me in the face and slammed me around something good." McKinney's lawyer interjected, "My client won't answer any more questions about what happened with Mr. Bentley."

"I don't need your damned advice," McKinney said to his lawyer. "I'm innocent of doing anything like what you say. Mr. Bentley attacked me and I fought him. That's it."

Peter continued, "How do you know Mr. Bentley? You seem familiar with him."

This caught the man off guard. "I don't know. He seems like some kinda big thing around here. Maybe he told me his name."

At this point, Judge Hastings chimed in. "This man says he doesn't have any information about drugs coming into the Reservation. He doesn't appear to have any material information that he is willing to share." McKinney chuckled and looked at George, but George managed to contain himself.

"Judge, since we're all here, I'm going to ask him about other criminal activity, okay?"

"I guess that's fine, Peter, since Mr. McKinney has a lawyer."

"Mr. McKinney, did you attack George Bentley and put a gun in his face?"

"No way."

"How long have you had that gun?"

"Years, I guess, I don't really remember."

"Did you borrow money from a rancher named Hamilton?"

"What's this about, Judge?" Mckinney's lawyer asked.

"Talk to your client sir, not me. I'm just here to watch."

"I don't remember anyone named Hamilton," McKinney said.

"So, you didn't borrow a thousand dollars from him and sign a promissory note?"

"I don't remember."

Peter was on a roll, and no one wanted him to stop except McKinney's court-appointed lawyer. Peter took out the promissory note and put it in front of the witness. "Will you verify that this is your signature?"

Miles studied the document. "I can't be sure, this paper looks awfully old, and has a date of over five years ago."

"Come on. We have a handwriting expert sitting out in the courtroom who says this is your handwriting. You're lying, Miles. Now why did you sign a note for a thousand dollars to a small rancher that probably had not much more cash to his name?"

Miles said, "I don't remember."

"Judge, what is this about?" McKinney's lawyer looked nervous.

"Yes, Peter, and Chief Richardson, what is this about? Is it relevant to anything here, 'cause I don't see any connection?" Judge Hastings was clearly amused.

"It's relevant, Judge. Can I keep going?"

"Yes, but you better explain the relevance to Mr.

McKinney's lawyer and the rest of us soon."

"That is your signature, isn't it Miles?"

"Could be. But I told you I don't remember."

"But you do remember giving rancher Hamilton a ring, don't you?"

"What?" Miles blurted out. "I didn't give him no diamond ring."

Peter smiled at his father, and Emery smiled back, knowing that Peter had said nothing about a diamond.

"You know Miles, the diamond ring that you stole from Steve Harris when you murdered him."

"Wait a minute," the court-appointed lawyer said. "Don't answer any more questions!"

Miles said nothing more. Judge Hastings smiled, thinking that Peter was smarter than he looked, but he decided it was time to stop the questioning. "Peter, why don't you or the Chief tell us about the ring so that Mr. McKinney's lawyer knows what's going on. At some point, the District Attorney will have to tell him anyway if this is headed where I think it's headed."

"Your Honor, found on the premises of the Hamilton ranch was a unique diamond, known to belong to Steve Harris before he was brutally murdered. The diamond came from a ring that was a family heirloom. It ties the thousand-dollar promissory note to Mr. McKinney here, or whoever he is. This man murdered Steve Harris, stole his diamond ring, and gave it to rancher Hamilton as a form of payment or collateral."

Judge Hastings sighed, then asked, "is that all you have, Peter? It's thin, but you can take it all to the District Attorney and see what happens."

Peter sat down in his seat, shuffled some papers around, found one, stood back up again and said, "Judge, George Bentley and the Chief are concerned that Miles McKinney or whoever he is will disappear if released. He has no known family or other connection to this County. It's obvious that he is involved in criminal activity. We ask that you continue the material witness warrant for some period of time."

"I've heard enough about that. I'm vacating the warrant and instructing Chief Richardson to release Mr. McKinney as a material witness. He's not cooperating with any drug trafficking investigation. That much is obvious." Miles McKinney grinned at George and sneered at Peter, "I told you I don't know anything." Judge Hastings rose and stepped out of the room.

Miles McKinney stood up and shook his lawyer's hand. "No offense, but I don't like lawyers much." Then he started for the door where he was met by Chief Richardson.

"Miles McKinney, you're under arrest for the attempted murder of George Bentley." The Chief turned McKinney around and put the cuffs back on him. McKinney was furious. "We'll see how long this sticks. I didn't do nothing to George Bentley that he didn't have coming."

Chief Richardson turned to Peter and George, "I'll talk to the District Attorney about murder charges for the Harris murder. That will take a few days, maybe more."

Outside the courthouse, George said, "Peter, you did a good job in there. You tied him to the diamond. That man is our killer, but now we have to prove it."

"Thanks George. I don't think the D.A. will want to file murder charges. Judge Hastings is right, there's a connection between Harris and McKinney, and it could show theft, but it's not enough to convince a jury of murder. In the meantime, Judge Hastings will set a bail hearing on the attempted murder charge soon, and this guy could be gone."

"I get it. We don't have much time. Peter, I do have one question?"

"Yes?"

"McKinney definitely wanted to kill me up there on Portal Mesa near the line shack. What do you suppose he meant when he said he didn't do anything to me that I didn't have coming?"

The call came just as Leon was locking up for the night. "Chief Richardson here, is Bill in, Leon?"

"No, he just left for the day, Chief. Can I have him call you in the morning?"

"Leon, this is kind of hot. See if you can find him, and have 'im call me?"

In time Chief Richardson and Sheriff Williams were talking together on the phone. The Chief said, "Guess what, Bill, Miles McKinney has a name."

"So I'm listening."

"Our poster paid off, his real name is Sean Mac Neal, and he has a rap sheet."

Sheriff Williams hung up and called George to pass on the news. George said, "I'll come on down, Bill, see you in thirty minutes."

49 | PETER

George called Peter Forbes, "Peter, are you available? If so, will you meet me in the Sheriff's office in thirty minutes or so. Something's come up you need to hear about."

"Sure, George."

The Sheriff was talking to Chief Richardson on the phone when George walked in. The Sheriff hung up the phone. He said, "I think we have enough on this character to keep Hastings off our back for a while."

George asked, "Where did they call from and who called about who he is?"

"Richardson's son-in-law lives in Denver. He is a police officer there, and has had Sean Mac Neal in their jail."

Peter walked in, looked guessingly at the two, and asked, "Something?"

George said, "Sit down, Peter, I have some work for you. The man we have in custody is maybe one of my kin. That puts even a more personal touch to the killing of Steve Harris.

"We need to tie this up a bit, and Peter, do what you need to do to trace back my ancestry. I don't think the name Sean Mac Neal is coincidental with my family Mac Neals. There has to be a tie in."

Peter sat down, poured himself a cup of coffee from the carafe that was on the table, and sipped a bit of the hot liquid. He waited, and it was the Sheriff who spoke, "Peter, killers often fail, but when they do, they nearly always try again. The man we have in jail tried to kill George Bentley, and if we let him go free he will try again. Maybe he will be successful the next time."

Laura Forbes at age sixty-two considered her two men as her boys. She was a retired school administrator, and knew those two well, so when Peter walked in she knew from the start that something was troubling him. After the routine items of arrival home were over, Peter plopped himself into a livingroom chair and closed his eyes. Laura noted, went on with dinner preparations and waited.

That's how Emery found them when he arrived home a short time later. He looked from his wife Laura to his son Peter for an explanation.

Laura said, "Don't look at me Em', Peter seems to have a problem."

Peter said, "I'd hate to try and hide anything dark from you two. You know me better than I do.

"Now you know that I have a retainer with the Arrow—B? Well I spent years going to law school to learn the law, but whenever the Arrow—B needs or asks for help I can't use any of that stuff. This time I am asked to research ancestry. I don't even know where to start with that one."

His Dad asked softly, "So, what's all that about?"

"My client is in trouble, and the need is for me to perform. The stakes are high, and I sit here asking how? I know I must figure out a way to keep that man in jail, and if he is set free he will try again to kill George. The law says I only have a matter of days to come up with something more than a fist fight to keep a killer in jail. I sit here fat and comfortable accepting a retainer from a very good friend, and I do nothing."

Emery asked, "So what's new? We knew all that yesterday. Three years in law school taught you the ABCs of law in the land we live in, but somewhere along the way, you were supposed to learn to think, and from what I've seen so far, you have . . . What started all this today?"

"You remember that wanted poster we put out a couple of weeks ago, well Chief Richardson got a response. Miles McKinney is really Sean Mac Neal. With that last name, there has to be a Sean Mac Neal in George's family line somewhere."

Emery Forbes had served the Arrow—B from its start and knew much of its background, "So what did George conclude from that, Peter?"

"He didn't say, just instructed me to trace things back."

"So start tracing." The father chuckled; the understanding mother served the evening meal, and the silent son ate.

After a sleepless night, and a skipped breakfast, Peter made his way to his office in Glencoe.

Peter had that wonderful relationship with his dad, which also included an irksome look at himself once in a while, and that was what he was doing this morning. So he took a look at the part of the Bentley family tree that he already knew. It started and stopped at Ellis Island.

Peter mused, since everybody knew all about families on this side of the big pond, my client must be expecting me to look back across the Atlantic, and every indication says Scotland. The man looks Scottish, the name sounds Scottish, and Scottish folk had been immigrating in numbers through Ellis Island timewise with the name I need to match to the man held in Richardson's jail.

The direct connection back to Scotland through Richard Bentley took Peter back over the water to Scotland. He paid a visit to the jail, and interviewed the prisoner, which visit produced nothing about the Mac Neals from the non-communicative prisoner. Peter did, however, get a good idea of his age and social background.

Peter next met with his client. He said, "George, I need to know as much of your past as possible. At this point the trail of your ancestors ends at Ellis Island. What did you learn from your father, Richard, while he was alive?"

"Peter, the death of my mother when I was twelve left my father sad and in some ways unavailable to me. We talked of his trip on the Metagama. We talked of his uncle, Leonard MacLaren. We talked a little about why he left home at age nine, and we talked a little about his birth father."

"So did he tell you why he ran away from home?"

"My father was a very positive person, kind of didn't like talking about bad stuff."

"But you do remember the name Sean Mac Neal. In what way?"

"I'm not sure, Peter, my father spoke almost lovingly of his foster parents. He lived with them for five years. They took him in when he ran away from home."

"Do you know anything about your grandparents?"

"Only that my grandfather died before my father left home."

"What happened to your grandmother?"

"Dad was quiet mostly about his life before he ran away from home."

Peter thanked George and left. He was beginning to see why his client needed to know the truth about the man in jail. If there was a kin of the family involved, he needed to know. There must be a yes or no here. He, himself, would be acting to research and legally protect his client. People who do bad things usually have a reason, and most of the time that involves money. The man in jail was guilty of one or both. George certainly interrupted his source of income, selling drugs. Peter further speculated: A family connection, if there was one, would be stronger only if there were a substantial sum of money involved, and certainly that could be so if you considered the worth of the Arrow—B.

Putting all this together, the question now becomes, who would benefit if George is killed or he dies?

Peter next turned to immigration records at Ellis Island. He found that the U. S. Navy Archives now contained the bulk of immigration records covering the time span involved in his search including those once contained at Ellis Island and other points of entrance into the United States.

Of particular interest to Peter were passenger lists of twentieth-century and later sailings from Europe. Peter filled out the required paperwork and forwarded it by express to 'Records' U. S. Navy Archives.

In a short time Peter got his answer. Of the several Sean Mac Neals found, one stood out. He entered the United States in 1925. His step mother was Mary Bentley Mac Neal and his father was Donald Mac Neal.

Peter called George, "I think I have found the family connection you want to know about. The man in Richardson's jail had a step mother, and her name is Mary Bentley Mac Neal. It looks like she was your paternal grandmother."

George said, "Nice work, Peter, now what can we do to keep Hastings from turning this guy loose. I'm certain that he killed Steve."

"I don't think this information changes the score on that one. Maybe we can establish a family connection to you, but it's still thin. And that, by itself, is not a strong motive to kill Steve Harris. So we are still a ways from convincing the District Attorney to bring charges for the murder of Steve Harris. I'll keep on that and keep you informed."

Of course, Peter had a girlfriend. Her name was Lois. She often was the recipient of Peter's uncertainties one of which happened as he hung up the phone call with George. Notwithstanding his protected attorney-client relationship with the Arrow—B, Peter did discuss situations using nondescript names with Lois. He called her, "Hi Sweetheart, can you meet me for lunch?"

"Sure Hon, where and when?"

"How about The Cattlemen's, 12:30?"

Lois was waiting in a booth. Peter leaned over and kissed her and sat down. He was quiet.

She said, "This is nice. I haven't seen much of you lately. What's been with you?"

Peter told her, not mentioning the client's name. They ordered lunch, wine for Lois and a coke for Peter. When the server retreated to do his thing, Lois said, "Since we are talking about the Arrow—B, Richard Bentley dies, and no one seems to know much back from there. As you said, George doesn't seem to know, or doesn't want to talk about it. Peter, are there no letters or other written material available to help understand what happened?"

Peter, still deep in thought, had to be reminded to pay the bill, helped Lois up and out to her car. Their kiss was matter of fact, Lois in frustration said to herself, "Oh that man."

He dwelled on what Lois had said though, "Isn't there some written material?" A picture of a rusty old safe flashed in his mind. His first assignment with the Arrow—B included going through fifty years of records, some of which were family personal. He had separated the letters and pictures from documents and financial records. All the non-business material went into a box.

He called the Arrow—B. George answered, "Mr. Bentley, what happened to that box full of letters and pictures we found in the safe when I went through it?"

George answered, "Probably up in the attic of the main ranch house."

"Mind if I come out and take a look? We may find something."

The box was hay bale size, and stuffed full of everything from letters to reminder notes like a grocery list. Peter sat down and started to examine the contents, missing nothing. At the end of the day he found what he was looking for. The letter was dated November 10, 1925. It read:

Dear Richard,

I received your last letter and am glad things are going well for you. Once again I must tell you that things are not that way here. Your step brothers, and particularly Sean, seek trouble as a way to get attention. Sean has been in gaol twice for thevin, and a third time will put him in prison. Your step father can't or won't do anything to make Sean straighten up.

Your loving mother, Mary

Peter found George and showed him the letter. "George, I think this letter proves for sure that the man in jail is part of your extended family."

"That's good work Peter. Any new ideas about why this so-called relative wants me dead?"

"I've been thinking about that a lot. He's not a blood relative, so he wouldn't have much of a claim to inherit from you, even if he killed your entire family. But he might not understand that, or maybe he just doesn't care."

George thought about his daughter, Eva, his son, John, and his beloved Joan. He thought of Betty who he still felt responsible for, and who suffered so much when Steve Harris was murdered. Were they all in danger? Could he really protect them all if Mac Neal were to get out of jail?

"Peter, he's from the same place as my father and my grandmother. How could he turn out this way?"

"Well that's another matter. He's not going to tell us, and anyone else that might, is dead. There's not much more I can do except pass this on to the District Attorney."

Chief Richardson had already received notice that his prisoner would have a bail hearing the next day, and he fully expected Sean Mac Neal to post bail and to be released from jail. Word got around fast. The bulk of the residents in the area knew this, and Betty through her caregiver did also.

Betty said to her live-in companion, "Marjorie, I'd like to go into Glencoe today. I want to go to church."

"Alright Betty, I'll get us ready."

The two women drove the fifty miles into Glencoe. Betty told Marjorie to let her off at the city police building, and she went into the front office and up to the desk sergeant, and said, "Hello officer, I'm here to see Sean Mac Neal."

"Ma'am, he's in a jail cell, and can't come out here. You'll have to come back tomorrow when this office is open."

"That's alright, I can go back there. I was told to see if I recognize him."

The officer said, "Lady, you'll have to wait until someone else is in the office, this is Sunday and we are only staffed for emergencies."

Betty said, "Officer, I just came fifty miles for this viewing, which I was asked to do."

The Officer, in frustration said, "Please have a seat." He picked up the radio and called the one patrol car that was available. "Sam, will you come on in. I've got a problem."

Patrol car one stopped in front of Police headquarters, Sam came into the office with a questioning look on his face. The desk sergeant said, "Sam, open up the jail cells gate, and usher this lady in to where Mac Neal is. Let her take a look and come on out. Watch her carefully."

Betty went ahead and up to the cell where Mac Neal was. She faced the bars and the figure of the jailed man, holding her purse in front of her. In the space of a few seconds, and hidden from the view of Sam, she took a pistol out of her purse, pointed it right at the bulbous, red face of Sean Mac Neal and pulled the trigger.

The resounding crack of the discharged weapon brought the desk sergeant into the cell area in time to see Sam carefully removing the pistol from a smiling Betty and a dead Sean Mac Neal. He said, "Jesus."

EPILOGUE

Whereas the act of killing the man she was convinced was her father's killer was justified in her mind, it was, of course, not justified in her real life. Betty Harris Bentley was declared mentally unfit to stand trial, and there was little doubt that getting a conviction against her anyway would be darn near impossible from a jury in Contra County. She was placed in a mental institution.

Peter Forbes struggled to accept the killing of Sean Mac Neal without condemnation by a jury of his peers. They would never have a chance to prove that this man killed Steve Harris, and Peter was left to wonder if Sean Mac Neal was truly guilty. So Peter started asking questions. Could they prove that this man killed Steve Harris, and why did he kill? And Peter also wanted to know if Mac Neal was alone when he killed? The people of Contra County didn't seem to share Peter's concern for courtroom justice, but they respected his honesty and sense of right or wrong.

Peter certainly had other matters needing his attention, and he would not be paid for the time he spent looking for answers. Peter first went over in his mind everything he had on Sean Mac Neal. Judge Hastings had put it this way, "I can't keep a man in custody over a fist fight." There were the diamond ring and the handwriting match. Peter next considered whether Mac Neal could have committed the murder of Steve Harris by himself, and this seemed unlikely because the body had been moved several miles. If there were two or more involved in the killing, who and where was the other? And what kind of hold did Mac Neal have on the other person that would keep him alive?

Peter paid a visit to a surprised Sheriff Bill Williams who had closed the book on the Sean Mac Neal case. He found out two things, first that unless there were more than one doing the killing, Mac Neal moving the body alone was not plausible. Second, two bullets had been found in Steve Harris's body, and those bullets were in a depository in Glencoe.

He next visited the police department in Glencoe, and began a conversation with Chief Richardson, discretely asking if the bullets taken from the body of Steve Harris had been compared against bullets from Sean Mac Neal's gun. Chief Richardson, having faced criticism for the failure of his department to keep a prisoner safe, bristled and told Peter it was none of his business . . . then asked, "Isn't the man dead?"

After Peter left the Chief's office and the Chief had calmed down a bit, he gave thought to what Peter had asked. He called in his secretary and gave orders to do the bullet comparison right away. Bingo, they matched. That evening, trying not to back down from his position of "why is this important, the man is dead," he called Peter at his home with the information.

The young lawyer, fresh from the University, idealist if you will, had properly sought justice for all involved. The man Sean Mac Neal was guilty. There was only one question left. Who abetted and where is he? This Peter left to law enforcement. He learned much about life, the law, and justice in those early years as the attorney for the Arrow—B. He went on to represent many of the state's largest businesses.

The Arrow—B as an enterprise continued as a respected icon throughout the last half of the twentieth century, providing food for our nation through war and peace. George Red Fox Bentley shepherded that western ranch with vigor, gradually turning over more and more responsibility to foreman Cliff and later to his son, Johnny. George continued to write for the papers in his area and later wrote fictional tales. His stories were westerns, and all took readers back to the mid-twentieth century.

Joan Bentley bore one more child, a girl, Sara. Joan loved and supported her man and their three children, and their family bonds of love and loyalty never wavered. Second to her family, as a veterinarian she managed to function well in animal care, her first love after family. Renee, her mother, stayed with her western family and played the doting grandmother during those early years with the three Bentley children.

The Cliff and Amy story was classic in a way, with both sets of parents trying to get in the way and not getting anywhere. Cliff and Amy loved each other with passion, and they drove their parents crazy before finally sealing their love in marriage. They were strong young Americans, Cliff becoming a ranch manager and Amy, who finished college, finding her place in business management.

Peter White and his charismatic wife Rosey lived out their lives in the house that Pete built, both giving of themselves as they had always done. Rosey went to town once a week to pick up supplies and continued to give counsel to town folk.

Bill Williams, the Sheriff, retired. He had saved for this time, and was able to travel, taking his long-time housekeeper to see the world.

Eva Bentley inherited the Harris Ranch, and eventually, the Harris diamond. She learned to ride and to love that ranch through her learning years, gradually becoming the cowgirl ranch owner.

ABOUT THE AUTHOR

Jack F. Kirkeby published his first full length novel in 2013, followed by his second novel later the same year. His three novels, including *Betrayal*, constitute a trilogy that tells the story of a rugged Western ranch family, blended from Scottish and American Indian roots, that overcomes threats, murder, prejudice, and all the challenges inherent in growing and running a large Wyoming cattle ranch in the early to mid-twentieth century.

From the start Jack F. Kirkeby's interests have been of the West. He grew up in an era of strong Western stories and movies. Later in life his writings would be of the West. Jack's motto, "Look behind you, there's no one there," is his way of reminding folks to accept personal responsibility for their successes and failures as adults. His principal characters embody this theme in their actions on the easily turned pages of his books.

Before he was twelve years old, Jack F. Kirkeby had lived in a plethora of homes and places as the product of fractured family conditions. Very early on this gave the author a desire to succeed and foster something more. Ultimately a sense of personal responsibility and gritty determination oozed from the six-foot, four-inch young man. In 1933 he entered Hollywood High School where he joined the ROTC. In

1935, mother and son Jack moved to Lake Geneva, Wisconsin where he finished high school, graduating in June of 1936. After a move to Chicago, the author lived with his brother and worked through the Depression years while he continued his education in after-hours college classes.

On June 9, 1941, Jack enlisted in the United States Army Air Force and served in the Pacific Theater during World War II for two years as an enlisted man. It was there, at an island base overseeing communications equipment, that Jack's early-life experience tinkering with radios and tearing apart equipment were truly appreciated. He then returned to the United States where he entered officer training.

At war's end, the author worked as a service manager for an appliance and radio company while he continued his education. He eventually entered the aerospace industry where his job with Northrop Corporation, later Northrop Grumman, included quality control, contract administration, and configuration management. His duties later included customer and government quality control issues, contract interpretation, and technical writing.

Jack F. Kirkeby is a lifelong student, a tinkerer, a fixer, and a writer. He currently lives in Mission Viejo, California, where at the age of 100 he remains active in his community and works on his next novel.